I0593680

A WARLOCK IN A
CURSED KINGDOM

WINTERTHORN
BOOK TWO

NATHAN TAYLOR

THE WINTERTHORN SAGA

A WARLOCK IN A CURSED KINGDOM

Copyright © 2023 by Nathan Taylor

All rights reserved.

No part of this book may be reproduced in any form or by any electronic
or mechanical means, including information storage and retrieval
systems, without written permission from the author, except for the use
of brief quotations in a book review.

ISBN (digital): 978-0-6457595-4-9

ISBN (paperback): 978-0-6457595-3-2

Cover designed by MiblArt

Edited by Falcon Faerie Fiction

Magpie Drive Press

🌸 Created with Vellum

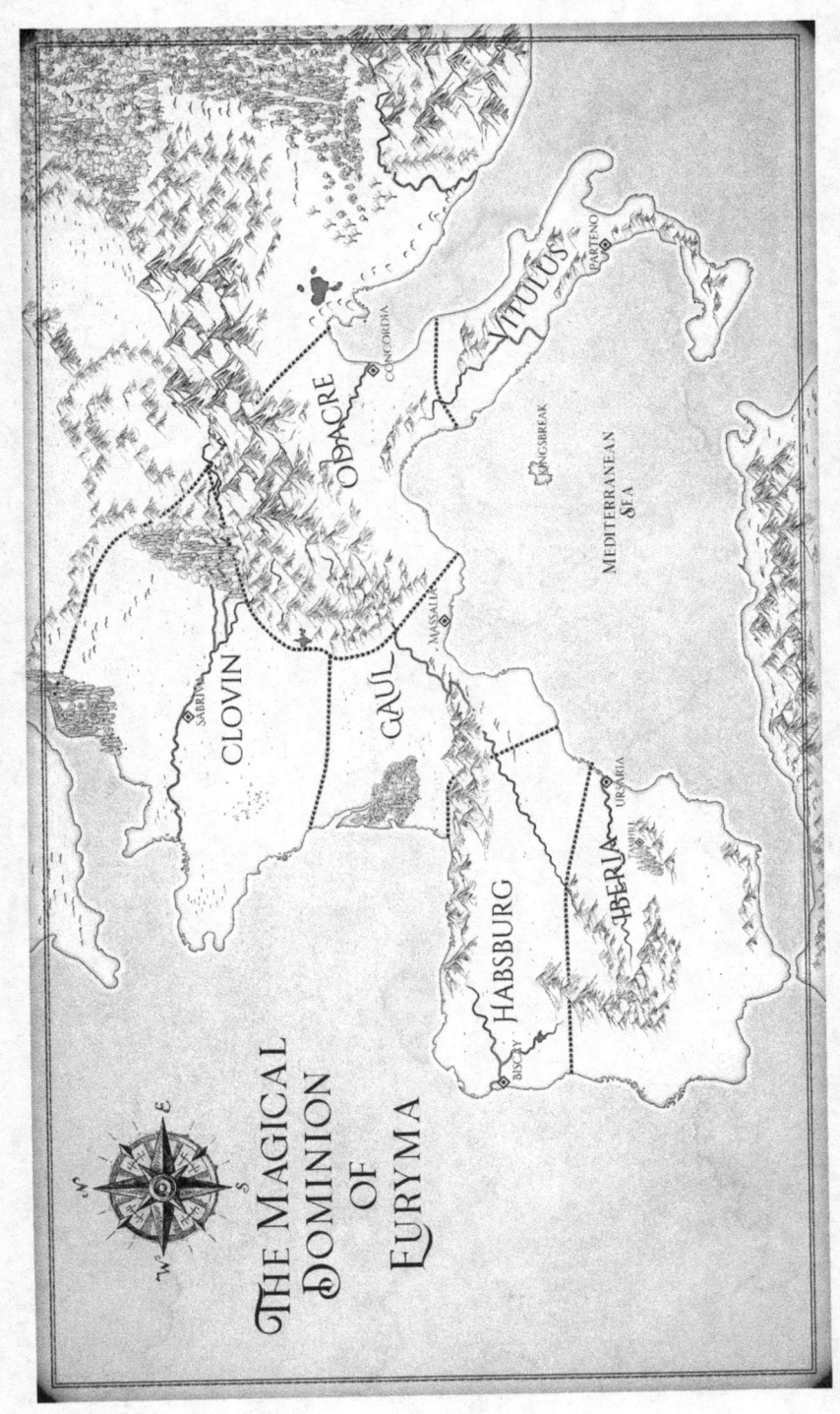

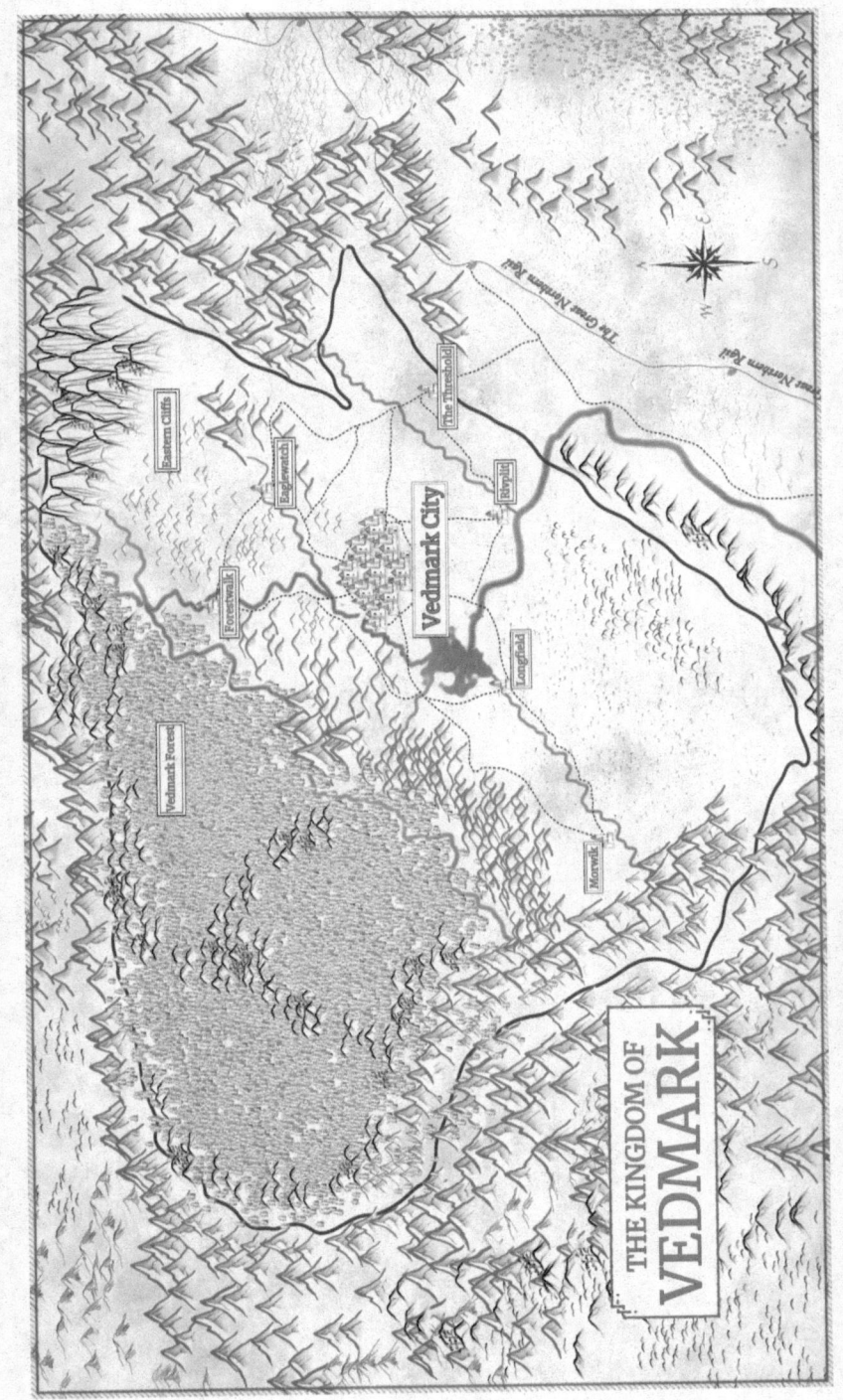

THE KINGDOM OF
VEDMARK

For Shirley, who always knew how to tell a good tale

A WARLOCK IN A

CURSED KINGDOM

WINTERTHORN
BOOK TWO

NATHAN TAYLOR

CHAPTER 1
RAUL

IN THE NEXT FIVE MINUTES, Raul would either kill the leader of the Fatesmiths or be killed himself. Fluorescent lights split the ceiling above the paper-thin carpet. The room was identical to every other room in downtown Biscay. He should have been nervous. He should have felt something. Raul didn't care. He only cared about the impostor seated by the window.

"Welcome, Mage." Haberdeen's face beamed through a scarred smile. "What brings you home?"

"Business, madam," Raul replied. Six weeks had passed since the boy—Declan Moore—obliterated their stranglehold on Euryma. That disaster at Anderma cost more than a few lives. It had opened the door for this serpent to slither into their ranks and undo years of planning. Raul knew how simple it was to disguise one's features with magic. This was not the real Haberdeen.

"And what business is that?"

"Nothing pleasant, I'm afraid." Behind his cool exterior, he rehearsed a simple pattern of movement. A flick of the wrist would release the fiery braid of pyronima and kinetic energy wrapped around the back of his hand. "I have word there is a traitor in Biscay. An impostor who has taken advantage of the recent chaos and slipped into our ranks."

The woman wearing Haberdeen's face nodded slowly. "A serious accusation. Do you know who the traitor is?"

"I do." Raul moved like a wound spring. His hands snapped like a whip. Fire burst from his palm and enveloped her. Beige paint curled off the walls as the room became a furnace. Raul leaned into the heat until a plume of acrid smoke forced him back. He released the pyronima, and the flames died.

Haberdeen stared back at him, unharmed in a smoking office chair. Her green eyes glowed violet. Purple light sparked off her like electricity.

Raul retreated to the door. "Who are you?"

The impostor tilted her head. Her amethyst eyes shone brighter. "I am Haberdeen." She raised a hand. Raul's arms snapped against his body. With a twirl of her fingers, she sat him into her blackened seat. It was still hot from the flames. "I know you feel guilty about Anderma, about losing so many Fatesmiths." She sighed. "And now it seems the trauma has taken its toll on you."

Whoever wore Haberdeen's face was powerful enough to weave nima and mask her spells at the same time. Raul struggled against bonds he could not see. "I know you're not her!" he shouted. "I know you're a liar."

A side door opened. A woman with auburn hair followed a balding man into the room. The fake Haberdeen nodded to Raul. "Do you believe me now, Ophelia?" she said. "I knew his failure to help us up north was a heavy burden. I did not expect him to spiral so fast."

Ophelia shook her head—pity etched into her expression. "He's lost his grip on reality."

Raul tried to break free from the chair. "Ophelia! Don't listen to her. She's lying." He turned to the man. "Benjamin, I'm not crazy. She's not Haberdeen. She's a fraud."

"But I am Haberdeen," the impostor said. She leaned back and tutted like he was a disobedient child throwing a tantrum. "Goodness, could you imagine the damage he could do in a state like this?"

"You're the one doing damage. You're a fake!"

"What are your orders, Madam?" Ophelia asked.

"Take him to the basement and fierise him. Hopefully, some time in stasis will help his mind make sense of recent events."

"No!" Raul strained against her magic. "NO!"

The pair took control of his bonds and carried him out of the room. Raul fought them to no avail, and Ophelia and Benjamin ignored his desperate attempts at escape. When they reached the elevator, Raul changed his approach. The moment the door closed, he gasped for air, sucking in shallow breaths like a fish out of water.

"What's he doing?" Ophelia asked.

Benjamin crouched beside him. "No idea. It sounds like his lungs?"

"His lungs? How?"

Raul jerked his head to the side and convulsed. Benjamin stood up. "He's having a seizure."

"Are you sure?" Ophelia frowned. "He... he could be faking?"

"Help," Raul wheezed. He thrashed violently against his bonds, then slumped forward. The lift stopped, a melodic chime played, and the silver doors parted.

"What do we do?" Ophelia asked.

"He's mad as a squirrel's mimic, but he's still a Fate-smith," Benjamin said. "I think we need to get him to medical."

"But Haberdeen said—"

"I know what she said. But we can't fierise him like this."

Raul waited. He felt fingers press against his neck.

"Pulse seems okay." Ophelia's voice was an octave higher than normal. "I still think he might be having us on."

"You decide," Benjamin said. "But whatever state he's in when we bring him back is your responsibility. I'm not taking the fall for fierising her first student on the cusp of death."

There was a long pause, in which Raul decided he would let Benjamin escape with only minor injuries. "Fine," Ophelia said. "Let's take him to medical."

The bonds holding him vanished. Raul fought the urge to fight; instead, he remained limp until they were back in the lift. When the doors slid shut, he wrenched on two handfuls of aeronima. The sudden gust of wind threw Ophelia and Benjamin against the elevator. With a delicate curl of his fingers, he condensed the gale into a solid wall of air. It trapped Ophelia and Benjamin, like flies in jelly. They stared at him in utter shock.

"Cheers," Raul said. With his left hand, he delivered a blow of pure kinetic energy to Ophelia's head. She slumped to her knees. "And you..." Raul loomed over Benjamin. "You should pay more attention to details before leaping to a medical emergency."

The lift chimed. Raul tied off the condensed air.

"Where are you going?" Benjamin called as Raul exited onto the second floor.

Raul considered a smart retort, but thought better of it. *Oh well.* He took an immediate left and headed down the fire exit. Out into the streets of Biscay, and away from the Fatesmiths— and their impostor of a leader.

CHAPTER 2
MARY-LOU

Between the white tile walls and linoleum floors, the Imbusion Lab was the perfect place to make a mess. A crate of onyxelles shuddered at Mary-Lou's feet; they snuffled and snorted like low-pitched pigs. "How are you feeling?" she asked.

Michael's lips were a thin line. He glanced up from the crate and offered a small smile. "Cautiously confident."

Laurefen stroked his curled mustache. "We'll soon find out..."

Two men, frozen in iron, stood in the room's centre. Laurefen circled them, spraying their casts with a yellow liquid that stank of rotten fruit. The ironhands had botched an attack in Sabriva's south and left behind two fierised wizards. One had a sallow face with a long nose; the other had wide eyes and held a curved cane. Mary-Lou did not recognise either of them, but that did not matter. Tonight, they had a chance to test Michael's mimicry. If he could recreate the power of a flarefly, they could undo fierisation as needed. *It should be possible. Ward had proved as much with Declan.*

A rush of anxiety followed the thought. Declan Moore had proven to be exactly what they needed—a force powerful enough to withstand the Fatesmith's magic—only to unveil himself as something even worse. A Knight of Despair. A danger to King's College—to the entire Dominion. And then he was gone. Spirited away by the Luck girl—Ava—before they could evaluate their options. *Maybe we could have saved him? Taught him to harness his power...* Mary-Lou let the unwelcome thought unravel. It would be easier to tame a poisonous viper.

Laurefen crouched beside the wooden crate. "This is it, what we've been waiting for." His eyes sparkled with anticipation. "I will let the onyxelles out. They will be attracted to these pheromones I have sprayed on our visitors. Once they're close, Michael will send them into a state of rage. Then we will see how effective the flarefly mimicry is."

"Are we going to be cleaning bits of onyxelle off the walls?" Mary-Lou asked.

"I certainly hope not," Laurefen said. "Ward performed this same magic on Declan. He emerged unscathed."

"But Declan's a—"

"Regardless," Laurefen continued. "You know why we have chosen these gentle creatures. As innocent as they are, they could be the key to rescuing thousands of magical brothers and sisters. Sometimes, sacrifice is necessary."

Mary-Lou hated the idea of hurting such beautiful animals, but she understood. The onyxelle's knack for invisibility was a strategic opportunity they could not afford to waste when they infiltrated the Smith's storehouses.

"What about you?" Michael asked. "I assume you have protective measures in place to avoid the spell's influence?"

"I believe so." Mary-Lou fished a transparent spike from

her coat pocket. It looked like a frosted icicle but felt warm to the touch. "Courtesy of Declan's friend."

Michael's shoulders tensed. "You trust it?"

"It seems potent." Laurefen held out a hand, and Mary-Lou handed him the spike. "I am confident it will protect us."

"Very well." Michael appeared unconvinced. "Let's get started."

"On my mark." Laurefen crouched by the box. "Three. Two. One."

As soon as the latch flipped, the crate snapped open. Four fat creatures with sleek black fur waddled out and vanished. The sounds of their sniffling wet noses circled the iron casts. Laurefen pulled Mary-Lou beside him, then thrust the spike into the ground. A clear bubble appeared around them. Michael's eyes narrowed in concentration. He raised his hands. The onyxelles sounded like a puttering motor. Their growls grew until they were snorting with rage. A nearby table burst into the air as if upended by a poltergeist. Mary-Lou's heart thrummed in her chest. "It's working."

"Poor creatures," Laurefen replied.

"Shield your eyes!" Michael shouted as brilliant white drenched the room. It was too bright. Mary-Lou squeezed her eyes shut—the insides of her eyelids burned scarlet. Then, nothing. Silence. She blinked the room back into view.

Two men fell to the ground. They coughed and sput-tered, eyes wide and wild. Laurefen pulled the spike free. The bubble vanished. "It's worked! It—"

One of the men whipped around with his cane. It caught Laurefen's head with a crack. He fell to the floor. The stranger moved his hands in an intricate pattern, a shimmering square forming before him. Laurefen attempted to roll away, but the spell engulfed him. An iron cast took his place.

"Laurefen!"

"Lou! Move!" Michael dashed out the door.

Mary-Lou hit the deck as another square hurtled after her. She rolled behind a fallen table and glanced back. The two wizards inspected the lab, perfectly at ease. "So here we are, the famous King's College. Who would've thought it would be so easy to get in?"

Mary-Lou made a beeline for the door. A surge of silver blocked her path—forcing her beneath a corner bench. The men laughed as their dim reflections on the tile walls edged in her direction. *Where is Michael?*

"We should've done this months ago."

They had her cornered.

The onyxelle's wooden crate hurtled through the air. The man with the cane turned too late. He disappeared in a cloud of splinters.

The sallow-faced man summoned a flickering square. Michael was gone. Mary-Lou took her chance. She popped up from behind the bench and grabbed a fistful of aeronima. With nimble fingers, she braided it into a heavy coil and looped it over the rogue wizard. His eyes bulged as it tightened around his throat. Mary-Lou gripped hard and yanked his head back, the man's long nose pointed up like a flagpole.

Michael appeared from a side door. He slid along the floor and pulled the glass spike from Laurefen's iron hands. The man thrashed like a hooked fish. Mary-Lou felt the thread fail. Michael raised the spike.

The other man emerged from the shattered crate. A silver square formed ahead of him.

"Michael!"

The spell streamed across the Imbusion Lab.

Michael dived forward and drove the frosted spike into Long Nose's chest. The wizard shrieked as the barrier blossomed around them. The fierisation square hit the barrier with a whip crack, spreading over it like a metallic spider-web. Michael compressed the shield into the spike and tossed it across the room.

It caught the other man in the shoulder. He dropped his cane and stumbled backward. Michael pinned him against the wall. The man roared in pain. Mary-Lou could see the fistfuls of aeronima holding him in place. "Who are you?" Michael's voice was venomous. Mary-Lou rushed to Laurefen's side, but there was nothing she could do. The Dean of King's College was an iron statue. The man moaned as Michael pressed the wound. "I asked you a question."

Mary-Lou checked Long Nose. He was dead. His living accomplice screamed. Michael drove the spike deeper. "Michael!" Mary-Lou dragged her eyes away from the corpse.

"Who are you?"

The man shook his head. Michael pressed harder. A crimson patch bloomed around the spike. "Stop! Stop!"

"Talk."

"Okay. I'll talk. STOP!"

Creases littered the man's forehead, tiny sweat-filled valleys. His breathing was labored.

"Who are you?" Michael repeated.

The man went quiet. Mary-Lou pursed her lips. *He's died too.* Then he looked up, and she gasped. Black fire burned in the Fatesmith's skull. They were the eyes of a man possessed, controlled like a puppet from somewhere else. The man smiled. "I'm here to deliver a message."

Michael's fists clenched. "Who are you?"

"I am a messenger," the man replied. Michael pushed on the spike, but it had no effect. "Ian isn't here anymore," he chortled. "You can't hurt me."

Michael stopped. "What is this message of yours?"

The man's face shone with moisture. His eyes burned with madness. "A truce of sorts. Remnant Magic is coming. The people of Euryma have spent the last thousand years using magic without regard, not believing it had a cost. The remnants of those spells have accumulated. The storms are coming. Swear to Haberdeen, and we will spare you. No violence, no fierisation, just a bloodspell oath that you will stop using magic. Help us save what's left of the Dominion."

He's lying. Mary-Lou shook her head. "Nonsense. You think we're stupid enough to walk right into your hands?"

"You were stupid enough to let us in," the puppet replied.

Michael pulled the silver spike from the man's shoulder and plunged it into his heart. The shrill cackle cut short. The man stopped in surprise, then smiled. A line of blood dribbled from the corner of his lips. "The storms are coming." His face grew pale. A dying breath rattled in his chest. "Remnant Magic is coming." He slumped forward— dead. Michael released him. He collapsed on the ground in a twisted heap.

"You fool!" Mary-Lou said, throwing her hands in the air. "We could have used him! There were more questions to ask!"

"He was a puppet! One we could not bargain with. Better off dead."

"You couldn't know that."

"What does it matter? It was nonsense!" Michael's eyes flashed. "The storm is coming? Remnant Magic? You've seen the Well, it's as high as ever. If magic were accumulating in the atmosphere, the Well would be empty." His chest heaved. He shut his eyes and took a long breath. When he opened them, the emotion was gone. "We can't let them get to us. It worked, Lou. It worked."

"It did." Mary-Lou scanned the room. No trace of the onyxelles remained. "Though it seems to have cost some innocent lives."

Michael crouched by Laurefen's cold, motionless figure and touched his arm. "Then I guess we're going to need more onyxelles."

Silence stretched between them. Three bodies lay still on the ground, two flesh and blood, one iron. Mary-Lou did not like death. Even on dangerous assignments with dangerous enemies, she always tried to keep everyone alive. The dead body smiled up at her. It made her skin crawl.

CHAPTER 3

DECLAN

DECLAN SWUNG DOWN. Hard. The axe head wedged into the wood with a dull thud.

"You do it again," Grigory groaned and shook his head. He was old, bordering on ancient, with sun-leathered skin, a ragged beard, and wispy, white hair. "Cut with grain, fellow."

The hardwood block creaked as Declan wiggled the axe free. "I'm trying," he grunted. The blade came loose, and he nudged the log back into place.

"Eyes on woodgrain." Grigory gestured to the textured rings within the wood. Corded muscles ran the length of his forearms. "Go on."

Declan changed his footing, then drove down once more. This time, the axe caught the right angle. It separated easily.

Grigory nodded. "Is better."

Declan gathered the split sections to add to his pile. He should have felt some measure of satisfaction, but he felt hollow. He always did. Ever since Anderma.

Once the kindling was stacked, Grigory pointed to the

13

remaining section of the log. "Now turn to find new grain to cut."

Declan reached down, but recoiled as something scurried up the woodpile. An armadillo. The telltale shine of its armor reflected the morning light. Grigory laughed. "Do not fear little demon, fellow. They are everywhere at moment. Plenty of grubs for them in there." The armadillo disappeared between fallen branches.

Grigory watched Declan split two more blocks, grunted his approval, and then left Declan alone. With just a shed of dry wood as company, Declan went on with his work. It had been barely a month since Ava—called away on 'business'—stashed him on Grigory's farm. He knew she was in Euryma, but nothing more. *She's busy helping. You're wasting time as a farmhand.* Declan pushed the thought aside and refocused on the woodpile. There was a welcome percussion in the axe's thud, a song that drowned his concerns. It didn't fill the empty hollow, but it subdued the voice in his head—the same voice that insisted helping an old goat farmer was a waste of time.

"Good, fellow. This is good."

Declan's sweat-soaked shirt stuck to his back. He had lost himself in the work's rhythm. The pile of split timber reached his waist. "Is that enough?"

"Is good. Will keep us warm and well-fed for a while longer." Grigory turned back to his cabin. "Come. Lunch is ready."

Tendrils of smoke crept off a stone chimney. Armadillos rolled into balls or scuttled into vegetable gardens as they passed. Grigory laughed. "People in City think they bring bad luck." He waved towards the creatures. "But they keep pests off vegetables. So, I don't mind so much."

The small cabin was housed in the hills south of Forest-walk. Three bedrooms—hardly larger than closets—and a kitchen extending into a sitting area. Stretched goatskins covered wooden walls, while faded floorboards creaked with every step. The delicious aroma of warm meat bubbled up from a cast-iron pot atop a wood stove.

"The same menu as always, I suppose," Declan said.

Grigory hung his heavy coat by the door. "Goat stew, fellow. Very best."

Declan took his seat at the table. His arms ached and his stomach growled. Grigory slid him a bowl of steaming brown meat, and a plate of buttered bread followed. "Thanks, Ory," Declan said.

The cabin fell silent save for their chewing and gulping. The food tasted amazing. It always did. Grigory had once told him that the secret to a delicious meal was to serve it *after* hours of hard labor. Declan found it hard to disagree. He had eaten the same meal daily for over a month and still enjoyed it, if only because he was always starving whenever it was served.

Three helpings later, he slid the empty bowl away. Grigory eyed it with concern. "There will be no goats left if you keep eating so much."

"Sorry," Declan said.

"No worry, fellow, you work hard. Hunger is price of work." Grigory cleaned the last remnants of stew from his bowl with a quarter-slice of bread. "And work never stops. Today, I show you to fix fence."

"Which one?" Declan bit his tongue. The question had slipped out.

Grigory rolled his eyes. "Southern questions," he muttered. He finished his bread, belched, then leaned back. "Fence not broken. Fence not working. Something is killing goats. Fence keeps goats in but doesn't keep something out.

That must be fixed before I lose any more goats." Grigory smirked. "Otherwise, you could bag manure."

"No. Not that," Declan said. "Anything but that."

For some unknown reason, Trevor, Grigory's lone donkey, saw Declan as a mortal enemy to be chased away whenever possible. Grigory laughed. "I will shovel. For Trevor's sake, not yours."

Declan nodded. He worked hard living with Grigory, harder than he ever had in Tamhill, but every day here nagged at him. *You shouldn't be here. People back home need you. Ace still needs you.* Declan ignored the thought. "I'll do the fences, and you'll deal with that donkey."

Declan cleared the table while Grigory vanished to get supplies. They walked out to a paddock behind the cabin, sturdy square posts thick as his arm bordered a level field, each post spaced five steps apart and connected by wooden planks.

"Whatever is taking goats is small enough to get underneath." Grigory waved to a large roll of wire netting. "I need you to join this along fence." He propped the roll up and unwrapped a section. Once he had positioned the wire against the wooden boards, he knocked three rusted nails into place with an old hammer. "Secure wire every eight paces. Four more rolls in toolshed." Grigory handed Declan the hammer and a heavy cloth bag; it held an assortment of different-sized nails. "Go on," Grigory said. "You do."

Declan copied him exactly. Grigory nodded. "Good. Remember, pull tight or it will be waste."

"Yes, Ory," Declan said. "Are you staying to help?"

Grigory sighed. "Questions, boy. This is Vedmark." He shook his head. "You do on your own. I need to go to City to buy claw trap for thing that is killing goats. I will be back in few hours to bag manure." Grigory held his gaze. "Don't waste wire, fellow."

"I won't."

The old man scanned the fence line before leaving. Declan started along the fence, first running the garden wire to the right length and then hammering it into place. By mid-afternoon, he had found a rhythm. His mind wandered while he worked.

What are you doing? Declan tried pretending that he could not hear the voice. It returned. Louder. *You need to learn how to be a Warlock. You need to save your friend.*

"And how am I supposed to do that?" Declan growled. A nearby goat tilted its head, then went back to eating grass. The voice fell silent.

Six weeks in Vedmark, but Declan still did not know how Warlocks were trained. From what he could glean, anything to do with Warlocks was an expensive secret. It had surprised Declan to discover jade mitka had no actual value. They were not even jade. Instead, the coins were carved stone tokens imbued with a very particular charm used to trade information. As long as the mitka stayed green, it had value. A grey mitka was 'spent', worthless, as was any knowledge that came with it.

Knowledge. Declan shook his head. That was the real currency in Vedmark. Mitka were placeholders for that knowledge. If you knew what others didn't, you had wealth. If you gave it too freely, your wealth became worthless. As far as Declan could tell, the whole idea had kept Vedmark living in the Iron Age.

Steal it, said an urgent voice in his head. *Grigory has mitka in his top drawer. Use that to buy what you need to know. You're wasting your time here.*

Disregarding the inner monologue, Declan swung the

hammer, caught his thumb—cursed—and dropped the nail. "I'm not stealing mitka," he muttered to himself. "Just shut up." He concentrated on the fence; a line of blood ran down his thumbnail. The sun blazed above, heating the wire until it was uncomfortable to handle. Declan was almost finished when a shadow appeared behind him. Declan couldn't tell if he was inspecting his work or surveying the fields.

"Curious words in City," Grigory said at last.

Declan hammered a nail into place. The blood on his thumb had dried dark maroon. He glanced back. "What are they saying?"

Grigory scowled. Vedmark wasn't like Euryma. It had its own customs, and one of those is that you didn't just ask questions. Asking for knowledge was akin to begging for money. "Remember where you are," Grigory said. "Curious, though. I have questions for you if you would care to earn mitka."

"Uh. Sure."

Grigory retrieved a small jade coin from his coat. "I have mitka for knowledge. Are you willing to trade?"

Declan struggled to recall the exact phrase. Slowly, it came back to him. "I am... willing to trade. This I know... uh... unsullied by untruth lest your mitka be spent."

Grigory handed him the coin. "They say Winterthorn is in Euryma. Is that true?"

"Um," Declan chewed on his lower lip. "I'm sorry. I don't know what that means."

"You do not know Winterthorn?" Grigory scratched his beard. "No mind. They say you battled one called Haberdeen, a witch from southern land."

Declan nodded. "I fought her."

18

Grigory looked satisfied. "Very well, confirm this for me, fellow. This witch, did she fight with a white dagger?"

That night in Anderma was one Declan would rather forget. He tried to be strategic, to focus only on the memories holding the answers to Grigory's question. He failed. All Declan saw were his parents melting away. All he felt was fury, loss, and emptiness. He wrestled that aside to picture Haberdeen, her fiery hair, her crooked smile. "She had a knife, a small one, though..." Declan shrugged. "I'm sorry, Ory. I don't recall what color it was."

"Very well. Rumors run through City like goats in a garden, and there is no way to know which is true. They whisper of you, too. You are not popular, fellow."

"What do they say?"

Grigory frowned. "Are you paying for questions, or am I?"

"Sorry, Ory."

The old man chuckled. "You will learn one day. Now, seal our exchange. You remember the words."

Declan held up the mitka and spoke with rehearsed eloquence. "I share this knowledge, true to my knowledge; let it show in green." The coin in Declan's fingers dulled for the slightest moment before returning to its soft, jade hue. Declan's honesty earned his coin. He put it safely in his pocket.

"Come, fellow, return to your work. Fence needs finishing, garden needs clearing."

You are not popular. What does that mean? How many people know about me? Declan picked up his hammer and nails. His unwelcome thoughts continued. *You're wasting your time here.*

CHAPTER 4
DECLAN

ANOTHER WEEK PASSED in a blur of sweat, stew, and sore shoulders.

Declan sat atop a circular wooden platform covered in pine needles. Below him, sheets of mist engulfed Grigory's cabin while the morning sun illuminated the higher sections of the surrounding fields. Goats wandered sleepily to these pockets of welcome warmth, and Declan watched them carefully.

Seven more were dead, one each day since Grigory had set claw traps, which had proved as useless as the fence Declan had rewired. The creature responsible for the deaths was clever; the old farmer responsible for the goats was angry. *You save my flock, fellow. I'll answer any question you want- no mitka required.* Grigory's words echoed in Declan's ears. If he could figure this out, he could finally ask about warlocks, his magic, and how he could learn to use it.

He breathed in the cold air. His nose twitched at the wood smoke rising from Grigory's cabin. He turned his attention to the forest's edge. "Okay, whatever you are," he murmured. "Where are you?"

A handful of older goats plodded along the field closest to the tree line. Grigory hadn't enjoyed using them as bait, but the frail beasts were easy prey. They should be irresistible so close to the forest.

Declan watched, waited, but nothing happened. The sun chased the fog away as it climbed. The old goats chewed on yellowing grass. Occasionally, a crow flew overhead. Nothing else. No bear, no wild cat, just silence. By lunchtime, Declan's rumbling stomach persuaded him to take a break. He swallowed his disappointment and started down the tree. Something moved below him. He froze.

A mass of brown fur stalked along the fence he had reinforced the week before. Young goats bounded through the fields, blissfully ignorant of something lurking on the other side of the wire.

Declan descended the rope ladder as quietly as he could. Grigory's axe sat propped against the tree trunk. He picked it up and circled the cabin—keeping low, moving slow. He took every precaution to avoid stray twigs and dry pine needles. When Declan reached the fence line, he gripped the handle and leaped out into the open.

Nothing.

The goats bleated at his sudden arrival. *Be quiet, stupid animals.* Declan craned his neck, searching the pen. The creature had vanished. *It must have heard—*

A hulking shadow appeared from nothing. Declan ducked on instinct. Brown fur and claws swept over him, grazing his back. He retreated behind the corner post of the fence as the creature charged. It split the corner post with a crack. Declan backed up quickly, axe tight in pale knuckles. A wolf as tall as a mule growled at him.

"ORY!" Declan shouted.

The wolf snarled, eyes gold, teeth razors. It lunged

21

forward. Declan swung and caught only air. The beast dodged and swiped with paws the size of saucepans. Declan stumbled back and swung again. The wolf backed away—a deep growl reverberated from the back of its throat.

"ORY! THERE'S A WOLF!"

Declan couldn't tell if he was shouting or not. His heartbeat thundered in his ears. The wolf circled left, then right, probing for a weak spot. Declan forced himself to stay calm, axe ready, and retreated to the cabin.

In a flash, the beast leaped at him. Declan swung, but the beast pulled up short. His swing caught nothing but exposed his shoulder. The wolf lunged forward, and Declan dived into the dirt, losing his axe as he rolled. With the weapon gone, the race was on.

The wolf skidded through loose leaves. Declan was already on his feet. He took off like a cannonball towards the front door. The beast bounded diagonally to cut him off.

Declan changed tactics. He dashed past the gardens at the front of the house. The wolf snapped at his heels. *It's too close.* He willed himself to go even faster, shooting through the trees to the woodshed. Teeth snapped at his heels. Declan reached out, caught a narrow pine in one hand, and used his momentum to spin back the way he came. The wolf scuffled to change direction. Declan sprinted towards the cabin. His feet moved too fast for his body. He stumbled, fell, and tasted dirt. Back on his feet, a moment too slow. The beast struck him like a bus. Declan crashed into a tree. Before he could move, jaws closed on his ankle.

The forest shrieked like a banshee. Teeth relinquished and Declan rolled away. It wasn't the forest. It was an armadillo. It attacked with spectacular fury. A blur, screeching and hissing, driving the beast into the trees.

Declan hobbled to the stairs, his right boot squelching with blood. The wolf reappeared, prowling straight out of thin air, blocking his path. Declan backed into a tangle of garden wire and fell to the ground.

The wolf pounced. Declan tried to roll away. It was all he could do to hold it off him. Hot, putrid breath filled his lungs. His free hand snaked through the earth and found the wire. Foul-smelling jaws snapped, inches from tearing flesh.

In a last-ditch effort, Declan threw the wire over the wolf's neck and pulled tight. The wolf jerked back. Its claws shredded his chest. *Don't let go. Let go and you're dead!*

The wolf dragged him around the clearing like a child's toy, doing its best to shake him free. Declan refused to release it. The wire cut his hands, but held the snapping jaws out of reach. His aching muscles trembled. *Don't. Let. Go.*

The beast started to whimper. Its movements slowed. Its weight pressed down on him. Warm drool mixed with the blood soaking his ripped shirt. The sky went dark, and the tall pine trees swam into a thick haze.

"Fellow!" Declan jolted awake. Grigory leaned over him. A blinding sun beamed behind him.

"Ory?" Declan squinted into the light. Pain flooded his body. Memories followed. "Ory! There's a wolf! We need to get inside!"

"There *was* a wolf." The old man patted a mound of fur to his left.

Declan's jaw dropped. "Did you kill it?"

23

"Questions, fellow." Grigory shook his head. "I did not. You did this."

"No..."

"I pulled him off you if that counts."

Declan let the words sink in. "I... I killed it..."

Grigory nodded. "Strangled with wire by looks of it."

Black bruises ran the lengths of Declan's hands, front and back. "I thought I was done for." He tried to sit up, but his body refused.

Grigory gestured to the three deep cuts running from his breastbone to his waist. "Those will make for impressive scars."

"They hurt."

Grigory didn't seem to hear him. He stared at the dead wolf. "We call these jumpwolves. Uncommon so far from mountains. This was just a pup."

"If that's a pup, I don't want to see an adult." Declan shifted his weight and winced. "It was fast. So fast."

Grigory laughed. "No, no, fellow. It is as you call..." he paused for a moment, "teleport. Only short distance though, here to tree." His expression soured. "Or through a fence."

Declan lay back on the ground. "No wonder. It came out of nowhere."

"Good skill for a hunter to have. Easy to eat my goats."

"You sound more worried about them than you are about me," Declan said. "I shouted for you."

"I was preparing lunch. I only saw you because I ran out of wood for stove." Grigory shrugged. "Wouldn't have mattered. You're a Warlock, fellow. You would have found a way."

A bolt of realization. Declan grinned. "Hey!"

Grigory raised his eyebrows.

"I did it! I saved your goats. You know what that means!"

"Yes, I remember."

Declan attempted to sit up, groaned, and collapsed. His cuts burned like hot wire.

Grigory placed a hand on his shoulder. "But not now. Save your questions, fellow, let's clean you up first."

———

An hour later, Declan sat buried beneath a collection of wet towels. Steam and smells made the air thick. Grigory squeezed another washcloth, and water splashed in the bubbling pot of fragrant herbs. "Here, last one for foot."

Declan laid the towel across his ankle. There was a momentary sting, and the pain faded. "Thanks."

Grigory stirred the liquid. "Very well, fellow, that is all of them. You have saved my goats. I am a man of my word. You may ask your question." He held a jade mitka up for Declan to see. "This I know, unsullied by untruth lest this mitka be spent."

Butterflies crowded Declan's stomach. *It's happening.* "Okay," he said, voice shaking with excitement. "How do I use my magic?"

Grigory's lips thinned. "Not that question."

"But you said—"

"I said I would answer a question. I cannot answer that one."

Declan deflated like a balloon. "What do you mean?"

"Warlocks. Knights. I am no part of this. I am a farmer. I keep goats, work land, and spend no mitka on what I do not need to know."

"But your son..." Declan trailed off, unsure of how to finish.

"Misha is Luck, not Warlock. Different."

Declan groaned, "You must know something."

Grigory stared into the simmering water. "I cannot answer your question, but I know who can."

"Go on."

"You have risked much pain to protect my flock, so I will do two things to help." He held Declan's gaze. "The first is an introduction. I will pay for you to sit with Irman. He is a trader now, but we worked silwood yard as boys. He knows of these things, but they are expensive."

"And the second?"

"As I say, this knowledge is expensive. I will organize work. It is dangerous but pays very well. After today, it is good job for you."

"That sounds fair." Declan fiddled with the corner of a towel. "Do you really know nothing about magic?"

Grigory laughed. "Fellow, you drive a hard bargain." He scanned the pile of bloody towels covering Declan's torso and sighed. "I do not know much, but I can tell you a little."

"Yeah, like what?"

"First, this is not magic. Magic is from south. Warlocks do not use magic, Warlocks use Sila."

"Sila?"

"Sila is what you call green magic. Knights use Sila when they want. Warlocks wield it when they must."

Declan nodded. He had only accessed his power under the weight of crushing despair. He pushed those memories away. "So, Warlocks learn how to use Sila?"

"Could be." Grigory shrugged. "I do not know. That is a question for Irman."

"What will it cost?"

"I expect many mitka."

Declan considered it. "Tell me about this job."

Grigory's grin returned. "You escaped a jumpwolf today."

"Barely." Declan shifted the towels draped across him. "And like you said, it was only a pup."

Grigory chuckled. "You are quick, Declan. Being fast can earn you a lot of money beneath cliffs along river."

Declan had always been swift on his feet. At school, he competed in district races. In the past months, his speed had saved him from both Fatesmiths and fire bears. "Doing what?"

"There is a bird that nests on Eastern cliffs. Opal eagles. They are rare, their eggs rarer. Make you much mitka."

The words sparked a memory. Declan remembered Laurefen calling him an Opal Eagle at King's College, now Laurefen likely wanted him dead. He ignored the thought. "What does an egg sell for?"

"Lots."

"Seems easy enough."

Grigory laughed. "Don't get ahead of yourself, fellow. Chasing eagles is no safe bet." As if to prevent Declan from getting ahead of himself, he winked and recited, "I share this knowledge, true to my knowledge. Let it show in green." The jade mitka on his lap glowed emerald. Grigory pocketed it, then handed him another towel. "Rest today. Will do you good. Tomorrow we will go to work answering your question."

CHAPTER 5
DECLAN

"WAKE UP, FELLOW."

Declan blinked the room into focus. The cramped space fit a bunk and wooden drawers. Grigory stood in the doorway, an oil lantern in hand. Out the window, the sky was ink-black.

"It's still dark."

"It is not yet dawn. If you want answers, we must go now." Grigory turned to leave.

"Wait." Declan sat up and winced. The herbs had worked wonders, but the sudden movement came with stabbing pain. "Why so early?

"I hope you have mitka for question."

Declan rolled his bleary eyes and considered an appropriate leading statement. "Uh... We are leaving very early."

Grigory smiled. "Irman is a trader, has many partners. He is busy man. He has agreed to meet before working day begins. For his line of work, time is much value."

"Okay. I'm coming." Declan willed himself upright. The cuts down his chest came to life. He hunched forward and

28

tried to breathe over the constant ache. "Just give me a minute."

"I will fetch Trevor," Grigory said. "Get ready quickly. Irman will not wait."

Grigory's land was a morning's ride from the City, but the path crossed dangerous terrain that made the journey slow. The old farmer steered the faded-yellow wagon down a knife's edge lit only by the promise of dawn. Declan held his breath. "You know, in Euryma, we have cars," he said.

"Yes, you tell me this." Grigory's eyes never left the road. "Mechanical carts that lead themselves."

"I expected Vedmark to be more..." Declan trailed off, unsure how to finish. "More advanced," he said finally. "You have magic here."

"Sila, not magic." The narrow path tightened, and stunted trees marked the track. Beyond those, a sheer drop into darkness. Grigory grunted, "Not me. I wield pitchfork and tend goats."

"Even so. The wizards back home create Openings in the air. They can go wherever they like at a moment's notice. We are riding an assortment of sticks down a mountain."

The cart's wheels squeaked as if in acknowledgment. Declan opened his mouth to apologize, but Grigory cut him off. "Just because it can be done does not mean it *should* be done. If we discard our ways, we forget where we come from. No coming back then, fellow. You lose your culture. You lose who you are."

"It's not about forgetting. It's about improving. New

things make life better. Imagine how much more time you would have if you could travel to the city in an instant."

Grigory nodded. "Many people visit southern land. They come back with bright eyes, big changes, but old ways continue."

"Maybe your old ways are all that can happen," Declan said. "It can't be easy to make progress in a country where everyone pays to ask questions."

"Questions are free, fellow. I pay for answers."

Declan sighed. "You know what I mean. In Euryma, you can ask whatever you want."

"People must struggle to guard knowledge."

"Not really. Just because someone asks something doesn't mean you have to answer. Sharing lets people do more. They can combine what they know to make things better."

"Maybe." Grigory stared straight ahead. Declan wasn't sure he was listening. The path took them atop an exposed ridge. Straying too far on either side here would equal certain death.

Declan didn't speak until they arrived on sturdier ground. "It just doesn't make sense, that's all."

"Perhaps that reflects your understanding."

Declan laughed. "You're as bad as this old cart, Ory."

Grigory held his head high. "I like my cart. It teaches me many things. Patience, trust, gratitude."

Dawn painted a luminous pink horizon. The road widened. They reached the peak of a small hill, and the city emerged. Vedmark. The word applied to both country and capital, and Grigory used the name interchangeably. After much confusion on Declan's part, he now referred to it as 'The City'.

From their vantage point, it could be a collection of

children's toys. Fairy-tale buildings crowded around a towering hall, or miniature wooden castles topped with rounded domes. Some were splashed with bright paint; those that weren't had a unique grey-green hue, as if the wood still lived.

The dirt road joined a path of interlinked hexagonal bricks. When it did, the shaking cart settled into a smooth glide. Declan watched, bemused, as they joined a procession of carts drawn by a horse or donkey. *They're all stuck in the Stone Age. Nobody wants to share their talents, so they all pay the price.*

When they reached the city wall, a tall man stepped up to greet them. He reminded Declan of a stick insect with tufts of wispy, white hair. "Welcome to Vedmark." The man's bored eyes brightened. "Ory! A pleasure to see a friendly face."

Grigory sat up a little straighter. "And you, Temfell. Your family is well, I hope."

"They are," said the thin man. "Ven is thriving, with continued attempts to kill himself. I trust Misha is doing fine."

"Misha is well, thank you. Is good to hear about Ven. He still runs for Erlo, I expect."

Temfell shook his head. "No, he has started his own guild. Erlo took too much mitka. Ven has staked a claim to the northern end of the cliffs."

"This is good." Grigory gestured to Declan. "If he needs a new runner, I have one right here."

Declan waved awkwardly, and Temfell's welcome expression faded. His pale lips turned down at the edges. "I had heard you were keeping a southerner with you." His eyes flickered to Declan and back. "I had thought you had more sense."

"More sense than superstition," Grigory replied. "Boy is good worker. Fast on feet, too. He outran jumpwolf yesterday."

This caught Temfell's interest. He considered Declan once again. "Ven is always looking out for new talent. He recruits at Fountain Square."

"I wonder if Ven is as superstitious as you," Grigory said.

Temfell's eyes never left Declan. "Ven's lust for gold outweighs his fear of southern curses."

"Then I will visit Fountain Square today." Grigory winked at Declan. "I think Ven will like this one. He is an interesting fellow— thinks our ways are outdated."

The hint of a smirk split Temfell's face. "Sounds like you replaced one Misha for another."

Both men seemed to find this hilarious. They went on, speaking as if Declan was invisible. It amazed him how the conversation flowed, despite a single question. At last, they said their farewells, and Grigory steered them into the city. "That encounter was good luck, fellow. Erlo would have hired you to run but taken half your mitka to do so. Running for Temfell's boy will fill your pockets much faster."

Declan smiled. His insides squirmed.

They traveled along the outer city and soon arrived at an aged brick building. "A storage house for goods," Grigory said. Declan followed him inside. A stocky man with a broad chest waited by the lone table.

"Good morning, Irman. Thank you for meeting."

"It is no hassle, my oldest friend." Irman's face was younger than Declan expected. Still, gray streaks winged his dark hair.

Grigory smiled and beckoned Declan forward. "This is boy I told you about, Declan Moore."

Irman took Declan's hand. The handshake felt like a vice. "A pleasure."

Declan fought to keep his face straight as Irman crushed his hand. His stomach lurched. Irman unsettled him in a way he could not describe. Grigory looked between them. "I will leave you to talk. I have business in Fountain Square."

Irman walked Grigory to the exit, speaking in muttered tones. When he returned, his smile was gone. Irman motioned for them to sit, then scowled at him. "Let me be clear, Declan Moore. I do not like southerners." Declan didn't know how to respond. Irman went on. "Yet Grigory is as a brother to me. I will humor you for his sake, but I do not approve of you being here. Vedmark is no place for your kind."

Heat crept up Declan's neck. "I'm sorry to be a nuisance—"

"Nonsense. The price is paid." Irman face was a mixture of curiosity and disapproval. "Ask me what you will."

Declan inhaled slowly, and the cuts on his chest made their presence known. "How do I use Sila?"

Irman's face darkened. "You have some nerve," he growled.

"I'm sorry. I'm sorry." Declan rushed to backtrack. "I can't afford that question. Sorry."

"If that is how you will start, this meeting will be short."

Declan nodded. "Sorry. What I meant was, *how much would it cost* to learn about Sila?"

Irman leaned back, still frowning. "Normally, I would

charge four hundred for such knowledge," a wry smile crossed his face. "For you, Declan Moore, double that."

Declan's jaw dropped. *Eight hundred mitka? Is he crazy?*

Irman smiled smugly. "It is reasonable to me. The ways of Sila should be *earned*, not *bought*. If it must be bought, it is reasonable that it should be a high price."

Declan struggled to hide his disappointment. "Could you lower that price?"

"Nine hundred."

"What? That is unfair!"

"A boy arrives in a new land and expects to be given their most prized secrets." Irman slapped his hand on the table. "Count yourself lucky I am even considering it. One thousand mitka!"

A muscle in Declan's jaw twitched. He wanted to punch Irman's stupid face and leave the building. Instead, he took a calming breath. "Okay. Pretend I can afford that. Will I be able to use your knowledge myself? Or will I need a mentor to train me?"

Irman considered him. He frowned, as if unhappy with the answer he had to give. "The knowledge I possess *may* be enough."

"What do you mean?"

"Knights' power comes at a terrible cost. If you want to be like them, you must be willing to sacrifice." He clapped his hands together. "I think that is enough. You have my price."

"One thousand mitka is a small fortune."

"I know many who would pay more for such power." Irman withdrew a mitka from a cloth pouch and held it at eye level. "I share this knowledge, true to my knowledge. Let it show in green." The coin glowed, but Declan ignored it. "That wasn't much of a negotiation."

"I am a trader. Negotiation is my profession. And I hold all the cards." He dropped the coin back into the pouch. "You know my price. One thousand mitka and I will tell you about our sacred power."

"That will take me years to earn."

"Then I guess this is farewell." Irman stood and left, not even sparing a second glance or glare. Declan sat cemented to his seat. Pain pricked his fresh scars. *A thousand mitka! What a scoundrel!* He was still fuming when Grigory returned.

"I trust it went well, fellow," he said. Declan knew enough to hear the question. The people here didn't ask questions. They made statements and waited to be corrected.

"Your friend is a thief."

"A trader," Grigory chuckled. "He is loyal to the Grand Steward. There is no place for men like you in *his* Vedmark."

"So why bother?" Grigory's eyes narrowed, and Declan realized he'd just asked a question. "Sorry. What I'm trying to say is that this was a waste of time. He asked for one-thousand mitka! It will take me years to save that Ory."

"Perhaps not." He paused long enough for Declan to raise a questioning eyebrow. "I met with Temfell's boy. Luck shines on you. They have opening in their guild, starting now."

Silence followed. Declan thought hard about how to phrase his query. "Somebody must have grown weary of earning so much mitka."

"No." Grigory grimaced. "Newest recruit was caught by eagle, carried four hundred feet into sky and dropped to his death."

"Oh." The blood left Declan's face.

Grigory shrugged. "Temfell's boy says it is what you might call, *occupational hazard.*

CHAPTER 6
DECLAN

VENWIN OSTROFSKI MET Declan in the shadow of the Eastern Cliffs. The 'egghold' was a three-room cement bunker reinforced with iron columns. Ven had a thick accent, bright eyes, and a mane of blond curls that bounced as he spoke with animated enthusiasm. Declan tightened a speckled brown breastplate while Ven explained his new job. The butterflies in his stomach seemed to dull his hearing. "Sorry. I missed that last part."

Ven smiled, revealing a surprising number of missing teeth. "I said leather armor will protect from anything eagles drop. That is good thing. But if they catch you, armor will make it easy for them to pick you up."

Declan chewed his lower lip. "They must drop some heavy things if I need this for protection."

"Mainly rocks from stone field. They're not large, just sharp."

Right. Declan's hands trembled as he adjusted the strap. He considered how to phrase his next statement. "Chain mail would be lighter."

"Sunlight catches metal, lights you like campfire. No runners get close to egghold in chain mail."

"Okay. So I climb the cliffs wearing this."

Ven shook his head. "No. You wait at base of cliff."

"Alright. So, I wait at the bottom, take the first egg I see, and then..."

"Run, like your life depends on it." Ven didn't seem to care that Declan was from Euryma, just that he was fast on his feet. He winked. "Because it does."

Declan felt sick. Ven secured his own breastplate and led them outside, where two young men waited. They wore crinkled gray cloaks that appeared to be made from stone.

"It's true then," one said. He spat on the ground. "A southerner. You bring us misfortunate Ven."

"He cannot be worse luck than our last recruit," said the other man. He looked at Declan. "Do not stop running until you get in bunker." He nodded to the ground. "Previous runner was taken from very spot where you stand."

Declan's butterflies had butterflies.

"Leave him alone," Ven said. "You know Erlo is quick to snap up new runners. Beggars can't be choosers." He tossed a reassuring grin at Declan. "He will be fine. They say he outran a jumpwolf."

This seemed to impress the men. Declan attempted to smile but couldn't. *If I open my mouth, I'll vomit.* Instead, he followed Ven and the cloaked pair towards a towering line of sheer cliffs. The trail ran parallel with a fast-moving river, then branched off onto a winding path of small flat stones. Declan struggled to stay upright on the loose rock. At one point, he lost his footing and slid ten feet backward. Still, they climbed—snaking around enormous boulders—higher towards the looming rock wall. "We will find the eggs on top of mountains."

All three men burst into laughter. "You are a joker." Ven clapped his shoulder. He must have noticed Declan's confusion. "Opal eagles' nest on cliff face," he explained. "But nobody goes higher. No man has ever reached its peak."

"Though many have died trying," said the shorter of the two cloaked men. "Eagles guard their young closely. Whatever is atop, they guard closer."

"Deathless Demon," mumbled the other. The air grew tense. Ven's smile faded. The two men pulled their cloaks tight. "You have heard of Deathless Demon, southerner."

Declan shook his head.

The cloaked man sneered at him. "I will tell you for mitka," he said. "It would explain many things. Explain why our people do not like your kind."

"I want to make mitka, not spend it," Declan said. He could feel the heat rising in his cheeks. "Maybe another time."

They started up that path, walking in silence. When they entered the cliff's shadow, the air became icy and still. "There they are." Ven gestured upwards. High above, wingspans like city buses patrolled the sky. The colors were brilliant, purples and greens as vivid as sunsets. Ven continued onward. Declan stood, transfixed. He took a breath and followed.

Loose gravel gave way to smooth stone when they arrived at the cliff's base. A series of dark ropes led up the wall, passing through small metal loops every few feet. Here, Declan realized the cloaks the other men wore matched the granite perfectly. They wrapped a short strap around their waists and clipped it to the rope. Hans pointed at him. "I will drop for you, wolf runner."

Declan raised his eyebrows.

Ven chuckled. "A dropper climbs cliff and gathers eggs.

39

When time is right, he will drop it to you. As soon as you catch it, you run. Don't stop until you're in bunker."

Sweat matted Declan's curls. He looked back at the twisting trail laden with loose stone. *I barely made it up.*

"Remember," Ven said. "Do not break egg. Broken is worthless. If you have to decide between breaking bone or breaking egg, choose bone."

"This job sounded easier when Grigory described it."

The dropper barked a harsh laugh. "If this was easy, every man, woman, and child in Vedmark would be rich."

"Declan, you are ready."

Declan knew the lie was a question in disguise. He nodded his own lie back.

The droppers began to climb. They ascended methodically. Slow but consistent, ever upwards. They stopped, only to vanish against the cliff face whenever an eagle passed overhead.

Ven settled into a crouch, his speckled leather breastplate camouflaged against the bare earth. "Be ready, Declan. They are nearly there."

Declan squinted up. Rainbow wings gleamed like stained glass as the eagles circled their nests. He watched one drop into a dive of screaming color, then rise with a fox in its talons.

"They're fast," Ven whispered. "We must be faster. Head down. Get to river as last resort."

"What do you mean?" Declan realized he'd asked a question, then blushed. "Sorry. I meant to say... I do not think I can out-swim the eagles."

"You do not need to, only to trick them. If you need to jump in river, loosen breastplate first. It will float downstream, and eagle will follow." Ven pointed up at the cliff. "Hans is ready," he said, pointing to Declan's dropper.

Sunlight danced off a small mirror above. "That is his signal to drop it, and I will catch it." Declan failed to hide the tremor in his voice.

"That is correct." Ven smiled. "Soft hands." He waved an open palm at the flashing light, and a large lavender egg fell towards them. Declan stepped back, stumbled, and scrambled to his feet, but he was too slow.

Ven leaped over him, caught the falling egg, and landed in a perfect roll. When he stood up, Declan's face was on fire. "Have no shame," Ven said, smirking. "Nobody catches first one." He handed it to Declan. It was surprisingly heavy. "Go. Run, now."

Declan cradled his prize and dashed down the path. Loose stones shifted beneath every step. He passed one boulder, then checked the sky behind. Eagles drifted around the cliff's peaks, ignorant of the theft. *This isn't so bad.* He slowed around a sharp turn and jogged down the track. He was already counting his mitka when the narrow straight appeared below. As he rounded the last bend, a shrill screech pierced the air. Declan's stomach vanished. A screaming rainbow blur plunged in his direction.

Declan held tight and sprinted down alongside the river. The eagle's cry filled his ears. He pushed his legs to move faster, faster, until his feet felt like they weren't touching the ground. A dark shadow enveloped him. Declan slid to the left. With a chaotic flap of giant wings, the bird shot past him. It was lime green and larger than a car. It dipped to the side, then circled back. Declan exploded forward. The bunker door taunted him ahead. The eagle appeared to his left and turned to scoop him up.

Egg in hand, Declan stopped on a dime. Bright plumage swept by him. The door was less than fifty paces away. The eagle shrieked, snapping at his heels. Declan sprinted ahead and leaped through the door. A roar of wingbeats and the bird was gone.

"That was close," said an unfamiliar voice. A blond girl sat, filing her nails, on a wooden chair.

Declan nodded, breathless. He checked the egg and sighed with relief. No cracks. He had done it. His heart pounded inside his chest. Declan lay on the floor for another minute while the adrenaline settled, then sat up. "I'm afraid I don't know you."

She smiled. "I am Fi. Ven's sister. I collect the eggs for the Ostrofski Guild."

She didn't look a day over twelve. Declan swallowed. "I imagine your brother feels better knowing you're safe in here."

"Ven would love me out there if it meant more mitka in his pouch. I'm just not stupid enough to risk my life for an egg."

"That's not a bad point."

Fi eyed the egg. "I can put that somewhere safe."

"Yes, please." Too exhausted to argue, Declan held it up for her, then lay back on the concrete. "I will wait for Ven."

"Good idea." Fi wrapped the egg in cloth and eased it into a wooden box. "He'll be waiting for commotion to settle before another run. Take off your armor, have something to eat. You'll need your strength for round two."

Declan climbed to his feet. His legs felt like jelly, but the scars along his torso burned worst of all. He loosened the breastplate, and his stomach protested loudly. "You mentioned food."

"There should be goat jerky in back room. Help yourself."

Great. More goat. Declan walked through the bunker. Iron rivets lined walls that smelled like a school shower. In the back was a small set of shelves with stacks of folded paper bags. The dried meat inside was closer to cardboard. Declan sat on the floor while he ate. *You need to do that nine more times. If you can do that and not die, Irman will tell you everything you need to know.* Declan frowned. He'd barely survived attempt one. *Is the mitka worth it?*

He tried to relax. The damp smell of mildew made him think of Ace's attic. Declan tried to shake the thought, but it took hold, dragged up memories he would rather forget. He pictured Ace being turned to iron in a narrow alley. *You need the money. Once you learn how to use your Sila, you can save him. You'll be able to save all of them.*

Declan's appetite vanished. Memories of Ace went in the same box as memories of his parents. Locked and hidden. He put the meat back in the bag. *But your parents are gone. Ace isn't.* The familiar hollow feeling set in.

A door clanged loudly. Declan sat up straight.

"Declan!" Ven called from the main entry.

Declan pushed himself to his feet. "I'm back here." He reached the front of the bunker as Ven slid off his breastplate. He held an egg of his own between his knees. "You survived."

"Barely."

"Your egg is undamaged."

"It is," Declan said.

Ven dropped his armor on a chair and scanned the room. "You have left your egg in the back."

"No..." He turned to the door. "I gave it to your sister."

"I have no sister..." Ven's forehead creased.

Declan's stomach fell. His words came thick and fast. "She was at the door when I came in. She said her name was Fi. She took the egg."

Ven started laughing. Fi stepped out from the side

room; she wore a wicked smile. "Just a recruit joke." Ven wiped his eyes. "Always fun."

"You nearly gave me a heart attack," Declan said.

"Ven's idea," Fi added. "Always fun to scare new runners."

Ven beamed at him. "You did well. Mother eagle noticed you earlier than normal and you still did not die. You have a future here if you want to earn much mitka."

Declan opened his mouth. A heavy knock on the bunker door interrupted him.

Fi glanced at the entrance. "We aren't expecting visitors."

Ven shook his head. "No, we are not. Probably Erlo." He peeked through a slot. His shoulders immediately straightened, and he swung the door open. Someone stepped through the entry, and both Ven and his sister dropped to one knee. "Mistress Drakonov."

The visitor was a young woman with short curls, dark skin, and brilliant blue eyes. While the others bowed, Declan couldn't hide his smile.

Ava.

CHAPTER 7
DECLAN

AVA'S EXPRESSION made no secret of her displeasure. Her lips were thin, her eyes were storm clouds. "Declan Moore. I have been sent to collect you." She stared at the lavender egg cradled in Ven's arms. "Your presence here has not gone unnoticed."

Declan blinked. "What... Ava. What does that mean?"

Ven groaned. Ava's eyebrows drew down. "Unless you're offering mitka, you would do well to keep your questions to yourself. I have been sent to collect you."

Declan stood rooted to the spot—his mind blank. "It is fine," Ven whispered from his kneeling position. "I will sell your egg and send mitka to Grigory. You best go with Mistress Drakonov."

"Who?" Declan asked, and Ven stiffened, as if Declan's direct question had doused him with cold water. Declan's face burned. "My apologies Av- uh... Mistress Drakonov. Uh, lead the way."

Ava scowled, shook her head, then left. Declan rushed to follow. Behind the egghold waited a handsome carriage attached to a chestnut horse. Dragons—the same as those

45

engraved on every jade mitka—were carved into the door. Declan followed Ava inside. Before he could sit down, she whistled, and the horse jolted to a steady trot. Declan tumbled into the seat beside her. Ava stared straight ahead, jaw set, shoulders tense. As soon as the bunker was out of sight, she started laughing.

She was joking? Declan glared at her. "You're so mean! I thought I was in big trouble!"

"I'm quite the performer, you know."

They traveled between grassy foothills—the city a splash of color on the horizon. "So, I'm not in trouble?"

Ava smirked. "Are you paying for those questions?"

"Are you paying for *that* question?"

Ava laughed. "I'm just as bad as you. Too much time in Euryma."

Declan felt a pang of homesickness. "So, why come to collect me? And why act so angry about it?"

Ava whistled again, at a lower pitch this time. The chestnut mare whinnied back, and the carriage slowed to a stop. Ava turned to him; concern filled her eyes. "Ory said you were here. I needed to talk to you and... people... they'd rather come up with their own conclusions than pay for the truth. It's safer for both of us if people don't know."

"Know what?"

"About us."

Something fluttered in Declan's stomach. "What about us?"

"So many questions! Sheesh, you must be flat broke."

Declan ignored the jab. "Is it because I'm from Euryma?"

Ava shook her head quickly. "No. It's not that..." She trailed off as an armadillo wandered down a nearby log.

They watched it in silence. Ava faced him. "The night we met. You asked me to sum myself up in one sentence."

"I remember."

"Do you remember what I said?"

Declan bit his lip. "Not word for word."

"Fair call." A fleeting smile crossed Ava's lips. "Well, I said I was the only hope of a family driven crazy by a misplaced sense of responsibility."

"Okay..."

"Well, that family includes me.... and the Grand Steward."

"The who?"

Ava raised her eyebrows. "Has Grigory told you anything about Vedmark?"

Declan's laugh sounded harder than he liked. "I can't afford to ask. I've been working non-stop so I can eat."

"Okay, okay." Ava bit her lip, and color darkened her cheeks. "The Grand Steward rules Vedmark... in place of a King."

Declan squinted at her. "You're a Princess?"

Ava snorted so loud, the armadillo outside curled into a ball. "No, no, no." She shook her head, chuckling. "Nothing like that. No, the Steward is a placeholder. There is no royalty in his blood, nor in mine. There *is* a King, but that's a whole other story." She sighed. "Declan, ever since my uncle discovered I was a Luck, I've been working in his service. They scrutinize everything I do. I don't want to pull you into that."

"Into what?"

"We don't exactly see eye to eye." She shook her head. "You know how things work here. It is cheaper to make assumptions. If word got out that we were close... It would be a disaster."

Close. Declan nodded. "Okay. So why come and collect me? When did you get back?"

"I got in early this morning. I have a summons to my uncle today—chances are they're going to send me away again. I wanted to see you. I dropped by the farm, and Ory told me you were running eggs." Concern creased her forehead. "I came to get you out of here. I don't want you to do this," she said.

"Get me out of here?" Declan leaned back. "Ava, I chose this. I need the mitka."

She didn't bat an eyelid. "C'mon, Declan. *Everyone* knows egg hunting is a loser's game. It's gambling. No, it's worse. Gambling, you just lose your money."

"Ava. I don't have a choice."

"Of course, you have a choice! There are plenty of jobs in the City."

"For a southerner?" Frustration sharpened his voice. "Nobody wants me here." He hesitated. "Speaking of which... what is a Deathless Demon?"

"Excuse me?" Ava's eyes were wide. "Where did you hear that?"

"One of those guys said it. He said it would explain why everyone hates me." Declan shrugged. "Why the surprise?"

Ava brushed a stray strand of hair behind her ears. It was the closest to flustered he had ever seen her. "It's... It's not something people talk about freely. Many think the name itself brings bad luck."

"So, it's a person?"

"Depends who you ask." Ava leaned forward until he could see the pale freckles on her nose. They were alone in the carriage. Still, her voice dropped to a whisper. "They say he was once a King. He grew too powerful and madness

48

took him. He cursed himself so that he could not die and now roams the Void."

"The Void?" Declan whispered, too, though he didn't know why. "What's that?"

"The Void. The Empty. The Nothing. People call it different things, but it's all the same. It's a barren section of the forest where nothing grows, nothing lives. My uncle sent Vedmark's strongest Knights there a few years ago..."

She stared out of the carriage. Declan waited. When she said nothing, he nudged her leg. "And? What happened?"

She shrugged. "None came back. Whatever it is, it's a death trap." Ava's gaze sharpened and fell on Declan. "And speaking of death traps—why are you running eggs?"

"I told you. I need mitka. Fast."

"Why?"

"So I can pay Ory's dumb friend to teach me how to be a Knight."

"Declan—"

"There are people in Euryma that need my help. Instead, I'm here mending fences, shoveling donkey manure, eating goat stew." It was all true, which is what made it such a convincing lie. Declan threw up his hands. He hoped the frustration would mask what he really wanted. What he'd always wanted.

"You can't save anyone if an eagle throws you off a cliff. Don't do this, Declan, it's too dangerous."

"Ace is still out there," Declan said flatly. "He's in one of those holding houses, trapped in iron because of me."

Ava fixed him with a sapphire stare. "That was outside of your control. You couldn't have known what was going to happen. You made the best decision you could with the knowledge you had. You can't blame yourself."

Declan's lips trembled. "He was supposed to go off to an

amazing Mag-Ed College, do whatever he wanted. He was going to get away from his awful parents. Away from his attic. He was going to make something of himself." A tear traced his cheek.

Ava squeezed his arm. "I'm sorry."

Declan forced the memory back into its box. "It's been months. I'm grateful to Grigory for letting me stay and for feeding me, but I need to do something. I can't hide in Vedmark forever."

Ava didn't answer. Birds chirped, and leaves rustled. Two more armadillos tiptoed across the clearing, noses pressed to the ground. They started digging into a decaying log. Declan couldn't bear the silence. "I thought armadillos were desert animals."

"And you'd be right," Ava said. "They were introduced and have adapted well. Probably a little *too* well. Most people hate them, but they seem to be everywhere this time of year." She looked him up and down. "Ory must be working you hard, Declan. You certainly look... stronger."

Declan blushed. "Amazing what a diet of goat and work can do," he muttered.

"Then why not get a job in the City? There's always demand for laborers. You don't have to tell them where you come from."

"I can't, Ava," Declan said. "That will take too long."

"Those eagles will not care that you're a Warlock. You're useless to Euryma if you're a splat on the ground."

"I'll be fine. I have no intention of getting caught."

Ava arched a single eyebrow. "Nobody ever *intends* to be a splat, Declan."

"I'm doing what has to be done. Grigory understands."

"He probably wants to be rid of the southerner that eats all his livestock."

Declan smiled, but it faded as his expression hardened. "Maybe. But I have to do this. You're not going to change my mind."

Ava studied him for a long moment. "You're as stubborn as a goat," she breathed. "I understand, but I don't agree. Look after yourself."

"I always do."

"No," Ava said sternly. "Promise me, if those eagles start chasing you, you throw the egg away and keep yourself safe."

Declan nodded. "I'll try."

"Good. And just to show you how unimpressed I am, you can walk back."

"What?"

"Out of my carriage, Southerner. Perhaps a stroll in the hills will clear your head of this nonsense."

––––––––––

Declan waited at the bottom of the cliff, leather breastplate pulled tight, butterflies secured in his stomach. He kept his eyes up, waiting for the flash of a mirror. *What if Ava was right? You can't save Ace if you're dead.* Her words ate at him the entire walk back to the bunker, circling his mind like the eagles patrolling the cliffs above. *You can't save him if you're stuck working for pennies, either. It could take years to save enough mitka to learn anything useful. There is no other way.*

A glinting reflection interrupted his thoughts. The dropper was ready. Declan waved in response. Time trickled like syrup. A lavender egg materialized overhead. Everything accelerated. Declan stepped back, positioned himself directly beneath the prize, and caught it against his chest.

He turned and ran. He'd barely made it to the first boulder when an abrupt scream pierced the afternoon air. Ignoring Ven's earlier counsel, Declan turned back to the cliffs. His blood turned to ice. An opal eagle had his dropper. Enormous talons wrenched the man off the cliff face. Thundering beats of colossal wings lifted them higher. The man thrashed in a wild panic that did nothing. The eagle ascended uninhibited until they were a speck in the cloudless blue.

High in the sky, one speck became two. The man flailed as he fell. His distant scream grew louder, louder, then silence. Declan fell to his knees and vomited.

A shrill screech echoed through the cliffs. More responded. Declan scanned the sky. Multiple eagles dropped into dives. Streaming towards him, riding the wind like a glittering storm-front.

Declan stumbled to his feet and sprinted down the path. The egg lay abandoned on the ground.

CHAPTER 8
DECLAN

THE WINDING PATH was not an option. Instead, Declan cut a straight line over boulders, loose shale, jagged edges, and steep slopes, part running, mostly falling, never stopping.

The eagle's shrill calls echoed off the rock. Declan didn't know how many birds hunted him, and he didn't dare turn to find out. His only chance of survival was to keep moving, weaving, tripping, and fumbling through the stone fields, shielding him from certain death.

A turquoise flash appeared beside him. Declan leaped away and slid over the ground. Razor-sharp granite tore his skin. Vivid feathers brushed over him, kicking up a haze of stone and dirt. A stream of blood ran down Declan's arm as he crawled through the haze. More wings. More squawks. Declan rolled over a short wall and squeezed into a shallow crevice.

Caked in blood and dirt, he surveyed the landscape below. A large chasm lay thirty feet below him. It looked like a giant had dragged a gargantuan pickaxe through the rock. It looked deep enough to hide him until the eagles lost interest. Declan struggled to breathe. His scars stung.

Something moved above him—a rush of magenta—and he jumped forward, dodging the eagle by inches. His armor buckled as he collided with a stunted granite shelf. He rolled left and leaped again, his arms flailing as the earth rushed towards him.

A magenta eagle plucked him mid-fall like some enormous insect. He jerked backward—the air forced from his lungs as bronze talons tightened on the leather breastplate; the granite field below him was a blur. With fumbling fingers, Declan wrenched on the laces until they snapped. The armor came loose. Gravity did the rest. Declan met stone with a dull crack. His right arm went limp, and the pain followed.

The bird dropped the breastplate. It bounced down the hill. Declan hobbled into the chasm as more birds flooded towards him. He cradled his arm, head spinning, and sheltered in the darkness. Sharp shrieks echoed along the narrow passage. Declan crawled in as deep as he could. Bleeding and dazed, he collapsed against the wall. *Ava was right. This is a death sentence.* Eagles landed above him, digging into the gap with their long claws, but he was beyond their reach. Declan slid to the ground. *They have to give up, eventually.*

But *eventually* felt like forever. Minutes trickled like treacle before the chasm fell silent. An undisturbed blue sky appeared between the rocks. Declan breathed a sigh.

A loud crack shook the chasm, followed by another, another. A small boulder hit the passageway like a cannonball, wedging itself in the chasm's opening. Bright plumage descended over it. Bronze talons wrapped around the stone and pulled it upwards. Once the eagle was gone, the thunderous avalanche resumed. Declan stared up in disbelief. *They're trying to break the place open.*

Flecks of dust filled his lungs. He coughed and crawled into the haze. The chasm walls closed in until he had to sidestep between the sharp granite and every rocky collision reverberated in his bones. Declan stopped short of a narrow exit and peered out. The bunker wasn't far off. One corner and then a straight trail back to safety. *You don't have a chance. They'll catch you as soon as you reach the path.* He turned his attention elsewhere. To his left, the winding trail ended in a sudden drop. *The river.*

The trembling chasm shook violently, and a sound like rolling thunder followed. The crevice walls were collapsing. A cloud of dust shot out behind him, forcing Declan into the open. When the haze settled, a small orange eagle stared at him. It tilted its head, then screeched an alarm.

The river.

Adrenaline dulled the pain, or some of it. Declan bolted. Head down, he willed himself towards the drop. At the loose rocks, he fell forward, sprawling face-first onto stone. A shadow overshot him, talons grabbing at empty air. The fall had saved his life, but the eagle's turquoise wings spread like a parachute. It stopped ahead of him, blocking his path.

Declan pushed himself up with his working arm. The eagle turned, fixing him with a chilling stare. Two more birds landed behind him. Declan squeezed his eyelids closed, seeking the deep despair that might unlock his power. There was none. No green coin, no Sila, only pain, fear, and the embarrassment that Ava had been proven right so quickly.

The turquoise eagle stepped forward, then shrieked. An armadillo clutched the bird's talons. The enormous bird shook its leg wildly—thrashed around—and took to the sky. With one mighty kick, it tossed the armadillo from its talons. It rolled into a golden ball that disappeared down the trail.

Declan didn't wait. Before the eagles behind him could react, he dashed to the edge of the cliff and jumped. A vast grey river coursed through the mountains. Chaotic rapids pitched and swirled. Declan braced himself, then wrenched backward.

An eagle had caught his shirt.

With a loud rip, the material tore loose. Declan plunged into the thrashing water. The impact knocked the air out of him, and the freezing rapids immediately sucked him underwater. His shoulder collided with something hard, slippery, heavy. The weight of the water pinned him in icy darkness, then dragged him free. He emerged long enough for a single breath before vanishing underneath. Declan shielded his head with his good arm as the current tossed him about like a feather in an updraft. *Hold your breath. Protect your head. Stay alive. Ava will kill you if you die.*

Declan did not know how far he drifted. The icy mountain water numbed his aching body, but he was too weak to swim. The rivers widened, the current slowed, and a shallow sandbar caught him near the shore. Declan crawled out of the shallows, then collapsed. Above him, a towering willow swayed in and out of focus. Its long curtain of leaves rustled in the breeze. Declan rolled onto his back. Pain shot down his side, and he shifted until the stabbing sensation settled. The sand was warm, the air cool. Everything faded to smells and sounds.

When he opened his eyes, a bronze armadillo sat on his chest.

Declan moved to shake it off, and exquisite pain filled every inch of his body. The armadillo crawled down his torso, fixed him with a knowing gaze, and started walking up the riverbank. Declan watched it go—certain he was dreaming.

The armadillo turned back. Declan didn't move. It stood on a patch of grass, watching with beady brown eyes. Declan ignored it. He focused on the golden sunlight glittering through the willow vines. When he looked back, the armadillo hadn't moved. It poked its snout at him, then swiveled its head as if motioning to go.

That armadillo is telling you to follow it. You have lost your mind.

It jerked its head again.

Okay. This is normal. You've smashed your head on a rock in the river, that's all.

The armadillo took a few steps, paused, and glanced back. Light pierced the willow's curtain, reflecting off its scales. They weren't bronze. They were gold. Declan blinked. "Are... are you... was that you that attacked the eagle?"

The armadillo dipped its head in a tiny nod. Then it walked up the bank. Declan's breath caught in his throat. *You've gone mad.*

The armadillo stopped again. It seemed frustrated. Declan labored to his feet. His muscles felt like shards of glass. He opened his mouth, then paused. *This is crazy. It's an animal. You're talking to an animal. Snap out of it!* The armadillo stood and stared. Declan sighed. "I suppose you want me to follow you?"

The golden armor glinted as the little head nodded. Declan rubbed his eyes, hoping the hallucination would fade. It didn't. The armadillo was still there. He shuffled towards it. "Okay then. Lead the way, I guess."

The armadillo teetered forward. Declan followed, grimacing with every painful step.

They walked beside the river at first. Willows of various shapes and sizes stretched over the banks, dipping their long, green strands into the water. The sandy riverbank gave way to soft patches of grass.

The wind picked up against the soaked remains of his clothing. Declan shivered. *You're following an armadillo. An armadillo that saved you from a giant eagle.* His little golden guide went away from the river to climb a steep hill. Declan groaned. The armadillo must have heard. It stopped and turned to face him. *Oh great,* Declan thought. *It's judging me.* He masked a wince and started up the path. When he reached the top, his mouth fell open.

A compact log hut, encircled by tall trees, waited on the hill's summit. It had two windows, a carved door, and a tilted, flat roof. Wilderness stretched out for miles around. He considered the way they had come. To the east, the eagle's cliffs were small enough to fit in his palm. *What is a hut like this doing in the middle of nowhere?*

The armadillo motioned to the hut.

"You want me to go inside?"

The armadillo nodded.

"Uh, okay then." Declan walked to the door, then stopped. *The Deathless Demon lives in the Void. A cursed part of the forest.* His hand hovered at the door. He checked over his shoulder. Birdsong floated out from the swaying evergreens. *This isn't the Void. This is fine. Everything is okay.* "Uh, should I knock?" He turned back, but the little golden creature was gone. Left with no choice, Declan knocked. No response. He tried again, but still nothing. The door swung open smoothly. "Hello?" he called. "Is anybody here?"

Silence.

"I don't know where I am. I woke up by the river. There

was a..." Declan paused. *Maybe don't mention an armadillo led you here.* "A guide showed me the way."

Still nothing. Declan stepped inside.

The cabin's interior comprised one large room. One corner housed a wooden table, the other, a low bed. The walls were empty, save for two short axes fixed to the wall. On one handle was a carved V, on the other was a W. The axe-heads were stamped with the symbol of a bull. *What is this place?*

In a wooden bowl on the table were three small melons, pale pink, each the size of a fist. Beside it, a fourth melon had been cut in half. Its lilac flesh smelled familiar. Sanarmelon. Ava used its juice as a healing remedy. Declan helped himself to the sliced half. The juicy flesh was heaven on his parched lips, sweet like watermelon, but creamier. As he ate, his weary body tingled. By the time the sanarmelon was gone, even his broken arm felt fine.

Declan searched the hut with fresh eyes. A folded cotton tunic lay on the bed. On top of that, a white card. Declan flipped it open. His jaw dropped as he read the message.

Welcome, Declan. Rest and recover. You are safe here.

CHAPTER 9
AVA

AVA HELD her head high as she crossed the Steward's Hall. An embroidered purple carpet muffled her steps while sunshine poured through circular windows, creating pillars of light on either side of her. Enormous silk banners lined the walls, each depicting scenes of Vedmark's greatest triumphs. It was a sight to behold, but Ava had beheld it more times than she could count. On a dais was the Emerald Throne, as glorious as its name implied. Sitting upon it was her uncle, Rasporvin Drakonov.

Rasporvin was a gaunt man, tall and thin. Tendrils of grey hair hung, like limp serpents, about his pallid cheeks. Ava had never liked her uncle, and she knew the Grand Steward of Vedmark felt the same about her. He was greedy for power, greedy for a kingdom that wasn't his.

When Ava reached him, she bowed. His beetle-black eyes made her skin crawl. His expression softened as she straightened. "My niece returns from the south."

"I return at your summons, Grand Steward."

"Such formality, Ava." Rasporvin leaned against his throne. "It is unnecessary."

"Apologies, Uncle."

"You have been gone for many weeks, my niece. Before that, you have spent much time in those wretched lands to the south."

"The Emissary keeps me busy."

"She does," he said. "So, tell me, the thief, Haberdeen. You have found her."

"No, uncle. Not yet."

Rasporvin clicked his tongue. "You come before me bearing failure."

"I come bearing your summons."

"Your failure is troubling indeed." Ava's uncle didn't seem to be listening. He pressed long fingers together. His expression darkened. "I have granted you more than enough time to retrieve my knife. Events are in motion. Winterthorn is crucial to Vedmark's success."

"Haberdeen is no easy target to track down."

"You wield the power of Luck," Rasporvin growled. "I question whether you wield it poorly or whether you have been deliberate in your failure."

Ava bowed. "I live to serve the Emerald Throne, Grand Steward."

"So you say..." Rasporvin stared over her, gaze fixed on something at the back of the hall. Ava turned to follow. They were alone.

She softened her jaw, arranging her expression into something she hoped would appear vulnerable. "Uncle..." she started. "I am curious about the boy I brought from Euryma."

"Ah, yes." Rasporvin's eyes narrowed as if she had interrupted some important thought. "You speak of Declan Moore."

"You've heard..." Ava's voice caught in her throat. *I*

61

nearly asked him a question. She feigned a cough to cover her slip. "You know who he is, yet do not seek to meet him. I expected the Knights to be thrilled with a Knight who could wield power outside our borders."

"He is an outsider." Rasporvin shook his head. "Declan Moore has no loyalty to Vedmark or the Drakonov line."

"But he's a warlock."

"A warlock, yes, but he will never be a Knight."

"How could you know that?" The question leaped from her lips before she could stop it.

There was a painful pause. Rasporvin's nose crinkled in disgust. "Listen to you. Asking questions like a beggar. You have been away from home for far too long.

"A thousand apologies," Ava stammered. "I did not mean to—"

"Perhaps it is time you put aside your travels and spend some time amongst your own people."

Ava couldn't imagine anything worse, but she knew her uncle. He was baiting her. She ignored her thundering heartbeat and forced a smile. "You may be right, Uncle. I have been gone a long time." Ava stared down at her feet, appropriately ashamed.

"I do not appreciate your reckless questions, despite that, I am certain. We have searched the boy's family tree. There is no path to Knighthood for him."

Ava didn't know how to respond. Knowledge of the Knights' inner workings was expensive and, for a Luck, irrelevant. Outside of public gossip, they were a mystery to her. "Declan will live out his life in Vedmark."

"He may. It is no concern of mine."

"It would be a shame, Uncle," Ava said. "His potential is vast. He cleared an enormous section of Anderma with no training."

Rasporvin chuckled, an uncomfortably high sound, like a hyena. "Any warlock looks powerful compared to those pitiful southerners. Their *magic* is no match for our Sila."

"Still..." Ava glanced up at him. "I cannot understand why you sent me to bring Declan here if you had no interest in using him."

"It was not *my* instruction for you to bring the boy to Vedmark." Rasporvin sat back in his throne. A loud knock interrupted them. To their right, a lacquered door swung open for a woman with dark hair, navy eyes, and a smile like winter. The Emissary.

"Ah, Samantha," Rasporvin said. "Your timing is impeccable."

The Emissary bowed her head. "My apologies for not being here sooner, Lord Drakonov. Euryma is a wildfire in the wind. As soon as I extinguish one flame, two more take its place."

"How unfortunate." Rasporvin didn't bother to hide his smirk. "You have spoken to their High Mage."

"He has had no luck finding Haberdeen or penetrating her order of Fatesmiths. I still believe Ava is our best shot." The Emissary's voice was matter-of-fact.

"My niece's failures are mounting." Rasporvin nodded at Ava. "You may leave." His lips twisted into something between a grin and a scowl. "Do not take that too literally. You will stay in Vedmark for now, reacquaint yourself with your homeland."

The Emissary's eyes flashed. "Grand Steward, I have need of Ava's service. Now more than ever."

"Ava has spent too long in Euryma. She needs to remember who she is."

"She is my only Luck with any experience. It would be foolish to remove her—"

"Enough!" Rasporvin thrust a bony finger at Ava. "Go." The finger slashed to the door. "You are dismissed."

Ava obeyed, or at least she started to. The moment she escaped their sight, she slipped up a short flight of stairs along a stone balustrade and down behind the hall's sweeping banners. Ava leaned on Luck to keep them still until she was within earshot of the throne.

"I need that dagger, Samantha," Rasporvin said. "Tell me what you are doing to find it."

"I have people searching, but it will take time. You are looking for a needle in a haystack." Exasperation tinged the Emissary's tone. "What I want to know is how the knife ended up in Euryma. The Knights took it into the Void."

"Knightmaster Korvan bore the blade. I would have trusted no other but him."

Ava could hear the Emissary's delicate footsteps, could picture her pacing the dais, forehead creased in concentration. "So Korvan disappears in the Void and Winterthorn with it. Then Winterthorn shows up a thousand miles south, and your Knightmaster is nowhere to be seen. It makes no sense."

"The Deathless Demon," Rasporvin growled. "He knew it was our only weapon against him, so he sent it beyond the reach of our Knights."

"I take your urgency to mean the Void is still growing."

Ava's jaw dropped. That was new information. Unsettling information. She strained to hear more.

"It is," Rasporvin said. "We need that knife back, Samantha. It is our only hope to stop the demon from destroying our land."

"Very well," The Emissary said. "I may have a lead. A sighting in the southeast. Parteno."

"A lead." Rasporvin's voice dripped with frustration. "I grow weary of leads that lead nowhere."

"It is not Haberdeen, but it is one of her most ardent followers. That's the best I have at present."

"You should have told me this sooner," Rasporvin said.

"I am telling you now," replied the Emissary. "Had it not been for your summons, Ava would be in Parteno as we speak. I sincerely hope our window remains open."

"Watch your tongue, woman. I am the Grand Steward of Vedmark."

"And such, you have never set foot in Euryma. You hired me for my expertise, Grand Steward. You said I could direct the Lucks as I please to accomplish your goals." There was a tense pause. "I respect your authority, but I have a job to do. If you insist on interrupting my work, it is not fair that you blame me for the lack of results."

Ava grinned. She had heard no one talk to her uncle with such bluntness. She just wished she could see his face.

"Very well," Rasporvin said coldly. "Command is yours, as is the accompanying responsibility. Investigate Parteno, but send the boy. My niece needs to remain."

His words were a punch in the gut.

"Lord Drakonov," the Emissary started. "Misha is not Ava. He has neither the experience nor the power that she does."

"I don't care," Rasporvin said. "Ava is a daughter of Vedmark."

"Be reasonable—"

"She asked me a question earlier. Straight out asked like a southern beggar. No, she will stay here until I deem her ready to leave once more."

Ava held her breath. She waited for the Emissary's plea.

Instead, the woman sighed. "Very well," she said. "I will send Misha to investigate alone."

"Very well."

"I only hope he is up to the challenge. As you have said yourself, most leads have led us nowhere. Opportunities are scarce. It would be disappointing if his inexperience proved the difference." The Emissary paused briefly, "and we lost the knife forever."

A new type of silence filled the room. Ava imagined her uncle weighing up the options. "Fine," he growled at last. "Ava will go with Misha on one last excursion. After that, she stays."

"Your wisdom is beyond reproach, Grand Steward."

"Don't patronize me," Rasporvin hissed. "I have concerns regarding Ava. She has questions about the boy. Declan Moore. She wanted to know why *I* brought him here."

Ava's ears pricked. She held her breath and listened.

"I expect you told her the truth," the Emissary replied.

"It was a fool's errand, sending her to retrieve him, Samantha. With his parents gone, there is nothing for Declan Moore in Vedmark."

"Perhaps." The Emissary sounded distant. "Perhaps one day, despite your doubt, he will prove useful after all."

———

Why would the Emissary send me to get Declan?

Ava sat on a sunlit bench outside the Steward's Hall. How she had got there was a question she could not answer. The revelation that the Emissary was responsible for Declan had caught her by surprise. The knowledge that

66

the Void was growing was also a concern. *Too many questions.*

"Hear anything interesting?"

Ava nearly jumped out of her skin. The Emissary swept her blue cloak aside to sit beside her. Ava tried to appear casual. "It is very bold of you to ask an outright question in this place."

The Emissary laughed. "Ava, please. It's bad enough I have to endure this backward nonsense with your uncle." Her smile faded. "Don't pretend you weren't hiding behind those curtains. What did you think?"

"Was I that obvious?"

"Only to those watching." The Emissary sighed. "Your uncle noticed nothing. His desperation blinds him." She shifted her skirt. "I imagine you have some question—"

"Why did you send me to retrieve Declan?" Ava stiffened. The words had escaped of their own accord.

"That didn't take long." The Emissary smiled sadly, then spoke in the softest of whispers, slowly, carefully, as if measuring every word. "That is one question I cannot answer."

"You don't know?"

"It is not *my* answer to give."

Ava raised her eyebrows. "That doesn't make sense."

"No, it doesn't. Not yet. I'm sorry. Keep your questions away from Declan Moore, and I will give you some better answers."

"Is the Void really growing?"

"It is." A troubled expression crossed the Emissary's face. "It has been for a long time, but recently it has sped up. The forest is being overtaken."

"How fast is it moving?"

"Impossible to say anymore. The cursed place has

grown too dangerous for Vedmark's Knights to monitor." Her lips were a narrow line. "Only a handful know about this; it must stay that way, or panic will envelop the city."

Ava silently agreed. If word got out that it was spreading, there would be chaos in the streets. "Is that why Uncle wants Winterthorn so badly?"

The Emissary nodded. "Winterthorn is his only lifeline. He is beyond desperate to find it, to destroy his demon and escape before the Void swallows his cursed kingdom."

Ava leaned away from her. "And you want me to find the knife and deliver it to him?"

"He is the Grand Steward. Those are his orders."

"But he's evil." Ava squeezed her palms against her eyes. "You're the Emissary to Euryma, and you're serving the man who wants to take your land."

The Emissary studied her intently. "What would you do instead?"

"Mess up on purpose. Lose Haberdeen. Let her get away. Whatever keeps that dagger out of his hands."

"And doom your people? I am no fan of Rasporvin, but he isn't interested in conquering Euryma. He wants to escape the Void. It is a noble goal to protect one's people."

"So he says." Ava's gaze fell to her feet. "But you've seen my uncle. The moment he can get the Knights into Euryma, he won't stop until the entire Dominion is his."

"Perhaps." The Emissary said. She let the words hang as a breeze rustled the trees overhead. "How's this for a compromise? I want you to kill the Mage, take Winterthorn, then hide it somewhere safe."

Ava's eyes snapped up from the ground. Her voice dropped to a whisper. "You want me to betray my uncle?"

"I want you to serve Vedmark. Your uncle is too

desperate to think straight. Do you know how he lost Winterthorn in the first place?"

"He lost it in the Void," Ava said, recalling their earlier conversation. "Sent it with Korvan and the other Knights."

"And why did he do that? Because they discovered the Void was expanding. He panicked. He didn't think, didn't seek counsel. He just threw it all away." The Emissary leaned forward until her lips were only inches from Ava's ear. "Rasporvin is not fit to wield that knife. If we give it to him too soon, he will do something foolish."

A solid silence settled on the sunlit courtyard. Ava could feel her heart in her chest. "And when I come back bearing failure? Uncle won't let me leave."

"He won't like it, but he'll come around. Especially if the Mage gave you some carefully crafted information before he died."

We'll send him on a goose chase. Ava smiled; she had never seen this side of the Emissary. She liked it. "What about Misha? Should he know too?"

"No, he should not. He will accompany you to Parteno, but I do not want him involved. Lie to him. Tell him to search for Haberdeen while you deal with the Mage yourself."

"You don't trust him?"

"I don't trust his boastfulness. One slip of the tongue, and we'll be labelled traitors."

Ava nodded. *Fair point.*

"The fewer who know, the better. I know we share a similar understanding of your uncle, and I know you want to do right by your homeland. Misha may earn that trust in time. For now, keep silent. Keep him safe. I'll organize passage through the Threshold for the morning. I will meet you in Parteno in two days for a report." She arched a perfect eyebrow. "Am I clear?"

Ava bowed. "Yes, Emissary."

CHAPTER 10
AVA

PARTENO WAS A BUST. Six hours on the Northern Rail. Six hours of Misha's non-stop talking. An entire day following dead-end leads, leaning on Luck until they chanced upon a Fatesmith who was, frankly, insane.

He grinned. His smile made her skin crawl. Sleeves frayed, buttons gone, oblivious to the iron chains wrapped around him. "Am I just going to sit here all night?" he asked.

"We will wait until you answer my questions." Ava gestured down the railway tunnel. "Or until you're a splat on the tracks."

The man relaxed against the chair, perfectly at ease. His breath crystallized in the cold air. "I have told you, I know nothing."

"Why are you in Parteno?"

"Madam Haberdeen sent me here to confirm it."

Ava glared daggers. "Confirm what?"

"The storm." The man's face split into an intense smile. "And I did."

"Where is Haberdeen?"

71

"She is wherever she needs to be."

"I'm not in the mood for riddles." Ava flicked a knife from her belt; she pointed its tip at the blackcoat. "Where is she?"

"No idea. Above my pay grade, I suppose."

"What about Mage Raul?"

The man blinked. "Mage Raul?" He squinted his eyes as if trying to remember something. "He's long gone. Lost the plot after Anderma. Haberdeen put him in iron."

Ava gripped the bands of Luck emanating from the seated figure; they rippled like molten honey. She tugged on the odds of the man slipping up. Instead, he just smiled. "I'm flattered you think I know anything."

She had half a mind to lodge the blade in his hand. "Well, what do you know?"

"That it's coming. The storm creeps closer. Closer and closer. Flashes fill this city, and soon it will be gone." His high-pitched laugh echoed through the tunnel. The moon pierced the clouds and spilled through the grate overhead. The blackcoat settled into his chains and started humming a tune.

"You've gone off the deep end." Ava slipped the knife back into her belt. This was a waste of time. She checked her watch. It was well past midnight.

"Death comes for one, death comes for all, the sky ignites, the city falls." The man chuckled at his own song and continued to hum.

"Where was Haberdeen when you received your orders?" Ava asked.

"A flash above. A flash below. Oh, fair farewell to Parteno." The Smith grinned. "Don't you understand? You're done. Finished." He laughed again, and this time, he didn't stop.

Ava rolled her eyes. *Useless. Absolutely useless.* A faint rumble echoed from the tunnel. A small light appeared further down the track. She glared at the man. "That train is as much as you deserve for the damage you've done."

The man beamed at her. Ava grabbed the chair and dragged him off the tracks. He landed with a thud, safe to the side of the rails. "You're prolonging the inevitable," he called from the cement. "Nothing here will last the week. Not you. Not me. The Flashfinders never lie!"

She ignored him as she climbed onto the platform. Grand Steward or not, this was her uncle's fault. If Haberdeen thought Parteno was unsafe, she would be long gone by now. Rasporvin's meeting had cost them, trading a promising opportunity for the ravings of a madman.

She couldn't wait to tell the Emissary.

The morning sun did nothing to warm the brittle air. Ava sipped her hot chocolate as the LAMPs filtered through the cramped markets. Families bustled with color and conversation in preparation for the annual Solstice Parade. The narrow brick alley hummed with activity.

"And they call themselves Fatesmiths," someone said to her left. A woman in a mustard cardigan spoke to her girlfriends. Ava leaned back and listened in. "They say the High Mage decided that magical folk have too much power." The woman's voice became a whisper. "The Fatesmiths are Johannasberg's private army. He's using them to put all the witches and wizards in prison."

"No," one of them protested. "Why would the High Mage do that?"

"Sabriva Tower doesn't like having a population who could undo them. They want us docile, like sheep."

Ava hid her smirk in the mug. The woman's story wasn't far from the truth. Haberdeen's stranglehold on Parteno had loosened since Anderma, but there were still thousands missing. Rumors ran wild in their absence. The group's conversation took a mundane turn, and Ava lost interest. She looked up as a mop of dark hair entered the cafe. Misha strolled in with rehearsed nonchalance and fell into the seat she'd saved for him.

"Interesting night," he said.

"Did you find something?"

Misha shook his head. "I found out a good portion of the beggars in Parteno actually live in nice city apartments."

Ava finished her drink. "But did you find something useful?"

"Nothing at all."

Ava fiddled with her mug. "It could be worse. I spent the evening with a lunatic."

Misha raised his eyebrows.

"Apparently." Ava lowered her voice, "Parteno is going to be destroyed by week's end."

"Destroyed?" Misha whispered back. "By who? Haberdeen?"

"Who knows? He spoke of storms..." Ava shook her head. "He was off his goat, singing songs about glowing skies and flashes."

"Singing?"

Ava nodded. "Like a drunkard loaded on silverberry wine."

"Did he sing anything about Haberdeen?"

"Nothing we can follow."

"Hooray," Misha said. "Another dead end. You would think the Emissary would've learned by now."

"It's not her fault," Ava said. "Rasporvin caused the delay. The Emissary would have had us here days ago if he hadn't summoned me to his stupid hall."

"Your uncle won't see it that way." Misha frowned. "It's going to come back on us. Or the Emissary."

"Maybe this will be enough to keep him out of our business. Enough to keep me in Euryma."

"That's a bit optimistic."

Ava flashed a bright smile. "Well, I get lucky on the odd occasion."

Misha laughed. "Well, here's hoping." He scanned the bustling markets. "Look at this place. No carts and donkeys, no cobblestone roads. Why can't Vedmark have this? We have the most powerful sorcerers in the world, and we live like peasants."

Ava shrugged. "Different customs. The people here work together, Mish. Our people... not so generous."

"I guess so. It just seems backward to me."

"It is. I like it here." Ava chewed her lower lip, careful not to say too much.

"I get it..." Misha said. "I thought you were crazy when you first left. I never really understood why you kept going back." He shook his head. "Ory made it sound like a nation of beggars."

Ava smirked. "Probably not enough goats here for Ory's tastes."

They sat in comfortable silence, absorbing the sights and sounds of Euryma's oldest city. Parteno had withstood millennia of wars and woes. A thousand years of brick stacked atop five millennia of stone.

If a storm was coming, Ava couldn't imagine it would do much to Parteno's ancient walls.

CHAPTER II
AVA

Music, laughter, and dancing filled the streets. The Solstice Parade painted Parteno in colorful banners, transforming the inner city into a series of vivid fabric snakes. Far below their balcony, a brightly decorated platform promised fireworks and fun. Ava sipped her lemon water, which tasted every bit as bad as she expected, and waited for the Emissary to finish on her laptop.

Misha sat on the balcony, face alight with childlike wonder. Motor vehicles and modern electronics were brand new to him. Ava's lips twitched as she remembered how she felt when she had first left Vedmark.

"Okay." The Emissary looked up from her screen. "Let's get started. Tell me about Parteno."

Misha turned away from the Parade; he exchanged a glance with Ava and then crossed his arms. "Parteno is a beautiful city, but Haberdeen is not here. If she was here, she didn't leave any evidence." He flashed his best smile. "Nevertheless, we will adhere to your wisdom, Emissary."

Ava pursed her lips at him. "Suck up."

The Emissary returned to her keyboard. "And you, Ava? Any luck on your assignment?"

Her assignment had been to take care of Mage Raul. Ava sighed. "Not at all. The closest I got was a crazy blackcoat singing about the destruction of Parteno."

The Emissary glanced up, lines of text reflected in her sharp eyes. "Say that once more."

"They were literally singing."

"I don't care about that," the Emissary said. "What did they say about Parteno?"

"Nothing worth our time. The ravings of a lunatic."

"Humor me."

Ava thought back to her failed interrogation. "He said a storm was coming. That Parteno would be destroyed. Something about confirming flashes, whatever *that* means."

The Emissary frowned. "Did he say when?"

"I... don't think so." Ava leaned forward. "You can't take this seriously. The man was a mess. He said the blackcoats had disowned Mage Raul."

"I must go to Sabriva." She closed the laptop with a snap. "You two, get the first train out in the morning. Head back to Vedmark."

"Vedmark?" Ava shook her head. "I can't go back. Rasporvin won't let me leave. You need to convince him to let me stay; we were behind here from the start. That was his fault."

"I'll deal with it later," the Emissary said. "This is important."

"We'll come with you. Let us come to Sabriva."

"Ava—"

"Uh, sorry," Misha interrupted. "But what is *that*?"

Ava scanned the scene below the balcony. An endless crowd writhed and jerked to the rhythm of the music. "Yes, Misha, that's what they call dancing here."

"Not that." Misha pointed at the horizon. "*That.*"

Ava peered out over the city. A glowing orange haze was swelling over the distant hills, like a sunrise in fast motion. "I... I don't know."

Misha squeezed the balcony rail. "Is it something for the Parade? Fireworks?"

"No." Ava squinted into the night. "That's definitely not fireworks."

The fiery wall continued to grow. The Emissary joined them, her lips paper thin.

"What is it?" Misha asked.

A door burst open, and Ava jumped. A man in a dark suit rushed inside. "Sam. We need to go. Now." He slid the Emissary's laptop into a bag. "Come on, there's no time to waste."

The Emissary shook her head. An avalanche of light surged towards them. "It's too late." She turned her back on the man to face the oncoming wave. "If we can *see* it, we can't escape it."

Ava's stomach tightened. *What is she talking about?*

"Nonsense. We'll make an Opening. We need to go."

"It won't work." The Emissary's voice sounded as if it came from very far away. "You are welcome to try."

The man frowned; his hands fell into a rhythmic weave. A small triangle formed in the room's center. "See?" he said, trembling voice triumphant. The triangle rippled and blinked out of existence. The man cursed and tried once more. The Opening failed again. "I don't understand," he said.

79

"It's pointless." The Emissary's hands fell to her side. "Nobody escapes Remnant Magic."

Ava's eyes snapped to the Emissary. *Remnant Magic?*

The man backed out the door and then left. The bag he held slumped, abandoned at the door. The cascading orange light was beautiful, a swirling wall of energy that turned the night to day.

A loud shriek shattered the silence. Below them, pandemonium had engulfed the Parade. People who were dancing joyfully moments earlier now fought their way down the narrow streets. Screams replaced songs as the stampeding crowd rushed to escape. Somewhere, a child wailed.

"We need to get away from here," Ava grabbed the Emissary's shoulders and steered her out the door. Misha followed. A dull roar washed over the city like an oncoming hailstorm. The walls rattled as they hurried down the stairs into a back alley. The street ahead was chaos. A young man ran towards them, carrying a small boy. A petite woman draped in silver necklaces held his hand, cold fear in her eyes. "Help us!"

"Follow me," Ava said. She led them deeper into the alley. Auburn light cast eerie shadows down the pathway, and the rumbling noise grew louder. When they came to the end, a massive throng of people carried them away.

"Ava!" Misha reached out. Ava grabbed his hand.

"Do you have the Emissary?"

Misha nodded. "She's here."

"What about that family? The boy?" Ava searched the mass of faces.

"I can't see them," Misha said. "They must have stayed."

"We need to get out of this crowd."

"Higher ground. Climb a building, and we'll roof-hop to shelter." Misha pushed his way to the edge of the crowd. "Up here, perfect." He started climbing the latticework of a nearby storefront. "I'm sorry, Emissary, but you must climb with us."

The Emissary seemed stunned. The light was so bright Ava had to squint to make out faces in the crowd. The little boy from the alley remained burned in her mind. She tested the chances of finding him, but the bands of Luck remained fixed. *They must have gone in another direction.*

She followed Misha to the side of a building. He was helping the Emissary jump to the next roof, then waved at her and shouted.

Ava pointed to her ears. "What?" She couldn't hear what he was saying over the roaring orange storm. She leaped over the gap to join them.

"It's too close!" Misha pointed down at the street.

Ava stared down at the nightmare below. People pressed together like chickens in a coop as Remnant Magic rushed towards them. Her heart lodged in her throat. This was it. This was how she died. *I'll never see Declan again.*

A hand grabbed her shoulder. Misha pressed his mouth to her ear. "Do you have a shieldshard?"

Ava shook herself back to reality. "Yes," she shouted. "Do you?" Misha pulled a clear spike from his coat pocket. Ava fumbled through her bag for hers. "Will it work?"

"How would I know? Maybe. Probably not. Who knows? We have to try!"

The Emissary's arms hung by her sides. Ava gripped her arm. "Come here! Quick!"

She didn't respond. Her eyes never left the street. "It would seem that this is the end of the line for us." The Emissary's skin blazed orange in the light. Ava stared, feet frozen. Remnant Magic coursed forward—a glowing tsunami.

"Get over here!" Ava pulled her close. The roof failed. All three of them crashed through the ceiling onto a polished stone floor. Intense light pierced the windows. Sprawled on the ground with the Emissary on top of her, Ava raised her shieldshard and nodded to Misha. "Now!"

Together, they stabbed their opaque spikes into the floor. A double-walled yellow bubble emerged around them just as the wave hit. Ava gritted her teeth and heaved on Luck. Shifting chance was normally like pulling on an elastic band. Now, it felt like heaving against a steel bar. She forced every ounce of strength she had into the insignificant odds that the shields would hold. Deep creases in Misha's forehead told her he was doing the same.

The outer shield quickly flaked away; small flecks flaked off like leaves in a gale.

"Focus. On. This. One," Ava stammered. The likelihood that the barrier would work was slim. She pulled on their chance of survival; it was so heavy. Misha nodded. Beads of sweat rolled down his cheeks. The outer barrier vanished, shredded like woodchips. One of the spikes shattered. Ava ignored it. She focused on her shield. Nothing else mattered. The swirling tempest, the Emissary's shallow breaths, Misha's groans. None of it mattered, only the shield.

Time moved like a glacier. Ava willed herself to fight on, to stay awake. Exhaustion clawed at her.

She could feel her body weakening.

The storm raged on. Torrential. Terrifying. Bands of Luck barely budged. It was all Ava could do to keep herself from letting go. She knew if she did, the odds would snap back into place, and they would be burnt to dust. *Just like that little family.*

Misha shook his head. Sweat beaded his forehead. "I can't. It's too much."

"Just..." Ava couldn't even finish the sentence. Every second lasted hours. Misha's eyes rolled backward, and he slumped to the side. Ava refused to let go.

Still, the storm continued. Ava's arms were wet tissues, her head a lead weight. Her body was a flickering candle. She hunched to the ground. She could see the little flecks of the bubble tear off in layers. A large crack appeared through the shieldshard beside her. *This isn't how it was supposed to end.* Her thoughts returned to Declan. *I'll never even get to say goodbye.* She closed her eyes; she could feel her Luck slipping. She would not let go.

The lights went out. As suddenly as it arrived, the storm was gone. Darkness fell over the city, and tiny diamonds twinkled above.

Ava curled into a ball and cried. Her body was so cold she shivered against the concrete.

"You did it," murmured the Emissary. "You actually did it."

Ava couldn't move, couldn't think. She was tired beyond description. Tears rolled down her cheek. Tears of relief, tears of guilt, they swirled together and pooled on the ground. *All those people. They were celebrating. They were happy. Now they're gone.* She tried to shake the thoughts away, the little boy, the little family. With eyelids too heavy to move, Ava sobbed on the floor and drifted into a troubled sleep.

"Are you alive?"

Ava opened her eyes. Misha crouched beside her, looking like he'd walked through a tornado. "Goats guts, Ava, you scared me."

She tried to sit up. White spots filled her vision, and pain flared from head to toe. She took a shallow breath that hurt her chest. "Do you have sanarmelon juice?"

Misha handed her a vial, and she forced it down. A welcome sensation cleared the ache, and her vision settled. "Thanks."

"It's fine," Misha said. Two more empty vials lay by the cracked shieldshard. "How did we survive?"

"Luck," Ava said. "Though it just about killed us." The roof they fell through was gone. As were the streetlights, buildings, everything. Ancient Parteno had been burned to ash. "How long was I out for?"

"No idea." Misha nodded skyward. "Sunrise isn't far off."

"Where's the Emissary?"

"I'm here."

Ava turned around. The Emissary sat with a portion of her torn dress wrapped around her ankle. Her hair was a bird's nest, yet her eyes were sharp. "Parteno is no more. People will soon come looking. We need to leave."

"Shouldn't we look for survivors?" Misha asked. Ava scanned their surroundings. A forethought of dawn cast a soft light over an endless plain of black dust. Not even rubble remained. There were no cries of children, no screams of panic, no shouts for help. Nothing.

The Emissary shook her head slowly. "There are no survivors here. I must report to High Mage Johannasberg. You should return to Vedmark."

Ava wiped a tear from her cheek. "I'm not going back. Not yet. We'll escort you to Sabriva and decide there."

The Emissary stared at her. "Fine. But we must move quickly."

"What will you tell the High Mage?" Misha asked.

The Emissary stood unsteadily and scanned their barren surroundings. "The truth," she said. "The Fate-smiths were right. Remnant Magic has arrived in Euryma."

CHAPTER 12
DECLAN

DECLAN ADJUSTED the odd tunic he had found back in the cabin. The midday sun beamed down on him, and an orchestra of birds and insects filled the surrounding forest. Declan looked back at the empty dirt path. The golden armadillo had long since vanished into the trees, but the occasional rustle in the branches made Declan question how alone he was. *Nobody will believe me*, he thought. *I don't even know if I believe it myself.*

Another hour of walking brought him to the familiar road leading to Grigory's cabin. When Declan finally reached the cabin, a chorus of bleating goats greeted him. Their enthusiasm must have been loud because the door burst open, and Grigory rushed to greet him. His old face split into a crooked grin. "Declan, fellow, you are alive." He pulled Declan into a rough hug. It felt like being hugged by a stone.

"That's quite the welcome, Ory."

Grigory clapped Declan on the back and let him go. A smile was still plastered on his face. "Fellow, I was worried! I thought you had died."

"I thought you'd be glad to be rid of me."

"You mistake. I worried what Ava would do when she found out."

Declan laughed. "Glad to know you have your priorities sorted."

"Young Venward delivered news himself three days past. He said they found your armor at base of hill." Grigory looked him up and down. "Yet you arrive in good health, in brand new clothes." His eyes settled on the cotton tunic. "Fellow, you must tell me your story."

Declan shrugged. "Oh, it was nothing exciting. I threw my breastplate as a distraction and jumped into the river. When I came out, I wandered to a nearby farm. A nice lady gave me this old thing and let me rest until I healed up."

Grigory gave him a knowing look. "That is how it is."

Declan fought to keep his expression level. *He wouldn't believe the truth. Led to a cabin by an armadillo? He'd think I was crazy.* "Ava was right. Running eggs is a loser's game."

"Very well, fellow." Grigory's gaze remained on Declan's clothes. "I'm glad you are safe. I am even more glad I won't have to tell Ava you were killed on my account." He turned and beckoned for Declan to come inside. "I will send word for Ven. I imagine he would like to know you survived."

"Thanks, Ory."

The familiar fragrance of goat stew wafted out the door. It smelled like home.

The campfire reflected in Ven's eyes as he listened to Declan's story. He gasped and laughed in all the right places. When Declan finished, he leaned back, shaking his head. "Amazing. We watched from bunker. There must have been six eagles after you. Fi swore she saw you in one's talons."

"She's right," Declan said. "One caught me. Well, it caught the breastplate. I slipped out."

"Incredible."

A crescent moon smiled down on them. For a long while, the crackling of the flames was the only sound between them. Without warning, a loud bout of laughter shattered the stillness. Grigory and Temfell were inside exchanging drinks they refused to share with the younger generation. Ven used a thick stick to shift a burning log. "What I don't understand," he said, eyes still on the dancing fire, "was how you convinced farmers to let you stay. Generosity to strangers is no common thing in Vedmark, especially for southerners."

"She was an old woman just looking for company," said Declan.

Ven nodded, "As you say. Yet few live by river. Its banks break in Spring, all know that." He searched Declan's face. "Unless there was no woman."

"The house wasn't right by the water." Declan knew he was speaking too fast. "It was a little way—"

"The house by river that is not by water, with lonely woman who lives in forest." Ven's smirk said enough. Declan's story was far from convincing. "And here you arrive in a tunic of curious cloth."

"What, this?" Declan tugged at the tunic. "The woman gave it to me."

"That is not ordinary cloth," Ven said. He reached out and rubbed the sleeve between his thumb and forefinger, then drew back as if bitten by an insect. "That is cotton. We do not grow cotton here. It does not do well in the cold."

Ven tossed his stick into the flame. "Even if we did, we would not. Cotton is bad luck in this land."

Instinctively, Declan touched his sleeve. "I don't know what you mean."

Ven's smile remained unchanged. "Let me ask you some questions. I brought mitka to share. You cannot lie to a jade mitka."

You can't go telling him about talking animals. Declan shook his head. "You won't believe me."

Ven dug a handful of jade from his pocket. "I have mitka for knowledge. Are you willing to trade?"

Declan considered the coins. He desperately wanted to say no, but he needed mitka, as much as possible. *What do I have to lose?* He held Ven's eyes. "Double that and I'll tell you everything."

"Done." Ven emptied the handful onto his knees and scooped a larger pile out of his inner pocket.

Declan stared in disbelief. "You carry a lot of coin."

Ven shrugged at the minor fortune. "Old Grigory let word of your coat slip. I feel this is a worthwhile investment." He smiled. "I have mitka for knowledge. Are you willing to trade?"

Declan nodded. "I am willing to trade. This I know, unsullied by untruth lest your mitka be spent."

"Excellent." Ven leaned forward, and the coins clinked in his lap. "Where did river take you?"

"I don't know exactly. It knocked me around pretty bad and washed onto the riverbank. I couldn't tell you how long I was in the water for."

"And then what happened?"

Declan hesitated. *You can tell the truth without mentioning the armadillo...* "A guide appeared and led me deeper into the forest."

"What type of guide?"

If you lie, it will show in the mitka. "Uh, they were short, rather hairy. Didn't speak, just motioned for me to follow to the cabin."

Ven grinned, almost as if he knew what Declan was trying to hide. "What was inside?"

Declan pictured the tiny hut's interior. "A bed. A table. A bowl of sanarmelon, I think. Clothes to wear. Two axes on the wall. They had pictures of a bull carved in the handles."

Ven's eyes seemed brighter than the flames. "A valuable investment indeed."

Declan shrugged. "I do not know what you're talking about."

"Can you find this place again?"

"I'm not sure..."

"Declan, you don't understand." A manic intensity smoldered in Ven's stare. "We could be rich beyond reason. Could you find that cabin?"

Declan stopped to picture it. The overgrown path he'd followed back to the road was faint, but it led straight to the cabin. If he could find it, he could get back. "I might be able to... But Ven, I'm completely lost. You need to explain to me how a cabin in the middle of the forest would make us rich."

Ven locked eyes with Declan. "I can tell you those things, but only under one condition."

"Okay..."

"You and I will form a partnership. I will tell you what you found, and you will lead way to cabin. We will split reward money evenly. Do you agree?"

"I agree."

Ven held up one of the jade mitka from the pile. "Seal it." He dropped the coin with a satisfying clink.

Declan felt as if he was diving into the river all over again. "I share this knowledge. True to my knowledge, let it show in green."

The mound of mitka in Ven's lap glowed like a tiny emerald throne. When it dimmed, Ven scooped the coins into Declan's lap. "This is excellent news. Soon neither of us will have to run eggs ever again."

"Uh. Okay."

Ven grinned at Declan. "Very well, I keep my side of bargain. Let me tell you story of the Deathless Demon." He tossed a new log onto the fire, and a puff of sparks danced around them. Ven cleared his throat, glanced at Grigory's window, then leaned forward. "One thousand years ago there lived a young Prince who was unsatisfied with his homeland. With two older brothers, the Prince had little claim to throne. With no duties, he chose to leave. His father granted him permission to depart Kingdom until Vedmark had need of him."

Delan scratched his chin. "I don't know what that has to do with the cabin I found."

"Perhaps you must let me finish," Ven said.

"Sorry."

Ven chuckled. "The Prince traveled south to land of warring tribes. In that age, southerners lived in constant war, endless squabbles over who owned what. It was odd decision for the Prince, but his choice to make. Many years passed until Vedmark needed him, but this Prince did not return when called upon. The King sent men in search of him, but they came back empty-handed. Vedmark considered him dead."

Declan went to speak, caught Ven's sharp look, and fell silent.

"Angry at their loss, the people of Vedmark sought

payment from the south for his death. But the King did not approve. He decreed the use of Sila for violence forbidden. Yet his eldest son, Morkurik, refused to waste such a gift. With the will of Vedmark behind him, Morkurik overcame his father and became King of Vedmark."

"Uh, explain what you mean by *overcame*."

"He killed him."

Declan's eyes widened. "That's dark."

"King Morkurik sought to avenge his brother. He assembled two ranks of Vedmark's strongest Warlocks to ride south."

"Two Warlocks is not much."

"Two ranks," Ven corrected. "Two thousand."

"Oh."

"The two thousand swore a blood-oath to obey the King. In doing so, they became Knights of Vedmark. They rode south for revenge, but found a land at war. King Morkurik, in his wisdom, abandoned his crusade to bring peace to the tribes. Soon, Vedmark became a mighty empire. Vedmark's army became known as the Knights of Despair—"

Declan's jaw dropped. "No."

"—And Morkurik's men wore the name proudly. But the southern wild men did not want their peace. As Morkurik pushed south, the savages united under the banner of Euryma."

Declan blinked, confused. "Euryma formed from a peace between nations, in response to an invading legion." The words left his mouth as barely a whisper. *This land, these people, they sought to conquer my home.*

Ven frowned. "Historians often leave out details to cover their failings. Perhaps it is same in your homeland."

He shrugged. "When King Morkurik learned of Euryma, he directed his Knights to destroy it. But there was one thing he did not count on."

"What was it?" Declan didn't even notice his question.

"The Prince was alive. Not only that, he served as Euryma's greatest General. A grueling war broke out that lasted many months and only ended when the Prince murdered King Morkurik, murdered his own brother to rob our Vedmark of southern riches."

The clearing was silent. Even the insects seemed to have stopped to listen. Ven's easy smile turned into a grimace. "The Prince took his place as King of Vedmark and used the Knight's oath against them. The tribes resumed their savage wars, our noble warriors lost the land they had earned in battle."

Declan replayed the tale in his mind. "But Euryma remained at peace."

"Vedmark was peace. Those ruins they call the powerless lands were thriving kingdoms governed by Morkurik's wisdom."

"The people must have been angry."

"They were. Vedmark sought to rise against him, but they did not have the power. The new King controlled the Knights. They were bound by their blood-oath to enforce his will." Ven smiled. "All except one. Vispa Drakonov, a recruit who had not sworn his oath. He alone had the agency to undo the King's will."

"Drakonov. Like the Grand Steward." *Like Ava.*

Ven nodded. "That same blood. Vispa challenged the King and defeated him, but his mercy was his undoing. The King fled to the forest. There, he cursed Vedmark so no Knight could wield Sila outside its borders. He cut the armies of Vedmark off at knees, their greatest power locked in our land."

"So that's why they never returned."

Ven nodded. "Vispa Drakonov became the Grand Steward. He was young, and thought he could wait out the King's curse, but Vispa would die waiting. That old, selfish King traded his soul for immortality. Less a man, more a demon, a creature that does not die, that holds the curse that keeps us trapped. The Deathless Demon."

A long moment passed until Declan remembered he was supposed to breathe. He stared into the luminous coals. "Wow."

"But we have a weapon, Declan Moore. A sacred blade charmed to kill the demon in his Void." Ven rubbed his hands together. "The Grand Steward just needs to find him. He has sworn on mitka that whoever locates the monster will earn a fortune beyond measure."

"A fortune beyond measure." Declan bit his lip. *Whoever lived in that hut saved my life.* He felt a pang of uncertainty. "I'm not sure Ven. The... thing... you're describing doesn't sound like what I saw. There was no Void, no danger, just an empty cabin with a place to recover."

"There would be nobody else who lives in that forest. Nobody who offers cotton garb. Nobody who sends their little armadillo devils to lead you."

Declan blushed. He thought he'd been smart to not mention the armadillo.

Ven nodded, hunger in his eyes. "If you can find the cabin, I can get word to Knights. We can split their reward equally. A fortune for us both."

Declan nodded. *With that much mitka, I can buy my training.* Another voice scoffed at the thought. *You'll betray the one who saved you?*

"Declan. We are in agreement."

"Right, yeah, sure." Declan struggled to hide his uncertainty. "I'll find the trail while you get the Knights."

CHAPTER 13

DECLAN

SMALL RIBBONS of steam curled above the chipped clay bowl, and the smell of cooked meat and onions filled the kitchen. Grigory spoke in the background; Declan stared through his dinner. *This isn't right*, he thought. *Whoever lives in that cabin took me in.* He pushed a chunk of carrot around with his spoon. *You need the mitka*, replied a decisive voice. *You need to learn to use your Sila.*

"You seem distracted, fellow."

Declan looked up. "Sorry, Grigory. I don't mean to be."

"Too busy staring into soup. You are worried."

Declan sighed and picked up his spoon. *How much longer can you live off goat and boiled vegetables?* "Oh, it's nothing."

"Tomorrow morning, you go looking for old King. Deathless Demon."

Declan's cheeks darkened. "I didn't think you knew..."

"Of course I know," Grigory said. "Temfell's a gossip, and his son is no better. Young Ven has been bragging about bounty since you made agreement."

Declan waited, but Grigory said no more. When the

silence grew untenable, Declan put his spoon down. "I'm not sure if I'm doing the right thing."

Grigory did not respond. They ate without speaking. Declan did his best to ignore his stirring stomach. When both bowls were empty, the old man crossed his arms. "The prize for finding him is a temptation, fellow, and you have good reason for seeking it."

"I know," Declan said. "But he saved my life, Ory. It doesn't feel right."

"Ven told you about the King's story."

Declan nodded. "Ven said he's a monster. He shrunk Vedmark's lands, locked all who could use Sila inside and threw away the key." He chewed on his lip. "But that makes no sense. I keep asking what type of demon would save my life for no reason—and I come up blank."

Grigory walked to the kitchen window and closed the heavy shutters. When he returned, his expression was conflicted. "What Venward says is one tale, fellow, and there are many. I could tell you another."

"Will it cost me?"

Grigory nodded. "This is Vedmark. All knowledge has a cost. But if you are troubled, I believe it a worthwhile investment."

Declan sighed. *How can I make enough to buy Irman's knowledge when I have to keep spending it on people's secrets?* He reached into his pocket and withdrew a single green coin. "I have mitka for knowledge. Are you willing to trade?"

"I am willing to trade," Grigory replied. "This I know, unsullied by untruth lest your mitka be spent."

Declan handed him the coin. "Go on then, what don't I know about this Deathless Demon?"

"The King witnessed great evil at the hands of the

Knights. Vedmark paints them as noble warriors. They were not. The Knights of Despair scourged southern lands, conquered like flames through dry tinder."

Declan listened in silence.

"Morkurik was a wicked ruler. His Knights followed his example. They ravaged cities, murdered innocents, and captured those with power they could not control. Vedmark took land they did not deserve."

"What do you mean capture those with power they could not control? I thought you could do anything with Sila?"

Grigory's voice fell even lower. "Lucks, fellow. Sila has no influence over luck. Morkurik stole Lucks from Euryma and sent them back to Vedmark. Men and women gifted to Knights, forced to bear children."

Declan's stomach lurched at the thought.

"The one they call demon did the right thing." Grigory's voice was a shadow of a whisper. "If the Knights find him, they will descend with entire army. They will murder him and be free to lay waste to world once more." Grigory scowled at the mitka in his hand. "I share this knowledge. True to my knowledge, let it show in green." The jade glowed and faded.

"I don't want to betray anyone, Ory, but I need the money."

Grigory held the coin up. "I have mitka for knowledge. Are *you* willing to trade?"

Declan rolled his eyes. *I guess I'll get my coin back.* "I am willing to trade. This I know, unsullied by untruth. Lest your mitka be spent."

Grigory held Declan's eye. "Is a bag of mitka worth more than your homeland?"

"Of course not."

"Then there should be no conflict. Simply do not take them to the King."

It's not that simple. Declan tried forming the right words to say, to make him understand. The seconds crawled by. Grigory waited. Declan shrugged. "I need the mitka."

"Why?"

"Because."

Grigory arched an eyebrow.

"Because I have to learn how Sila works so I can help my friend." Declan's gaze darted from Grigory to the coin. *I need to stop this. He's asking too many questions.* Grigory tried to speak, but Declan cut him off. "I share this knowledge. True to my knowledge, let it show in green."

Grigory's eyes narrowed.

A long moment passed, and Declan felt his stomach sink. The coin dulled to a grey pebble. He had lied. Grigory flicked the spent coin into his palm. "A spent mitka is a tenth of the debt owed," he muttered. "You owe me ten of these, fellow."

Declan's cheeks burned. "I'm... I'm sorry."

"Keep your apology. I want truth. Explain why you need mitka so bad."

"I... I can't tell you. I'll give you what I owe..."

"You have lied to me. Tell me truth."

"I just want to save my friend."

"Liar!" Grigory shot to his feet. A tempest stormed behind his old eyes. He dropped the spent mitka on the table. It landed with a thud too loud for its size. "You spent this mitka telling that lie! Say it, fellow, tell me you are just hungry for power!"

Declan's face was a furnace. He stumbled out of the chair, out of the room. "I'm sorry. I..." But he didn't finish, he couldn't. Instead, he turned and ran out of the cabin and into the night. Grigory called from behind, but Declan didn't listen. He dashed through the clearing into the trees. Salty streams flecked off his cheeks. He ducked under branches and jumped over fallen trunks until Grigory's cabin was a speck of light in the dark.

You idiot.

Declan fell to the ground and cried. *You haven't changed a bit. You're still the weak boy from Euryma. You've known it all along.* Declan couldn't fight it. He collapsed. A blanket of wet leaves soaked his back. Tiny diamonds twinkled in the sky. *Lie to Ava. Lie to Grigory. Lie to the world. You can't lie to the mitka. You can't lie to yourself.*

Declan closed his eyes to stop the tears. They still leaked through. In the darkness, for the first time in months, Declan let himself remember. Memories tumbled out. His parents sat at the breakfast table, smiling, laughing, teasing each other and themselves. For a moment, they filled the cavernous hole inside him. Then, other memories followed. The iron casts, the melted puddle. *You've learned nothing from their death.* Memories washed over him like waves on a beach. He remained there for a long time, remembering. *What would they think if they could see you now?*

He ushered the memories carefully back into their box and closed the lid. The forest wasn't right. The smells were the same, the blinking stars the same, but it was quiet. Too quiet. The songs of insects, the hoots of birds, the sounds of the night were gone.

They've abandoned you. You're sentencing Euryma to destruction for your own magic. You're so selfish even the creatures of the night can't bear your presence.

Declan ignored the thought.

This is my power. I've done enough to deserve it.

Have you?

Declan stood and squinted into the darkness. Nothing was there. No-one. Just him. He started the shameful trek back to Grigory's cabin. He did not dare try to enter, but at least the wood shed would give him somewhere dry to sleep.

The sun rose, and Declan with it. His bed of hay had not been comfortable. When he stepped into the morning sun, Grigory waited on a wide stump, a small knife in one hand and a gnarled wooden figure in the other. "You could have slept in your bed, fellow." He whittled the stick, his gaze fixed on the knife's edge.

"Uh, I... I didn't think I should."

"I suppose you feel bad. Off to betray your home for a rich payday."

"Grigory, I—"

"Save your apologies." Grigory pressed the blade into the wood. "You'll need them for your kinsmen."

"I'm not apologizing. I deserve this power. It's mine, and I'm going to use it to help Ava. To save my friends. To help Euryma."

"Spoken like a true Knight."

Declan stood awkwardly outside the woodshed. "Ory, you're from Vedmark. It should not matter to you if Euryma falls."

"You owe me ten mitka," Grigory said.

Declan reached into his pouch and counted ten green coins. He tossed them at Grigory's feet, then left.

Ven waited by the water when Declan arrived. Beside him stood six men, all clad in forest green armor. Their helmets had thin horns that curled like an insect's antennae.

One man stepped forward. He had a short black beard and his hair hung by his shoulders. "Welcome, Master Declan."

"Uh, hello."

Ven stood by his side. "Big day today, Declan. Exciting day." He gestured to the man with the dark beard. "This is Knight Urik. He's the group commander."

Urik scowled. "Thank you, Master Ven." His gaze was intense. "The Grand Steward Drakonov has sent us to investigate a lodging you have found in the wilderness. Master Ven believes it may be home to the Deathless Demon."

Declan waited for Urik to blink. He did not. They stood in silence until Ven nudged Declan's ribs. "Oh. Yes. Yes, that is correct."

"Very well. Today, we will scout what you have seen. These are my companions." Urik introduced each of the hard-faced men by name. Declan struggled to keep up. Their names escaped him almost immediately. When Urik finished, the men fell back in line. "If you lead the way, we will follow."

Declan considered Urik's fish-scale armor. "Ven and I are not prepared for battle."

"There is no risk of violence. We are here to investigate. Observe unseen."

Declan nodded.

"Tell us about the reward," Ven asked.

Urik's jaw tightened. The question seemed to frustrate him. He exhaled through his nose, one long breath. "Once we have confirmed the lodging belongs to the demon, the Grand Steward will give your reward."

Ven grinned at Declan. "Well, no need to stand around. Let's get moving."

"Wait," Urik said. "We must first silence our footsteps."

Declan exchanged glances with Ven. "Uh, okay."

A strand of green light threaded its way across the back of Urik's hands. He clicked his fingers, and the ground blazed green. The light flickered, then faded.

Declan stared, amazed. *That was Sila. He just used Sila.*

Ven took a step forward and his grin grew even wider. "Incredible." He stomped his feet on a patch of dry leaves; they disintegrated under his boots without a sound.

Urik's eyes narrowed. "If you cannot control yourself, Master Ven, it is best you remain behind."

Ven stopped stomping. "Apologies, Knight Urik."

Urik ignored him, instead turning to Declan. "Lead on. We shall follow."

The small party followed the faded path. It felt surreal to walk in absolute silence. He felt the forest floor crunch beneath him, but heard nothing. The absence of accompanying noise was unsettling. He also glanced over his shoulder far too frequently, checking to make sure that Ven and the Knights were still there.

"We will not abandon you," Ven called. Urik silenced him with a glare.

The narrow path split in two directions, and Declan stopped. Something gold caught his eye, but when he looked again, there was nothing there. *It's just your imagination.*

"You are certain you know the way, Master Declan," Urik whispered.

Declan hesitated. "Yeah, uh, sure." *Are you really going to do this? You're going to doom all of Euryma because you still want to do magic?* Declan stood at the fork. *How could you live with yourself if you take them to the cabin? Whoever lived there saved your life. Is this how you repay them?*

"Master Declan."

"Sorry, sorry." Declan bit his lower lip. "I just have to get my bearings." *I have to do it. I lost my parents chasing this. Doesn't that count for something? I have to!* Declan pointed left. "It's this way."

They crossed through dense forest and open clearings. Up steep hills, and down lazy slopes. The sun reached its peak in the cloudless sky as Ven's breathing grew louder and louder. Declan started up yet another hill when one of the Knights tapped him on the shoulder.

The others were ten steps back. Urik pressed a glowing hand against Ven's chest. His eyes bulged, and his jaw grew slack. Sweat faded from his face, and his pale cheeks colored. "Amazing, thank you."

"Apologies, Master Declan," the Knight said. "Master Ven was growing too loud. We must be silent." He looked ahead. "We have walked a great distance. We should be close."

Declan nodded, deciphering the question. "We are. Not far now."

They continued up the rise. The narrow track curved and took them down through an overgrown clearing and out by a sandy riverbed where he had washed up. Declan nodded to himself. The sand became patches of grass. The sun drooped, and at last, they reached the bottom of a steep hill.

Declan turned back to the company. "The cabin is up there."

"Very well." Urik's face didn't change, but his shoulders

tensed, and he stood a little taller. "We shall see if your claims are correct." Urik faced the others. "Blend in. Check perimeter. Touch nothing."

"He may be ready," said one of the Knights. "He is a crafty demon."

"Do not make your presence known. If he is here, we will return in legion." Urik looked back at Declan. "Remain with Master Ven. We will—"

Declan blinked.

Urik was gone.

With a shout of surprise, the remaining Knights fanned out around the base of the hill. They shouted instructions and moved in formation. Flashes of green pulsed beneath their armor, and their hands ignited like emerald torches.

"He's here," one of them growled, snapping his face-plate closed. "The Deathless Demon is here!"

CHAPTER 14

DECLAN

DECLAN BACKED AWAY WITHOUT THINKING. A clod of dirt exploded to his right. The force of it threw him left. He scrambled for cover as geysers of earth erupted throughout the clearing. Declan sprinted for the trees, vaulting a fallen trunk before sliding behind it. His heart thundered in his chest.

A visceral silence fell over them; it pressed against him like thick smog. Declan peeked through the branches of his barricade. A fine mist of wood and stone lingered in the air, illuminated by the columns of afternoon light that could penetrate the canopy. Otherwise, the forest was empty. But not. Movement caught his eye. A hunched figure limped through the haze.

The forest held its breath. A long beard hung beneath a green hood, but the figure's face hid in shadow. It stopped in the center of the clearing and then laughed. Goose pimples appeared on Declan's arm. The laugh was rolling thunder. Trees trembled. Pine needles fell to the ground. "It is folly to seek me out," spoke a voice, deep like an ocean trench.

Declan didn't dare move. *The Deathless Demon.*

"Hide if you wish, *Knights*," thundered the figure. "It does you no service. I see with more than eyes."

In a burst of movement, the six Knights attacked. Emerald plumes of Sila shot from their hands.

The Deathless Demon swirled its cloak and transformed into a flaming vortex that roared like a gale. The Knights leapt back. One threw a glowing blade into the fire. It went straight through and lodged in a tree. The tree exploded with a whip crack, and wood-chip confetti rained over the battle.

The flame flattened against the ground and rushed around the clearing. It knocked most of the Knights off their feet. Two leaped onto branches, pointing and gesturing. They summoned large chains that finished with a gleaming hook. The Knights tossed the hooks into the flame and pulled tight. The chains tensed. For a moment, Declan thought they had him trapped. The chain links rattled, faster, faster, vibrating in protest like a musical instrument. With a single crystal chime, they shattered. Those holding them tumbled from the trees.

The flame swirled into the clearing's center, and the Deathless Demon reformed into a cloaked, bearded figure. The Knights scrambled to their feet. Panic replaced their stern masks. From high above came a desperate shout. A man plummeted towards them. His scream grew louder as he descended until, at the last moment, he stopped. An inch from the ground, an inch from his death. With a thud, Knight Urik fell into the dirt.

"Leave," boomed the voice. The Knights exchanged glances. "Leave with your lives. Your King commands you."

Urik spat a mix of soil and blood. "You do not command

us!" he bellowed as he staggered to his feet. "You are no King!"

A jagged spike of green ice burst through the earth. It impaled Urik's shoulder, lifting him off the forest floor. He roared in pain.

"I will suffer you no more!"

The Knights backed away. The towering shard of Sila dissolved into a fine spray. Urik fell to the ground.

"Take him. Heal him. Then LEAVE!" The world shook with the avalanche of his voice.

Two of the Knights dragged Urik back. From the corner of his eye, Declan saw Ven crouched behind a mossy log—eyes as large as eagle eggs.

The Knights retreated the way they had come. Once they were gone, the Deathless Demon turned to the fallen tree where Declan hid. Declan held his breath; his heartbeat pounded in his ears. "I am disappointed in you, Declan Moore." The voice sounded old, tired, normal.

Declan caught Ven's eye. They exchanged shocked glances. *How does he know me?* When Declan looked back, the figure was gone. He scanned the trees. They were alone. Ven dropped beside him. "I don't believe it," he whispered.

Declan nodded to the slope; his mouth was dry. "I need to talk to it. I need to apologize."

Ven's eyes bulged to the point Declan worried they would fall out of his head. "You are a mad man," he stammered. "It knows you by name! You have angered the Deathless Demon! you saw what it did!"

"I know. I have to explain."

Ven's head shook too fast. "No, no, no. It will kill you."

Probably, it's as much as I deserve. Declan gritted his teeth. "I need answers." He stood, but Ven grabbed his arm.

"Then come back to Vedmark," he pleaded. "We found

the Deathless Demon. We'll get a hall of mitka to split. We'll never need to run eggs again. I will be able to look after father."

Declan paused. "Temfell doesn't need your mitka."

Ven's hand fell loose. "Father has watched Vedmark's gates for many years with none to show. It pays a pittance." He shook his head. "He is growing old. Running eggs, chasing bounty, it is for him. Please. Just come back with me."

"I can't," Declan said. "But you go. Catch up with the Knights. They'll lead you back. Tell them we got separated in the trees. I'll come back." *Maybe.*

"You don't have to do this, Declan."

"I do."

Ven frowned. "There is nothing I can do to change your mind."

"That is correct."

He ran a hand through his hair. "I will respect your wishes." Ven squeezed his shoulder. "Good luck, Declan Moore. I will wait for your return."

If I return. Declan smiled. "Thanks Ven. Now go. If the Knights get too far away, you will have to find your way home in the dark."

Ven hurried the way they had arrived. Declan stood and took a long breath. *Why are you doing this? You're going to get yourself killed. Turn around and follow Ven back. Grigory will be happy the Knights failed. Things will go back to normal, better than normal. You can probably get a reward for finding the cabin, and you can buy your Sila. Why are you doing this? Do you want to die?*

Declan started up the hill.

The Deathless Demon knows who I am. He saved me. I need to explain. He paused. *It's what my parents would expect.*

109

He stopped at the top of the path. The small cabin appeared identical to the day he arrived injured. Declan wondered if the man inside was expecting him. He started forward, then jumped at a loud hiss. It was the cabin. It was shrinking. In moments, it was gone.

Declan stood rooted to the spot. Nobody came out, and nobody went in. It had just vanished, leaving an empty clearing like a thousand others in the thick forest. The setting sun cast vibrant pink light over the slopes. Declan searched the area, unsure of what to do next. Something ruffled in the bushes ahead. *The armadillo. It will lead you after him.* Declan rushed over. An ordinary squirrel stepped back—an acorn clutched in its tiny claws.

The Deathless Demon was gone. Declan's shoulders slumped. He turned away from the sunset and made his way into the darkness, trudging in the footsteps left by the Knights of Despair.

CHAPTER 15
AVA

THE CAFÉ WAS CROWDED, but quiet. Ava sipped her hot chocolate as she took in the room. A somber weight hung over the people—all eyes were on the images of Parteno flashing on a television behind the counter. Ava didn't look. The memories were still too fresh. *I should have done more.*

"How can magic do so much damage?" Misha's eyes were glued to the screen.

"I don't want to talk about it," Ava said.

"What are we doing here, Ava?" Misha whispered. "Parteno's gone. The Emissary is busy with politics. We have no purpose here."

"I don't want to go back."

"You never do. There's nothing for us here. No leads, no mission. Father's running the farm himself. It's getting colder. We need to get home."

Ava looked down at her drink. "Ory could use your help, but I can't leave. Not yet."

"What are you going to do?"

"I need to see the Emissary again."

"Why?"

111

"Damn it, Misha, because I just have to. Okay?"

Misha blushed. A group of people opposite stared at them. Ava exhaled, then leaned forward. "I'm sorry. I'm just... Tired and frustrated, and I know if I go back, Rasporvin won't let me leave."

Misha relaxed. The neighboring table lost interest, and their attention returned to the television. Ava swirled her drink while Misha fiddled with a small sachet of sugar. "Hey, Ava," he said at last.

"Yeah?"

"Do you ever think about what it would be like if she hadn't found us?"

"Who? The Emissary?"

"Yeah."

Ava considered it. The Emissary was the reason they'd escaped the silwood yard. "I guess so, but we left for the better. I never enjoyed carting wood for builders."

"Me neither. Wild odds, though. Two Lucks in one place."

Ava snorted. "Are you kidding?"

"What?"

"We're Lucks, Mish." Ava laughed. "The odds are always in our favor."

Misha stared for a moment, cogs turning. Realization spread across his face, and he grinned. A woman in a pinstriped pantsuit glared at them. "I never thought of that. Seems it was less luck and more inevitability."

They talked for a little longer. Ava had finished a second hot chocolate when Misha stood to leave. "Anything you want me to say to Declan?"

Ava stood to give him a hug. "Tell him to stop pestering eagles." She bit her lip. "And send Ory my best."

Misha nodded. "Be safe, Ava." He waved goodbye and slipped out the door.

Ava considered a third hot drink, then thought better of it. She carried her empty mugs to the front counter with a generous tip. Sabriva had relied on magic for centuries to keep evenings comfortable. Now, the air was biting cold. Ava pulled her coat tight and reached out for Luck. The familiar golden bands were pliable, a world of difference from their rigidity in the Remnant Magic storm.

But something felt different. A new path to follow. This could be what she was waiting for—a way to justify her presence in Euryma for as long as possible. Or it could be something else, a shortcut to danger, or worse, back to Vedmark. Luck was a tricky thing, and Ava had learned the hard way that trusting it blindly was a mistake.

To her right, Sabriva Tower glimmered over the skyline. The Emissary would be there right now, and unless Ava came up with something useful, the Emissary would have to send her back. With that thought in mind, Ava checked the knives in her belt and followed the golden trail into the cold night.

Sabriva wasn't just a big city. It was an enormous city. From Ava's vantage point on the ridge, it was a sea of twinkling lights. From this distance, Sabriva Tower was now just a glittering candlestick in the night. Ava took it in, then turned towards Kannidy.

Unlike Sabriva Central, nothing glittered in Kannidy. The main road looked like a giant baby had knocked over a pile of blocks, except instead of blocks, they were houses— ramshackle tin boxes that smelled like public restrooms.

Ava wrinkled her nose and walked a step faster. She immersed herself in the stream of Luck that had tugged on her since leaving the cafe.

Nobody lived in Kannidy by choice. Ava passed three men arguing over plastic bags of bread. Around a corner, a young woman sat on the ground. She was thin as a broomstick, cradling a baby in withered arms. The trail stopped at her feet. A shimmering golden cloud hung over her head.

"Can I help you?" Ava asked.

The girl lifted her chin to reveal milky white eyes. "Money for my baby?" she asked in a hoarse whisper. She grasped at Ava's coat with fingers like fishhooks. Ava dropped a wad of Euryman bills on her lap. The moment she did, the golden haze vanished. Brittle fingers felt the notes. The blind girl gasped. Ava rushed ahead before she could attract attention.

"That was awful generous," called a sharp voice from behind. A stocky man with an unkempt beard emerged from the building's shadow. He wore a too-tight jacket with patches across the front. Over his shoulder, two men crouched by the girl. They stood up, laughing. One of them slapped the stack of money against his open palm.

Ava's eyes narrowed. "That wasn't yours."

The leader of the trio chuckled. "You're right, it wasn't." His two friends stopped by his side. He took the money and held it up to her. "But it is now." Golden luck swirled around them; a gentle vortex invisible to everyone but Ava.

"Hey honey," said one of the others. His patchy mustache was more fitting for a teenager. "What's a pretty girl like you doing out here by yaself? Need a bit of company?"

Ava adjusted her feet ever so slightly. Waves of chance rippled around them. Instinctively, she started tugging on one, moving it with her mind. To her delight, it moved easily. *These thugs are all show.* Ava smiled sweetly. "Come get me."

One man lunged forward. His foot caught a shallow pothole and he fell to the ground. His companion stumbled over him. Their leader scowled. "Get up, ya idiots."

Ava leaped forward, driving all her speed and strength into one compressed fist. It met the man's jaw with a wet crunch. Ava landed as the other two climbed to their feet. Two swift kicks—one to the face and one to the groin—left both men in a heap. Ava tugged the wad of notes from the man's limp hands and walked back to the girl. She was gone.

A slow clap came from a nearby alleyway. A bald man stepped into the street, followed by the thin girl with milky eyes. "Very nice," he said. "Very, *very* nice,"

Ava scowled back at him. "Who are you?"

"Maurice," said the man.

He looked at her expectantly and seemed disappointed when Ava shrugged. She nodded over his shoulder. "I hope this young lady is being taken care of."

"I compensate my daughter well for her performances." Maurice motioned to the pile of men in the street. "You've done quite a number on my muscle."

Ava smirked. "That's the muscle, is it?"

"Unfortunately, the pickings are slim in slums like this. Mage Raul has a dangerous reputation. The information I'm selling would be useless if you couldn't handle yourself."

Ava fought to keep her jaw from dropping. Her Luck had outdone itself this time. *Mage Raul is here? And this man is handing him to me on a platter? Why?*

"As for compensation." Maurice held out his palm. "I trust *that* is the amount we agreed on."

"Naturally." Ava handed him the bills.

"I have sent transfer details to Laurefen. I expect the second payment tomorrow by sunset. That is more than enough time to confirm my information is accurate."

"Very well," Ava said. She forced her voice steady, unable to believe her good fortune. Laurefen was the Dean at King's College. She had intercepted their deal. *They must be hunting Raul, too.* "Tell me about the Mage."

"He's here. He may hide in the shadows, but twice a day —morning and evening—he visits a house."

"Where?"

"Thirty-eight, Arbour Crescent. Upper east of the suburb."

"That means nothing to me."

Maurice waved to his daughter. "Add another hundred to the pot, and Marni will guide you."

"I'll have Laurefen add it to your second payment," Ava said. The girl, Marni, stepped forward with a cane in front of her. She offered a skeleton arm. Ava worried she might break her wrist just by touching it. She gripped Marni's sleeve and nodded to Maurice. "Thank you for your business."

Maurice bowed with a mocking smile. "The pleasure is mine, Ms. Hall."

Ava waited on the corrugated iron roof of a nearby house. Arbour Crescent was a mismatched arrangement of poorly built hovels and empty blocks. Number thirty-eight was a collage of flaked paint and rust. It looked like it should have collapsed a decade ago. Beside it was an abandoned yard piled with scrap metal and stacks of rotted timber that reminded her of the piles she would dig through as a girl— back when she first met Misha. Ava smiled and let the thought take her back to her childhood.

Beads of morning dew clung to the smooth beams of gray-green silwood that Grigory had cut the night before. Misha rushed to one end, Ava to the other. Together, they lifted. Grigory watched on with bright eyes. "Very good, you two," he said. "We need sixty beams from this pile and thirty-four from others. Stack them out front for carpenters."

Misha nodded, always eager to please his father. Ava wasn't so sure. "That's ninety-four beams!"

"It sure is, work as a team. It will go fast."

Misha was already moving. Ava followed down the hill, past the sawmill and into a dirt square on the edge of the road. They lowered the beam and walked back. "One down, ninety-three to go," Ava said.

When they reached the silwood stack, Grigory was gone. Misha hurried to the bottom of the pile; it was more than triple his size. "Take one from the bottom, I guess." He shrugged at her, the question bright in his eyes.

"Sounds okay, I guess," Ava said. "This is your yard, not mine."

Misha blushed. "But you're nine! You know way more stuff than me!"

Ava stood a little taller, emboldened by her age. "Okay. Grab the other end."

Misha bent down low, and together they pulled. Ava heard it before she saw it. The lumber creaked and tilted. The stacked wood began to tumble. As it fell towards her, everything slowed down. The creamy fragrance of sawdust filled her nostrils. Heavy beams sunk through the air as if caught in syrup. Golden lines fanned out from them like honeyed ripples. Ava reached out and grabbed at them. They felt... bendy.

She gripped tight and pulled. Bronze shadows flowed out of the lines; she watched the beams fall a hundred different ways. Most of the time, they crushed her own glowing shadow. She continued to pull on the line until she found what she was looking for. Her shadow-self, surrounded by wood, unharmed. Something locked into place. She let go of the bendy gold band and squeezed her eyes shut.

When she opened them, a cloud of sawdust blocked her vision.

"Ava! Misha! Call out to me!" A voice called from her left. It was Irman. "Misha! I see you!"

As the dust settled, Ava could only blink. She was alive. Snapped lengths of silwood lay scattered around her, but she was fine. She turned to Misha. Broken wood surrounded him, too. "I'm... fine..." she panted. Her legs felt weak. "And so is..."

"Misha! Ava!" Grigory ran up the hill. He jumped over the pile and scooped them up. "I heard... I saw it fall. You are okay. You are okay! It is miracle!"

Ava watched Irman shake his head. "More than a miracle," he said, his voice faint with disbelief.

Grigory shook his head. "Nonsense. It is a miracle." He squeezed them tight. "They are safe—that is what matters."

Ava stared at her hands while Irman and Grigory discussed the matter. Their words faded as she puzzled over what had happened and how she could do it again.

A man entered Arbour Crescent. Ava snapped out of the memory. The visitor wore a black sweater with the hood drawn. He crossed the street, completely at ease. In his hands were two paper bags. He walked to the front door of number thirty-eight, put the bags on the ground, and left. As he did, Ava caught sight of his face, a smooth-cheeked teenager, not Mage Raul's ginger beard. *Not him. Not yet.* Ava settled back into a comfortable crouch and returned to her memories.

"It felt the same for me!" Misha's eyes burned with excitement. "Like I was pulling on a rubber rope... Maybe I am a warlock!"

Ava shook her head. They were sitting on a hill overlooking the lumberyard. "No, you can't be. I felt the same, and you know what they say- girls can't be warlocks."

Misha looked at her like she'd eaten his pie. "I don't know what else it could be."

"We should ask Grigory."

Misha scratched his head. "I'm not sure pa will like that. He doesn't like Sila."

Ava snorted. "That doesn't make sense. Someone who doesn't like Sila wouldn't own a silwood yard!"

Misha shrugged. "It's not pa's yard- it's grandad's yard. Pa wants nothing to do with it. He wants a farm, wants animals and a garden."

"That sounds silly."

"I wouldn't mind having animals. Baby ones are cute."

Ava squeezed her hands into tiny fists. "I wonder what it is."

"Baby animals."

"No. Not baby animals. Us. This thing we did. I wonder what it is."

"Maybe we're both warlocks."

Ava replied with an elbow. "I'm not a boy!" Misha rolled away, laughing. Already, the broken silwood beams had straightened and repaired themselves. "But whatever it is, it saved our lives today."

Misha sat up and nodded. "Maybe it's luck."

119

Another man entered the Crescent. He wore a short green coat, patched at the elbows. His face was uncovered, his red beard clear under the streetlight. *Raul.* Ava touched the knives at her belt.

Raul walked up the driveway of number thirty-eight, stopped to pick up the paper bags at the door, and slipped inside. Ava waited until the door closed behind him, then dropped off the roof and crossed the road. She rushed to the splintered wall, tugged probability in her favor and moved to a side window, lucky not to crunch a single dead leaf beneath her feet.

A deep voice rumbled inside the house, too muffled to understand. Ava moved further along the wall; the voice grew louder. Whoever was talking, they were at the back of the house. Ava climbed a rusted downpipe and crawled towards them. When she reached a cloudy plastic panel patching the roof, she flattened herself against it to listen.

"You must eat. Your body needs strength." There was a long pause. "Yes, Parteno is gone. That doesn't matter now. You need to rest, and to eat."

Ava frowned. As far as she could tell, Raul was the only person inside. *Who is he talking to?*

"I will leave this here. Please do not let it go to waste. You can't fix *anything* until you fix yourself. I have business tonight. I'll be back in the morning to check on you." Footsteps moved to the front room. Ava unsheathed a knife and crept after them. She positioned herself right above the door. The door creaked open, and Raul stepped out.

Tense like a spring, she prepared to attack. *What is he hiding?* Ava pushed the stray thought away. She leaned forward. *Don't kill him. Not yet. You don't have all the information yet. He'll be back tomorrow.* Ava considered it. The Mage *was* hiding something. A corpse couldn't answer questions. She gripped chance and pulled it towards her. The odds were slim. She felt it burn in her muscles, but it worked. The door shut, but the lock didn't click. Raul left the way he'd arrived, none the wiser that he'd left the house unguarded.

Ava waited until she was certain Raul was gone. She scanned the street one last time, then dropped and slid inside. To her surprise, the inside of the house resembled a country manor. Soft lamps lit a handsome walkway, complete with mahogany floorboards and framed paint-ings. *It's all a front.* The corridor branched off into several spacious bedrooms. Partway down the hall, she stopped to listen. A rasping noise scratched its way from the back of the house. Ava tiptoed to the doorway.

"Raul?" called a voice as dry as chalk. Ava froze. "Raul, is that you?"

Something creaked behind her. Ava spun on her heels. Somebody was in the walkway—a dozen distinct possibili-ties splayed out in the open. Ava dived right, wrenching on Luck to keep the spell hurtling her way off target. It missed, splitting the wall over her shoulder. A framed picture broke against the floorboards. Ava dived to catch the figure around the waist. She held tight and dragged the person to the ground.

Ava climbed on top, raised a clenched fist, then stopped.

A familiar woman with a long brown braid lay beneath her.

The woman used the moment to flick her fingers in an intricate motion. Ava shot backward, pulled by invisible hands. She hit the wall with a thud.

The woman climbed to her feet—her eyes narrowed. "I

know you," she said. "You're the girl who took Declan." Ava couldn't move. Magical bonds held her against the wall. The young woman stood over her. "What are you doing here? Where's Mage Raul?"

"That's none of your business," Ava replied. Her chances of escape were slim; it would cost a lot of energy to get away now.

The woman took a step closer. Suddenly, the odds didn't seem so bad. "Where is Declan?"

Ava answered with a swift headbutt. The woman cried out in pain; the magical bonds dissipated. Ava wrapped an arm around the woman's neck and held tight. They fell to the ground, and Ava gripped tighter.

"Let... me... go..." she choked.

Ava saw her hands go to work. "Don't be stupid. Anything you do to me, you do to both of us!"

With a loud bang, the mahogany boards snapped up from the floor and smashed into them. Ava rolled through a nearby door as more floorboards rocketed up at her. They crashed into the room and splintered against a bed frame.

Ava crouched behind the door and waited for the attack to slow. When the young woman poked her head inside, Ava grabbed her shoulders. The woman shoved her off, backing away. Ava tugged Luck, and she stumbled, falling through a section of missing floorboards. Ava scooped up a length of wood to finish the job when the woman raised her hands. "Stop!"

Ava paused. "No." She swung down. The board exploded in her hands. She picked up another one.

The woman held her hands high, palms out. "I won't hurt you, and you don't attack me. Let's just talk, okay?"

Ava held the floorboard still. "Why should I trust you?"

The woman kept her hands held up. "You are Declan's friend, right? He's safe, isn't he?"

Ava nodded.

"Well, I am Declan's friend too. I was there in Anderma." The woman chewed on her lower lip. "I think we may be on the same team."

"The same team?"

The woman nodded. "I'm trying to save the people who Haberdeen fierised. I'm here searching for a man named Raul. He knows where those people are."

She considered the woman. *She was in Anderma. She was one of the King's College people, the Directive. She must have been the one Laurefen sent, the one Maurice mistook me for.* "Are you Katie?"

The girl lowered her hands slowly and climbed out of the broken floor. "I am. And you're Ava, right?"

"How do you know my name?"

Katie smiled. "Declan talked about you." Her eyes narrowed. "How do you know my name?"

Ava shrugged, unwilling to admit she had intercepted the woman's messenger. "Just got lucky, I guess."

Katie nodded slowly. Her eyes wandered up and down the ruined hall. "Seems we've done a good job announcing our arrival. Is Raul still here?"

"He'll be back in the morning, but..." Ava pointed to the back of the house. "There's somebody else down there."

"You lead," Katie said.

Ava didn't move. "No offense, but I don't trust you. If we're working together, let's go together."

There was an awkward pause, and then Katie nodded. They walked to the end of the hall and entered a grand kitchen. It had sapphire-flecked stone tiles, a marble bench, and three small chandeliers. In the dining area, in a partially reclined chair, lay a woman wrapped in blankets. A long scar ran along her left cheek. Between shallow breaths, her eyes bulged.

Katie gasped. Ava's skin crawled. After months of searching, she'd found her mark.

Haberdeen.

CHAPTER 16
AVA

HABERDEEN BREATHED in shallow rasps with eyes like headlights.

"What happened to you?" Ava asked.

Haberdeen said nothing. Only stared. She looked like a mouse cornered by cats.

"This doesn't add up." Katie stood over the frail shell of a woman. "We had reports of you in Biscay last night. If you are here, who is leading the ironhands?" Again, Haberdeen refused to speak. Katie turned back to Ava. "Do you know when Raul is coming back?"

"In the morning," Ava murmured. *Raul is unnecessary now. We have Haberdeen. If I take her back, Rasporvin will get his knife, and I'll be stuck in Vedmark forever.* The leader of the Fatesmiths sat swaddled and helpless. "We have until sunrise to get something out of her." *Or some excuse to stay in Euryma.*

Katie stepped up to Ava's side. "If she even knows anything."

"What do you mean?"

"Look at her. This may be Haberdeen's body, but who

can say what Declan did to her? For all we know, she's a breathing corpse."

Ava squatted to Haberdeen's level. Ribbons of gold swirled about her frail frame. She tested one. It didn't budge. "You have information that we need." She procured a vial of sanarmelon juice from her back pocket. "This can heal you, but only if you will answer our questions."

Haberdeen's gaping eyes went from Ava to the vial in her hands. She dipped her head in the smallest of nods.

"Very well," Ava said. "What happened to you?"

Haberdeen inhaled a rattling breath. "Anderma," she rasped. "That boy... attacked me."

Declan. Ava exchanged a knowing glance with Katie.

"Escaped through an... Opening. Raul... brought me here." Haberdeen coughed; flecks of blood marked her blanket.

Ava popped the lid open. "Lean back. Don't spill any."

Haberdeen swallowed with a loud gulp. Ava only used a third of the juice; the change was immediate. Color returned to her pale skin, and her breathing steadied. Haberdeen exhaled deeply. "Remarkable," she whispered. "No improvement for months, and all it took was a drop of Vedmark juice."

"Glad to hear you've recovered," Katie said. She didn't bother to hide the sarcasm in her voice. "Now, where are the holding houses? Where is my mother?"

Haberdeen sagged into her chair. "Dear, I wish I could tell you."

Katie's eyebrows drew down. "You're lying."

"I don't remember."

Katie raised her hand, and Ava rushed to step between them. "Calm down," she hissed in the shorter girl's ear. "This is not the time to do something rash."

"Fine." Katie took a calming breath and stepped back.

"What about the knife?" Ava asked, turning back to Haberdeen. "The white dagger, Winterthorn."

Haberdeen shook her head. "I don't remember that either."

Katie's eyes narrowed. "Seems convenient of you to forget anything useful."

"I've been on death's doorstep for days." Haberdeen blinked at the vial. "This... this is the clearest my mind has been in months. Everything before now is... nothing... gone."

Katie gritted her teeth. "You took my mother. The only thing keeping you alive right now is the knowledge to deliver her safely home. If you don't have that information..."

Ava watched silently. The odds weren't in their favor. Even now, in the shadows of likely events, she could see Katie snapping the woman's neck. *Not yet. She's still useful.* "Katie," Ava interrupted. She pulled Luck as hard as she could to move them in a more rational direction. "Can I speak to you for a moment?"

Katie tore her eyes away from Haberdeen, her balled fists relaxed. "Just a moment."

They walked to the corner of the kitchen. "You're too close to this," Ava whispered.

"What do you mean?"

"I mean, you're about to kill the woman."

"No more than she deserves."

Ava nodded. "But not yet. She has the information I need."

Katie squeezed her eyelids closed. "Okay, fine," she said at last. When her eyes opened, the fire in them was gone. "What do we do?"

"Let me do the talking. You watch for anything I might miss."

"Okay." Ava turned, but Katie touched her shoulder. "Ava?"

She glanced back. "Yeah?"

"Thanks for keeping me in check."

Ava blinked. "Uh, sure, no problem."

When they returned to Haberdeen, Ava didn't waste any time. "Tell me about Anderma. What *do* you remember?"

"Like I said, there was a boy. He was standing over me, and I had a nasty gash in my side."

"A gash? What do you mean? Show me."

Haberdeen hesitated, then wriggled free of the swaddling blankets. She lifted her loose shirt to reveal a gauze wrap over her ribcage. Ava leaned down to inspect it and noticed something small and silver tucked into the blanket. Ava snatched it. Haberdeen cried out, and Katie pinned her to the chair with a wave of her hand.

Ava turned it over. It was a LAMP phone. The tiny green screen displayed an ongoing call. The timer read ten minutes. "Who did you contact?"

Katie yelped in surprise. Ava whirled and watched her crash into the chandelier. Glass crystals scattered everywhere. Katie disappeared behind the marble bench. Raul stood in the doorway. His dark eyes flickered to Ava. A shimmering silver square appeared in front of him.

Ava stumbled backward. Haberdeen had her ankle. She delivered a sharp kick to her hand and wriggled free. She rolled behind the chair as a second fierisation square shot past. Haberdeen sat, sobbing. The woman's fingers jutted at awkward angles. *Serve you right.*

Raul and Katie were tossing spells back and forth. Ava

squatted beneath the chair, positioned its weight over her shoulders, and charged.

Raul shouted in surprise. They collided, he fell backward and Ava drove her elbow into his neck. He roared in anger. Magic propelled Ava backward, her shoulder caught the window frame. She felt the bone break.

The kitchen faucet tore away. A large ball of water formed between Katie and Raul, each trying to force it onto the other. Haberdeen sat in a corner, cradling her hand. Her hair resembled a bird's nest.

The watery orb inched closer to Katie. Ava dug through her pocket for sanarmelon juice. A quick gulp and her shoulder reset with a painless click. The moment the pain faded, an invisible force dragged her to the ground. Ava tried to roll away but couldn't move. Raul's spell pinned her torso. Through the window, she watched Katie edge backward. The swirling sphere of water loomed over her. Her drawn face went pale. She was trapped.

Ava reached around in the dirt. Her fingers closed on something sharp, a jagged shard of corrugated iron. Ava lined up her target and let fly. She pulled chance like a bowstring and felt the projectile connect.

Raul faltered as the iron shard lodged itself between his thumb and pointer. The pressure on Ava's torso vanished and she rolled to safety.

Katie tried to make a dash for it, but the water was too close. The rippling orb engulfed her and its surface froze over. Ava watched, horrified, as Katie's cloudy outline fought to break the spherical prison.

Raul turned to the window. A series of shimmering squares formed around him. Ava moved without thinking, plucking Luck like a harp. Dodging, diving, and spinning, all the while conscious that Katie was drowning. She rolled away from another square and felt something hard below her. Another iron sheet. Ava grabbed the corners and pulled it up just in time to shield her from attack.

She huddled underneath it. The metal shuddered beneath every spell.

"Your friend is dying, lass," Raul called. "Come out and I'll let her live."

Katie was running out of time; Ava considered her options. *Screw it. I'll just kill him now.* She raised the iron sheet and charged. It trembled under a magical onslaught, but still it held. Two steps from the house, she thrust the panel in Raul's direction and leaped, pulling herself up to the roof and crashing down through the skylight. She hit the frozen bubble, slid down its side, grabbed a metal stool, and smashed it into the icy orb.

A crack appeared in the bubble, extended, like cobwebs, then shattered. Katie's limp body slid to the tiles as a tide of frigid water flooded the kitchen floor. Raul spun it into a large wobbling ball. Ava dashed beneath the kitchen bench and helped herself to a block of knives.

The first knife brushed Raul's ear and lodged in the wall. He rushed back to the safety of the dining table as blades billowed from behind the bench. The watery sphere collapsed and lapped across the floor. When the knives ran out, Ava dug into the drawers, relying on Luck to find anything sharp, iron or both. Katie lay motionless between them.

"You put up a good fight," Raul shouted. "I'll give ya that."

Huddled by the bench, Ava searched the kitchen. She had emptied every drawer and cupboard. The only object left in reach was Haberdeen's phone.

"All out of luck?" The small splashes of Raul's footsteps

grew closer. "You should have taken my offer. Your friend is dead. Now, it's your turn."

Ava slipped into a cupboard.

"Tell me, was it worth it?"

Raul rounded the corner. Ava listened, counting the seconds, not daring to breathe. The cupboard door darkened in his shadow. Ava coiled like a spring. *Three. Two. One.* Haberdeen's phone alarm erupted in a shrill ring. As Raul spun to confront the noise. Ava leaped from the cupboard and dropped an elbow into the back of his neck. Raul's head straightened; his shoulders went slack. His knees barely touched the ground before Ava delivered a swift kick to his head.

Raul landed with a splash. Ava smiled as he splayed out in the water. *Totally worth it.*

She rushed to Katie's side. Her skin was freezing, her chest still. Ava pressed the last of her sanarmelon juice to her stiff lips. A moment later, Katie coughed and spluttered back into consciousness. "Wha- what happened?" she said, looking around at the flooded room.

"Raul nearly got the best of both of us."

Katie followed Ava's gaze and gasped at Raul's unconscious body. "You beat him?"

"I got lucky," Ava said, the corners of her mouth twitched.

Katie searched the ruined kitchen. "And Haberdeen?"

Ava nodded to the hall. "Hear that?"

Someone was sobbing from the other room. Katie's mouth fell open. "That's her?"

"I think I broke her hand."

"I thought she'd be..." Katie shrugged. "Tougher?"

Ava stood and helped Katie to her feet. "I don't..." she trailed off and listened to the soft sobs. "I don't think that's the Haberdeen we remember. She seems different. Broken."

They walked out of the kitchen, over the ruined floorboards, and into a spacious bedroom. Haberdeen pressed herself against the corner. Cloth wrapped her hand. Her puffy eyes were bloodshot.

"You need to come with us now," Ava said.

Haberdeen shook her head.

"That wasn't a request."

"What's the point?" Haberdeen moaned. "I know nothing! I have no magic, no memory, I'm nothing!"

Katie frowned. "What do you mean, he took your power?"

"The boy!"

"Declan?"

"I don't know his name," Haberdeen hissed.

Katie looked at Ava. "A word outside?"

They walked into the hallway. "What do you think?"

Katie bit her lip. "I think she's telling the truth."

"I agree." Ava checked the kitchen. Raul was still unconscious on the floor. Katie had bound him in coiled air just to be safe. "What's our play?"

Katie looked back into the room. "There are two potential sources of information here, and there are two of us. Raul clearly knows more. He seems to have his memories intact. He might know where my mother is, but..." her cheeks colored. "Well, you saved my life. If you really want Raul, I'll take Haberdeen."

Ava considered the choice. *Raul will have answers. Haberdeen will raise more questions. Questions I'll need to investigate here in Euryma.* She grinned at Katie. "If you want Raul, take him. My people will want to see Haberdeen in the flesh."

Katie's eyes bulged. "Really?"

"For sure, it's for the best... for both of us." Ava walked back into the kitchen. Raul's unconscious figure twitched on the floor. *I guess you'll live another day, Mage Raul.* She picked up Haberdeen's phone and dropped it in her pocket.

"What's that for?" Katie asked.

Ava shrugged. "You never know who might try to call."

Kannidy was no place to be after sundown. Cars, like people, avoided its streets, separating it from the bustle of Sabriva's sleeplessness. Haberdeen snored on the bed, seemingly oblivious to the binds on her wrists and ankles. Ava watched her from the lounge and listened for any sign of trouble. A lone jewelry stand rested on a cabinet. Amongst the silver chains, a topaz pendant caught her attention. It was the type of necklace the Emissary would wear on occasion, even back to their first meeting.

"It is a delight to meet you both. My name is Samantha. I am an Emissary between Vedmark and Euryma."

Misha beamed at her with enormous brown eyes. "What's a memissary?"

The woman's shoulders shook with silent laughter, and the sapphire pendant bounced against her chest. "Em-Iss-Air-Ee. That's a good question, Misha. Ava, do you know what an Emissary is?"

Ava shook her head.

"An Emissary is kind of like a friend from somewhere different. Like I said, I come from a place called Euryma. Have you heard of it?"

"I have." Ava nodded eagerly. "Uncle said Euryma is our land, that one day we'll get it back."

133

The Emissary's smile flickered for a moment. "Well, that sounds like an interesting story."

"He's very busy. He's the Grand Steward."

"Yes, he is. Tell me, Ava, why do you think he sent you here to work with Misha?"

Ava felt her cheeks grow warm. "Because I'm a girl."

The Emissary squeezed her shoulder. Ava met her twinkling blue eyes. "That's right, a very special girl. You are what we call a Luck."

"A what?"

"A Luck. It means you have a wonderful power. You can change what will happen to make the world better."

Misha smiled, showing a mouth of gaps. "Me too. Me too. I can do that. Am I a Luck too?"

The Emissary patted him on the head. "Yes, Misha, so are you."

Ava frowned. "If I'm so special, why doesn't Uncle want me?"

"It's not that," she said. "As you told me, the Grand Steward is very busy. But I'm here, Ava, and I want you to come with me. I will give you the time and space to learn how to use your gift so that you can help the people of Vedmark and the people of Euryma." She knelt down, Ava caught her reflection in her sapphire necklace. "You are going to help so many people, Ava."

Haberdeen groaned. She was still asleep but struggling against her binds. Her bruised eyes snapped open in the moonlight. For a moment, Ava thought she would scream.

"You're fine," Ava said. "It's just me."

Haberdeen stared at her, then fell back to the bed. "Can you at least untie me?"

"Nope." Ava tested the bands of chance around her. Right now, they were as pliable as ever. She leaned on one as she leaned back in her chair. "Were you having a nightmare?"

Haberdeen's lower lip trembled. "I was... remembering." She took a deep breath, and her voice grew a little firmer. "I'm there, surrounded by people. It's snowing. The ground is solid glass."

"Anderma?"

Haberdeen nodded. "I'm bleeding. There is a gash in my side, a young man standing over me."

"Declan?"

Haberdeen shrugged. "I don't know his name. He is confused. He's holding a blade. It's white."

Winterthorn.

"The boy gets distracted as the people wake up. I run. He chases me. There's an Opening ahead. He's just about to get me and I... I wake up."

Ava walked to the window. Clouds rolled over the city, illuminated in shades of yellow and orange by Sabriva's lights. For a moment, she was back in Parteno. Ava closed her eyes and shook the thought away. "It's just a nightmare, that's all. Declan didn't see you. He didn't stab you. He—"

A knock at the door interrupted her.

Ava glanced down the hall. "Are you expecting company?"

"No," Haberdeen murmured. "Raul was the only one who knew I was here."

The knocking grew louder. Ava tugged on probability. The visitors were not friendly. "We need to go."

"Why would I go anywhere with you?"

Ava's eyes narrowed. "Because it's in my best interest to keep you alive." She tilted her head toward the hallway.

"Those people, I'm not so sure." She grabbed her knife and cut Haberdeen's bonds.

A loud bang echoed through the house. Haberdeen paled. "What was that?"

"Sounds like someone kicked the door in. Hide." Haberdeen slid under the bed. Ava grabbed a chair and threw it through the window. The crash set footsteps rushing towards them. Ava climbed into a closet, pulled the door ajar and pulled on Luck with all her strength.

"Here! They've gone out the window!" A pair of black-coats rushed to look outside.

"I don't see anyone."

Ava heaved on the golden band. Something clicked into place. "They've probably slipped around the back. C'mon, before they get away."

"You think Maurice lied to us?"

"Haberdeen will have his head if he did."

The blackcoats are after Raul. At Haberdeen's request? Ava waited until the men were gone, then waited some more. She emerged from the wardrobe as Haberdeen wiggled out from beneath the bed. "What was that about?"

Haberdeen struggled to her feet. "An imposter is running the Fatesmiths now, someone bearing my likeness."

Ava considered it. "We need to leave."

"And go where?"

Ava looked out the window, past the lights of Sabriva. *To Declan. He already beat you once, Haberdeen. He's the best chance we've got... if he hasn't killed himself chasing coins.* She turned back to the pitiful woman. "North."

CHAPTER 17
KATIE

MICHAEL WAITED under a flickering street light on Kannidy's edge. He raised his eyebrows as they approached. "That's not watching from a distance."

Katie shrugged. "Events spiraled out of control." She tugged on the aeronima wrapped around her wrist. A long strand of kinetic energy kept Raul's unconscious body upright. From far away, they could be lovers on a late-night stroll. Up close, Raul's feet dragged like a bad dancer.

"Even so..." Michael eyed Raul's drooping figure. "I'll bet you an Iberian Dime Lou won't be pleased."

"Is an Iberian Dime worth anything?"

"It's solid gold."

Katie grinned. "Then I'll take that bet."

The rusted metal bench creaked as he stood up. "Raul is a Mage, Katie," Michael said. "And Lou will not be impressed that you went up against him without our help."

"But... I've got him."

"Indeed." Michael nodded. "How?"

"How what?"

"How did you beat him?" His gaze wandered up the

empty street behind them. "The title *Mage* is not given lightly."

Katie considered it. For a moment, she wondered if it would be best to lie about the encounter. *No. As soon as we start lying, the whole thing will fall apart.* "Ava."

Michael's eyes narrowed. "The Luck?"

"She was tracking him too. Michael, I have news. Can you save your lecture for later?"

He must have heard the urgency in her voice. "Very well." He moved his hands with rehearsed perfection. A small triangle rotated into a circular doorway. A towering cedar waited on the other side. "But the lecture will be waiting once we get there."

Mary-Lou stared daggers across the table. "Katie! What were you thinking?"

Katie opened her mouth, Michael nudged her. "You owe me a gold coin," he whispered.

"This is not a joke!" Mary-Lou snapped. "Raul is a *Mage*. He could have killed you."

"He almost did," Katie admitted. "But he didn't. I had help. That's what I need to talk to you about."

Laurefen stroked his moustache. "Katie, I think what Lou is trying to say," he shot her a glance, "is that we worry about you, and that we are glad you are safe."

Mary-Lou pursed her lips. "What I'm——"

"Regardless," Laurefen continued. "You said this cannot wait. What have you learned?"

Katie nodded, eager to move on. "Raul was hiding out in Kannidy with Haberdeen."

Michael straightened. Mary-Lou's eyes bulged.

"You saw her?" Laurefen asked.

"I did. She is powerless. She claims to have no memory of anything. She says Declan took her power."

"Impossible," Michael said. "She was playing you for a fool."

Katie met his eyes. "I don't think she was. Raul attacked me, he beat me, but Ava—"

"That same Ava that took Declan?" Mary-Lou's eyes grew wider. "Was Declan with her?"

Katie shook her head. "No, but Ava saved me. The whole time though, Haberdeen hid in a corner. She could have helped fight. They would have beaten us easily, but she didn't, she couldn't. She was... weak."

Laurefen touched the star-shaped scar at his temple. "A blow to the head can play havoc with memory, but that doesn't explain the weakness."

"Green magic?" Michael asked. "Did Declan rob her of her power? Who knows what it can do?"

"Where is Haberdeen?" Mary-Lou asked. "If she is as feeble as you say she is, then she must have been easy to capture."

Laurefen caught Katie's gaze. He held it like a magnet. "Ava took her."

"No." Mary-Lou's lips pressed into a grimace. "You wouldn't be so foolish."

"He's right." Katie said. "Ava took her." Michael walked to the window. Katie's stomach dropped. *I hadn't even considered Michael. Haberdeen killed Dreyfus.* "I'm sorry Michael."

"For what?"

Katie fought to keep her voice steady. "For not thinking about you, or about what Haberdeen did."

Michael turned back, knelt, and put his hand on her

shoulder. "You did the right thing. I miss Dreyfus. But I have found peace knowing that he did the right thing. Green magic or not, Declan saved us. He gave us a chance, and now, by bringing in Raul, so have you."

Katie didn't reply.

"I agree," Laurefen said. "If Haberdeen has lost her memories, she is useless to us for now. It raises an interesting question about who is leading the Fatesmiths, but that is for another time. Mage Raul may know where the holdhouses are."

"Where is he now?" Mary-Lou asked.

Michael returned to his seat. "I secured him in one of the containment chambers."

Katie dabbed her eyes. "Containment chambers?"

"The containers in the Imbusion Lab for improperly imbued objects."

"Those small Perspex boxes in the back corner?" Katie tilted her head. "You fit him in there?"

Michael shrugged. "He won't be comfortable when he wakes up."

Katie decided not to pursue the subject. She glanced at the empty chair across from her. "Where's Amber?"

"She is in Massalia," Laurefen said. "Following up on something that suddenly seems less important."

Katie nodded. She looped the thread connecting her palm to Amber's and tapped a rushed message. *Found a lead, real game changer. We may need you back here soon.* She looked up. "Any news about Parteno?"

Michael shook his head. "Whatever spell was used to destroy Parteno was unimaginably strong. I still cannot create an Opening there. The High Mage is keeping a lid on specifics."

"The great buffoon." Mary-Lou rolled her eyes. "The

Fatesmiths are using the event at Parteno to spread lies about Remnant Magic storms. They are desperate for followers. They are recruiting anyone who will listen, even LAMPs."

"LAMPs?" Michael stiffened. "What would the iron-hands do with LAMPs?"

"Your guess is as good as mine."

Katie chewed her bottom lip. "How can we be certain that they aren't telling the truth?"

"Katie..." Mary-Lou shook her head. "How many times must we go over this? Remnant Magic can't destroy anything. It is a breeze that carries leaves across a park lawn, that's all. This dangerous lie is a story of Haberdeen's invention, a fabrication for the fickle masses!"

"Yes, Lou, I accepted that." Katie turned to Laurefen. "But that was before Parteno. Michael said it himself. Whatever did that was beyond anything we've ever seen. If we can't be open to evaluating our ideas when new information comes to light, how can we be sure that we're doing the right thing?"

"I understand what you're saying, Kate," Laurefen said. "But there is no evidence..."

"What destroyed Parteno then?"

Michael crossed his arms. "The only magic that can do that kind of damage is from the North."

"Vedmark?"

"It's the most likely explanation," Mary-Lou said. "Green magic was all but a myth. Then Declan shows up. Less than six months later, a city is destroyed. What are the chances?"

"A possibility but not a certainty," Laurefen said. "We don't want to make assumptions. We have no reason to believe that Vedmark wants anything to do with Euryma."

"With all due respect," Mary-Lou said coldly. "My conclusions have turned out fairly accurate in the past."

"Why would Vedmark come against us?" Katie asked. "Why now?"

"We can only guess. Perhaps all the Knights of Despair died out and now they have Declan, they're ready to take over."

Katie shook her head. "I can't believe that. Declan isn't a bad person."

"The Declan we knew *was* a good person," Mary-Lou said. "We have no idea what they've done to him."

"It doesn't matter," Michael said. "We don't know what happened in Parteno. We don't know why the Luck took Haberdeen. We don't know what Declan Moore is up to, and this idle speculation is a waste of time." He looked to Laurefen. "What we have is a man in our possession who may well have the location of every holdhouse."

Laurefen nodded. "Michael is right. We will deal with Parteno when we can. Arguing helps nobody. Let's focus our attention on what we can control. I think it's time we have a discussion with Mage Raul."

The Imbusion Lab smelled of bleach. Small green lights blinked off the glossy white tiles. Raul was still unconscious, cramped into a box half his height, bloody hand wrapped and pressed flat against the plexiglass door. Katie frowned. *Michael must have bandaged it.*

"Now Michael," Laurefen started. "That looks terribly uncomfortable."

"It's as much as he deserves."

"We are not savages," Laurefen said. "Let him out. Let's hear what he has to say."

Michael slid an iron key into the door. As soon as the lock clicked, Raul's eyes opened. With an almighty roar, he threw himself forward and knocked Michael to the floor.

Mary-Lou and Laurefen trapped Raul in nima before he hit the ground. Together, they carried him across the room. Katie rushed to Michael's side. "Are you okay?"

Michael brushed himself off. "Stupid of me to let my guard down." He removed a yellow tub from the top of a white cupboard, its contents jingled with every step. He reached inside and withdrew a long chain. Laurefen nodded, and Michael bound Raul to the chair.

Raul fought it. His face darkened, muscles tensed, veins bulged. For a moment, Katie expected he would pass out. Then Raul gave in. His shoulders relaxed, but his chest heaved. "What do you want with me?" he growled. His dark eyes fixed on Katie. "Well, well, how impressive of you to come back to life." Something invisible slapped his face.

"You will not speak unless spoken to." Mary-Lou's lips were pencil thin.

"I will speak whenever—" A second slap cut him off. He cursed and spat at them.

"Mage Raul." Laurefen spoke softly.

Raul chewed on his bloody lip. "If it isn't the Headmaster," he sneered. "Going to make me write some lines? Clean the chalk dusters?"

"That is not the subject we are here to discuss," Laurefen said. "Mage Raul, I want you to tell us about the holding houses."

"The holdhouses..." Raul attempted to shrug. The chains held fast. "Not my domain, sorry."

Laurefen remained calm. "We are not playing games.

Tell us exactly how many holding houses there are and their locations."

"I can't help you. The Fatesmiths tossed me aside months ago. For all I know, they've moved them."

Michael retrieved a set of silver spikes and a mallet from the tub. Raul's eye twitched. "What is this?"

"This is me being persuasive," Michael said.

Raul shook his head. "You can't do that. This is Euryma. There are laws—"

"You speak of law?" Michael growled. "Let us just pretend we follow the same rules you did when you turned innocents into iron and melted them for scrap." He stepped forward, spike in hand.

Veiled panic flashed behind Raul's eyes. "You're actually gonna do this?"

Laurefen didn't move. Michael lined the spike up with Raul's left knee. "You're not giving me a reason not to."

"So much for scholarly ethics."

Michael raised the mallet. "This is your choice."

Raul's gaze darted from the spike, to Michael, to the gleaming mallet in his hand. He breathed a long sigh and nodded to Laurefen. "The Fatesmiths and I aren't quite on speaking terms. I can tell you what I remember, but that information is outdated. I need your word that your attack dog here," he gestured to Michael, "won't skewer me if what I say is not accurate."

Laurefen raised an eyebrow at Michael, who shrugged. "It's a start."

"Very well, Mage Raul," Laurefen pulled up a seat. "You tell us what you can, and you have my word that Michael won't *skewer* you. Agreed?"

Raul's eyes never left the spike. "Agreed."

CHAPTER 18

DECLAN

You are summoned to the presence of Lord Drakonov, son of Orovin, Grand Steward of Vedmark, at noon tomorrow. Present this summons to enter. Declan glanced up from the parchment in his hands. An imposing building towered over him. "This is it," he said, with a finality that masked the question.

Ven beamed up at the door. "The Grand Steward's Hall." He held an identical summons. "They took their time notifying us."

Declan nodded. Three days since their ill-fated journey in the forest. Ven was convinced they were there to collect their bounty. Declan wished he shared his optimism. They ascended the polished steps. A single guard waited at the cavernous entrance; he raised an eyebrow as they approached. "I require your summons to pass."

Ven handed his parchment to the Knight. Declan did the same, and he stepped aside. "Wait before the throne. The Grand Steward will see you when he is ready."

The hall was enormous—larger than two houses—and

more ornate than anything Declan had ever seen. Intricately chiseled archways bordered every window. Long silk banners hung from the ceiling, stitched with artworks of raging battles and glorious feasts. A nearby banner depicted a crowned man holding a white knife to the sky.

It was beautiful. Magnificent. Declan's head swiveled back and forth, up and down, as he tried to take it all in. A purple carpet, softer than lamb's wool, split the polished marble floor. At the front of the hall, on a stone dais, was an enormous emerald throne. It glowed green in the morning sun. Declan imagined the boulder of a gemstone that could have birthed such a thing.

They stopped at the dais as instructed. One banner caught Declan's eye. It did not look like the others. Sections were missing, though Declan noticed a familiar building. *Sabriva Tower? What is that doing here?*

Seven Knights entered through a wooden side door, led by Urik. Their armour clicked like chattering insects as they formed a line behind them. Declan fought the impulse to turn around. Still, his neck prickled at their presence.

An older man dressed in maroon robes arrived soon after. Declan studied him carefully. *So, this is Ava's uncle.* They bore no resemblance. The man climbed the staircase to the top of the dais and settled into the gemstone throne. Ven winked at Declan, his eyes bright with excitement. Declan bit his lip. It felt like a trap.

The Grand Steward stared down at him. His eyes were set deep in his head, his pale skin looked cold. Declan couldn't help but imagine this man as a living skeleton. Yet when he spoke, his voice was firm. "Declan Moore. The Southern Warlock. We meet at last."

Declan bowed. "An honor, your Highness."

The Grand Steward's expression remained unchanged. "I have called you here to discuss the ambush you organized with the Deathless Demon."

Silence. The words took a moment to settle. When they did, Declan shook his head quickly. "No. No, no, no. No, there was no ambush. I—"

The Grand Steward thumped a gnarled fist on his throne. "You cannot deceive me, southerner. You visited the demon's lodge and together you concocted a trap for my Knights. Do not lie."

Declan's heart sprinted in his chest. "That's not true," his voice cracked in panic. "You have it all wrong."

"Declan speaks the truth," Ven interrupted. He bowed to the Grand Steward. "Your Majesty, Declan knew nothing of the Deathless Demon. I had to tell him the story myself. Only then did he understand what he'd stumbled on."

The Grand Steward shook his head. "You have been fooled, boy. This southerner has fooled you, just as he seeks to deceive us now."

"I'm not fooling anyone," Declan said. "You're right. I found the King—"

"Demon," Ven interjected.

Declan nodded. "Yes. Demon. I found his cabin. I didn't know what was happening. I accepted food and shelter to stay alive." He stopped to breathe, sweat wicked against his collar. "I only realized who he was after Ven told me. Then I said I would help. I would lead your Knights to him. And I did."

The room fell silent. The Grand Steward's eyes were shrewd and calculating. "Urik, bring it to me."

The Knight ascended the dais and handed a folded slip of paper to the Grand Steward. He opened it and read out loud. "You have done well, Declan Moore. It is as we planned. Go back to your lodging and await further direction."

Declan's stomach sank. "No," he said faintly. "That's not true."

The paper strip erupted in flame. The Grand Steward glared down from his throne. "We intercepted that message yesterday. Yet you say you are not deceiving anyone." His gaunt eyes narrowed. "Explain yourself."

This must be his revenge. Declan stumbled to find the words. "The demon... It's setting me up! It gave me food and shelter and I brought the Knights to its lodging. It's getting back at me!"

"More lies!"

"No! No, I'm not lying. He's the liar! The demon is the liar, not me!"

The Grand Steward studied Declan intently, his eyes bored into him like a drill. He spoke in a whisper, "I am a merciful ruler, Declan Moore. I believe you. I believe you because I know of the depravity of the Deathless Demon. It will use you and throw you away without a second thought. It has done it before, and unless we can undo its selfishness, it will do it again."

Declan nodded. "I see that now. Thank you, your Highness."

Urik stepped forward. "Your Majesty. We know where it lives. Let us take this demon by storm. It cannot resist the full force of Vedmark's Knights. We can fall upon him in our hundreds and finish this today."

The Grand Steward shook his head. "Be silent Knight Urik."

"But my Lord."

"Yes, my King." Urik bowed his head, but his jaw

tensed. His armor clicked as he returned to stand alongside the Knights behind them.

"An attack now is pointless," said the Grand Steward. "The demon is a coward. I am certain it has already moved on, fled to the refuge of the Void as it has done so many times before. It will not return."

The Grand Steward was right, the cabin was gone. Declan considered confirming his suspicions. *No, don't do that. He'll ask you why you went up there. Just play dumb.*

Ven stepped forward into a flamboyant bow. "Majestic Highness. I inquire respectfully about our payment."

The Grand Steward leaned back in his throne. "There will be no payment."

Ven's cheeks flushed. "My pardon, your Majesty. I am sure you offered the reward for *locating* the Deathless Demon."

"I did." The Grand Steward's eyes scanned the hall. "I see no demon here."

Ven shook his head. "No, but your oath— "

The Steward clapped his hand together. "Very well. No payment necessary."

Ven's eyes darted from the Grand Steward to Declan. Declan tried to catch his gaze, tried to send a clear message. *Don't do anything stupid.*

"Enough of this." The Grand Steward waved a hand. "Leave now. If it contacts you again, you will alert my Knights."

Ven squeezed his fists. "Please. Your Highness. The reward. Just a small percentage."

Declan grabbed his arm. "Come on, Ven," he whispered. "It's fine."

"Listen to the southerner," the Grand Steward said. He was grinning. "It's fine."

Ven pulled away.

The Grand Steward's face darkened. "Leave," he growled. "Last warning."

Ven ignored him. He took a step towards the throne. "You made an oath! You owe us—" With a crack like lightning, a green spike erupted through Ven's chest and lifted him from the floor. Ven's eyes expanded. He glanced down in surprise, then his head slumped to the side.

Declan stood, frozen in shock. His entire body trembled. He didn't know what to do, what to say. The magical shard vanished. Ven's body dropped to the ground, sprawled on the polished stone. Declan stumbled backward in horror. The Grand Steward seemed unperturbed. He turned to Urik. "Get rid of this mess. This hall is no place for a corpse."

Declan couldn't believe it. He rocked on his heels. He tried to breathe, but his lungs weren't working.

Another flash of Sila and Ven's body shrivelled into a pile of black powder. Urik thrust out a hand. What remained of Venward Ostrofski rushed into his palm, solidifying into a small, dark rock. The Knights left the hall without a word. Declan struggled to keep himself from vomiting.

"A shame," said the Grand Steward. "It does not reflect well on you to align oneself with such greedy youth. Vedmark has no need for people like that."

Declan's mind no longer worked. He nodded, half in shock, half in fear. "Y-yes, your Highness." A stray thought bubbled up. His logical brained rejected it. *You're going to get yourself killed.* He tried not to stare at the spot on the floor where Ven's body vanished. "Your Majesty..."

The Grand Steward glared at him.

"I... I have delivered information about the Deathless Demon. I do not seek any reward."

"Good. You are not as daft as your companion."

Declan continued. "I do not seek payment, but I have one question. One that has been on my mind since I arrived here." Declan took a steadying breath. "With your permission, your Grace. I would like to ask it."

The Grand Steward's expression remained passive. "I will allow it. I am nothing if not merciful. You come to me with humility, and that *is* a quality of Vedmark. Ask your question."

Declan nodded. "How do I become a Knight?"

The Grand Steward considered him, long fingers stroking his pale chin. For a moment, Declan thought he had gone too far. Then the Steward's shoulders shook. Harsh laughter echoed down the hall. Declan waited in silence. "I am afraid that is not an option for you."

Declan frowned. "You have me confused, your Highness."

The Grand Steward withdrew a silk handkerchief from his maroon robes and dabbed at his eyes. "I am correct, Southern Warlock, knowing that your parents no longer live."

Declan nodded, unsure of what that had to do with anything.

"And you have no siblings."

Declan nodded again.

"No aunties, no uncles, no blood relatives."

Declan frowned. "No. None."

The Grand Steward's smile was cold and hard. "You are an orphan, boy. A single, lonely branch on a barren family tree. With no bloodline, you cannot perform the requisite sacrifice. Becoming a Knight is not possible. Not for you."

The words were a knife in the stomach.

The Grand Steward didn't seem to care. "I have answered your question. Now go. As you have witnessed, my patience is not unlimited. Go."

Declan nodded. The memory of Ven made his insides squirm. He bowed and left on trembling legs. As soon as he got outside, he emptied his stomach into the garden.

CHAPTER 19
DECLAN

By THE TIME Declan reached Grigory's farm, he had vomited three more times. He couldn't close his eyes without picturing Ven's final moments, or Rasporvin's indifference. Declan rushed to some bushes on the side of the road and vomited again. Stomach long since emptied, the bile burned in his throat.

Lantern lights beamed from the cabin windows. Grigory only bothered with the lanterns when he had visitors. Declan's heart dropped as he pictured walking into a surprise greeting from Grigory and Temfell, celebrating their new wealth.

To Declan's relief, he entered to an empty room. Almost empty. Misha looked up from an armchair, a smile split his face. "Hello, Declan." The smile vanished, Misha stood up. "Something is wrong. You look unwell."

"No, I'm okay. I'm..." He trailed off, then forced a grin. "Welcome back, Misha. You must be glad to be home."

"I am glad. It is good to see father and the goats. He says you have done well helping." He settled back into the threadbare seat. "In other ways, I am not. Euryma is an amazing place. I miss the generosity."

"Generosity." Declan ignored his shuddering stomach. "I'm not sure I'd call Euryma generous."

"When you live your whole life paying for questions, a land that gives them away certainly feels generous."

"I'd never thought of it that way."

"I wouldn't expect you to," Misha said. "A fish would never think its home wet and refreshing. Why would we be any different?"

Declan blinked. The rising pitch of Misha's voice gave him pause. It took him a moment to realize he had asked a direct question.

"Sorry." Misha blushed. "A slip of the tongue."

Declan grinned. "Don't worry about it. That *is* refreshing. Pretend you're still there and ask all the questions you want."

The door behind Declan creaked open. "Ah, I thought I could hear nonsense talk." Grigory said. "Welcome back, fellow. I could use your help to hang meat." Grigory's arms were bloody to the elbows.

Declan nodded to him, still unsure where they stood. "Hi Ory," he said, tentatively.

Grigory grunted, then walked past him. There was a clattering of pots. A rich aroma wafted through the door. "Stew is ready," Grigory called.

Misha smirked. "Some things never change."

It had been three days since he'd stormed out of the cabin. Three days since he'd lied to Grigory. Neither of them had spoken about it. Declan did not know what he could say.

They sat around the kitchen table, eating in silence. Misha inhaled his bowl, then helped himself to more. "I never thought I'd miss your cooking," he said, settling back into his seat.

"Euryma still stands," Grigory stated.

Misha nodded. "It is a wondrous place. Full of marvels. The non-magical people there have harnessed natural power for many things."

"Laziness," Grigory said.

"No, not lazy. Clever."

Grigory rolled his eyes.

Misha nodded to his bowl. "You could have cooked this on an open flame, but you did it on the woodstove. I wouldn't call that lazy."

Grigory tapped his gnarled finger against his chest. "But I still cooked it. Those southerners probably put goat in box and come back when it's ready."

"Maybe." A smirk formed on Misha's lips. "I'm not sure they eat goat in Euryma."

Grigory's jaw dropped. "That's even worse than laziness." His attempt to look indignant slipped behind a small smile. The room relaxed. Grigory turned to Declan. "You met the Grand Steward today."

Misha glanced up from his bowl. Declan nodded. He hadn't touched his dinner, but could still feel the stew churning in his stomach.

"What's wrong, Declan?" Misha asked.

"Misha!" Grigory scowled at his son. "Keep your questions in the south."

Misha ignored him. "Are you okay?"

"Misha!"

"No, Father. This entire country is backward. There is

155

nothing to gain by paying to ask someone if they're okay."
He frowned at Declan. "Are you?"

Declan slumped forward. "No, not really."

"It is not proper," Grigory snapped.

Misha kept his eyes on Declan. "What happened?"

Declan pretended he could not see Grigory's scowl. "We
went to the Grand Steward's Hall. Ven and I. There were
Knights there. Ven... Ven asked for the ransom and the
Steward said no. When he pushed for it... one of the
Knights... killed him."

Grigory's anger melted away. "No."

Tears blurred Declan's vision. "I... I should've done
something. It happened so fast."

"You fool." Grigory shook his head, lips pressed
together. "You chased riches and now someone is dead."

"I didn't mean—"

"I told you." Grigory said. "I warned you not to go. Ven's
death is on your hands, fellow. *Your* hands."

"Father!"

Tears streamed down Declan's cheeks. "I know. I—."

Misha slapped the table. "No. It's not!" He gripped
Declan's shoulder. "The blame is on the Steward. No one
else." He glared at Grigory. "Shame on you, Father."

"Rasporvin is a monster," Grigory said. "You cannot
bring a mouse to a cat and blame the cat for its nature."

"The Grand Steward isn't a cat. He's a man. He is
responsible!"

"They should have never been in that position."

"This is not Declan's fault."

"I told you!" Grigory glared at Declan. "I told you not
to go."

"Stop blaming Declan," Misha said, thrusting a finger at
Grigory. "Blame your damned brother."

Declan blinked. *Brother?*

Grigory's demeanor darkened. "You know that's not true."

"It might as well be."

"What... what do you mean?" Declan asked.

"More questions!" Grigory threw up his arms in indignation. "This is Vedmark!"

"Goats guts, Father. Let him ask his questions." Misha nodded to Declan. "Rasporvin's brother married Grigory's sister—Eve."

Declan tried to connect the dots. *Rasporvin's brother married Grigory's sister.* He puzzled it over, then glanced at Grigory. "I didn't know you had a sister."

Grigory's eye twitched.

"She is no longer with us," Misha said. "Eve was my auntie, but she died when I was young. She was Ava's mother."

Ava's mother is... Misha's auntie? Declan felt like he was unraveling a tangled spool of garden wire. Then it clicked. His jaw dropped. "Ava's your cousin?"

Misha nodded. He chewed on his upper lip. "She is, but... she doesn't know that."

"What? Why not?"

"It's complicated." Misha's eyes darted to Grigory, who appeared on the cusp of an explosion.

Declan looked between them. "Why can't she know you're related?"

"That's your story to tell," Misha said to his father.

"Leave me out of your reckless questions."

"Fine. Then I'll tell him. But first, I need a tea." Misha gathered their bowls and vanished into the kitchen. Declan didn't dare look up from his dinner. Misha returned with three mugs and a clay teapot. A wisp of steam curled from the cracked spout. "Ava's tale is a sad one," he said. "Ava's father was a man named Dimenus. He was much younger than Rasporvin. Probably twenty years between them."

"Thirty," Grigory corrected.

Misha poured his tea and smiled. "Are you telling the story, or am I?"

Grigory's eye twitched again.

"Dimenus was young. By the time he married Auntie Eve, Rasporvin had inherited the title of Grand Steward. Rasporvin was obsessed with the Deathless Demon. As soon as he took power, he started sending Knights— including his baby brother—into the forest to find it."

"Ava's dad was a Knight?"

"He was." Misha leaned back, savoring his drink. "Ah, that's good. The tea in Euryma is dreadful." He took another sip and murmured his approval. "Anyway, one day, on one of those ventures, Dimenus was killed."

"By what?"

"According to Rasporvin, the Deathless Demon."

"Nonsense," Grigory interjected. "Rasporvin organized death. He was jealous of brother's power. Afraid he might take throne."

A smirk tugged at Misha's lips. "You'll take it from here then?"

Grigory huffed, then continued. "When my sister first met Dimenus, I told her just how I felt about Drakonov family. After that, she wanted nothing to do with us. Eve exiled herself from own blood. When Rasporvin killed husband, she had nowhere to turn."

"What about Ava?" Declan asked.

"Only a baby," Misha said. "She doesn't remember her father at all."

"Eve begged Rasporvin for help. Rasporvin refused. He

cast her out. She came to me but..." Grigory fell silent. He poured a mug of tea and took a long drink. When he spoke, his voice was heavy. "But I... we had... grown distant. I told her she had abandoned us for riches of royalty." Grigory set his mug down. "When I didn't hear from her, I assumed Rasporvin had taken her back..."

"And?" Declan whispered.

Misha put a hand on Grigory's shoulder. "For eight years, Eve lived as a beggar. Ava too. They survived on Vedmark's streets until one bitter winter, which killed Auntie Eve."

Grigory dabbed at his eyes. "Men from the City came to tell me Eve had died. I did not know... I did not know how she had been living. They said Ava had been *lucky* to survive. I took her in."

Declan leaned in; stew forgotten. "Then what happened?"

"Back then, we worked silwood yard. Ava believed us kind strangers. I planned to tell her, but as time went on, it grew harder. I couldn't. I didn't want to crush her heart. I didn't want Ava to know my betrayal."

Misha rubbed Grigory's back. "Soon after that, we discovered that Ava and I shared some abilities. We were lucky. More than that, we were consistently lucky. We avoided death and injury in the most peculiar ways. When Irman sent word to Rasporvin, we were recruited to serve the Steward."

"Irman?" Declan faced Grigory. "Your friend, the trader?"

"Irman and dad were partners in a silwood yard," Misha said.

"So Rasporvin trained you?"

"Rasporvin knows nothing of Luck," Misha said. "However, he convinced an ambassador from Euryma to teach us what she knew. She had worked with Lucks before. She accepted a role training us. She met with us as children. Two years ago, when Ava turned sixteen, Rasporvin sent her south on her first assignment. Since then, she's barely spent two weeks in Vedmark before heading off again."

Grigory sighed. "This place holds much pain for Ava. I understand why she would want to leave."

Ava's loyalty to Euryma, her disinterest in Vedmark, it made sense. Declan leaned back in his seat. "Ava told me she was the last hope by a family driven mad by a misplaced responsibility."

"Rasporvin," Grigory said. "As her power grew, he became more and more interested in her."

"He wanted her to join his crusade," Misha added. "To do what her father couldn't. Find the Deathless Demon, undo the curse keeping the Knights trapped in Vedmark, weaken Euryma, create a way so he can invade. The Grand Steward thinks it's his destiny to rule the land Morkurik conquered."

"A fool," Grigory said quietly.

Misha smiled. "But Ava has no interest in that. She wants Euryma to remain as it is, and I would bet Father's best goats it is because she wants to escape there."

"Leave my goats alone."

Declan looked at Grigory. "Why didn't you tell me this earlier?"

"You didn't have the mitka."

Declan rolled his eyes. A stray thought struck him. "Ory. You're from Vedmark. You despise questions, you rant about traditions, *but* you also wanted me to keep the Knights away from the Deathless Demon. You call the

Grand Steward a monster and wish for him to fail. Whose side are you on?"

The cabin was silent. Grigory examined his fingernails for a long time, then cleared his throat. "I have answered many questions tonight." Grigory's eyes were hard. "But some questions are best left alone, fellow. It is safer that way."

"Declan, listen." Misha said. "You can't tell Ava any of this. It would destroy her. I hate that it's a lie, but there is no upside to her knowing the truth."

Declan nodded. "I understand."

"Promise me."

"I promise."

Misha's easy smile returned. "Excellent. Now. We have answered a lot of your questions tonight, free of charge. Now, I have a question for you."

Declan blinked. "Uh, yeah, sure. What is it?"

"What do *you* think of Ava?" Misha's grin grew.

The question caught Declan off-guard. He turned bright red. "What do you mean?"

"You know what I mean," Misha said.

Declan's crimson cheeks somehow burned hotter.

Grigory chuckled; Misha smirked into his mug. "Well, that's definitely one way to answer. Say no more, Declan, we hear you, loud and clear."

CHAPTER 20
DECLAN

ONE WEEK LATER, Declan woke with an anvil lodged in his skull. He, Misha and Grigory had spent the night with Temfell.

Ven's death had been a crushing blow to his father; what started as a toast to Venward's life had ended in the early hours of the morning afloat a fragrant river of red. Declan had never drunk wine before. Now, judging by the fantastic pain in his head, he never would again.

He closed his eyes, tried to stay still. It did nothing to dull the ache. When somebody knocked on his door, it felt like hammer blows to the brain. "Come in," Declan rasped. Blinding sunlight assaulted his senses. Declan retreated beneath his blanket as someone entered.

"Good morning," Misha said. "Sorry for interrupting. This arrived from the Grand Steward."

Declan squinted from his refuge. Misha held a slip of parchment. "What is it?"

"No idea. Want me to open it?"

"Better you than me. My head is on fire. I'm not sure I could even read it."

Misha laughed. "Vedmark's wine hits hard." He unrolled the parchment, read in silence, then clicked his tongue. "A summons to meet with the Grand Steward."

"Again?" *He probably wants you dead after all.* Declan ignored the thought. "When?"

"Noon. Today. That is sudden."

What does the Steward want with me? I haven't heard from the demon. I can't learn magic. I haven't said anything. His stomach slipped. *Maybe I wasn't supposed to tell Temfell about Ven.* He stared at the ceiling until the panels blurred.

"Do you know why he would summon you?" Misha asked.

"Not a clue," Declan lied.

Declan cursed under his breath as Trevor wandered off the road again. *Stupid animal, I'll disguise you as a goat and let Ory put you in a stew!* The donkey chewed lazily on a bush, unfazed by Declan's urgency.

While the four-legged-menace had no qualm pulling a loaded cart, it clearly despised carrying a single person, especially him. It bucked its way down the hills, making Declan's sore head worse. By the time they reached the city gates, Declan had given up riding and led it by hand. As he approached, he saw Temfell standing at the gate. Their eyes met, Temfell's face darkened. Whatever goodwill he had earned the previous night was gone.

"Morning, Temfell. I hope you are well."

"Do not speak to me, southerner," he said. "I am only here because my expenses have no sympathy."

He can't even afford to grieve. Declan didn't know what to say. He reached into his coat and tossed him a small cloth

163

pouch. It was the last of his jade mitka. "It's not much. Still, I hope it helps. Your son was a fine man." He stood there awkwardly, then tugged the donkey onwards into the City.

Declan left Trevor at the first public stable he passed. "Good riddance," he muttered, closing the booth door. The way to the Steward's Hall was easy. Follow the widest road to the largest building. With no donkey to fight, Declan soon arrived at its towering doors. The square courtyard was empty, bordered by thick hedges trimmed in gentle curves. It had four stone benches arranged in two rows. Declan took a seat on the nearest bench. His head hurt, his stomach quivered; he tried to think of something else.

When the sun peaked, a bell-tower chimed twelve. With shaking legs, he stood, summons in hand, and approached the entrance. A guard stepped out to greet him; he scanned the parchment, face unreadable. "The Grand Steward is waiting."

Declan could only nod. His skin felt cold. He shivered as he walked down the purple walkway, eyes down. The Hall seemed different this time, its grandeur dimmed by unpleasant memories. Someone gasped and Declan looked up. The Grand Steward sat on his throne, but Declan only had eyes for Ava.

"Declan!" She slipped down the steps, Declan rushed to meet her. "Declan! You're safe!" Ava pulled him into a hug. He hugged her back. She smelled sweet, like sanarmelon juice. After a long moment, she stepped back. "Why are you here?"

"No idea," Declan whispered. "They summoned me this morning. I was hoping you might know."

Ava glanced back at her uncle. "I was not expecting you." Her smile faded into an uncertainty. "Declan, there's something you should know."

A line of Knights entered the hall, drowning out Ava's words. Their armor clicked as they bowed to the Grand Steward. A Knight with a sharp chin approached them. He knelt and kissed Ava's hand. Declan felt a pang of jealousy. "Mistress Drakonov, the Steward demands your presence."

Ava let him lead her back to the dais. Declan could see the worry in her eyes. *What is going on?*

"Welcome, Declan Moore," boomed the Grand Steward. "Come closer. We have much to discuss."

Declan did as he was told. The Grand Steward's gaunt eyes glowed with a manic fervor. He pressed his spindly fingers together, touching their tips to his lips. A cloud must have passed between the sun outside because the room darkened without warning.

"Such a remarkable coincidence to see you again so soon."

Declan forced a thin smile. "I'm honored, your highness."

The Grand Steward gestured to Ava. "And of course, my beautiful niece, back from the south. You are home, Ava Drakonov. For a long time, no doubt."

Ava did not look pleased.

The Steward's attention returned to Declan. "I am curious, Declan Moore, about your brief visit north, to Anderma." He leaned forward in his throne. "My Emissary has told me the story, but I am curious to hear it in your own words."

Declan's heart drummed in his ears. *I've been here for months. Why ask now?*

"Tell me, Declan Moore. Tell me about the night your parents died."

Those memories lived in a box Declan did not want to open. Slowly, painfully, he recalled the night in Anderma.

"They tricked me. The witch Haberdeen lied to me. She fierised me, turned me to iron, then a wizard..." Declan bit his lip. He hated the name. "Ward. He killed my parents. Killed them on Haberdeen's command."

The Grand Steward nodded. "Yes, but you took your revenge."

Declan nodded. "I... I did. I killed Ward—"

"And Haberdeen too."

"I don't know what happened to her. I never found her. Ava helped me escape. We fled to Vedmark soon after."

The Grand Steward waved his words aside. "Tell me about Haberdeen."

"She was the leader of the Fatesmiths. They were taking people from—"

"I do not care about that," The Grand Steward growled. "Tell me about your battle, about your victory over her."

"Oh." Declan shrugged. "She tried to stop me, but she was no match. I remember... throwing her across the dome. I never saw her again."

"And you took something from her."

Declan frowned. "Uh... A decent amount of Fatesmiths? I suppose."

The Grand Steward's eyes flashed. "Do not lie to me, Declan Moore. You have seen how I deal with those who do not respect their leader. I know you have Winterthorn."

"I-I don't know what this is, your Highness." Declan could feel his heart thumping in his chest. "After I threw Haberdeen, I didn't see her again."

The Grand Steward leaned back against the gleaming throne. "Bring her in," he said.

"Uncle, no!" Ava burst out.

"Be silent," the Grand Steward growled. Two more Knights entered through a side door, a third person between them, a prisoner dressed in rags, head covered by a hessian sack. The Knights marched the individual onto the stone dais. A flash of green forced the pitiful figure to their knees, bands of light secured ankles to stone. The Grand Steward removed the sack. Long, red hair spilled loose.

Declan stepped backward. "What... What's she doing here?"

Haberdeen squinted into the bright hall. Her hair was tangled, her face bruised. Declan's heartbeat thundered in his ears. *It's a trap! A trick!*

The Grand Steward grabbed Haberdeen's ear and turned her to face Declan. "This is him. This is the boy that took your power."

Haberdeen stared at Declan. She mumbled something inaudible.

"Speak up, witch. This is the one. The one who has Winterthorn."

Haberdeen shook her head. "I... don't know." Her eyes closed. She slumped forward.

The Grand Steward pushed her aside. "Somebody revitalize her."

One of the Knights rushed to obey. A thousand questions whirred in Declan's head. "No!" he shouted. Blurred scenes from Anderma flooded his mind. "No! Don't heal her. She's dangerous."

The sharp-chinned Knight ignored him. His hand blazed green. Declan started towards Haberdeen. Someone grabbed him from behind. He tried to pull away, more hands grabbed hold. Ava was shouting. Declan couldn't understand it. The Knight put a palm to Haberdeen's chest. Emerald light filled the hall. Haberdeen's back straightened and their eyes met.

All at once, everything returned. The dull haze, the

shrinking mass of his parents' sculpted figures, the pain of their loss. Repressed memories burst from their box and sucked Declan down into crushing hopelessness.

He opened his eyes into the blackness. A glowing green coin hovered ahead of him. He snatched it and electricity surged through him. His bones imbued with power beyond description. "No!"

Whoever held him back fell away. Declan spun as two Knights slid backward into the banners lining the walls. Bright pulses ignited in the Knight's hands. "Release your grasp on the Sila," said one of them. "Do not be a fool."

Declan looked back at the dais. Haberdeen climbed gingerly to her feet. "She killed my parents," he said. He turned to face her. Green vines erupted from the floor, wrapping around his legs, extending back to the Knights behind him. "Let me go!"

"Release the Sila. We will not ask again."

Declan glared at Haberdeen. *Neither will I!* He tensed his fists and let go. Like a bowstring snapping into place, a wave of energy burst from his body. Declan saw Ava leap to safety as the Knights blocked the attack.

The glowing vines vanished. The three Knights stumbled backward. As quickly as they hit the ground, they were on their feet, but even that was too slow. Declan acted on pure instinct. He hurled torrents of power across the hall, scorching silk banners, and shredding sections of the wall. The Knights shielded the bulk of his attacks, doing their best to protect the building. He had to drive them off. Only then could he avenge his parents. Only then could he kill Haberdeen.

The building's walls shook. Declan thrust a pillar of green light upwards, carving a hole in the hall's rooftop. Intricate masonry tumbled over them. The Knights caught the collapsing roof in clouds of Sila. Declan just broke more. With a searing pulse, he shattered the entire ceiling. The Knights shouted over one another, overwhelmed by the damage. Declan turned back towards the dais. The Grand Steward was gone, Haberdeen was not. Sila still bound her ankles to the floor. Her eyes darted frantically around the hall—like a caged animal.

Declan raised a hand; crackling green light filled his palm. Someone stepped in front of her. "Declan. Don't."

It was Ava.

Declan brushed her aside. *I have to do this. For my parents.* He raised his arm, then realisation of what he'd just done gripped him. He turned around, his heart stopped. Ava lay thirty-feet behind him, crumpled in a torn silk banner. The emerald orb vanished. The surging power vanished. In the blink of an eye, his Sila was gone.

Declan slid through the shattered stone toward her. "Ava! No! Ava, no, no, no! No!"

A ribbon of blood wound its way down her temple. Her eyes were closed. "No. Ava. No." Declan cradled her in his arms. His sobs echoed in the damaged hall. He pressed his trembling hands against her neck, feeling desperately for a pulse. Nothing. He couldn't find it. He pressed his hand to her chest. Relief flooded him. A faint heartbeat, but definitely there. *Oh Ava. I'm sorry!*

A large grinding sound caught Declan's attention. The collapsed stone was shifting, reconfiguring itself into the ceiling. Declan shifted Ava into his lap and something tinkled across the floor. A small crystal vial. *Sanarmelon juice!*

The stones were slowly rising, crushing groans echoed off the walls. Declan tilted the vial to Ava's lips. Powdered dust hid them from view. Declan emptied as much as he could into her mouth. *You'll be okay. I'm sorry. I'm sorry Ava.* She stirred, groaning softly as Declan lowered her to the ground. He waited long enough for her eyes to open, then ducked beneath a torn banner and fled through a hole in the wall.

Shouts chased him away from the hall. After five frantic minutes, Declan slowed to a halt and slid against a brick well. Deep, gulping breaths burned his lungs. *What have you done?*

He buried his head in his hands. *They're going to hunt you now. They'll search Ory's house. You'll need to flee Vedmark. You idiot.* Shouts echoed a street over. Declan climbed to trembling feet and moved in the other direction. Careful to appear casual, he wandered past a row of storefronts, stopping at a butcher's window and pretended to inspect the slabs of red meat decorated with sprigs of green herbs. *Just get out of the City. You can figure out the rest later.*

He continued to the stable, stopping often enough to blend in, never lingering long. Trevor did not seem pleased to see him, but Declan didn't care. He rushed the kicking beast out into the streets towards the city gates. When he got there, his stomach tightened.

Four Knights guarded the exit. Declan turned down a side street and went east. The next exit had just as many. He tried again. This time there were six Knights, dressed in full armor. They searched the crowd with stern faces. Declan tied Trevor to a post and assessed his options.

Where are you going to go? They'll be looking for you at Grigory's cabin. The Directive wants you dead. Your home in Tamhill is just rubble. You have nowhere to go.

Declan buried his head in his hands. *You idiot. Why did you do that?* Something tapped his shin. Declan froze. A golden armadillo lounged against a paved gutter. It stood on its hind legs and shrugged tiny armored shoulders.

That's it. You've lost your mind.

The armadillo wandered to the corner of the street and glanced around the building.

Declan frowned. "I can't go out there. They have Knights at every exit!"

The armadillo turned back to him with beady eyes like tiny black marbles.

Declan squeezed his eyes shut and opened them. Sure enough, the armadillo remained. It shook its head. Then— in a green puff—it was gone. A moment later, in a second flash of emerald light, a man stepped out of thin air. He wore a faded green robe, one that looked to be made of cotton. He had a long beard and dark eyes.

The Deathless Demon.

Declan stood rooted to the spot, utterly speechless. This was no demon. He knew that face. He knew that beard. He knew those sharp eyes. He had eaten his lunch in the shadow of this man's statue every day at school. It was impossible. The man stepped forward, Declan stepped back. "You're... It can't be."

The man's lips curled beneath his beard. "You look as if you have seen a ghost."

Declan couldn't believe his eyes. "You're... Arman Moore," he whispered.

The old man nodded. "I am."

Declan couldn't believe his ears. *The armadillo made more sense than this.* "You're dead," Declan said, shaking his head. "Long dead!"

Arman smiled sadly. "Some may say it would be better I

171

was." An elderly couple stopped to stare at them. The woman murmured something to the husband, whose face drained of blood. Arman sighed. "Come, Declan. It is time we left this place."

"Where are we going?"

Arman Moore gestured to the horizon. "To safety, grandson."

CHAPTER 21
DECLAN

THEY WALKED ALONGSIDE THE RIVER, snaking through valleys shrouded by auburn leaves. Dead foliage blanketed the path. The gentle crunch of dry leaves underfoot kept the silence at bay.

Declan could not believe what was happening. *The Deathless Demon is my great-great-great-great-grandfather. I'm dreaming. Any moment I'll wake up in Ory's cabin.* He pinched his arm, to no avail.

Arman marched ahead; his cloak swayed like liquid as he moved. Declan followed, Trevor resisting behind him. The donkey seemed most unimpressed with their adventure. Questions tumbled through his mind. *Where are we going? How is he alive? What is he doing in Vedmark? How did he find me? Why has he just made himself known now?*

They walked until Declan's legs were spent. His feet were heavy and his head light when Arman vanished through a curtain of flowering vines. Declan hurried after, then stumbled to a standstill on the other side.

The small cabin from the hill hid in an overgrown clearing. A tiny brook bubbled alongside it, bordered by a low, moss-covered wall. A pair of squirrels squeaked down a nearby pine. Arman produced a handful of dried fruit from his coat. They chittered with glee as they ate. "It is good to be home." He looked back at Declan. "You have my leave to enter, though please refrain from inviting more soldiers to my dwelling. It is tedious to clear such old forest for my home."

Speechless, Declan settled for a frantic nod. After that, he tied Trevor to a tree and followed his grandfather's grandfather—or whatever they were—inside. The cabin's interior was as he remembered, a single room, a bed, a wooden table. Two axes hung on the wall, engraved with two letters. Only this time, Declan realized it wasn't a 'V' and 'W', it was 'A' and 'M'. *Arman Moore.*

Arman shrugged off his cloak. Underneath, he wore faded trousers, matching suspenders and a cream shirt. His beard almost touched the floorboards as he removed his boots. Declan waited by the door. "This must be confusing for you, Declan," he rumbled.

Declan nodded.

"Vedmark's custom of purchasing knowledge is not an old tradition, Declan. In my Vedmark, questions were free, and so they remain. If you are confused, you may ask and I will answer." Declan nodded again. Arman's laugh was buoyant thunder. "Oh, come boy, you look as if I consumed your donkey." He motioned to the seat. "Rest your weary body. Ask what questions weigh on your mind. I will do you no harm nor ask for your mitka."

Declan did as he was told. His aching legs appreciated the chair, he savoured the relief and for a short time they sat, silent, still. Finally, Declan tilted his head. "So you're not a demon taking me into the Void, then?"

"The Void..." Arman Moore shook his head. "That is an

evil place, a name I would rather not taste on my tongue."
He shook his head. "No. I am not taking you there. I would
not set foot in that wretched slice of forest."

The awkward silence threatened to return. Instead,
Declan opened the floodgates. "How are you alive? And
why are you here? And how did you find me? And who was
that armadillo? Was that you that saved me? Why? Are you
the reason I can use—"

Arman's face brightened. He raised an enormous hand,
chuckling. "Steady there. Allow me the courtesy to answer."

Declan's jaw snapped shut. "Sorry."

"There is no need. Each of those questions deserves an
answer. I will begin with the first. How am I alive..." Arman
gazed thoughtfully at his hands. "Long ago, I sought to rule
two kingdoms. I failed both. Now, I pay the price for my
arrogance and live on, cursed to watch everyone and everything I love fade to dust."

Declan frowned. "I'm sorry, uh..."

"Grandfather," Arman said. His eyes twinkled. "You
may call me grandfather."

"My apologies, grandfather, but that doesn't explain
why you're here."

Arman scratched at his beard. "My history is a long tale,
Declan."

"I already know some of it."

"You do, do you?" A small smile appeared on Arman's
lips. "I am interested in hearing it. The Steward's story
shifts from generation to generation. Tell me, grandson,
what do they say about me in the City?"

Declan clenched his hands in his lap and leaned
forward. "They say you were a Prince in Vedmark but you
didn't like it here. You left and they thought you died. Then
your brother formed the Knights of Despair and traveled

south. You formed Euryma and stopped him. You defeated your brother and became King."

Arman nodded. "That is all?"

"As King you forced the Knights to give up their land, which made you unpopular with the people. One of the Knights challenged you and defeated you," Declan considered how to word the next part. "And.... then you cast a spell to keep the Knights from leaving Vedmark forever."

"A worthy attempt, albeit with some error." Arman nodded to himself, a smile still on his lips. His eyes were as bright as a full moon. "Would you like to hear what really happened?"

"Yes, yes please."

"Very well. Let us start at the beginning, with my family." Arman leaned back in his chair. "Even as a boy, my eldest brother's soul was wed to bloodlust. We would hunt in these forests every day. Morkurik always killed more than he required. He took immense joy in doing so. My other brother, Imond, took it on himself to rescue any creature he could, but I saw Morkurik's thirst. It was only a matter of time before his dark desires extended to people. I did not request leave of my father because I did not like Vedmark. I love this land. No, I requested leave because I feared my brother. I wanted no part of his bloodlust, so I sought sanctuary in the south."

"With the tribes?"

"The tribes." Arman chuckled. "Many nations ruled the land south of Vedmark. The Grand Steward branded them as tribes to undermine their culture. The south was no continent of barbarians. No, it was a land of impressive cities filled with innovation, philosophy and art. Empires stretched far across it, full of rich customs and beliefs of their own." He smiled and stared into the distance. "It was a place of beauty, a place of history."

Every word turned the world Declan knew upside down.

"I built a life in Hispania, the kingdom of Luck. I found favor with their King and wed his daughter." He breathed a long sigh. "My Maria. She was fierce, intelligent, beautiful, kind. Maria saw wonder in all things. My life was good." Arman closed his eyes, the small smile fell away. "Then he came."

"Morkurik?"

Deep creases split Arman's brow. When he opened his eyelids, his grey eyes resembled troubled skies. "Dark rumors accompanied traders. Tales of war in the north, of a conquering legion wielding green flames that obliterated all in its path. Men. Women. Children. It didn't matter. He murdered all without mercy. The stories left no room for hope. The Knights of Despair earned their name under Morkurik's bloodthirsty rule." Arman shook his head. "When word reached my ears, my heart grew heavy. He had no interest in land, only death. My brother's soul delighted only in fear and slaughter."

The room fell silent. Arman's expression darkened, and the cabin seemed to grow dim. Declan felt his chair shudder. "But... but you beat him. You united the south and won."

Arman breathed a deep sigh. "I rode north to meet him. Morkurik. He welcomed me. We exchanged pleasantries. I tried to convince him to go back. He would not..."

Declan couldn't take it. "And?"

"We fought, but I could not defeat him. I was driven back. I was not brave, Declan. If there was another way, a way to save my family and people, I would have taken it.

But I knew my brother. There would be no end while he lived. I had to stand against him, and unlike the helpless men he had fought before me, I had Sila of my own. Tales of our battles set across the land like a spark in tinder. Word of the Southern Knight spread like wildfire."

"How did you win?"

"As great kingdoms fell, people fled south, to Rome. The ancient heart of the Empire became a sanctuary... and Morkurik fell upon it with everything he had. Every man, woman and child died. Every brick and statue became dust. In this desperate hour, emperors, kings and rulers pledged allegiance to unity, to Euryma."

Declan leaned so far forward he risked falling. "Then what happened?"

"We prepared for a war of magic. Hispania had Luck and with that we found magic in others. We assembled those who could use the magic and marched to meet the Knights."

"How many did you lead?"

"Twenty thousand. The Knights had a tenth of that. It was an even match. Vedmark had grown complacent with the ease of their conquest. We used this to our gain. With strategy and numbers, we drove the Knights back. For seven months, we fought a desperate campaign. Many died. We drove them to the northern border of the Franks' Kingdom. Our force was nearly gone. Less than a thousand of us still stood."

"And the Knights?"

"An identical number, with reinforcements on their way. We had to act."

"Act?"

"We had to cut off the serpent's head."

"Morkurik."

Arman nodded. "What remained of our army had one job. Keep the rest of the Knights occupied. I would challenge my brother alone."

"And it worked."

"It did." Arman's gaze wandered to the axes mounted on the wall. "On the Plains of Sabbrevan we fought. It was a battle for freedom, for land, for family, and I was the victor. I bought my Sila by spilling my brother's blood."

Declan sat in silence. In his mind, he could see Arman Moore, as tall and imposing as the statue in his hometown, standing victorious on a field of battle. It took a moment for his words to sink in. "Bought your Sila? What does that mean?"

Arman locked eyes with Declan. It was like looking into the sun. "Sila is powerful—and like all power—it comes with a price. It is granted freely in times of need, but to use it at will, one must pay in blood."

"Wh-whose blood?" Declan struggled beneath his grandfather's gaze.

"Your own. The blood of your family." He sighed. "I never wanted this power. I left Vedmark because I did not want to spill blood."

"So, to become a Knight, you have to sacrifice a family member?"

Arman nodded. "A terrible price for terrible power."

Declan remained silent.

"After I killed my brother, I tried to right his wrongs. The rulers of the southern kingdoms created the Dominion of Euryma, but I went north, I returned to Vedmark. I disbanded the armies and set strict laws about leaving the borders."

179

"What about your family?"

"They remained in Hispania—now renamed Iberia—and I would return as often as I could, but this became less and less. My Maria grew weary of time spent between kingdoms. She resented my victory on the Sabbrevan Plains, and the people of Vedmark grew to hate what I had taken from them." Arman's shoulders slumped, the creases in his face deepened. Songbirds sang gentle music in the trees outside while the setting sun ignited the windows in orange and magenta. Arman hesitated, and his voice dropped to a whisper. "I had an idea. A plan to seal Sila in Vedmark so I could remain in Iberia assured of the peace I had helped create. I shared my intentions with Vispa—"

"Vispa Drakonov?"

"My only friend among the Knights. My one loyal soldier. So I believed. He entered our ranks after the battle. He seemed to hold no contempt. He seemed a kindred spirit."

Declan wondered what his grandfather would say if he knew about his connection with Ava. He didn't know what to say.

"Vispa betrayed me." Arman's voice was thick with sorrow. "He travelled to Iberia disguised in my armor. He murdered my Maria in the presence of witnesses. When I returned, the people were livid. The Lucks set upon me, carved a curse in my bones."

"A curse?"

Arman nodded. "Iberia's daughter feeds the earth, struck down by Vedmark's sword. For this, their King must roam the Earth until his tower falls."

"What does that mean?"

"In the spot where my brother died, the Sila burned so

hot it forged a large platform, a foundation more dense than any natural stone. On that spot where I took his life, the people of Euryma built a tower to mark our victory. Maria hated that tower. She hated what it represented. Among her people, that hate was no secret." Arman wiped a stray tear from his eye. "My understanding, my grandson, is that I am cursed to walk the earth until the tower in Sabriva falls."

Declan's jaw hung open as the words sank in. He closed it with a snap. "So that's how you're alive."

"Destroy your legacy or live to see it fade away." Arman laughed bitterly. "Of course, Vispa expected the Iberians to kill me. They did far worse. I arrived at Vedmark possessed by the fury of loss. I enacted my plan, barred the Knights from leaving. I alone could wield Sila in Euryma..." He paused, a fleeting smile returned. "At least until you came along."

Declan nodded slowly. Realization dawned on him. "And that's why they overthrew you."

"It had been Drakonov's intention from the start. Befriend me, destroy me, return to Euryma to finish the fight." Arman smiled darkly. "But he never continued Morkurik's campaign. He spent his life rotting on my throne, trapped in a prison of his own making."

Outside, an orange moon peeked over the trees. "And that's why the Knights never returned."

Arman nodded. "While Sabriva stands, I live. While I live, the Knights are trapped here. While I live, Euryma is safe." He followed Declan's gaze out the window. "It would seem the answer to your first question has taken us into the night. Perhaps it is wise to revisit this conversation in the morning."

Declan glanced at the waning moon. A wave of tiredness washed over him. "Why am I here, grandfather?" he asked through a stifled yawn.

"Take rest, young Declan," Arman replied. "We shall talk more tomorrow."

CHAPTER 22
DECLAN

DECLAN WOKE TO AN EMPTY CABIN. Morning light beamed through the window, splaying over floorboards while forest creatures chattered from the trees. The previous night was a blur. *My grandfather is the King of Vedmark. A thousand-year-old King.* It sounded like something from a fairy-tale. Declan rubbed his eyes; the room's interior had grown overnight. There were two chairs in the corner, the square table was now rectangular. He climbed out of bed as Arman arrived with an armful of fruit.

"Morning's greetings," he said. He bit into the odd fruit, tossed another to Declan, then arranged the rest in a bowl. "Help yourself to more."

It was vivid turquoise and smelled of lavender. "What is this?" Declan asked.

Arman took another bite. "It's a sky apple. You've never seen one before?"

Declan tried a bite. The sky apple tasted like herbal tea. "It's... fragrant," he said.

"An acquired taste, perhaps. Sky apples were common

183

in Iberia. I introduced them to Vedmark myself. I am surprised you are unfamiliar."

"When was the last time you were in Iberia?"

"You stop counting years when the years cease to count," Arman said. "Maybe three hundred winters. I gave aid when Will Fendragon dissolved Euryma's monarchy..."

"The Rainy Rebellion," Declan said.

Arman barked a laugh. "I'm glad the name stuck." He finished his apple and helped himself to a second. "It was indeed a rainy battle."

"That was over four centuries ago."

"Four hundred years..." He paused thoughtfully. "An interesting time in Euryma's history. Many did not want democracy. The rule of the King was all they had ever known. We met Lord Arthur at the settlement Tamhill and claimed victory."

"I grew up in Tamhill," Declan said. He swallowed the last bite of his sky apple, but did not ask for another. "You said, Lord Arthur?"

Arman nodded. "Lane Arthur had a loyal contingent of kingsmen. They did not want democracy. They thought it would make Euryma weak."

"I went to school with his great granddaughter, Lyle." Declan paused to think. "Eight or so times removed." He shook his head. "She hated me. Seems grudges last a long time amongst that family."

"Honor is a funny thing. Losing it can leave traces over generations. Lane Arthur pushed us hard, becoming something of a monster in the process. It was not enough, and we won the day."

The whole situation seemed so surreal. "Why didn't you come back? You know who I am. You could have visited."

"It is hard." Arman's smile fell away. "I have known many who profess to envy my situation, who wish to live forever. They have never seen their grandchildren grow old and perish." He looked out into the sunlight. "At some point, it became easier to stay away."

"I can't imagine," Declan said.

Arman nodded. Their conversation went no further. Sitting in the silence, Declan's mind strayed to Ava. He bit his lip. "Grandfather..."

"Yes, Declan?"

"I have to go check on someone. If I go, will I be able to return?"

Arman smiled. "Of course. You are no prisoner. You are my grandson. You may come and go as you see fit. Just remember to come alone."

"Thank you. I won't be long." Declan glanced out the window into the tangled forest beyond the clearing. "Though I might need some directions."

———

I will send Lancelot to guide you to the river. From there, walk southward until you pass a tree that resembles a giant's hand. Follow that southeast to a hunter's trail that will lead you to a main road. Declan considered the crooked willow. Five stunted branches jutted out from its trunk. "That's as close to a giant hand as I'm going to get," he said to Trevor. The donkey seemed to roll its eyes, somehow unimpressed. Declan glanced back the way they had come. Lancelot, Arman's golden armadillo, had been a much friendlier companion.

Eventually, Declan found the path leading back in the general direction of the City. A tightness in his chest faded as familiar landmarks came into view. They trudged through winding hills that flattened to grassy plains, Trevor struggling all the way. The donkey didn't settle until they reached the trail to Grigory's cabin.

Declan had barely tied Trevor to his post when the door banged open. Misha marched out with Grigory close behind. "What are you doing here?" Misha's face was red, his fists clenched in white-knuckled balls.

Declan paused, "I came to—"

"To what? Attack us? You're not welcome here, Declan."

Grigory held Misha back by his shirt. "Misha, calm yourself."

"No, Father." Misha pulled away. "Ava could have died."

"How is she?"

Misha jabbed a finger at Declan's chest. "You don't get to ask questions about her."

"I'm sorry. It was an accident. I didn't mean to hurt anyone."

"You think that matters? Do you think if you killed her, it would've been okay because you didn't *mean* it?"

Grigory stepped between them. "Calm yourselves."

"I know I messed up." Declan looked from Misha to Grigory. "It was Haberdeen. She killed my parents."

"I don't want your excuses!" Misha shouted. Flecks of spit sprayed off lips. "Get out of here!

"Just tell me if she's alright."

"Get out of here!"

Declan opened his mouth, Misha dodged underneath Grigory's arm and threw a well-placed fist into his jaw. The clearing shifted out of focus. Declan stumbled back, tasting blood on his tongue. *I came here to make amends, you idiot!* Declan recovered his balance, then tackled Misha around the waist.

Grigory shouted. Declan couldn't hear a word he said. He was trying to wrestle himself on top to sock Misha in the nose. Grigory continued to yell.

"WHAT ARE YOU DOING?"

Declan froze. So did Misha. Ava stood in Grigory's doorway. She wore a loose blue shirt, bandages hung off her body. She looked terrible.

"I.... I'm..." Declan was at a loss for words. He pointed at Misha. "He started it."

Ava took a deep breath and winced. "Declan, please leave."

Grigory pulled Misha from the ground. Declan couldn't look at either of them. He climbed to his feet, focused entirely on Ava. "I'm sorry, Ava."

"So am I Declan. You weren't supposed to be there."

"Can we talk?"

Misha struggled forwards but Grigory held him firm. Ava bit her lip; tears formed in the corners of her eyes. "No, Declan. Not yet. Sila hits harder than most things. I'm not better yet."

"Ava..."

"You need to go." A crystal drop rolled down her cheek. "We can talk. But not yet."

Declan stood rooted to the spot. Birds sang, goats bleated, everything slowed down. "I understand. I'm sorry, Ava." He turned to Grigory. "Sorry Ory, I didn't mean to bring violence to your home." He ignored Misha and went back the way he came.

By the time he found Arman's lodging, the failing sun had painted the sky purple. His jawbone ached, his legs burned, but he was too lost in his own thoughts to care. *Alone. No Ava. No Grigory. Misha hates me. The Directive thinks I'm dangerous. They're right. Look at what I did to Ava. I couldn't save my parents. I can't save my friends.* Arman opened the door as Declan arrived. He frowned at Declan's bruised face. "What happened?"

"Punch in the face."

"Was it earned?" Arman grinned when Declan shrugged. "Some things do not change."

"Yeah, like what?"

"Young men fought over pretty girls a thousand years ago too."

"How do you know it was about a pretty girl?"

Arman's eyes twinkled. "Am I wrong?"

Declan had to grin. He shook his head. "No, you're not."

Arman stepped aside for him to enter. The cabin's interior had changed again. Now, the living area had a bench and fireplace, with two panel doors on the opposite wall. One door carved with an intricate 'A' and the other the letter 'D'. Declan raised an eyebrow. "You've been busy?"

"Sila makes things easier."

"You did this with magic?"

Arman winked. "Sila. Not magic."

"There's a difference?"

"The difference between a candle and a wildfire."

Declan let the words settle. "So Sila is just a stronger version of magic?"

Arman shook his head. "Magic is what is. Sila is what could be."

"That sounds like Luck."

"They're not so different," Arman said.

Something crossed his face so fast Declan wondered if he had imagined it. A rumbling gurgle interrupted them.

"Sorry. I haven't eaten since this morning. What do you do for dinner?"

"The fruit bowl is always full."

Declan blinked. "You live off fruit?"

Arman laughed. "I live off a curse. Food is a luxury, a sensation of flavour."

"But what about meat?"

His grandfather shrugged. "Why should I take the life of another needlessly?"

Declan's stomach rumbled again. "I'm not sure I can survive off just fruit."

Arman's left hand glowed green. A loaf of bread unfolded from empty air, then hovered towards him. Declan accepted it with wide eyes. "How did you do that?"

"The same way I built this house."

Declan bit into the bread. It was soft with a crunchy crust. He nodded his appreciation. "Amazing. Can you do drinks as well?"

Arman waved a glowing hand, and a wooden mug appeared on the table. A wobbling orb of water formed above it and dropped inside. The sight reminded him of his mother—how often she would perform something similar with a glass of juice. "Grandfather..."

"Yes, Declan."

"How are we connected?"

"What do you mean?"

Declan tried to simplify his question. "You're a thousand-year-old king of a magical kingdom. I'm a seventeen-year-old kid from Iberia. How does that happen?"

Arman settled into a seat. He gestured for Declan to do the same. "I never sought to be the ruler of Vedmark. It was a title born of obligation. I gave my heart to Hispania." He snapped his fingers and the fireplace burst to life. "Uncertainty plagued Euryma's early history. The Dominion formed as a desperate last resort, and many expected it would collapse soon after the threat abated."

"But it didn't," Declan said. "It still stands today."

"Yes," Arman nodded. "But at significant cost. You must understand, Euryma was a union of kingdoms and empires that had not always agreed. It did not take long for the old differences to arise."

"What happened?"

"So much. From early on, I would frequent Euryma to advise Arthur Fendragon on leadership of the young Dominion. This continued for his eldest son Matthew, his son Rand, his son Percival."

"That sounds exhausting."

"It is the weight of duty. I felt I owed Euryma. I paid for its existence in my brother's blood, and that obligation drew me back." Arman sighed. "But Euryma was not mine to coddle. It was a Dominion capable of governing itself. When young Will Fendragon sought my aid, I nearly didn't come."

"Why did you?"

"I don't know. Loyalty to generations of Fendragon kings? Perhaps. Yet even then I told myself I would not return. And then I met her."

Declan smirked. "Her?"

Arman laughed. "Yes, a woman. A wonderful woman named Evangeline Moore." Arman's bearded face split into a warm smile. "I saved her during the uprising at Tamhill. She had put her life on the line for a flock of burnt sheep. She loved life, she loved nature, animals and every living thing."

Declan shifted in his chair. "And that's why I'm here."

Arman's beard trembled. "In so many words. Yes. After

hundreds of years of solitude, I had found a soul that allowed me to heal. I decided I could stay a little longer. We had a son, for a moment all was well."

"What happened?"

Arman's smile faded. "Immortality. Eva grew older. I did not. My son became an old man. My grandson withered with age. Still, I did not." He stared into the fireplace. "The curse of immortality is not living forever, Declan, but outliving those you love. I had fought in countless battles, bore the burden of a thousand deaths, but this burden was too heavy. I returned to Vedmark and commissioned southerners to watch over the Moore bloodline."

"Did you ever come back?"

"Never. I returned to Vedmark, where I have since remained." Arman shook his head. "Enough talk of the past. Let us ponder the future." He paused. "It appears, my grandson, that you have committed high treason against the Grand Steward. The Knights will hunt you, as they have me. You have my leave to remain here, but hiding in the wilderness is no life for you. What is your plan?"

Declan stared bleakly out the window. "I'm not sure."

"Understandable. Perhaps it is something you must think on. While you stay, I thought I might instruct you in a skill that may prove useful."

"Like how to use Sila?"

"One does not *learn* Sila. It grows in you. It develops like a tree that blooms when the time and conditions are right." He leaned back in his chair. "No, that power is beyond you at this point in time. You are the last of my bloodline, Declan, and I am immortal. I am afraid your only option is to father a child whose blood you could spill."

Declan paled. "What?"

"Be at ease." Arman's lips curved at the edges. "It is not a decision to make today."

Declan stiffened. "I would never..."

"It is irrelevant. No. What I want to teach you is what my people taught me." Arman's eyes wandered to the top of the fireplace, where two axes glinted in the firelight. "Tell me, grandson, have you ever fought with an axe?"

CHAPTER 23
DECLAN

DAWN PAINTED THE CLOUDS GOLD, illuminating the small valley clearing in soft light. Declan's breath crystallized in the morning air as Arman drew a large circle with the handle of his axe.

Declan held another axe. His finger traced a simple carving on the wood. "What does this bull mean?"

"The bull was the mark of Hispania. It is strong and relentless, like the people." Arman finished his circle and beckoned Declan to its center. "Show me how you hold your weapon."

Declan held the handle tight. "Like this?"

Arman chuckled. "Tight is tense. Tension is wed to error." He swung it around in his palm. "See this? It is as you would grasp a fish. Secure. Safe. Not strained." Declan imitated his grandfather's grip. Arman adjusted his hands, then stepped back. "Perfect. Now..." Arman took a broad stance. "Strike me."

"Excuse me?"

"try to hit me with that weapon."

Declan glanced at the razor sharp axe head. "But what if I cut you?"

"It is more likely that you will cut yourself."

"That doesn't sound great either."

Arman chuckled. "It is easy enough to heal you. As for me..." Arman wedged his axe into his ankle. Declan's stomach turned. Arman winked, then pulled it free. The wound rippled like a disturbed puddle and healed. "Your blade will not undo this curse, grandson, I promise."

Declan looked from Arman's untouched leg to his devilish grin. "Okay then." He leaped forward and swung for his chest. The chest vanished before contact. Arman's axe appeared an inch from Declan's neck.

Arman lowered the weapon. "What did you do wrong?"

"I attacked too fast?"

Arman shook his head. "No. There is no sin in moving quickly. Your error was more elementary. Your grip tightened from the outset of your attack. A tight hold will fail."

"Got it." Declan softened his grip.

"Your second error was that you failed to counter."

"Counter?" Declan swung the handle in a small circle. "How do I counter with an axe?"

Arman rotated the axe head. "This is the weapon of Hispania. As with the bull, it is a weapon of power and passion. A warrior must be relentless, must always be the aggressor. If you halt, you are exposed, and the fight is over."

"So, I just keep swinging?"

"Not swinging, countering." Arman spun his axe in perfect rhythm. "Watch." The old man attacked empty air in slow motion. The axe floated from his left shoulder to his right hip, only to change hands at the last moment. Its head looped to his right shoulder, then drifted to his left hip.

"Observe. Always on the attack." Arman moved smoothly, never exposed to harm but always pressing forward. The blade moved like a dancing pendulum. The glinting silver head transformed into a screaming blur that found its mark, a mighty pine, with a satisfying crack.

Declan's jaw hovered by his feet. "How do you do that?"

Arman levered his weapon from the tree. "Soft grip, smooth counter. Watch once more. I shall do it slowly. Then we shall practice together."

A noonday wind whistled through the pines. A blanket of clouds had crawled over them as the morning wore on, promising an afternoon storm. Declan practiced under Arman's watchful eye. While his grandfather made changing from one hand to the other look effortless, to Declan, it felt like juggling egg-yolks.

"Slow yourself. Perfect the movement first. Haste creates poor habits."

The axe arced forward at a snail's pace; Declan eased the handle from hand to hand and concentrated on the pattern.

"Excellent. Test a little faster, maintain your rhythm."

Declan followed the circle—around and around—until the sun crowned the forest. When Arman called him to rest, he collapsed

"That went well." Arman tossed him a waterskin. "You are a fast learner."

"It's... fun." Declan took a long drink. "When you get the movement right, it just flows."

"It is easy to be caught in the dance."

"It's a welcome distraction from... everything."

"The pretty girl?"

Declan took another, longer drink.

Arman chuckled. "She must be special, to inspire such devotion to hydration." He sat on the ground across from Declan. "Tell me about her."

Declan ignored his burning cheeks. "I... I don't know... She's always happy to see me and, well, she makes me feel like I've got someone. Like I'm not alone."

"How did you meet?"

Declan recounted meeting Ava in Tamhill. A small wren landed on Arman's shoulder and entertained itself with his hair. When he finished, an odd expression crossed his grandfather's face. "What's that look for?" Declan asked.

"What look do you speak of?"

Declan laughed. "The one you are doing right now. Like you know something."

"Lucks are a curious type. That is all."

Declan paused. "Curious? How?"

Arman didn't answer straight away. He traced his axe-handle. "My Maria. My first wife was a Luck."

"She was?" Declan let the question hang in the air. Arman had said very little about his first wife.

"Yes." He closed his eyes. "Lucks were different back then. Vedmark coveted such power." His expression turned stern. "The Knights made particular effort to capture Lucks and bring them to Vedmark. Many escaped by virtue of their abilities, but not all."

"What happened to them?"

"Terrible things. The men were scrutinized. The women gifted to those favored by the King, and forced to bear children that might pass on their gift."

The thought made Declan feel sick. "That's horrible."

"My brother was an evil man, Declan. Understand that

this was a dark time in Vedmark's history, perhaps its darkest part. They committed many wrongs." Arman held out a hand and the bird on his shoulder hopped into his palm.

"Is that why you locked them in? As punishment."

"Perhaps," he said, he stroked the bird's feathers. "At first it was for safety, then for revenge. Now, centuries later, I do it because it is all I know." The little wren flew away. "Enough talk. Are you refreshed?"

Declan nodded.

"Then let us return to your instruction."

"Same thing?" Declan stood, then winced. Blisters lined the edge of his hand. His legs felt like concrete. Arman squeezed his shoulder. In a burst of green light, the pain melted away. Declan's hands remained hard and pale.

"Warriors earn their calluses through time and effort. Time, we have little. Effort alone will suffice."

Declan squeezed the axe handle, stepped forward and returned to rehearsing the movements. The axe cartwheeled in an endless loop, one hand to the other. Clouds thickened above them, and a strong wind rushed through the pine needles.

"Excellent work." Arman said. "Your grip and counter have rhythm. Now add haste. Make your axe a force to be feared."

Declan launched the axe from palm to palm. He followed the line in the dirt, circling the clearing again, again, until his mind cleared and everything faded into movement. Somewhere in that circle, it swallowed his loneliness and guilt. He forgot about Ava and Ven, Grigory and Misha, Ace and the Directive. There was him, the axe, the next strike.

When Arman called for him to stop, it was dusk.

Thunder rumbled in the distance, a haze of drizzle hid everything beyond the trees. Declan slowed to a halt before stumbling to the ground. Exhaustion crashed over him. His legs felt like water, his arms trembled beneath the axe's weight. "How long was I going for?"

Arman beamed at him. "Hours."

Declan dropped the axe and lay on the ground. The wet earth cooled his hot skin. "I didn't realise…"

Arman lowered himself to lie beside him. "You have picked up the Bull well."

"The bull?"

"The Bull."

With all the effort he could muster, Declan raised an eyebrow. "What is that?"

Arman laughed. "You are tired, and that is good. You shall rest well tonight." He picked up Declan's axe and traced the carved bull. "The bull is a form. There are many forms, but all are variations of four animals. The Bull, the Bear, the Lion and the Armadillo.

"The armadillo?" Declan rubbed his eyes. A tired thought bubbled to the surface. "What is your connection to armadillos?"

Arman winked. "They come from Hispania. The armadillos of Vedmark are my doing, my way of keeping Hispania close."

Declan fought to contain a yawn. "What about that golden one? You called him Lancelot?"

"Lancelot is a very old companion."

"He saved me from the eagles."

"He did. A loyal friend too." Arman smiled. "You did well without him."

"Not well enough." Declan yawned. "But thank you."

"I will pass on your gratitude." Arman stood and started talking more about the history of the axe. Declan attempted to follow along, but his grandfather's words faded into meaningless babble. Arman must have noticed because he startled Declan with laughter. "Is my knowledge so uninteresting?"

Declan took a long moment to understand his words. He shook his head. "No, no. Sorry Grandfather. I'm just... exhausted."

"Very well." Arman nodded and climbed to his feet. "Let us take leave and rest. We shall continue tomorrow."

Declan smiled. With gargantuan effort, he staggered upright. A gust of wind rushed through the valley. "Grandfather... How long can I stay?"

Arman stroked his chin. "When you have lived as long as I, time means little. I am wary of keeping you here, Declan. A brief stay—in my mind—could be your entire lifetime."

"Would that be a bad thing?"

"You have a life to live, grandson. It will do you no favors to spend it hiding in the trees."

Declan nodded. "I understand." He waved to the axe in Arman's hand. "What if I stay long enough to master the axe?"

Arman chuckled. "Grandson, I have lived many lifetimes and not mastered the axe."

"Well, get a handle on the basics. The different animals. The Bull, Armadillo... I forgot the others."

"The Bear and the Lion."

"Yeah. How long will that take?"

Arman stroked his beard. "It depends how hard you train."

"Give me four months. A month for each Form."

Arman rubbed the back of his neck. "I am surprised you want to stay."

Declan shrugged. Tiredness weighed on his shoulders. He smiled at his grandfather. "It's nice to be with family."

"Four months," Arman agreed. "Though you may tire of me before then."

CHAPTER 24

KATIE

THE ONYXELLE'S greasy fur stank. Katie couldn't see it, but she could smell it. She cornered the beast in the pen and then pounced, wrapping her arms around its neck. "Amber!" she called, holding tight as the onyxelle strained against her. "I've got one. Take it."

The onyxelle whimpered as magic pulled it away. Over the wire-link fence and into a long, wooden crate. Katie straightened and dusted off her jeans. *That should be enough.* Every onyxelle she caught was going to die. She felt a weight of sadness thinking about it, but it had to be done. Katie needed her mother back. It had to be done. "How many is that?"

"This is number eight." Amber's fingers plucked the air. The crate's lid swung closed.

"Perfect." She looptapped the messaged to Michael. As she did, butterflies erupted in her stomach. Tonight, she could be laughing, crying, hugging her mom. *Control your expectations*, she told herself.

Amber slid the brass lock into place. "Well, this feels different," she said.

"What?"

"Being on the front foot for once. Saving people, having a plan. It's refreshing."

Katie nodded, stomach aflutter. "We can't get ahead of ourselves though," she said, more for herself than for Amber. "One step at a time."

A gate behind them opened with a piercing creak. "You girls moved fast," Mary-Lou said. Her eyes settled on the crates. "Michael sent me to collect these. Were there any troubles loading them?"

"Just the smell," Katie said. "Are we still on schedule for tonight?"

"We are..." Mary-Lou trailed off.

"Is everything okay?" Amber asked.

"I hope so," Mary-Lou said. "High Mage Johannasberg has requested a meeting with Laurefen."

Katie bit her lip. *No. Not now. He'll ruin everything.*

"That buffoon is the reason we're in this mess," Amber said. "What if it's a trap?"

"After everything that's happened..." Katie chose her words carefully. "Are we certain that the High Mage is on our side?"

Mary-Lou shook her head. "That's what they're discussing right now."

"But tonight?" Katie asked. "We're still going tonight, yeah?"

"Tonight will go as planned," Mary-Lou said. "I'll make sure of it. I know how long you've waited, Kate. I know how bad you want Lisa back."

Katie nodded, jaw clenched tight. It had to be done. She needed her mother back.

The wind had teeth. Katie stumbled through knee deep snow to a towering concrete dome. Laurefen pressed his hand to the wall. His eyes narrowed in concentration.

"W-what is it?" Katie pulled her outermost layer tighter.

"Movement inside," came his muffled reply. He pulled the scarf below his chin. "It's faint. Likely nothing."

"Worth the r-r-risk?"

"Let's give it a few minutes." Laurefen redirected the aeronima around them and the biting gale ceased. When Katie's jaw stopped chattering, she turned back the way they had come. The Pechora River was solid ice. Even so, the wall of snow and wind masked anything out of arm's reach. Katie glanced up at the dome. "Mary-Lou said the High Mage contacted you."

"He wants to meet tomorrow."

"That's soon."

"Extremely. And uncharacteristic. I have wasted a lot of effort trying to reach him these past two years."

"Why do you think he's contacting you now?"

"I wish I could say," Laurefen pressed his hand back against the building. "He says he has a proposition. The optimist in me hopes he may know something about the Fatesmiths that we don't. The pessimist suspects an ambush." He slipped his hand back inside his gloves. "The realist expects neither. The most likely explanation is he needs something from us."

Katie nodded. "So you're going to go?"

"I'm undecided." He nodded to the holdhouse. "But I would consider us safe to proceed."

"Any idea how we get in?"

"We follow the warmth." Laurefen tugged on a thread of aeronima. Katie considered the transparent spaghetti strand that ran through his loose grip. "What are you doing?"

"Shhh," Laurefen closed his eyes.

"Laurefen?"

He didn't respond. The minutes marched by. Katie leaned against the dome. Even under six layers, the cold gnawed at her bones. She was ready to call it quits when Laurefen's eyes snapped open. "There."

The aeronima flattened out, like a glass ribbon, it snaked its way around the building. Laurefen followed it and Katie trailed behind. "You're following the air?"

"I'm following the warmth," he said. "Cold air comes from outside, so warm air—"

"Must come from an entry." Katie smiled. "Genius."

They marched through the deep snow, up a slight slope and down again to where the strand of air vanished into the ground. Laurefen pointed. "That's our way in."

Katie grabbed fistfuls of hydronima and pulled the ice loose, revealing a metal trapdoor with three narrow vents. She wrapped kinema between the vents and let the kinetic energy do its job. The trapdoor groaned, then popped open. Welcome warmth rushed past them. Katie peered down into darkness. Her mother was down there. She knew it.

"At least we'll be free of this cursed cold," Laurefen said. With a precise twist of his hand, a column of snow formed an icy ladder. Laurefen disappeared into the tunnel.

"What do you see?" Katie called.

"It's a ventilation shaft," he called. "Come on down."

Katie ignored the growing butterflies and climbed into the dark. The slippery ladder threatened a sudden descent. When she reached the bottom, she wiped her hands on her coat. Beads of photonima from above were knotted along the roof—they looked like fairy lights.

Their footsteps reverberated off the curved concrete walls. The tunnel was an enormous concrete pipe leading to the surface. When they reached the end, a large metal grate led into the cavernous dome. *Mom is in here, somewhere.* She shook her head. *Maybe, don't get ahead of yourself.* She peeked through the metal bars. Nothing moved. Nothing made a sound. As far as she could tell, it was empty.

Laurefen pulled the photonima, illuminating the tunnel through the grate, like a procession of fireflies, beads of light streamed up to the roof, lighting the floor. "And there they are."

Thousands of iron casts glinted in the dim light—they seemed to crowd every inch of the enormous building. Katie's heart skipped a beat. She wrapped Amber's strand across her palm. *We've got another full house. How are you and Lou doing?*

A prodding sensation returned. *Still finding our way in.*

Follow the warm air, Katie tapped back.

Laurefen shifted the grate enough for them to slip inside. The soft light made the casts appear like sculptures of a master craftsman. Katie tried not to think about how each one of them was a person imprisoned in their own skin. She leaned close to see if she recognized any faces, if her mother was among them.

"Michael is on his way," Laurefen announced in a whisper. "We'll want to set up the onyxelles in the center of the dome."

"Got it." Katie traced her way through the figures, searching for her mother's face. Laurefen dragged more photonima in from outside, but despite the growing brightness, a shadow seemed to follow her. A pang of anxiety. Katie couldn't find her mother. *There are fifteen other domes like this,* she told herself. *Mom's probably in one of those.*

"Here's a suitable spot," Laurefen called. He stood in a circle free of casts and looptapped against his palm. "This should be enough room for the onyxelles."

Odd place for a gap, Katie thought. As far as she could tell, the holdhouse was bursting at the seams. A rotating window of light appeared by Laurefen.

Michael whistled as a crate floated alongside him. "This is fantastic." He nodded to Katie. "Credit where credit is due, Kate. You capturing that Mage was a game changer." He lowered the crates. The imbued boxes shook noiselessly, the onyxelle's grunts masked by Amber's charms.

Katie scanned the empty clearing. *Something's not right.*

"Shield yourselves," Michael called. His arms were already moving, the wooden crates rocked from side to side. Beside him, shimmering air condensed around Laurefen.

A group of casts caught Katie's eye. "STOP!"

Michael paused mid-swing. "What is it?"

Katie pointed to a group of casts directly in front of them. "Look at what they're wearing." The four figures wore regimental coats with a hammer and anvil embroidered in iron on their chest. "They're ironhands!"

Laurefen stepped through his barrier of compressed air to inspect the casts. "You're right."

"You said you heard movement earlier?" Katie asked. "What if they arrived just before we did?"

"Why would ironhands fierise themselves?" Michael asked.

"It wouldn't be the first time." Laurefen touched the star-shaped scar on his temple. "The bigger question is, how did they know we would be here?"

A cold sensation ran down Katie's spine. She quickly

looped Amber's thread and tapped an urgent message. *Fatesmiths are fierising themselves in holdhouses. It's an ambush.* A moment later, a reply returned. *Good to know. We're waiting on Michael.*

"Could be rogues." Michael suggested. "Fatesmiths who tried to fight back?"

"Perhaps," Laurefen said. "Though it is suspect that they are here, right near this clear space in the dome's centre. It all appears too convenient."

"So, what's the plan?" Katie asked.

Laurefen looked to Michael. "You said compressed air is enough to stop the spell?"

"The spell will dissipate the aeronima. Everything beneath it will stay unchanged."

"Then the solution is simple," Laurefen said. "We comb through the casts, encase the Fatesmiths in air. They will remain in iron. We can send the innocent witches and wizards of Euryma home."

Michael scanned the floor. "Searching the entire place will take hours."

"Then we best get to work." Laurefen smiled at Katie. "Excellent catch Katie. Once again, your eye for detail has saved the day."

Katie did not know how long it took to search the holdhouse—she didn't care. She was thrilled about the chance to save her mother, but Lisa Hall was not in the dome. By the time they were done, they had isolated two-dozen more men and women dressed in telltale black coats. To the south, Amber and Mary-Lou were doing the same. They had been equally unlucky. *You'll find her. Just keep looking.*

"They're not too clever," Michael said. He enveloped the last pair in a bubble of aeronima. "You'd think they'd be smart enough to change outfits."

"The probably weren't expecting us to inspect every single cast." Katie knotted her own shield and surveyed the holdhouse floor. "Even so, there's still the chance some of them did change."

"I agree," Laurefen said, his voice muffled by his own shimmering globe. "Keep your wits about you. Are you ready, Michael?"

"Ready as I'll ever be." Michael dragged the crates towards him and went to work. They trembled as his spell took hold, then rocked back and forth, faster and faster, until they threatened to buckle and crack. Katie closed her eyes as a brilliant blaze scoured the holdhouse. When her vision returned, an enormous crowd blinked at the strange reality of their awakening. A steady buzz filled the dome as the crowd questioned their surrounds.

"Ladies and gentlemen," Laurefen's amplified voice bounced off the ceiling. "You are victims of a hostage situation. We will soon create Openings to the northern suburbs of Ursaria. Please remain there for the next seven days to enable us to rescue other hostages. More explanations will follow. For now, remain in Ursaria while we deal with the situation."

The message was short, sharp and instantly drowned out by the crowd's confusion. Katie searched for Fate-smiths, waiting for a cry of panic. There was none. People herded like sheep through a series of Openings into the early morning sunlight of Iberia. In under an hour, the holdhouse was empty save for Katie, Laurefen, Michael and twenty-eight iron casts.

"What do we do with them?" Katie asked.

Michael shrugged. "We could toss them in the river. Would serve them right."

"I cannot condone that," Laurefen said. "They are defenseless."

"So were the people they took," Michael said. "If they are here on purpose, their suspicions will be confirmed as soon as the ironhands check back."

"What about an earthquake?" Katie suggested. "We could take these casts back to King's and then collapse the dome. Make it seem like a natural disaster."

Michael scratched the back of his neck. "It's not a bad idea." He nodded to the remaining casts. "If we defierise these, one at a time, we might be able to work out what the Fatesmiths have planned."

Laurefen nodded. "Very well." He sighed and tapped a quick message on his palm. When he looked up, exhaustion masked his smile. "It's past time you helped Lou and Amber. Thank you, Michael. We will clean up here."

Once he left, Laurefen considered Katie with a curious glint in his tired eyes.

Katie frowned. "What is it?"

"You did well today, Katie," Laurefen said. He paused; eyes fixed on his open hand. "How would you like to join me for a meeting tomorrow?"

CHAPTER 25

OPHELIA

OPHELIA STOOD at the plain office door. It was particle board, covered in cheap vinyl to give an appearance of value. She searched for a metaphor in that, but she was delaying the inevitable, Haberdeen waited on the other side, and Ophelia's news would not to be to her liking. She inhaled through her nose, held the breath for a count of five, exhaled, and entered.

Haberdeen sat at a desk, reading through paperwork. Behind her, notes and pins littered a corkboard map of Euryma. "You have an update?" she asked without looking up.

Ophelia paused. *Yes, and you will not like it.* "A fleet of vans have looptapped in."

"Looptap," Haberdeen glanced up, her eyes narrowed. "Are we such hypocrites?"

"It's the fastest way to communicate, Madam."

"The LAMPs have electrical devices. They call them phones. We've got towers all across the Dominion you can use to communicate. No magic needed. Why aren't we using those?"

"I... I don't know." Ophelia shuffled, then shook her head. "Madam, one of the holdhouses is gone."

Haberdeen looked up from the pile of paper. "Gone? How?"

"Early suggestions are an earthquake. The dome is shattered, the citizens in stasis are buried."

"Have you confirmed it? Are there any records of an earthquake to the north?"

Ophelia blinked. The thought hadn't even occurred to her. "We don't keep records of geological activity in other countries."

Haberdeen scowled. "Then perhaps you should find someone who does. How soon can we dig them out?"

"I beg your pardon?"

"The iron casts." There was an edge to Haberdeen's voice. "How long will it take us to remove the casts from the rubble and send them to a safer spot?"

"We... we weren't planning on..." Ophelia trailed off beneath the heat of Haberdeen's gaze. "Madam, they're the reason we're in this mess. If an earthquake buried those casts, it serves them right. Leave them underground. The world will thank them."

Haberdeen dropped the papers on the desk with a snap. "If we're leaving them buried, we might as well bury whichever foregone soul *looptapped* you this information."

Ophelia's cheeks burned. "That's different—"

"No, it's not. Either we're all guilty, or none of us are." Haberdeen stood up. "Those people are in stasis so that we can fix the problem. When the Dominion is safe, we bring them back. All of them. Are we clear?"

"Yes, madam."

"How soon can you recover the casts?"

"With or without magic?" Ophelia regretted the question the instant it left her lips. Haberdeen's flat stare nearly put a hole in her. "Could be a month, I am not sure."

"Then find out," Haberdeen said. She turned to the corkboard and traced her fingers up the map. "And follow up on that earthquake, Ophelia. I want to know what happened."

"Of course, Madam." Ophelia bowed and backed away —all the while wondering what caused Haberdeen's change of heart.

Finding the reports didn't take long. Ophelia slapped a printed sheet on Haberdeen's desk. "You were right. No earthquake recorded."

Haberdeen held the page between razor red fingernails. Her eyes darted across the graphs and charts; her lips pressed so tight they risked disappearing. "No geological activity. No casts recovered." She stared at the passage; her brow creased. "Where are the casts?"

"Ursaria," Ophelia said. "A crowd of strangers walked out of thin air a few days ago."

"Walked?"

"They're not casts anymore. They've been pulled out of stasis."

A muscle in Haberdeen's jaw twitched. She stood at the window and scanned the bustling streets below. Downtown Biscay could have been any city in the Dominion, and none at the same time. It was a flavourless collection of steel and concrete boxes. Ophelia waited, wondering if this would nudge their leader back to her old ways.

Haberdeen turned back to her. "What is wrong with

these people? Do they not realize the gravity of the situation?"

"You would think what happened at Parteno would give them pause," Ophelia said.

"All I'm trying to do is save them."

"I understand Madam." Ophelia didn't dare say more.

Haberdeen crumpled the seismology report. "How could this happen?"

The answer was simple. Haberdeen had changed since Anderma. It started with pulling back on raids, focusing only on high-volume magical users. Now, there were whispers the High Mage had gone rogue. *What if Mage Raul was right? Maybe this isn't her at all.* The thought was laughable. Mimicking a face was child's play, but Ophelia had witnessed Haberdeen's power in full force. Nobody could mimic that. *Then she's just gone soft, too much blood on her hands.* Ophelia longed to say it aloud, but bit her lip and opted for a gentler approach. "Perhaps we should adjust our strategy. An aggressive stance may send the message we need."

Haberdeen tilted her head. "What kind of message?"

"A message that we are still here. That we are intent on stopping Remnant Magic. That we have magic that normal witches and wizards cannot stop."

"The last thing we need is to add more magic to the storms." Haberdeen shook her head. "No. We need to trust the process. LAMPs are joining in record numbers. The tide is turning."

LAMPs? What use are they? Ophelia held her tongue. "Whoever did this will not be satisfied with one holdhouse, Madam. What happens when they're all set free?"

Something dangerous flashed in Haberdeen's eyes. The

stretching silence made Ophelia's skin crawl. "Sometimes I think these fools don't deserve to be saved," Haberdeen said at last. "Okay, Ophelia. You get your wish. Organize a team of Mages to leave within the hour."

Ophelia bowed. "Yes, Madam."

CHAPTER 26
KATIE

FOOTPATHS AND FOUNTAINS filled Sabriva Central. Manicured grass lawns stretched around perfect circular lakes, all hidden in the shadow of Sabriva Tower. A behemoth that rose into the clouds like a glistening geyser.

Tourist brochures described it as a wonder of the world, but Katie had never liked Sabriva Tower. Maybe it was the jagged spires, maybe the man who occupied it. She followed Laurefen up the steps and paused beside him at the door.

"Have you met Reginald Johannasberg?" Laurefen asked.

"Never face to face. I've been in the crowd for some of his speeches. Why?"

"Keep your wits about you." Laurefen said. "He may be cowardly, but he is also cunning. Do not tell him anything about the holdhouses. Do not agree to anything, no matter how reasonable it may seem at that moment."

"Okay..."

Laurefen nodded, then led them through a busy lobby and into an elevator. A silver panel illuminated green at his touch, and up they went. "Your critical eye saved us yester-day," Laurefen said. "Johannasberg will make a convincing case. His persuasion will be perfect, his argument iron clad. I need you to unravel them. Use that critical eye to find the hole in his reasoning, the manipulation in his method."

"I'll try." Something fluttered in Katie's stomach. She watched the numbered floors blink higher, the lift walls seemed to press in on them. When the doors opened, Katie wanted to leap out.

Laurefen led her into a waiting room full of brown leather couches and frosted lamps. "Welcome to the Office of the High Mage," drawled a silky voice from behind a desk. "Dean Ember, an honor to see you again."

"Good afternoon Annabelle," Laurefen said. "How are the grandchildren?"

"Growing up, causing trouble. What can you expect from kids?"

Laurefen chuckled. "Never a dull moment, no doubt."

Annabelle was an elderly woman with a brilliant nest of golden curls "Allow me to introduce my associate, Katie Hall. Katie is a junior member of our staff who will serve as an extra set of ears today."

"Delighted," Annabelle said. Her right index finger looptapped her palm.

"A pleasure," Katie replied.

"Is Reginald ready for us?"

Annabelle nodded to her hand. "He said you could go straight on in."

"Wonderful. Lovely to see you again. Give my regards to Peter and Beth."

Laurefen led Katie down a corridor lined with gilded frames. Portraits of previous Magistri were succeeded by larger, more extravagant paintings of the Fendragon Kings and Queens. Laurefen strode through a double door; Katie felt like she'd walked into a maritime museum.

High Mage Johannasberg's office was a study in nautical decor. Dark blue carpets beneath white furniture embellished with gold fixings. Ornamental anchors, clumps of dried coral and miniature ships lined the shelves while rope accents hung from the curtains. The High Mage, it seemed, had an affinity for the ocean.

"Welcome, my old friend!" The High Mage's voice was melted butter. "A pleasure to have you here. And Katie Hall, such a delight, to meet another member of the Directive, and one so young."

His massive hand engulfed Katie's. A waft of sandalwood flooded her nostrils. The High Mage stepped back and fixed her with a beaming smile. Katie bowed her head. "It is my honor to meet you, High Mage."

High Mage Johannasberg raised a brow. "You training a bunch of stiffs, Loz?" He shook his head. "Please, call me Reginald. None of this High Mage nonsense. Come, be seated."

He directed them to a luxurious blue couch. Katie sat while Reginald sank into an armchair opposite. Laurefen remained standing. "I would love to banter over formalities, but our time is precious, Reginald. Why have you called us here?"

"The world is an interesting place of late." He winked at Laurefen. "How's that Well of yours holding up?"

Katie thought she caught Laurefen's eyes flicker towards her as he cleared his throat. "Why didn't you contact me months ago?" Laurefen's voice was terse. Anger bubbled beneath his calm demeanor. "I have things to do. Important things. You are no fool, Reginald, you know what's been going on in the Dominion. Why has it taken you so long to ask for my help?"

"Haberdeen came out of nowhere. She targeted the Magistri's best Mages to start. She turned those who wouldn't join her to iron before we even knew it was possible. By the time the Fatesmiths were fierising citizens, the Government was on its knees."

"And why am I hearing about this now?" Laurefen said. "How many times did we seek an audience with you? Myself? Mary-Lou? Dreyfus?"

"If I had taken those meetings, you would be dead."

Laurefen paused. "I beg your pardon?"

"They took our most competent Mages, Laurefen. They had us. Hook, line, sinker. I was a placeholder, kept in office to keep up appearances, but I've been under twenty-four-hour surveillance for three years. Every meeting, every looptap. I couldn't buy a sandwich in the square without them knowing what type of relish was on it."

Katie remained silent. She held tight to Laurefen's words. *Use that critical eye, find a hole in his reasoning.*

Laurefen settled into a chair. "So, why are we here now? What changed? I assume you're not throwing us to the wolves."

"I figured out their trick." Reginald leaned back with his hands behind his head. "I worked out fierisation."

Katie snapped to face him. "You know how to do it?"

Reginald nodded. "Inverted magic. They pull nima in on itself and that creates something new."

Katie's jaw hit the floor. Laurefen looked as shell-shocked as she felt. *It's really that simple?*

"Show us," Laurefen said.

Reginald waved a hand, and his door bolted shut. Katie's

stomach dropped. *It's a trap!* But instead of doing anything remotely dangerous, Reginald crossed the office and opened a cupboard door with no cupboard inside. Instead, a cement stairway led down into darkness. Reginald turned back to them. "I figured out their spell, and with it, their doom. I can destroy Haberdeen and the Fatesmiths, but I require your help. Before that, I need your word. If you follow me, you're agreeing to go through with my plan. If winning this war is not to your liking, then you are welcome to leave."

Katie waited for Laurefen to speak. He stroked his moustache, well-rehearsed nonchalance. "An intriguing offer, Reginald. But I reject your terms. You cannot coerce us into collaboration."

The High Mage stiffened. "You would throw away the chance at saving the Dominion?"

"I'm throwing away nothing," Laurefen replied. "We are happy to see what you have to share, to weigh it on merit, but the Directive does not make blind promises."

"I will not risk giving this information to someone on the outside."

"We are not *on* the outside," Laurefen said. "Nor are we sheep."

Reginald closed the door. "I am sorry, old friend."

"As am I." Laurefen turned away from him. "Come Kate, we have work to do."

Katie looked from Reginald to Laurefen. *He has a plan! A solution! He can beat the ironhands!* It took all her self-control to put one foot in front of the other and follow Laurefen to the door. *What are you doing? You're going to throw away our chance!*

Laurefen gripped the door handle. Katie longed to pull away. She wanted to accept the High Mage's offer and join

219

him, to learn how to defeat the Fatesmiths, to win the fight they had been losing for months.

"Wait."

The corners of Laurefen's mouth twitched. Katie gawked. *It was a bluff.*

"Yes?" he asked.

"Will stubbornness be your legacy?" Reginald growled.

"I am not being stubborn. You are being unreasonable."

The two men glared at each other, then a smile cracked Reginald's expression. "You are insufferable." He shook his head, his thick braided beard swayed side to side. "At the very least, you must commit to secrecy. Word of what you see does not leave this building. Are those terms to your satisfaction?"

"I suppose that is fair." Laurefen nodded. "Lead the way, Your Excellence."

The cement stairs didn't lead far. Twenty feet down, they reached a concrete room with watermarks on the walls. It held a waste disposal chute and a service elevator. Reginald slid a small panel out of the waste disposal and produced a key from his pocket. A fake wall shuddered open, revealing a hidden door.

"Very secure," Laurefen noted.

Reginald swung the door open. It appeared to be iron—at least five inches thick. "The Fatesmiths have done terrible things. While I do not doubt some are more innocent than others, by donning the hammer and anvil they are taking upon them the sins of the whole."

He beckoned for them to follow. As they did, Katie struggled to make sense of the scene inside.

Two rows of massive water tanks lined a long room. Each lit dimly with the same orange light; a lifeless body of a man or woman clad in the Smith's signature coat suspended within. Past the haunting vista was a large glass cylinder.

"What is this?" Laurefen's voice trembled.

"Justice."

Katie felt sick. She wanted to turn tail and run, but Reginald blocked her path. He swung the iron door closed.

"The Fatesmiths had me in their pocket for years. They fierised my staff, my friends, my acquaintances. I was powerless to do anything but bide my time." Reginald pulled a narrow lever and a strip of lights flickered to life. The Smith's coats swayed like seaweed in the water. "So, I waited. I listened to their conversations and, slowly, I pieced together the puzzle of their power. They weren't pulling *on* nima, they were pulling *through* nima. And every time they did, they changed themselves in some distinct way."

"Ire tides?" Laurefen asked.

Reginald shook his head. "No. Not dissimilar, but no. This is something else. Each time they reach through a strand of nima to fierise an innocent man or woman, it leaves a mark." He walked past them and put a hand to the glass pillar. "If someone is marked, we can find them."

Laurefen stepped back. Katie thought he may have tripped, but then she saw the fear in his eyes. "No," he whispered. "This is your conduit attack all over again, isn't it? That's why you need my help?"

"It is." Reginald's face was grim. "And I need your piece of the puzzle, before it's too late..."

"What are you talking about?" Katie said. "What is a conduit attack?"

"Years back, when we were both students, Laurefen and I were business partners. It came after we developed a way to imbue stone conduits to exterminate common pests. Cockroaches, mosquitoes, all eliminated with magic in an instant. A college project that became a lucrative source of income."

Laurefen still looked shell-shocked. When he spoke, his voice was distant. "Even as foolish teenagers, we understood the necessity of working in isolation. Reginald would develop the conduit, and I developed the spell that triggered it. We kept our work separate for safety. And for good reason." Laurefen blinked, and his eyes focused on the High Mage. "It took less than twelve months for Reginald to take things too far."

"I was being proactive," Reginald said. "Ire Tides were getting out of control. Too many people were falling apart chasing power, trying to be more than their Potential allowed."

"You wanted to commit mass murder." Laurefen turned to Katie. "When Reginald proposed using our pest-control treatment to murder thousands, I removed myself from the partnership."

"You destroyed our office," Reginald snapped. "Because you cared more about your legacy than the innocent people being attacked by power-blind criminals."

"And we went our separate ways." Laurefen continued, ignoring the High Mage's words. "And now, I fear you want to do it again."

"Only once," Reginald said. "Sabriva Tower is the perfect conduit. All I need is your half of the equation." He waved to the bodies floating in the tanks. "The Fatesmiths are here, preserved. They'll give you everything you need to isolate fierisation's unique mark. Then, one simple spell and this war is over."

A shadow of alarm crossed Laurefen's face. "What you're describing is genocide."

"What I'm describing is victory. Swift, immediate victory of a war fought in the shadows." He punched a fist into his palm. "Haberdeen has been ahead of us from the get go. This time tomorrow, the war could be finished."

"Mass murder will not be my legacy," Laurefen said.

"You would trade the blood of our enemies for defeat?"

"There are other ways to win."

Reginald grimaced. "You haven't seen what I've seen."

"And you haven't seen what we've done."

"What you've done?" Reginald laughed. "You think I don't know? A few thousand wizards show up in Ursaria. You think that will stop anything? For every thousand you save, Haberdeen draws five thousand LAMPs to her cause. We could stop her before those numbers grow beyond our control, before the LAMPs rise against us."

Katie felt ill. She wanted to leave, to be out of the awful room surrounded by corpses. Laurefen squeezed the bridge of his nose. "How long before the LAMP component of the Fatemiths grows too large?"

"Three weeks," Reginald said. "A month, if we are lucky. They're growing fast. Too fast."

Laurefen hesitated. "I need time to think about your offer."

No, you don't. Katie fought not to shout at him. *This is lunacy.*

"Remember our deal," Reginald said. "What I have told you cannot escape these walls."

"You expect me to walk the Directive blindly into a mass extermination?"

"I do." Reginald's face held no amusement. "Extraordinary times demand that leaders lead, Laurefen."

Laurefen nodded. "I will consider it and decide on the Directive's behalf."

Katie sat in Mary-Lou's living room, feeling dizzy. People spoke around her, but it was a muffled mess of sound. She missed her mother. *She would know what to do.* The meeting with the High Mage had left her wanting to vomit. She couldn't bring herself to look at Laurefen. *What is he thinking?*

Michael was the last one to arrive, smeared in dirt and onyxelle fur. Mary-Lou raised an eyebrow at his muddy boots. "Sorry," he said. "Your looptap sounded urgent."

"Just.. don't sit on the couch,"

Michael took a seat at the table. All eyes turned to Laurefen, all except Katie's. Her gaze remained fixed on the floor, her stomach in knots.

"The High Mage has lost his mind," Laurefen said. Katie blinked. "He's developed a weapon and needs my help to finish it."

"What kind of weapon?" Michael asked.

"He has discovered some sort of marker left behind by using fierisation. Reginald wants to use Sabriva Tower as a conduit and kill every witch or wizard who has used the fierisation magic."

"So, we could... defeat the ironhands." Michael chewed on his lip. "It's not a terrible idea."

Katie shook her head. "You're talking about murdering thousands. Laurefen called it genocide."

"This is not our path to victory," Laurefen agreed.

"I'm not saying it's not horrible," Michael said. "But do you think the ironhands would do different if the situation was reversed?"

"They already have," Laurefen said. "The Fatesmiths have blood on their hands, but they have elected to capture most victims in place of murder."

Mary-Lou fiddled with her braid. "What's our alternative then? You mentioned a way to victory. Do you have a plan?"

"We stay the course." Laurefen scanned their faces. "First, we rescue those trapped in holdhouses, then we beat the Fatesmiths on our terms."

"And if we lose?" Michael whispered. "If history looks at us as the fools who threw away their chance?"

"Then we do so on the right side of history," Laurefen said. "Reginald expects our answer in three weeks. That gives us three weeks before he does something terrible. Michael, where are we with onyxelles?"

"Packed in crates, ready for another expedition."

Laurefen clapped his hands together. "Then we have no time to waste. There are a pair of domes opposite one other at Anabar Bay. Mary-Lou and I will take the western bank. Michael, you take Amber and Katie to the east."

Katie nodded. *Tonight is the night. We're going to find you, mom.*

225

CHAPTER 27
KATIE

ANABAR BAY WAS a powdered ocean of snow. Katie fought to keep herself from sinking under the snow as she followed Amber through flurries of dagger-cold wind. A glistening white pyramid beckoned from the horizon, apex ignited by the midnight sun.

"Why isn't it a dome like the others?" Amber called ahead.

"I don't know." Michael shouted back. A thread of aeronima trickled up his wrist around a small silver device. "Your compass is incredible, Amber. This way."

Amber had tweaked Laurefen's idea of tracking warm air and imbued a compass to make it sensitive to changes in temperature. They chased the warmth to a familiar grate and were soon underground. Katie drew two strands of photonima down with her. One traced her pointer, the other her thumb. She pressed them into bulbs of light that chased the darkness ahead of them. Her heart raced with a mixture of hope and anticipation.

"This feels smaller than the last one," Amber whispered when they got inside.

Katie nodded. "Wall to wall, I'd guess it's half the size."

"Could be the shape of the building." Michael stopped and looked at his palm. "Something's wrong."

"What is it?" Katie asked.

Michael turned back to the tunnel. "Lou just sent out an emergency tap." A spinning triangle formed behind them, an identical pyramid loomed on the other side. Snowflakes blew through the magical doorway.

"We'll come with you," Amber said.

"No," Michael replied as the Opening grew larger. "Stay here. Stay out of sight. I'll looptap when things have settled."

"But—"

"No. You're safe here. Stay and wait." Michael pulled down his scarf and stepped into the snow.

The doorway blinked away. Amber turned to Katie. "I'm so tired of his over-protective-man-shtick."

Katie laughed. "He doesn't do it on purpose. Or maybe he does. I don't know." She considered looptapping Mary-Lou to learn more. *I would just be a distraction.* "I'm sure they'll work it out. They're used to sticky situations." Katie nodded to the nearest group of iron casts. "Well, we might as well check for Fatesmiths." *And Mom.*

"Michael said to stay out of sight."

"We're fine. We'll stick together."

They worked slowly, one row at a time. Katie tried to temper her expectations, fighting the urge to go faster. The Fatesmith's regimental coats made them easy to find. They uncovered six in their first sweep, four men, two women.

"Why do you think they're here?" Amber asked as Katie marked a round-faced woman with a photonima knot.

"I'm guessing they are either here as sleeper agents designed to protect the holdhouses from people like us, or they're ironhands who went rogue and got fierised like any other witch."

"Or," Amber said, grinning. "They're witches or wizards who dressed up as Fatesmiths to infiltrate their creepy organization."

"Stranger things have happened." Katie checked a group of casts huddled together. "Yep, here's another one." She tied a bead of light to the iron woman.

A loud click echoed around them. The western wall of the holdhouse rumbled to life. A strip of snow and daylight poured inside as a rolling door started to open.

"Hide!" Amber said.

Katie untied the beads of photonima as fast as her hands would let her. They would have to go through every cast again, but she had no choice. She rushed after Amber and ducked behind a vast ventilation pipe. With a mechanical hiss, the top of the western wall vanished. A silver vehicle with enormous treaded tires drove to a halt and a half-dozen blackcoats climbed out.

Taps tickled the inside of Katie's hand. *What are they doing here?* Amber's eyes darted up at her.

Katie looptapped back. *I have no idea. We just need to lie low.* She swapped Amber's thread for Mary-Lou's. *Ironhands have arrived. We are hiding. What's happening over there?*

Footsteps echoed off the walls. Fatesmiths swept the floor with military precision before doubling back to their vehicle. "Looks fine here," announced a woman with auburn hair.

"Should we defierise the volunteers?" asked another.

"No," said the woman. "Not yet. Give them until they end of the month, as agreed."

Katie held her breath. Mary-Lou's looptap tickled her

palm. She fought to hold a gasp. *Haberdeen is here. Hide somewhere safe. Report when they're gone. Michael will come get you.* She passed the message along to Amber and watched her face pale.

I thought you said Haberdeen was powerless, Amber tapped back.

It could be the imposter, someone wearing her face, the way Ward did with John. Katie peeked over the pipe. The iron-hands were opening the vehicle doors when one paused. "Wait. What's that?"

Katie followed the man's pointed finger. Her heart stopped. One of the fierised ironhands had a single bead of photonima pressed to their neck.

"Somebody has *marked* her. Was that you, Ophelia?"

"No." The auburn-haired woman marched through the line of bodies to inspect the solitary knot of light. Guilt crawled in Katie's stomach. "Alert Haberdeen, search the building. Whoever is stealing our casts may still be here."

The panic in Amber's eyes said it all. Katie wound Mary-Lou's strand across her palm and tapped a hurried message. *They know we're here. Help.* She waited. Ten seconds, no reply. Footsteps approached either side of them.

"This is like Anderma all over again," Amber whispered. "But this time we don't have Declan."

"Quiet," Katie replied in an even smaller whisper. "C'mon. This way." She wrapped two pads of air beneath her feet and crept to the back wall. "We need to get over there." She pointed to the place where they had entered.

"So we should cause a distraction over there." Amber nodded to the opposite wall. "If we can get the ironhands chasing ghosts, we can slip out the way we came."

"We can't do anything from here. They'll trace the nima back to us. What did you have in mind?"

"How about a loose knot?"

Katie nodded. "That might work."

They crouched and returned the way they had come. The Fatesmiths moved at a snail's pace, checking every shadow. Katie crept as close as she dared, then wrapped a group of casts in loose strands of kinetic energy.

"Ready?" Amber whispered. She had done the same.

"Ready." Katie's braid of kinima began to unravel the moment she let it go. She rushed behind Amber, careful to keep out of the light. They had reached their starting point when a clatter of casts rang out from the opposite wall.

"Over there! Northern wall!"

Katie raced in the other direction, following Amber through the ventilation grate. There, she hunched forward, hands on knees, and tried to catch her breath. The grate creaked closed. Before they could move, something shoved Katie against the wall. It knocked the wind out of her. Amber gasped as a slow clap echoed from the depths of the passage.

The auburn-haired woman—Ophelia—stood before them, her face creased with disgust. "Who would've thought?" she said. "The cause of all our headaches, a couple of teenage girls." She walked past them and leaned through the grate. "In here! I've caught two of them!"

Katie focused on breathing. A slab of compressed air pressed both her and Amber into the tunnel wall. Five iron-hands entered ahead of them. "This is it?" one said. "A couple of girls?"

"I doubt this is it," Ophelia sneered. She stepped forward until they were an inch apart. The pressure on Katie's chest increased. "Who are you working for?"

The aeronima pushed harder. Katie's vision blurred—she felt like her ribs were going to break. "We work alone," Katie said. "We're here by ourselves."

"Nonsense," Ophelia said. "You're in over your head, girl. If you're honest with us, you'll find we're more than reasonable."

"I'm telling you the truth." Katie's lips trembled. "We are on our own. Searching for our friends."

"And yet you are marking Fatesmiths in stasis with knots of light." Ophelia shook her head. "I get it. Somewhere somebody has told you that you need to save these people. That the big, bad Fatesmiths have taken them all hostage. But that's not true. These people are here for their own safety, here out of reach of Remnant Magic storms, where they won't make the problem worse."

"Remnant Magic's a lie," Katie said.

"You can't still believe that?" Ophelia said. "Have you seen Parteno? An entire city turned to ashes. What single person could do something like that? Now our flashfinders tell us that Massalia is next..." She held Katie's eye. "We are not enemies. The enemy is the magic that risks destroying our home."

"You're holding these people against their will!" Amber said. "How can you justify that?"

"We tried to do things the diplomatic way," Ophelia replied. "We went to the High Mage. We showed him the evidence. What did he do?"

"Nothing," one of the ironhands growled. "Called us a bunch of radicals."

"That's right," Ophelia said. "Sometimes you have to be cruel to be kind. Keep a toddler from an open fireplace is the right thing to do, no matter how much the toddler wants to play with the flames."

Katie shook her head. "That would be very convincing if you had any proof. But you don't. There's nothing to say Remnant Magic exists."

"You tell that to the good citizens of Parteno," Ophelia said flatly. "No wait. You can't. They're dead."

"We're not joining you," Amber said.

"We're not asking you to," Ophelia replied. "We will fierise you, but first, you need to tell us who you are working with."

"You might as well turn us to iron," Katie glared at the woman. "We're not telling you anything."

"That doesn't sound very helpful, dear." A sickly sweet voice floated down the tunnel. Haberdeen swept into the light, exactly as Katie remembered her. Red hair, crooked smile, except a curious glint of purple sparkled in her eyes. Bile crawled up Katie's throat.

"Madam," Ophelia bowed, as did the other ironhands. "These two girls tried to escape. They marked one of our fierised decoys."

"You have done well, Ophelia." Haberdeen's gaze rested on Katie, but if she recognized her, she did not show it. "I imagine you explained our cause and offered them the chance to join our ranks and save Euryma."

"I gave them the short version," Ophelia said. "They're stubborn. They both refuse to say who they're working for."

Haberdeen clicked her tongue. "Ah, well, let's see what we can do about that." She produced a white dagger from her dress and held it up to the light. "This is a marvellous weapon," she said with a small smile. She flicked the blade so its tip touched Katie's chest. "I could plunge it into you and you would die, but as you did, every single thing you knew would transfer to me. Your favorite color, first kiss, everything would be mine, including the names and faces of the people who sent you here."

Katie's watched the knifepoint like a viper. Her heart thundered through her body.

"So how about it?" Haberdeen asked. "Are you going to tell me what I need to know? Or am I going to take it?"

"You ironhands are all the same," Amber said. "You talk about how noble your cause is, then you murder innocents at the drop of a hat."

"You may be the center of your universe, darling, but the world is bigger than you, or me, or any of us. One life for a million, ten million, a hundred million? The answer is simple." She turned back to Katie. "What will it be, dear?"

Katie opened her mouth. A gentle pressure on her palm stopped her. It was Mary-Lou. *We're here. Get ready to move.* Katie rolled the words over in her mind. She smiled. "I'll take my chances."

Haberdeen raised an eyebrow, then vanished in an explosion of dust and wind. Katie stumbled through the gale into the darkness. *Get to the wall. Now.* Katie hurled herself to the left as a hailstorm of stone screamed past her. She struggled forward, Amber on her heels. As suddenly as it started, the storm was gone. Mary-Lou hugged her and pulled her through an Opening. Katie landed in an empty car park. Mary-Lou dragged her up through a second Opening, this time in the welcome shade of Cedrus.

"That was close," Michael said. His chest heaved, dirt covered him from head to heel. Laurefen looked just as disheveled. His curled mustache looked like frayed wires on a broken cable.

Katie collapsed onto a bench. She pressed her hands to her head and coughed up a mouthful of brown gunk. "You got there just in time. Are you okay Amber?"

There was no response.

Mary-Lou's face dropped. "Where's Amber?"

"She was with you," Michael said.

"I grabbed Kate."

"No, you grabbed both." Michael shook his head faster than normal. "You grabbed both. You pulled them through."

Katie jumped to trembling legs. "Amber! We left Amber!"

"Did she go through the first Opening and not the second?" Laurefen said. "She may still be in Sabriva."

"We need to go back," Mary-Lou said.

"Stand back." Michael worked an Opening into existence and jumped into the empty carpark. Katie watched him scan the area. She felt like someone was squeezing the air out of her. Michael called out, then shook his head. "She's not here."

"We have to go back to Anabar Bay!" Katie shouted. Hot tears blurred her vision. "We left Amber!"

"How could this happen?" Mary-Lou said "We weren't supposed to leave until—"

"It happened so fast." Laurefen's voice was a trembling whisper.

"We have to go back!" Katie looptapped Amber. There was no response. Her eyes leaped between the three of them. They weren't listening. *Why don't they understand?* "WE HAVE TO GO BACK!"

Laurefen's eyes were hollow. "We can't Katie," he said. "They'll be waiting for us now. We'll walk right into an ambush."

"Amber wouldn't want us to go back," Michael said. "Not now. We'll wait for them to fierise her, then rescue her with the others."

234

"No." Katie spoke between sobbing breaths. "We have to. We can't leave her." Someone touched her shoulder, but she pulled away. "We have to go back," she sobbed. "We have to go back."

CHAPTER 28
AMBER

DARKNESS, the smell of dirt, a ringing in her ears. Amber opened swollen eyes and groaned. Iron rings forced her hands open; they were fixed to an iron plate. Her wrists were likewise bound. Somewhere, someone was speaking in muffled tones.

Amber squeezed her eyelids shut and tried to make sense of the situation. *Snow, lots of snow, a holdhouse, ironhands... Haberdeen.* Something sharp shattered her thoughts. The woman had slapped her!

"Are you listening?" Ophelia asked.

"Where are my friends?"

Ophelia squinted at her. "You don't remember?"

Amber didn't respond. She couldn't remember what had happened. Bits and pieces fit together then fell apart. "Where am I?"

"Anabar Bay," Ophelia said. "You were trying to defierise our casts. We caught you and your friend. She escaped. You did not."

Kate's face flashed in her mind. They were in the ventilation shaft of the pyramid shaped holdhouse. Amber held the woman's eye with what she hoped was a level gaze. "They'll be back for me."

Ophelia nodded. "We are counting on it." She stepped closer, dropping her voice so only Amber could hear. "Either you tell us who you're working with, or we'll find out ourselves next time they try to save you. They are your only bargaining chip. Don't waste it, girl."

"And what if they don't come?"

"Then Madam Haberdeen will take your memories in blood."

Amber wanted to focus on a way to get free. Instead, her mind wandered to everything she knew that Haberdeen couldn't find out. The holdhouses, Mage Raul, the entry point to Kingsbreak, the Directive. With a stab of realization, she remembered their last meeting, Laurefen sharing the High Mage's plan to destroy the Fatesmiths. "If I tell you what you want to know, will you let me go?"

Ophelia shook her head. "No, but we won't kill you. You'll be fierised and stored in a new holdhouse. One that is not compromised."

"Fine." Amber took a deep breath. "What do you want to know?"

"Smart girl." Ophelia turned to the dark ventilation shaft. "Fetch Madam Haberdeen," she announced. "Tell her the girl is ready to speak."

Butterflies and other fluttering sensations filled the time spent waiting for Haberdeen's arrival. The ironhands spoke amongst one another in hushed tones. It didn't seem real.

Their muffled words were background noise to Amber's pounding heart. Haberdeen swept into the crumbling cavern. The long scar running along her cheek contorted in a crooked smile. "I would like to talk to the girl alone. You may leave."

An awkward pause followed. Haberdeen's request appeared out of the ordinary. "Yes, uh, of course Madam." Ophelia raised a questioning eyebrow before following the other Fatesmiths back into the holdhouse. Haberdeen closed the ventilation door behind her. Amber's pulsed thundered in her ears.

"I need to send a message—" An invisible force clamped her mouth closed.

A deep purple glittered behind Haberdeen's eyes. "I decide when you speak," she said. Anger bubbled beneath her serene smile—it made Amber's skin crawl. "I have spent months trying to save Euryma, months putting witches and wizards in safe stasis, moving them out of harm's way. We have had no help from our so-called 'leaders' and now you've started undoing all that hard work. Why?"

The gag around Amber's mouth vanished. Haberdeen's smile vanished.

"You took people against their will. We were trying to get them back, to free them."

"Free them? From what? Safety?" Haberdeen shook her head. "You don't realize what you've done. Who else was involved? Who do you answer to?"

It was time to figure out how much Haberdeen knew. Amber bit her lip. "I work for High Mage Johannasberg. I'm part of a special task—"

Exquisite fire flashed down her spine. Amber's bones felt like molten metal. She convulsed—tried to scream—

but the invisible gag returned. She arched her back and thrashed against the plates holding her hands. The burning sensation melted away, the gag did too. "Do not lie to me," Haberdeen said. She produced a white dagger from her cloak. It was carved from top to bottom in intricate lines. "There are other ways we can do this."

Amber forced herself to silence. She trembled, terrified of the cost that came with that white blade. "I work for the Directive. It's an organization from King's College."

"Who is the leader?

"The Dean of the College. Other staff have senior roles."

"And who is that?"

Amber struggled to hide her confusion. *What is she talking about? Haberdeen knows Laurefen. They fought in Anderma.*

"Speak, girl." Haberdeen pointed the dagger in her direction. Light glinted off its tip.

"Laurefen! Laurefen Ember."

The knife point retreated. "How did you know where to find the holdhouses?"

"We've been looking for months. I imbued compasses to follow threads of warm air through the ice and snow." She waited for another onslaught of agony. It never arrived. A small bubble of hope ballooned in her chest.

"Interesting," Haberdeen said. "I hadn't thought of heat escaping. We will need to remedy that." She held Amber's eyes. "Which holdhouse will they attack next?"

"I... I can't tell you."

Haberdeen flourished the dagger. "Is this really something you're ready to die for?"

"I can't tell you because I don't know. Laurefen knows where all ten of the holdhouses are. He tells us where to go and when."

"Ten holdhouses, you say?" Haberdeen flashed a tight-lipped smile. "Darling, we have over thirty. I do hope you are not lying to me."

Amber shook her head. "I'm telling you everything I know."

"Very well. How are your Directive defierising my casts?"

"Some of the Directive members learned to mimic flare-flies. They're using that spell to undo them."

Haberdeen nodded. "Impressive." She glanced back down the tunnel. "But there's something I don't understand. If you have been searching for months to locate my holdhouses, following traces of heat on the air, how did you miss the new ones? The ones the LAMPS are making with common tools. Those use much more heat than *anything* inside these walls."

Amber's mind jammed. She couldn't think of a lie. There was no lie to tell. "I lied. We have—"

"You did," Haberdeen said. "And if you lied about that, who knows what else you lied about?"

Amber's voice rose in panic. "It's Mage Raul. We caught Mage Raul in Sabriva. He told us everything."

Haberdeen raised an eyebrow. "Now I know you're lying."

Amber's heart stopped. "It's true."

"Mage Raul is an iron cast, packed away in a basement in Biscay."

"No. It's true." Amber said. "He gave us the locations for the holdhouses."

Haberdeen sneered at her. "If you won't tell me the truth, I will take it." In a flash of movement, the white dagger slid to Amber's chest. It pierced her like a shard of ice.

"I'm telling the truth." Her voice was weak. Everything seemed so large. The room grew dark, Haberdeen's eyes expanded, a green light flared inside them. Amber felt like she was drifting away.

I'm telling the truth.

CHAPTER 29

OPHELIA

THE GIRL'S bone-white body lay on the tunnel floor, her long hair rippled across the ground in a pale fan. Ophelia had seen her fair share of death since joining the Fatesmiths. This felt unnecessary.

"She was a liar," Haberdeen said. There was a dangerous quality to her soft voice. "Although... she did not lie about everything."

"What did she lie about?" Ophelia wasn't sure what to make of Madam Haberdeen. Volatile undercurrents seemed to threaten her calm demeanor.

"Holdhouses," Haberdeen said. "She tried to hide the amount of holdhouses..." she trailed off and closed her eyes. Ophelia waited for her to process the girl's memories. When they opened, they were an unsettling shade of violet. "You told me you fierised Mage Raul."

"I... I beg your pardon?" Ophelia maintained her composure, but it was too late. Something in her expression had slipped.

The tunnel ceiling fractured in a jagged fork. A vein twitched in Haberdeen's jaw. "You said he was in iron," she whispered. Her hands gripped the white dagger, knuckles pale as its blade. "Yet this girl's memories confirm he is on Kingsbreak. With the Directive. Spilling our SECRETS."

The roof shattered with a thunderous crack. Snow and ice buried the outer half of the ventilation tunnel. Ophelia backed away. Haberdeen advanced on her. "WHY DID YOU LIE OPHELIA? WHERE IS YOUR LOYALTY?"

"Madam, please, I swear I didn't know."

A purple blaze pinned Ophelia to the tunnel wall. Haberdeen thrust the dagger into the concrete by her head. The blade cut through it like cheese. "Shall I confirm that?" Haberdeen sliced the wall until the pale blade touched Ophelia's ear.

"Please Madam. I am loyal. I would never—"

Haberdeen drew the knife from the stone and held it to her throat. "You would never what? Lie? Reflect on your next words, Ophelia. They may be your last."

Ophelia closed her eyes and pictured a small campfire. It was a mental exercise she had learned from Haberdeen in their first lessons. She fed her worries into the hungry flames, watched them curl and die. She met Haberdeen's furious gaze. "You are right. I have lied, but every lie has served our cause. I can see you are upset. It must be exhausting to be undermined by the people you're trying to protect. I am not undermining you, Madam. We walk the same path. We want to save Euryma from Remnant Magic."

"They don't understand! They don't realize the danger ahead of them. They undo our work and now this!"

"This?"

Haberdeen leaned back against the tunnel wall, the spell surrounding Ophelia vanished. "High Mage Johannasberg seeks to destroy us—he has the tools to do so."

"How?" Ophelia asked.

"He played us for fools."

"He lied?" A spark of anger ignited in Ophelia's belly. "But no! He swore allegiance after Parteno. Handed us his Cabinet of Mages on a silver platter. He—"

"He went to spectacular lengths to earn our trust," Haberdeen said. "He may profess to be Fatesmith, but it was all so he could learn our secrets. Now he wants to use them against us."

Ophelia wanted to destroy something, to wrap something in air and crush it to dust. *Madam would not approve. Every spell counts.* "Can we stop him?"

Haberdeen closed her eyes, face contorted in concentration. "The High Mage's plan hinges on Sabriva Tower," she said. "If we take the tower, he cannot stop us."

"We're going to wage war on Sabriva?" Ophelia stared at the dead girl's body. "What about her friends? What about the holdhouses?"

"A distraction." Haberdeen's voice sharpened. She stood at the grate, staring into the holdhouse floor. "We've spent far too long trying to save these non-believers. We give them safe refuge, they spit in our faces. Now, our own seek to murder us where we stand. No more! If Johannasberg wants to fight, we will follow his example."

"Madam?"

"Melt them down. All of them. Send word to the others to do the same. Let the Directive uncover their fate for themselves. Perhaps then they will realize the gravity of the situation."

A shiver ran down Ophelia's spine. A thousand thoughts followed, but words escaped her. How long had she complained about Haberdeen's mercy? Now it was gone. Ophelia had gotten exactly what she wanted, and now she had it, she wasn't sure she wanted it. "Yes, Madam." She bowed. "It will be done."

Haberdeen nodded her acknowledgment, then swept out of the tunnel. Ophelia considered the dead girl on the floor. *You thought you were saving these people, now you've sealed their fate.* When she was certain Haberdeen had left, Ophelia wrapped the girl in a ribbon of kinima and led her to the door. Her memories had likely saved their skins, and the entire Dominion of Euryma. *The least I can do is send you south for a proper funeral.*

CHAPTER 30
KATIE

KATIE STOPPED dead in the snow. Amber's thread was gone. Either someone had cut the nima between them, or she was... Katie didn't want to think about it. She couldn't bear the thought of her friend imprisoned in iron.

"Come, Kate, we need to move fast now." Mary-Lou called back. "I think I've found it." She dug out a heavy grate and wrapped it in kinima. The door groaned and sprang open. "Down we go."

The concrete tunnel was the same as the last one. Katie kept her eyes on the ground and followed the muffled footfalls of Mary-Lou's boots. They stopped at the holdhouse entry.

"There are people inside," Mary-Lou whispered.

Katie's stomach tightened. The element of surprise was gone. Every holdhouse crawled with ironhands. "What do we do?"

"We wait for them to check and leave."

They traded shifts watching. until finally, the Fatesmiths packed into the oversized vehicle and disappeared into the snowy haze. Something was wrong. They waited for the rolling door to close, then opened the ventilation grate, its shrill wail echoed in the cavernous room. Katie pulled a thread of photonima into the holdhouse, its faint light illuminated an empty floor. Her stomach sunk. "There's nobody here."

Mary-Lou stepped behind her. "Where are they?"

Katie walked to a center panel. She drew the light in around her, found a switch and flicked it. High above, fluorescent lights flickered to life. The dome's interior was a colossal stretch of empty space. "Gone."

"I don't understand," Mary-Lou said. "Laurefen and Michael scouted every house. Why would they send us to an empty one?"

There was nothing. No place for an ambush. No room to hide. The dome was identical to most of the others they had visited. The only difference was the absence of iron casts. An icy shiver ran down Katie's spine. "Could they have taken them somewhere else? A new holdhouse?"

Mary-Lou didn't respond.

Katie turned to face her. The older woman stared at the ground, a portrait of horror.

"Lou, what's—" Katie froze. She took a step back. Her heart shattered on the iron floor. "No," she whispered. "No. Mom. No." Tears filled her eyes..

Mary-Lou trembled. Head shaking from side to side. "What has she done..."

Katie couldn't speak, couldn't think. She wanted to scream. To cry. To yell. To curse. She opened her mouth, but nothing came out. The entire floor, end to end, was solid iron. The swirling, rutted remains of a thousand melted people.

A fire burned in the corner, yet the room seemed dim. Hopelessness throbbed in Katie's chest like a stumped toe. *We were so close.*

Laurefen stared into the flames. His shadow flickered against the walls. Michael held his head in his hands. Mary-Lou sat opposite. Nobody spoke. There was nothing to say. Months of searching, preparation, action. All undone. It was over. Hours passed. The logs in the fireplace served as the only sign of time. They crumbled to glowing coals, Laurefen added more, they too burned to ashes.

Mary-Lou's soft croak broke the silence. "You checked them all?"

"We did," Laurefen murmured. "It was the same. Melted pools of iron."

"What about Amber?" Katie's voice sounded so small.

"I wish I knew," he replied.

"What... What do we do now?" Mary-Lou asked.

"We take the High Mage up on his offer," Michael said. "Two can play at this game."

Laurefen shook his head. "We can't..."

"We could have stopped this Laurefen. We could have saved them."

"Not like this," Laurefen said.

Michael jumped to his feet, his chair clattering to the ground. "Then we do it a different way. We get more information, and we strike where it hurts." He stormed out the front and slammed the door behind him.

"What does that mean?" Katie asked.

Mary-Lou's eyes widened. "Raul!"

They rushed after him. Their steps echoed off the stonework as they crossed the campus. "What is he going to do?" Katie called from behind. Neither Laurefen nor Mary-Lou answered. When they reached Raul's cell, Katie staggered in shock. Blood covered Raul's face, and an iron chain was wrapped tight around his neck.

"Michael, stop!" Laurefen shouted.

Michael looked up. The chain dropped to Raul's chest with a rattling clink. The bloodied man gasped for air. "HE KNOWS!" Michael roared. "HE KNOWS WHERE TO FIND THEM!" He held a metal spike in his hand, it trembled with rage.

"I don't," Raul said in a hoarse voice. "The Fatesmiths own downtown Biscay. They change to a new inner city location every few months. I can't help."

Michael yanked on the chain and Raul's head jerked back.

"Michael!" Mary-Lou shouted.

Michael wasn't listening. "Tell us everything you know. The buildings they use. The security plan. Everything."

"I know nothin'," Raul repeated.

Michael shook his head. "You're a liar!" In one swift motion, he drove the spike into Raul's knee. Raul roared, his body convulsed against the chains, jaw clenched so tight the veins popped in his neck. "I don't know what happened out there and I don't care. This whole Dominion is going to burn, and I can't wait to see you suffer."

Michael pulled the spike free, bright red blood covered its tip. Katie felt like she was going to pass out.

Raul's eyes were wide and wild. "Remnant Magic is on its way. Its surge will tear the flesh off your bones and you will feel every painful moment."

Laurefen stepped forward, but Michael beat him to it. With a sickening crunch, his enormous fist collided with Raul's face. Raul's head lolled to the side.

Mary-Lou gasped. "You've killed him."

Michael felt for a pulse, then shook his head. "No. Just shut him up."

"We need to bandage that up," Laurefen nodded to his leg. "He's no good to us dead."

"He's no good to us now," Michael replied. He used Raul's torn shirt to wipe the spike clean. "You heard him. He's insane."

"Insane or not, he's all we have," Mary-Lou said. "I'll get the bandages."

Katie ignored the blood and focused on Laurefen. "What if he's right?"

"Right?" Michael cleared his throat. "Right about what?"

"About Remnant Magic." Suddenly, Katie felt very nervous. She shrugged. "If the Smiths had the power to destroy Parteno, we would have lost a long time ago. Surely—"

"Katie," Laurefen interrupted her softly. "That's what they want you to believe. What they've always wanted you to believe."

Katie shook her head. "I'm not so—"

"Don't be an idiot," Michael growled. "That's the first step to getting sucked in."

Katie exhaled. *You're being an idiot.* She pursed her lips tight as Mary-Lou returned with an armful of bandages. She glanced at their faces, her eyes narrowed. "What did I miss?"

"Kate wants to discuss Remnant Magic," Michael said.

Mary-Lou sighed. "Oh dear." She crossed the room and went to work packing Raul's wound. After she'd wrapped it tight, she turned back to Katie. "Haberdeen. The ironhands. They've created a beautiful, logical lie. Don't fall for it. It's fake."

Katie could feel tears coming. "And what if you're wrong?"

"Kate..." Mary-Lou started, but Katie couldn't bear to hear it. She rushed outside, salty droplets rolling down her cheeks. Amber was missing. Her mom was gone. She felt more alone that she could put into words. Cold stars glittered between the clouds overhead.

CHAPTER 31
KATIE

AMBER'S BODY lay on a table. Laurefen said it had arrived in a crate by boat. Michael said the ferryman had passed out when he saw what his cargo held.

Katie's mind was blank. She wasn't speechless, wasn't shocked, she had no emotions at all. She was empty. Ten minutes earlier, things still mattered. Now, they didn't. Part of her had ripped away, something that would never regrow. With trembling hands, Katie touched Amber's fingertips. They felt like ice. Her skin was snow. Her hair robbed of color. "We should have come back for you." Tears streamed from red eyes down wet cheeks. "I'm so sorry."

Mary-Lou hadn't said a word since she brought her in. Katie thought she was in trouble for yesterday's outburst, for considering the possibility of Remnant Magic. That didn't matter anymore. Katie sat with Amber's body for as long as she could stand it.

"I'm sorry Kate," Mary-Lou said. "I know how close you were."

Katie couldn't hear it. Not now. She ignored her. Then,

when the emptiness was too much, she fled. Out the door and into something tall and solid.

"Woah, Kate," Michael said.

Katie tried to sidestep him. Michael wouldn't allow it. He held her still and leaned down to meet her downcast eyes. "This is tragic. First Lisa, now this... It's unfair beyond words." He squeezed her shoulders. "Do you want to talk about it?"

Katie shook her head. Michael's hands kept her steady. "I just want to go."

"This isn't something you beat by yourself." He released her and tilted her chin with his fingers. "When Dreyfus died, I spiralled into a dark place. Laurefen was there. He let me get it all out. The anger, the sorrow, all of it."

Katie nodded. The tears would not stop.

"I'm not saying I'm that person Kate, I can be, but I don't have to be. But there needs to be a person. It's raw now. Nobody expects you to open up just yet. When the time comes, you need to. If you don't, it will destroy you." Michael's eyes were wet. "And Amber wouldn't want that. Nor your mother."

Tears blurred Katie's eyes. She wiped them on her sleeve. "Okay, Michael."

"None of this was your fault. It wasn't. And if Lisa or Amber were here, they'd say the same thing." He placed his hand on her arm. "It's not your fault."

Katie nodded. Michael stepped aside so she could leave. She stumbled down the stairs of the administration building with no idea where her feet would take her. *They killed her. No fierisation. No chance. Just murder. They murdered her; they murdered mom.* The cobblestone paths were slippery, curtains of sleet should have chilled her to the bone, yet she felt nothing. When her wandering legs came to a halt, she stood at the front entry of the Imbusion Lab.

Don't be a fool. Laurefen warned you. You need to stay away from him. Katie's footsteps matched her pounding heart. Up the stairs, down the hall and, with a deep breath, she entered Raul's improvised cell.

He stirred in his iron chains, dry blood matted his beard. "Nice to have a visitor," he said. Some teeth were missing since their last encounter.

"Shut. Your. Wretched. Mouth."

Raul's grin faltered. "That's not very—" A loud slap cut him off, and a distinct hand print bloomed on his cheek. His smile was gone. "You little—"

A second slap swallowed the words. Katie's palm burned. "You're going to shut your gob and listen, or I'm going to remove your face with my hand."

Raul's eyes grew wide and Katie felt a momentary surge of satisfaction. *Michael couldn't shut him up half as well as this.* She dragged a chair across the room and sat in front of him. Fiery rage replaced the emptiness in her chest. "Who leads the Fatesmiths?"

Raul squeezed his eyes, then began blinking rapidly.

"What are you doing?"

"Trying to get my damned vision back."

"Then hurry up," Katie snapped. "Why did the iron-hands get rid of you? You were looking after Haberdeen in Kannidy. Why did she turn on you?"

Raul continued to blink. "Haberdeen never turned on me."

"She's still leading the ironhands."

"That's *not* Haberdeen."

Katie repeated Raul's words in her head. "What?"

"Whoever is leading the Fatesmiths is a fake. An impos-

254

tor. You saw the real thing in Sabriva. She's a shell of herself. A shell of a shell."

"A fake? Then who is it?"

Raul shook his head. "I don't know."

Katie stood up. "That *doesn't* answer my question!"

"I can't answer your question!" Raul shouted. "I took Haberdeen into hiding to help her recover. When I went to confront the liar wearing her face, I was damned near turned to iron."

"What?"

"That's why they got rid of me. Said I was crazy. They told me the guilt of not helping in Anderma had addled my brain." Raul rolled his eyes. "Truth be told, here's a safe place to be."

"What are you talking about?"

"Everyone knows about the old magic protecting Kingsbreak," Raul said. "Here is one of the few places I can sleep knowing I'll wake up in the morning."

Katie sat back down and buried her head in her hands.

"What's going on out there?" Raul asked.

Katie slumped against the chair. "My friend was murdered." The rage drained away, leaving her empty once more. "Her body arrived in a box an hour ago."

"My condolences."

"Like you care."

"Doesn't matter whose side you're on." Raul frowned at her. "It's never good to lose a friend." He leaned forward as far as the chains would allow. "You think Haberdeen did it?"

"I know she did," Katie said. "She had us at the holdhouses near Anabar Bay. "We got out..." A wave of nausea washed over her at the thought. She took a long breath until it settled. "She didn't."

255

"That wasn't the real Haberdeen."

"Then who is it? Ward? He disguised himself as John for months."

"Your boy Declan killed Ward." Raul frowned. "I don't know. Still, it's not like the Fatesmiths to return bodies. Did they send a message?"

"I don't know."

Raul frowned. "What... what did your friend's body look like?"

Katie shot to her feet and raised her palm. "You foul-mouthed—"

The color drained from Raul's face. "I don't mean any disrespect. It's... well... was your friend pale? So pale, almost transparent?"

Katie paused. Her chest swelled with emotion. She nodded slowly. "Does that mean something to you?"

Raul's bloodied face darkened. "She used the knife."

"Knife?"

"Haberdeen has a dagger that takes memories. It uses green magic, like your boy. You stab someone, it absorbs their blood, you can see everything they've done. Once their memories are gone, it leaves a drained corpse."

"The white dagger. She showed us..." Katie paled. "You're saying that whoever killed Amber, they have her memories now?"

Raul nodded.

"So, whoever she is, she knows everything about fierisation? And everything about the Directive? She knows who I am, who you are. Everything?"

Raul nodded again.

Katie collapsed into her chair. *Amber knew about the High Mage's plan.* Her blood ran cold. If he was telling the truth, they may have lost their only chance at winning. "I have to go," she said.

"Good luck, girl," Raul said. And in that moment, he seemed genuine.

"Kate!" Mary-Lou wore a thick coat and held a large red umbrella. "Where were you? I've been looking everywhere."

"Lou, I need to talk to you, and Laurefen and Michael."

"Katie, dear, it's been a rough—"

"Now!"

Mary-Lou's back stiffened. "Of course, dear, of course. Laurefen and Michael are still inside."

Katie climbed the stone stairs two at a time. They rushed through the administration lobby, down a spacious corridor, past the room housing Amber's body and into Laurefen's study. Michael stood at the window, Laurefen sat at his driftwood desk. The deep creases in his brow smoothed when he looked up. "Hello Katie." His eyes darted to Mary-Lou, then back to her. "How are you?"

Katie wasted no time. She told them about the interrogation at Anabar Bay, the threats Haberdeen had made, and the white dagger that transformed blood into memories. When she finished, the room fell silent.

"Do you suspect this dagger killed Amber?" Laurefen asked.

Katie nodded. "I heard the knife's victims lose all color."

"Did Haberdeen tell you that?"

Katie met Laurefen's eyes with a stubborn stare. "Mage Raul did."

"You went to Raul?" Michael said. "What were you thinking?"

Katie turned her steely gaze to him. "What I was thinking was that Amber is dead and we know nothing."

"Raul is a Fatesmith, Katie, a Fatesmith! He'll feed you lies until the world stops turning."

"He's not an ironhand! Haberdeen has been replaced with a fake. He was the only one who noticed, so they forced him out. They tried to fierise him, but he escaped."

"Or so he says," Mary-Lou said softly.

"This is what we warned you about," Laurefen said. "Raul knows how to use your emotions against you?"

"For what purpose?" Katie said. "What would he have to gain by telling me this?"

"We can't trust him," Michael said.

Katie stamped her foot. "If they used the dagger on Amber, the ironhands know everything. They know about us, about Raul." She turned to Laurefen. "They know about the High Mage's plan for Sabriva Tower."

Laurefen leaned back in his chair. "An unsettling possibility," he said. "Yet a knife that turns memories into blood... I can't even imagine how that would work."

"Raul told me it uses green magic," Katie said.

"Of course he did." Michael muttered.

Laurefen interrupted the dagger on Katie's tongue. "We cannot risk it," he said. "As much as I hate to admit it, Johannasberg's plan may be our only hope. If there is the slightest chance that Haberdeen knows about it, we must act fast."

"How?" Katie asked.

Laurefen stood up. "I will talk to Mage Raul myself. Let me see if I can get to the bottom of his tale."

"And me?"

"You've done well." Laurefen said. "You've done

enough. Go and process what has happened today. Lou will go with you while we work out the next step."

"But..." Katie searched their faces. Mary-Lou watched her with concern. *They think you're a stupid little girl who knows nothing.* Disappointment ballooned inside her. *They're never going to listen.* "I'm... okay. I'm fine. It's fine Lou, I'm okay by myself."

"Keep away from Raul," Michael said. He looked her up and down, then followed Laurefen out the door.

Mary-Lou remained behind. "Do you want to talk?"

"No." Katie left the room before she could respond. Eyes on feet, she wandered back to her home in the Academy Village. In the frigid evening air, the reality of Amber's loss returned—and with it, a fresh wave of tears. *I wish you were here*, Katie thought. *You would believe me.*

CHAPTER 32
KATIE

THEY HELD the funeral the following morning. Mary-Lou had prepared Amber's body; Michael had carried her outside. She was beautiful, dressed in a silk gown with small white flowers braided into her long hair. Laurefen spoke of her bravery, her generational talent imbuing items in creative ways, her insatiable desire to do the right thing. Michael made them laugh. Mary-Lou made them cry. When it was Katie's turn to speak, she could barely manage the words.

"You are my best friend," she whispered. "I love you." The soft goodbye amidst a torrent of tears was all she could manage. She sat on the cold grass as the last remnants of the pyre collapsed. A thin trail of smoke curled into the bleak sky. "I'm sorry," Katie said to the lapping waves.

Mary-Lou soon joined her on the hill. The two women waited in silence until the fire burned out.

"I let her mother down," Mary-Lou said at last. "I promised I would protect her daughter. I failed."

Katie nodded. There was nothing more to say.

"Laurefen and Michael finished with Raul this morning. They suspect you're right. Haberdeen—"

"It wasn't Haberdeen," Katie muttered.

Mary-Lou pursed her lips, then continued. "Just listen Katie. If Hab—"

"Not Haberdeen."

A shadow crossed Mary-Lou's face. She took a long breath. "If whoever it *is* knows about Sabriva, we need to act."

Katie swallowed. "Act? How?"

"High Mage Johannasberg has the means to stop this."

"Laurefen's changed his tune then?" Katie's insides lurched. Part of her agreed every Fatesmith needed to die. Another part couldn't stomach being responsible for that much death.

Mary-Lou nodded. "He's seriously considering it. We had time on our side before. Now we don't and we are faced with an impossible choice."

An impossible choice. Mary-Lou had used the same words a lifetime ago when deciding the fate of surprising college application. Declan's application. Katie bit her lip. "What about Declan Moore?"

A long silence passed between them. "An interesting possibility." Before Mary-Lou could continue, Michael called out from behind. They turned as he ran to greet them. "What is it?" Mary-Lou asked.

"Massalia," Michael said between deep breaths. He leaned forward and sucked in the morning air. "Massalia is gone, destroyed by ironhands."

"What? When?"

"Word's just come through now. The entire city wiped clean off the map. Levelled just like Parteno."

Mary-Lou responded, but Katie wasn't listening. The

words of the auburn-haired woman in the holdhouse were bouncing around her head. *Have you seen Parteno? A whole city turned to ashes. Now our flashfinders tell us that Massalia is next.* She looked up at Mary-Lou and Michael. "It's not the Fatesmiths," she said. "It's Remnant Magic."

"Kate, please." Mary-Lou pleaded. "Not again."

"The woman at Anabar Bay. She predicted this. She told us Massalia was next."

"That confirms it," Michael said. "Of course, they knew it would happen. It's their doing."

"If it is Remnant Magic... How do we stop it?" Katie's thoughts were too fast for her to catch up. "I don't think we can. I don't think anyone can, except maybe Declan? Who knows? It doesn't matter, we need to contact—"

"Enough!" Mary-Lou stamped her foot. "Katie, they have sucked you in. Your little chat with Raul has you caught in his web of lies. You need to stop this nonsense talk now. You're going to get yourself killed."

Katie blushed crimson. "But Lou!"

"No!" Mary-Lou snapped. "I've already lost Amber; I will not lose you to some foolhardy idea about something that isn't real!"

Katie fell silent. She gazed out to where Amber's body used to be and clenched her teeth. "No, Lou. You're the one being a fool." She watched the smoke rise from the broken pyre. "Amber's dead—"

"Don't you dare bring Amber into this?"

"You brought her into it." Katie said. "She's a part of it. She was murdered because we left her behind. We should have gone to find her, but we didn't. We were waiting, watching, like we always do!"

"We did what we could with what we knew," Mary-Lou said.

"WE SHOULD HAVE DONE MORE!"

Mary-Lou stepped back, stunned by Katie's outburst. Michael scowled down at her. "Katie."

"No. I'm done. I'm finished with the Directive! I'm done with your inability to accept the truth in front of your eyes!"

"You're abandoning us?" Mary-Lou said. "You're abandoning the cause your mother gave her life for?"

Tears filled Katie's eyes. "My mother didn't die for you to bury your head in the sand." She stood and walked down the hill. Mary-Lou called after her, but Katie refused to look back. She shook her braid loose, then rushed towards the Imbusion Lab.

Raul's eyes narrowed as she entered. "Back to slap me s'more?"

Katie pulled up the same chair from the previous day. "Tell me about Remnant Magic."

Raul raised a questioning eyebrow. "What do you want to know?"

"What is it?"

"It's all in the name."

Katie gritted her teeth. "Okay, so how does that destroy a city?"

"Well, it's like a raindrop." Raul shrugged. "A single raindrop is nothing. Put enough together and you get a flood. Same thing. If everyone is pulling on nima for every minor task for a thousand years, it builds up. Enough magic in one place—things turn violent. Nobody can stop a millennium of magical build up. Nobody."

Katie sat in silence.

"You don't believe me."

Katie turned from the chair and rummaged through a nearby cabinet. With shaking hands, she found what she was looking for, a pair of bolt-cutters. Raul paled as she advanced on him. "Uh, what're you... stop. Stop!"

"Shut up and listen," Katie said, positioning the blade to his chains. "I need to talk to Haberdeen. The real Haberdeen. If I let you go, can you help me?"

Raul's mouth dropped open. "Are you crazy? Why would I leave? This is the safest place for me."

"Do you think you can hide here forever?"

Raul stared at her. "Maybe."

Katie's gaze darted to the door. She knew Mary-Lou and Michael would check in on Raul at any minute. "If you're right. Remnant Magic is coming and there is nothing any of us can do to stop it. If it doesn't get you here, the ironhands will. If the Fatesmiths have Amber's memories, they know you've betrayed them."

"So, my option is to leave and die or stay and die? Girl, you're not too convincing."

"Once we find Haberdeen, you can both leave. You'll be free to go wherever you want. How's that for convincing?"

"I don't believe you."

"Damn it, Raul, we don't have time. Are you in?"

Raul pursed his lips. "Why?"

"Why what?" Katie snapped. Somewhere in the distance, a door closed.

"I'm not going anywhere with you until you tell me why you need to talk to Haberdeen."

Katie rolled her eyes. "Because Haberdeen is with Ava and Ava can find Declan."

"Declan? You mean the kid who knifed her in the first place?"

"He's the only one strong enough to stop the storm."

"And how do you expect me to find her? I don't exactly have a magical bond that points me in Haberdeen's direction."

"But you have a phone number. Haberdeen had a LAMP phone that night in Kannidy. Ava took that phone."

Raul raised a single eyebrow. "You're risking my life on some LAMP doodad?"

A door down the hall banged open. Katie's eyes shot to the entrance. "Time's up. What will it be?"

Raul's eyes darted from Katie to the bolt cutters. "I might just kill you as soon as you cut me loose."

"I doubt it," Katie said. "Ava will bring Haberdeen to me. Not to you. If you want her, you need me, and once we get her, you're free. I swear it."

Footsteps clattered down the linoleum floors as Katie cut the chains free. "I'm going to regret this," Raul growled.

They dashed through an adjoining door and out a back exit, just in time to hear Michael's shout of surprise.

"Where are we going?" Raul whispered.

"To Cedrus." Katie pointed to the ancient cedar that marked the only spot on the island Kingsbreak where witches and wizards could create Openings. "From there, wherever you want. As long as it has a phone."

"WELL, THIS IS DELIGHTFUL." Katie looked from the crowded bar to Raul's bruised face. "I can't believe you chose Ursaria."

"If I recall correctly, you said our destination didn't matter as long as it had a phone." Raul took a long gulp of his smokey drink and wiped his beard. "What's wrong with Ursaria?"

"It's in Iberia. Vedmark is north of the Dominion. Why would you take us south?"

"South is safe, no Directive, no Fatesmiths."

Katie bit her tongue. "Fine."

"If anyone should complain, it's me," Raul muttered. "You said you'd get me to Haberdeen. Fifty phone calls later, I'm still stuck with you."

"Then leave."

Raul shook his head. "You owe me. I got you out, I gave you that number. You're going to get Haberdeen back. You gave me your word."

Katie wanted to scream. *This is not how this was supposed to go.* Over the road, a lone streetlight illuminated a

266

payphone. "Well, I guess I'll try again. The sooner we part ways, the better. For both of us."

"Don't wander too far. I'm watching you."

"Yeah, whatever," she muttered.

Ursaria's reputation was one of hot days and warm nights. Tonight, that reputation did not match reality. Katie began shivering the moment she stepped outside. She wrenched the phone off its holder and mashed the number she had memorized onto the keypad. *C'mon Ava. Pick up. Pick up, pick up, pick up.* The call rang out. A loud beep cued her to hang up and try again. *Pick up the phone.* Three more attempts and her hands were numb. Katie tossed the receiver back on its hook, then stopped dead. Four ironhands walked down the path. She held her breath, willing them to keep walking. Instead, they entered the bar. *Damn you Raul, why did you bring us to Ursaria?*

A looptap prickled her palm. It was Mary-Lou. *Please come back. Laurefen is meeting with Johannasberg tomorrow morning. We need you.* Katie considered replying, then thought better of it. She brushed off her concerns and stepped into utter chaos. Bar stools flew around the room like a whirlwind. Raul stood on one side, surrounded by ironhands, the rest of the bar's patrons huddled opposite. A golden tsunami sloshed past her. Katie frowned as the wave threw a blackcoat into a wall. *Is that beer? What does it matter? Focus Kate!* The remaining ironhands pushed Raul into a corner. Nobody noticed her arrival.

I should run. I've got Ava's number. It's as much as he deserves. One of the Fatesmiths thrust a shimmering square towards Raul. He dodged right. A sharpened pool cue speared his shoulder. Raul dropped to a knee.

Katie clenched her fists and stepped into the battle. First, she took control of the wave of alcohol. A burly blackcoat drew the pool cue back and threw it again. Katie caught it an inch from Raul's chest and snapped it in two. The Fatesmith spun to face her as a frozen orb of beer flattened him. That got the other's attention. Katie threw out both arms. A battalion of glass bottles surged from behind her. The ironhands hit the floor and crawled to safety as expensive drinks exploded all around them. Katie drew the shards of glass together into a razor-sharp tornado.

Something latched onto her ankle. Katie skidded to the ground; glass tinkled to the floor. A Fatesmith had wrapped aeronima up her leg. He charged forwards, then stumbled, a splintered pool cue protruded from his chest. The man collapsed, face down, in front of her. Raul climbed to his feet with a bloody smile.

Katie picked up where she left off. A vortex of spinning glass formed in the bar's centre. She directed it into the remaining Fatesmiths. They retreated into Raul's waiting hands. With a twist of his wrist, he threw one into the whirlwind. Katie turned away as the glass engulfed him. The other made a dash for the door. Raul caught her with a wave of beer and began forcing the liquid inside her. The poor woman tried to cover her mouth; Raul let her drown where she stood.

Katie watched in horror. *This isn't right.* "Stop it!" She screamed. Raul didn't listen. Katie hurled a chair into his back, knocking him forward. The fountain spilled all over the floor. "I said stop!"

A silver square filled her vision. Raul dived and knocked her to the ground. The beer-soaked woman turned from them and fled out the door.

Katie glared at him. "You didn't have to kill them!"

Raul rolled over and groaned. "You're welcome."

"I'm welcome? Don't you mean *thank you*? I saved your skin!"

Raul climbed to his feet. "And I—" he touched his shoulder.

"What is it?"

Raul pulled his shirt to the side. Katie gasped. The top of his arm was metallic grey. He glared at her. "Look at what you've done, girl."

Katie rose to her feet. "Excuse me!"

"We should have stayed on the island."

"Whose stupid idea was it to come to Ursaria?" She imitated his deep, accented voice. "Let's go to Iberia, no Fatesmiths there." She rolled her eyes. "Don't blame me for your bad ideas." She breathed deeply through her nose, then nodded to his shoulder. "Does it hurt?"

"It's not the pain I'm concerned about."

"What does that mean?"

Raul dropped his shirtsleeve. "It means until someone rids me of this curse, I can't do magic."

"What?"

"And the only ones that can get rid of it, as you just saw, are the people who want me dead."

Katie groaned. "And that means you can't make Openings any more..."

Raul laughed bitterly. "You said we needed to go north?"

"Don't say it."

"I hope those short legs like walking."

Katie buried her head in her hands. *Damn it, Raul! Why did you bring us to Ursaria?*

Empty farmland stretched out on either side of the dirt road. Plowed fields in all directions. Katie scanned the horizon for any sign of movement. Raul occupied himself with her backpack.

"I thought you said you had food." He tossed a handful of carrots to the ground and continued digging.

"That is food." Katie snapped. "I'm terribly sorry. I didn't have time to pack a gourmet lunch." They had been walking for hours. Her legs were on fire. "Aren't you glad you took us to Iberia?"

Raul didn't respond. His focus was on the bag.

"That's all there is."

Raul scowled at her. "What's the point of a bag o' food if there's no food in it?"

"There is food."

"I don't eat rabbit food."

Katie tried not to growl. *It's like babysitting a toddler.* "If you're not hungry enough to eat carrots, then you can't be that hungry."

Raul tossed the bag into her chest. "Never mind."

She bit her tongue and shouldered the backpack. He limped beside her in silence. The wound from the spike in his leg had healed, but it had not healed well. "How's the shoulder?"

Raul muttered something under his breath.

"Pardon?"

"I said it's fine."

"How does it work?" she asked. "Fierisation."

Raul looked at her, eyes empty. "What do you mean?"

"I mean, iron resists magic, yet here you are doing spells that create iron out of nothing." Katie shrugged. "I know it uses inverted weaves."

"I'm not showing you how to do it."

"Like you even could."

Raul didn't reply. He just walked. They had caught the train at first, then spent an hour running from Fatesmiths. There were eyes everywhere. After that, they resorted to stealing bikes, until Katie blew a tire eight miles from the nearest town. Now they were stuck walking. Katie gave up on a response and focused on the road ahead.

"We came up with fierisation as a shield." Raul kept his eyes forward while he spoke. "You College people think of it like a weapon, but it was never supposed to be that. It's a safe state, safe from magic, from Remnant Magic."

Katie frowned. "Safe how?"

"Remnant Magic can't hurt you if you're fierised. It will undo the spell, but it won't kill you, won't turn you to a cinder."

"I can't believe it's real."

"Welcome to reality." Raul limped onward. "You live in your perfect bubble while a third of the world is gone."

"What?" Katie stopped in her tracks, but Raul didn't. She hurried after him. "No. That can't be real. If a third of the world is gone, why hasn't it made it into the papers? Or on the news? Where are the refugees or survivors?"

"Survivors?" Raul barked a bitter laugh. "What survivors?"

"But... Surely someone would notice—"

"Noticing isn't the same as caring."

"What does that mean?"

Raul stopped and turned to her. "It means your precious leaders have known for years. They've known the powerless regions have been torn to pieces. They've known LAMPs have been dying by the millions. They don't care. Because caring would mean to stop using magic. And that's

what makes Euryma great. Magic." He spat on the ground
and kept walking.

They reached the top of a hill; more fields greeted them.
The path wound down a slow curve to a narrow stone
bridge. It looked ill-used and centuries old. For the first
time in days, Raul smiled.

"You know that bridge?" Katie asked.

"I don't give a damn about the bloody bridge. It's what
goes under it."

"Water?"

"That river runs north."

Katie glanced down at her tired legs. "We're just going
to float up the river to Vedmark?"

"You've got a better idea."

"No."

"You want to keep on walking?"

"Not in the slightest."

Raul nodded to the river. "Then shut your mouth and
do what I say. It's time to build a raft."

———

The raft Katie built was neither good nor bad. It just was.
Conjured from a fallen cottonwood tree, it was the plainest
raft to ever exist. Raul barked instructions as branches
shaved themselves into panels and slid together while sap
filled the gaps. The end-result was long enough for both to
lay toe-to-toe and wide enough for Katie to spread her arms
without touching either side.

They boarded on the western shore and a rode north on
a thick strand of hydronima. After a few hours, the gentle
swaying was having an undesirable effect. "I think I need
some dry-land time," Katie said.

"No time," Raul replied. "You'll be fine. If you're gonna be sick, do it over the edge."

Fluffy clouds decorated the azure sky. Katie tried to find pictures in their shapes, but her stomach refused to be ignored. It didn't take long for her to lean over and add to the river.

"Delightful," Raul said.

Katie glowered at him, then vomited some more. She lay back quivering, her stomach muscles ached. The fresh air cooled her head. Her eyelids felt heavy. Everything slowed to nothing.

She woke up shivering in the dark. Clouds hid the stars from view. The only sound was the gentle lap of the tide breaking around them. Raul sat with a small phone in his hand. Its tiny blue screen reflected in his eyes.

"You've had a phone this entire time?"

Raul pocketed the device. "Look who's not dead after all."

"Why did you make me use payphones?"

"Why would I share my phone?" Darkness shrouded Raul's face. Katie could not tell if he was joking or not.

"Still, we could have been calling Ava this whole time." She scanned the darkened horizon. "What time is it, anyway?"

"Nearly midnight," Raul said.

"Midnight? Where are we?"

"Habsburg. Fatesmith territory. The further we can travel under cover of night, the better."

Katie rolled into a seated position. "And then what?"

"We continue north, through Clovin and out of Euryma. You fulfil your side of the bargain. I get Haberdeen back."

Katie considered his silhouette. "Do you love her?"

It was too dark to see Raul's expression. When he spoke, his voice was soft. "It's not that type of relationship."

"What kind of relationship is it?"

"You ask a lot of questions."

Katie shrugged. "Apparently, I have a lot to learn."

Raul chuckled but said no more. He returned to his small phone's screen; the sounds of the river filled the silence.

"You're going to run the battery dead doing that," Katie said.

"Not this one." Raul's eyes never left the screen. "Imbued to run forever. It will call anyone from anywhere too."

"Oh." The darkness masked her embarrassment. She considered him, his face illuminated by the phone's blue light. "How did you end up being a Fatesmith?"

Raul sighed, a long, exasperated sigh. "If I answer, will you go back to sleep and leave me alone?"

"Deal."

He switched off the phone. The night went black. "Where to start? I was excluded from Euryma's Magical-Education system. They told me my potential was dangerous. They told me *I* was dangerous. I applied for private tutelage, but my family was poor. We couldn't afford the asking price. Then, a girl came to me, freshly expelled from college herself. She wanted to work with people like me, but she had no experience and nobody to vouch for her. She convinced my parents that I would be her first student— her lab rat—and in return, the instruction would cost nothing."

"And you took it?"

Raul nodded. "Of course. She took me under her wing. There were mistakes, growing pains, but I learned to manipulate and mimic. In the end, we departed as friends. My teacher used the experience to make a reputable name for herself."

"I don't see what that has to do with you being a Fatesmith?"

"After I finished my formal education, I traveled. I made my way to Briton, west of Euryma, where I found my love. One thing led to another, and we married. Not long after, we learned we couldn't have children. My Kairi wanted them so bad, so I told her I'd come back here, back to Euryma to find magic to heal her."

Katie waited for him to go on. Water sloshed across the raft. In the distance, an owl called to the night. Raul didn't speak. "What happened?" she whispered.

"I got what I needed, but when I returned..." He shrugged. "Everything was gone."

"What do you mean?"

"I mean something massive wiped Briton off the map. I went searching for answers. Between stories of monsters that swallowed entire cities and demonic curses, I found nothing of substance. Nothing until my old teacher reached out with a magic dagger and word of Remnant Magic."

Katie's jaw dropped. "Haberdeen was your teacher."

"And I became a Fatesmith." Raul paused. "I answered your question. Go to sleep, girl. We have a long journey ahead of us."

Katie bit back a flood of questions. She stared at the starless sky and her mind ran wild. *Maybe the Fatesmiths aren't evil after all.* She peeked at Raul, a motionless silhouette in the darkness. *At least not all of them.*

CHAPTER 34

AVA

A GENTLE BUZZ shattered the silence in the cramped cabin bedroom. Ava stirred, rolled to the side, then opened her eyes. The sound persisted, as it had intermittently for the past three days. Grigory suspected rattlemites in the floorboards. Ava wasn't so sure. The soft vibration ceased the moment she climbed out of bed.

"Morning, Ava," Grigory said when she reached the kitchen. He sat in his nightclothes, drinking from a cracked mug. Last night's dinner simmered on the woodstove. "You rested well."

"I could have slept until midday if that noise hadn't woken me up."

"Rattlemites." Grigory said. "It is on my list."

"No rush, Ory." Ava helped herself to an empty bowl. "I don't see Misha."

"He's gone to the city for supplies."

"That is good of him." Ava buttered a slice of bread, then spooned herself some stew.

Grigory smiled as she took a seat beside him. "You are moving better. Your body healed well."

276

Ava winked. "I guess I'm just lucky."

Grigory had always dreamed of farming his own plot and Ava had done everything in her power to push the odds in his favor, an unspoken thank-you for his kindness. But Grigory was growing old, and Ava could see it in the broken posts and garden weeds. She hefted a roll of wire over her shoulder and started down to the paddocks.

She began with the fences, then raked a blanket of pine needles into the compost. After that, she headed to the vegetable patch, weedsack and fork in hand.

"Look who's out and about," Misha called from atop Grigory's yellow cart. "You've been busy."

"We can't all go gallivanting off to the City." Ava poked out her tongue. "Someone around here has to keep this place in order."

Misha laughed. "That's rich after a single morning's work."

Ava scratched behind Trevor's ears. The donkey nuzzled her cheek in return. "Any news from the City?"

"Not really. Repairs to the Steward's Hall are finished. They're still saying it was a structural failure." Misha rolled his eyes at these last words. "There's a bit of panic about the Void. Whispers that it's growing."

Ava said nothing, uncertain how much the Emissary wanted her to reveal. After a momentary pause, she changed the subject. "What about Haberdeen? Any changes?"

"Still locked away in the cells beneath the Knight's barracks."

"And Declan?"

Misha's lips thinned. "The Southern Warlock is tending goats in the mountains. Why do you care?"

"It was an accident."

"He could've killed you."

"They threw the witch responsible for his parent's death in front of him. If anything, it was Rasporvin's fault, his stupid idea to put them in the same room." Ava dropped to her knees and started pulling weeds. "You shouldn't have hit him."

"He shouldn't have hit you."

"Drop it, Mish. I told you. It was an accident." She tossed a handful of dandelions into the weed sack. "Once you've packed away the cart, you should come be helpful."

"Packing the cart away is helpful."

Ava cleared two garden beds before Misha returned. Together, they cleared the final three. Misha fetched mulch; Ava spread it. By the time they finished, the sky was turning purple. Ava stepped back and clapped her hands. "That is so much better."

Misha arched his back with a loud crack. "The goats will be thrilled next time they break out."

"Ah-hah, but they won't!" Ava pointed to the fences. "Because I fixed those first."

"Just a regular farmer, aren't you?" Misha teased as they walked inside for the nightly ritual. Goat stew with Grigory, who had spent the day tending his flock. The food tasted the same, delicious, but the same. Then afterwards, they filled the old bronze bathtub that washed away the ache of hard work.

Ava had just finished dressing when the persistent buzz return. *Cursed rattlemites.* She tracked the noise to the room's edge when it stopped. *Must've scared it off.*

She turned to go, then it started again, like a bee stuck

in a jacket. Ava rushed back to the corner and tugged on a strand of Luck—it led her to the bag she'd brought back from Sabriva. Something small vibrated in the front pocket.

Inside was something Ava had forgotten existed. Haberdeen's silver LAMP phone. It fell silent.

Ava flicked the screen open. *Three-hundred and eighty-nine missed calls.* She glanced at the door. *How are calls even getting through?* She owned a LAMP phone herself, but that only worked in Euryma. Ava sat against the door and returned the most recent call. A voice answered instantly. "Hello?"

Ava didn't reply.

"My name is Katie Hall. A man named Raul gave me this number. I need to speak to Ava. Ava from... Vedmark. Is she there?"

"Katie?"

"Ava?"

Ava bit her lip. "Yeah... Katie... what are you doing? What are you doing with Raul?"

"Ava, I... It's a mess, everything's going wrong. I need you to bring Declan to me, and Haberdeen too."

"Bring Haberdeen back? Why?"

"I made a deal with Raul."

"Why?" Ava repeated. She didn't know what else to say. "Katie, what's going on?"

There was a long pause. When Katie spoke again, she sounded on the verge of tears. "Ava, I've left the Directive. They aren't seeing straight. They don't understand the danger of Remnant Magic. Someone pretending to be Haberdeen killed my friend Amber. Now that person knows that the Directive want to help the High Mage kill them all, and she killed all the people in holdhouses because—"

"Katie. Slow down."

279

"I can't," Katie said. "There's no time. I need you to bring Haberdeen, and I need you to bring Declan. He's the only one that might be able to stop the storms."

"I..." Ava sighed. "I don't know where Declan is."

"What do you mean?"

"It's complicated."

"Ava, I don't care about complicated. Don't you hear me? Remnant Magic isn't a story. It's real. We *need* Declan."

A loud knock at the door made Ava jump. "You are talking to someone," Grigory said.

"I'm talking to myself," Ava squeaked. "But I'm, uh, still getting dressed."

"Oh," Grigory suddenly sounded very flustered. "No worry. Just checking. Sorry."

Ava waited until Grigory's footsteps were gone, then dropped her voice to a whisper. "Okay, okay. I can't help you with Declan, but I may be able to get Haberdeen. Where are you?"

"There's a settlement in the Northern Remnants called Bruxelle. Do you know it?"

"I do."

"Meet us there. Your phone is imbued so you can reach us at any time." Katie's voice cracked, and she coughed. "We're running out of time, Ava. You need to find Declan and Haberdeen. We'll meet you at Bruxelle."

Ava hung up the phone, then stared at it. The mere mention of Remnant Magic summoned unwelcome memories of Parteno. She collapsed on the bed and stared out the window, where a crescent moon sailed over a sea of clouds. *How on earth am I going to find Declan? And get Haberdeen out from the Knight's barracks?* As she considered the predicament, an idea popped into her head. An idea so outlandish, she couldn't help but chuckle. It was a bold plan—one she could not do alone. *Misha's going to think I'm crazy.*

"You are crazy." Misha sat at the window, shaking his head. "You are actually crazy. Tell me you're kidding."

"Do I look like I'm kidding?"

"No. But stealing Haberdeen from the Knights of Despair? The idea is ludicrous. You're going to get yourself killed." He looked pale, though Ava wasn't sure if it was because of her or the brilliant moonlight.

"All we need is a little Luck."

"A lot of Luck."

"And that's why I need your help!"

Misha ran a hand through his hair. "You're serious?"

"Deadly."

He leaned back in his armchair, shaking his head. Grigory's soft snores drifted through the walls. After an enormous stretch of silence, Misha sighed. "You're doing this, with or without me, aren't you?"

"I am."

Misha groaned. "I suppose I don't have a choice. I assume you have a more detailed plan."

Ava smiled. "Actually, I do."

"And?"

"We're going to need manure. And copper. Lots of copper."

"Copper?"

"*Lots* of copper."

CHAPTER 35

KATIE

THE MORNING AIR was thick with woodsmoke and the mouth-watering scent of baked goods. Elderly neighbors talked over a fence; a young couple walked their overly fluffy dog. Katie sat in the shadows, admiring Laroa's small-town charm.

Raul stood a pace behind her. "We're too exposed," he said. "Let's get breakfast and get back on the river."

"Agreed." Katie's call with Ava had left an anxious kernel in her stomach. *What do we do without Declan?* She brushed the thought aside. A looptap tickled her palm. Mary-Lou, again. *Check the news*, she said. *We need to talk.* Katie ignored that too. Something guttural rumbled behind her. She scowled at Raul. "Was that your stomach?"

"And rightfully so," he said.

Katie sniffed the air. "Come on, whatever is cooking, it's coming from that way."

They exited a walkway into a row of shopfronts, including a news booth. Something caught Katie's eye and her appetite vanished. "Raul. Look."

Reginald Johannasberg stared at them from a half-dozen newspapers. The headlines left little to the imagination. 'Dominion Mourns High Mage', 'Age of Johannasberg Over', 'Assassination in Sabriva Square'. Katie turned to Raul. "He's dead."

Raul's eyes narrowed. "Is this your lot?"

"I beg your pardon?"

"The Directive. Did they kill him?"

"Why would we do that?"

Raul checked over his shoulder, then bent down to whisper in her ear. "Because the High Mage was a Fatesmith."

"What?" Kate shook her head. "No. No, he wasn't. No. He had a plan. The Fatesmiths did this. They would know that he was a threat."

"What does that mean?" Raul asked, suddenly suspicious.

Katie pursed her lips and shrugged. She had not told Raul about the High Mage's plan—she had not planned to —but it seemed there was no other choice. "Johannasberg figured out how to use Sabriva Tower as a weapon against the Fatesmiths." Katie hesitated. "Amber knew some of the specifics. The ironhands got her memories." She nodded at the newspapers. "Now he's dead."

"He double-crossed us?"

He tried to. Katie felt a pinch of guilt.

Raul picked up a newspaper and flicked to the major story. "No mention of Remnant Magic or Fatesmiths. They're blaming a group of LAMPs called the Young Scholars."

Katie reached for a newspaper of her own, caught sight of movement in the news booth's reflection, and hit the ground on instinct. A fierisation square shattered the store. Magazines and newspapers went everywhere.

Katie rolled away. Raul turned around as if nothing had happened. "Why hello there, Benjamin."

"Shut your mouth, Raul. You're coming with me."

"You could have asked," he said. "You know some poor sap's gonna have to clean all this up."

Katie slipped into the man's blind spot as Raul leant down and picked up some newspapers. They had discussed this. He would distract, she would attack. Raul went on picking up magazines, moving left, moving the man's attention further from her. The blackcoat watched him like a hawk. "I'm taking you back," he said. "Haberdeen knows you're roaming free, there's nowhere in the Dominion you can hide." He raised his hands; Raul raised a finger.

"Don't you remember what happened last time you tried to one-up me?"

"It's different this time," the Fatesmith said. "I know you can't do magic."

Raul waved his finger. "You should have waited for help."

"You're my mess to clean up."

"Mess?" Raul took another sideways step. "I prefer the term bojangle."

Bojangle. The word was her cue, and Katie whipped a club of geonima into the back of the man's head. He stumbled into Raul's waiting fist. Katie wrapped him in air before he landed. Raul nodded to the walkway. "Well done, girl. Let's get him off the street."

Katie nodded. Another looptap pricked her palm. *It's urgent. We need to talk.* She ignored Mary-Lou and wrapped the unconscious ironhand in a hammock of kinima. As soon as they were out of sight, Raul unbuttoned the man's coat and searched his pockets. He found a small LAMP phone and crushed it beneath his boot.

"What are you doing?" Katie asked.

"Haberdeen imbued these. The real Haberdeen." Raul continued his search. "Saved us adding more Remnant Magic to the world every time we wanted to talk."

"So why did you destroy it?"

"Because I'm betting that's how he found us so fast. I don't know how these LAMP gadgets work, but there's no other way he'd know we were traveling by water."

Katie considered the ruined mess of plastic and metal. "How many others are there?"

"At least another dozen." Raul finished his search. "The sooner we get out of the Dominion, the better. But first, let's wake young Benjamin up and find out what he knows."

"Are you sure?"

Raul nodded. "Just keep him bound. I assume you want to leave him alive."

Katie raised an eyebrow. "Uh. Obviously."

"Then hide somewhere. Wouldn't do you any good for him to recognize you."

It was sound advice. Katie ducked behind a large bin, then pulled a stream of cool water from the air. She wound the hydronima up Benjamin's sleeves and around his neck. He woke with a start. "What are you doing?" He strained to see her, but the compressed air held him in place. "Who are you working with?"

"Enough questions," Raul said. "Time to give me some answers."

"I don't have to tell you any—" The Smith's head jolted left. Raul rubbed his knuckles. The man glared at him. "I'm not—" Raul hit him again. "Damn it, Raul, stop hitting me!"

"How did you find me?"

"You were seen. One of our people saw you floating in northern Habsburg. I waited by the river. When I got within fifty miles, I could track your cell."

"My what?"

"Your LAMP phone."

Raul nodded, seemingly satisfied with himself. "Who else is looking for me?"

"Everyone. We know you're headed north. We know you're traveling by river." A purple lump had formed under Benjamin's eye. "Where are you going?"

"No questions," Raul said. "What happened with the High Mage?"

"Haberdeen took care of it."

"Why?"

"He betrayed us. He was going to kill everyone. Anyone who has used inverted weaves," Benjamin said. "He figured out that fierisation leaves a mark, and how to target that mark."

Raul's eyes flickered to Katie. "Is that true?"

Benjamin fought his bonds. "Who are you talking to?"

Raul swung his fist and Benjamin the Fatesmith fell silent. Raul turned to face her. "Is that true?"

An unpleasant sensation chilled Katie's chest. "It is. Johannasberg wanted our help to do it. Laurefen said no— said it was genocide."

"Not just genocide. Suicide." Raul looked down at Benjamin's slumped figure. "Johannasberg was a Fatesmith. He used fierisation himself." His gaze snapped to Katie. "What will the Directive do now he's dead?"

"I have no idea," Katie said. "They were considering his plan again when we left."

Raul gestured to her hand. "Well, you should probably find out what they decided."

Katie shook her head. "I'm not talking to them." She had not replied to a looptap since fleeing Kingsbreak. The moment she did, that dam would break.

"Excuse me?" Raul stepped towards her. "My head is on a magical chopping block and you can't tell me where the axe is? Because you aren't on speaking terms with the executioner?"

"Calm down," Katie said. "Johannasberg's dead. They can't do anything without him."

"You're sure of that? Absolutely positive?" Raul's hard eyes drilled into her skull. "You have no clue what they're planning, do you? Find out, right now, or—"

"Or what?" Katie snapped. "You've got the magical potential of plaster board. I could wrap you up here and leave you for dead." She met his gaze with steely resolve. "Right now, you need me more than I need you. I don't want to talk to the Directive and there's nothing you can do to make me."

A trio of women peeked into the walkway. Raul's glare sent them scurrying. "Let's get back to the river," he muttered. "The sooner we end this arrangement, the better."

"You don't want to get some food?" Katie glanced longingly back down the street.

"Not as much as I want to get rid of you."

CHAPTER 36

AVA

THE DRIED manure smelled as putrid as it was potent. Trevor, the source of the manure, led the cart toward the gates. Ava dipped her nose beneath her shirt and inhaled. She couldn't avoid the smell, but she could blunt its edge.

Moonlight illuminated the city wall. A young guard waved them to a halt. His nose crinkled as he stepped forward; Misha greeted him cheerily from the top of the cart. "Our greetings, fine watchman."

The man held his nose. "It is a late hour to enter Vedmark."

"Manure delivery, fresh from Eaglewatch. We were told to deliver our product while the City slept." Misha winked. "For obvious reasons."

"Very well." He waved them forward. "Through you go."

Misha whistled to Trevor, and they entered the City. Ava smirked at the revulsion on the guard's face. *No Luck necessary.*

High above, the moon vanished. A wall of clouds drifted overhead, just in time to blanket them in darkness. The cart creaked through the silent streets. "Which way?" Misha whispered.

"Keep going straight. There's a coppersmith two streets from the Knight's barracks. Stop there and we'll get to work."

"You can unload the bags of poop."

Ava rolled her eyes. "Fine."

The coppersmith's workshop was a one-story building with an impressive display of metalwork in the front window. Misha steered the cart as close as he could, then climbed down from the driver's seat. "I'll get the door."

Ava took one last breath from inside her shirt and started unloading bags onto Grigory's rusted trolley. By the time Misha had picked the lock, the trolley was full. Even in the dim light, the workshop glowed with burnished warmth. Everything—from pipes to plates—was copper.

Ava felt a pang of remorse for the poor coppersmith whose wares were about to go up in smoke. She finished unloading the sacks of manure and wheeled the trolley back for more. "Start stacking everything around the bags," she whispered. "As much as you can."

They worked fast. Ava fetched three more loads, while Misha shoved every ounce of copper he could find between the sacks. As Ava heaved the last bag of manure into the pile, Misha squeaked with glee. "What is it?"

He held up a small metal cylinder. "Furnace dust. That should make things easier."

Grigory had always warned them about the dangers of furnace dust. "Go for it." Ava shot him a sweaty thumbs-up. "The hotter the fire, the better the show."

Misha emptied the cylinder around the pile. The powder smelled of dried rosemary. Ava blinked. "Was that the whole vial?"

"Almost." Misha made a small trail of dust out the front door. "I'll move Trevor somewhere less conspicuous."

Ava tossed the last of the copper items onto the stinking heap of metal and manure. Outside, she pulled a mitka from her pocket and balanced it on the side of the curb.

"What's that for?" Misha asked.

"Goats guts, Mish." Ava looked up, startled. "I didn't even hear you arrive." She shook her head, then gestured to the mitka. "That is your signal. I'll head down to the barracks. Once I'm in position, I'll tug on Luck and knock it flat. When the coin drops, start the fire, and hide."

"How long will it take to burn green?"

"As soon as the copper ignites, the fire should change color. The furnace dust will help with that. Stay hidden, use Luck to make the flames seem magical. We want the Knights thinking that Declan has come for them."

"And when they rush out..."

"I'll get Haberdeen. You head to the southern exit."

Misha frowned. "And what if only a few of the Knights come out?"

"The Knights of Despair were just embarrassed in front of their steward by a teenager from Euryma." She smirked. "They're all going to want a piece of him."

"Alright." Misha looked from the coin to the copper-smith. "I guess this is it, then."

Ava pulled him into a hug. "Stay hidden. The plan won't work if I must come back and break you out too. I'll see you at the southern gate."

Misha nodded. "Good luck. For both of us."

Ava squeezed him tight and turned down the street. The night air was brisk on her cheeks. Down a winding alley and up a side-lane. Ava had spent her childhood roaming these streets. They offered memories she would sooner forget. When she reached the Knights' barracks, she tucked herself into a brick alcove.

It was an imposing building, built from ancient silwood and topped with six onion domes. Exits led out on all sides. Ava watched a Knight walk the length of the building's perimeter. Then, quiet as a shadow, she concentrated on Luck. The effort required to move the coin was tiny, like pulling on a loose thread. Two blocks away, the jade mitka fell to the ground. Ava held her breath and waited.

And waited.

And continued to wait. *Maybe Mish got distracted, maybe he hasn't noticed the coin, mayb—*

A thunderous explosion rocked the street. Windows shattered, flags flailed and the Vedmark City shook. Behind her, a swirling tornado of green flame rose like a pillar in the night. Ava was impressed.

Armored figures flooded from the barracks—like ants defending their nest. The fire burned brighter, a brilliant green that stretched high into the cloudy sky. More Knights rushed towards it. As the stream thinned, she pulled on Luck to rouse every man from the building. *I hope you're hiding well, Mish.*

A pair of stragglers were the last to leave. As soon as they vanished around the corner, Ava made her move. Out of the darkness, into the open doorway. She double-checked her surrounds, then slipped inside.

———

Haberdeen sat alone in a cramped wooden cell. Finding her was easy. The hard part was getting her out. Ava dashed through a long tunnel, one of many that ran deep below the

City. In one hand she held an oil lantern, in the other she gripped Haberdeen's wrist.

"What do you mean Bruxelle?" she asked. "What's in Bruxelle?"

"Shhh!" Ava kept the lantern behind her ear so she could see the way ahead. The Knights would have extinguished the green flames long ago. Once they checked the barracks, they would raise the alarm.

"I don't understand." Haberdeen said. "We traveled all this way for you to take me back?"

"Stop talking. I'll explain later. Just move." Ava had not missed the woman's questions. She had not missed the woman at all. Ava navigated by lantern and Luck, but leaning on Luck was taking its toll. Her legs were heavy. Their tunnel started going up, Ava pushed pain aside and kept going—the slight ascent felt like a mountain trail.

They rounded a sharp bend, and the tunnel ended. Ava nearly cheered with relief. A rusted ladder led up to a hexagonal exit. Sunlight slipped through two holes in the grate. It was morning. *No wonder I'm so tired.* She herded Haberdeen up into an empty street.

The Luck worked. They were in Southern Vedmark. Ava crouched in the shade of a nearby building. Haberdeen scanned the empty road. She wore a plain white tunic and, somehow, resembled a panicked chicken. "Stay down, Habby."

"That's not my name." The nickname was more suited to a house cat than a witch. Haberdeen hated it. Ava used it whenever possible. "What's in..."

"Shhh!" Ava glared at her. "Not now. There's a day's journey ahead of us. We'll talk later."

"A day's journey. Walking?"

A gentle clopping answered the question. Ava smiled. *Timed to perfection.*

Misha sat in the cart, smiling. "Morning ladies." He threw a bag to Haberdeen. She caught it, opened it, and frowned. "What's this?"

"It's your disguise." Misha threw another bag to Ava, who took one glance inside and groaned. Misha laughed. "Don't worry, I've got one too. We're going to look fantastic!"

The journey to Vedmark's border was an uneventful one. Ava napped while Misha steered. When she woke, the Threshold loomed ahead.

Misha was dressed like a peacock. He passed her a water skin as she stretched. "Feeling better?"

Ava took a sip. Her own colorful coat felt like a warm hug. "Much better. How's Habby?"

"That's not my name," came a muffled voice from behind.

"She's an excellent rug." Misha grinned. "All things considered, that went surprisingly well."

"Don't speak too soon." Ava nodded to a small group of Knights guarding the Threshold's colossal doorway. "That's not great."

"You think they're here for us?"

"I guess we'll soon find out." Ava leaned back. "No sudden moves, Habby, or we're all dead."

She turned her attention to the archway. The Threshold never failed to astound her. A single wall—thirty feet high—made of smooth white quartz carved in angular runes. Both sides stretched into the distance.

There were two lines. Entry and exit. Misha joined the line leading out of Vedmark. It was a mess of trader's wagons. They were common at the Threshold. Their businesses could not thrive on Vedmark alone, so they roamed into the wider world, trading with outsiders to make their living.

Clay pots towered atop the wagon ahead of them, the precarious piles wobbling as they crept up the line. Ava caught Misha's eye and nodded to the wagon. "Just in case."

Their wagon appeared full of a mountain of colorful rugs. In reality, there were eight rugs folded artfully over planks of wood. Underneath, dressed as a rug herself, lay Haberdeen. The illusion was convincing enough, though Ava doubted it could stand against closer inspection.

The Knights worked in pairs, examining two wagons at a time. In the other line, wagons returned unnoticed. Ava's heart thumped louder. *They are only checking departures. They must be looking for us.* Two Knights searched the pottery ahead, while two more approached their wagon. Ava gripped Luck and waited.

"Hail, fine Knights," Misha called. "We welcome a thorough inspection, but I beg you to make haste. We were delayed this morning and are in a rush to fill an important order."

The Knights nodded in reply and circled the wagon. Ava tugged on chance.

Shouts erupted as a pile of narrow vases tilted and fell. With an almighty crash, hundreds of clay pots clattered to the ground, shattering in every direction.

Silence followed, then a high pitch wail pierced the haze of dust. The Knights inspecting their wagon hurried to help, then exchanged uncertain glances. "You said you had a large order to fill."

Misha nodded. "We do, sir, though we will wait if required," he paused. "Though the delay will cost us dearly."

The Knight nodded at the mess of broken clay and turned to Misha. His eyes brushed over the stacked rugs. "Go ahead. This will take some time to repair."

"Thank you, an honor, lord Knight."

The Knight waved the compliment away. Ava kept her face rigid as Misha led them around the queue and through the archway. She felt a surge of relief as they came out the other side. "We made it," she said.

"Can I come out now?" Haberdeen said.

Ava smiled. "Not yet," she whispered sharply. Misha's shoulders shook with silent laughter. They continued at a steady pace until they reached the decrepit train station. "Ah, the Northern Rail. The finest rust bucket on tracks." A wicker basket hit the back of his head.

Haberdeen took a gasping breath. "That was awful."

"I thought you made a wonderful rug." Ava unravelled herself from the colorful garbs. "Where did you find this stuff, Mish?"

Misha laughed. "The Knights arrived sooner than I expected. My hiding places became more and more creative and in the madness I happened upon this stuff."

"Trust a Luck," Ava said.

Haberdeen thrashed free of her outfit.

"Now what?" Misha asked.

"We go south. You need to get back to Grigory."

Misha's face fell. "What?"

"Rasporvin's smart enough to suspect something. As far as he knows, I'm still with you. If he sends anyone to Ory and you're not there, he won't have a leg to stand on. Get back there before the Knights do."

"And what do I tell them if they ask about you?"

Ava chewed her lip. "Tell them I went looking for Declan."

Misha's face soured.

"Tell them I was trying to bring him back to face punishment."

"You think they'll believe that?"

"The easiest lies to believe are the ones we want to hear." Ava turned to the Threshold. "C'mon Mish, I'd never forgive myself if something happened to Ory."

Misha nodded. "Fine. Just... look after yourself, okay?"

"I will. You too." Ava pulled him into a tight hug. "I couldn't have done this without you."

"I know. Good luck Ava."

Haberdeen waited in silence until Misha had gone. "What's in Bruxelle?"

"Raul, for starters. Katie, the girl from the night we found you. Questions about Remnant Magic."

"Why do they want me?"

"Who knows?" Ava led them to the train station. Dead vines strangled a crooked sign reading *Platform One*. "Same deal as last time. We stay together. I'll keep you alive. You try to take off and you're on your own. Got it?"

Haberdeen nodded.

"Here's hoping the northern rail still runs." Ava led them through a partially collapsed doorway. "While we wait, I suggest we change into less *noticeable* outfits."

CHAPTER 37

AVA

PALE ASH CRUNCHED beneath Ava's feet. She ignored the pounding in her chest. This should have been Bruxelle. A settlement of those unwelcomed in Euryma's magic-centric society. Now, it was nothing.

Haberdeen followed behind like a flame-haired duckling. Ava dug the phone from her satchel and called Katie. A gruff voice answered. "Are you here?"

"Put Katie on."

"I—"

"Put Katie on."

There was a brief pause, a scuffling sound, a familiar voice. "Ava, where are you?"

"I'm in Bruxelle. But it's gone. Destroyed. It's like..."

"Remnant Magic. Yes. We're here too."

"When did it happen?"

"No idea. Could be the storm that destroyed Massalia came through here. It was like this when we arrived."

"Massalia's gone too?" Ava's heart skipped a beat. Euryma was being erased, one city at a time. Pathways between the mounds of ash were all that remained of the roads. "Where are you?"

"Can you find your way to the old square? We're camped out where it used to be."

"We'll arrive soon."

"Any luck with Declan?"

"I'll talk to you when we get there." Ava closed the phone and checked the knives on her belt. Last time she'd encountered Raul, he was determined to kill both Katie and herself. She turned back to Haberdeen. "C'mon. They're waiting for us."

A gentle breeze stirred loose ash along the ground. The square was ruin and rubble. Katie sat in the shade of a jagged stone pile. "Ava!" She stood up to greet them. Behind her, Raul looked like he had aged ten years. Skin mottled, hair tangled, he walked with a steady limp.

Haberdeen rushed forward, Ava barred her way with an outstretched arm. "Just a moment," she said. "What's going on? It wasn't easy to separate these two," she motioned from Haberdeen to Raul. "So if we're just going to pair them up again, I want to know why."

"The girl wanted to see you." Raul took a swig of water, which dripped down his beard and formed tiny craters in the dust. "This was my price. Haberdeen for a meeting." He turned to Katie. "She's here, we're square."

Katie nodded. "It was the only way."

Ava eyed them both. Her hands twitched at her waist, strings of Luck hovered about them, waiting to be plucked like harp strings. "Why did you need to talk to me?"

"It's a long story." Katie's gaze shifted to Raul. "Our deal hasn't changed, but you need to stay for this. You know things I don't. Once it's finished, you can take Haberdeen and go."

Ava pursed her lips. "I never agreed to that."

Katie's expression darkened. She seemed harder than Ava remembered—something had happened to her. Something terrible. "Remnant Magic exists," Katie said.

"I know," Ava said. "I was doing business in Parteno when it hit."

"We thought it was Fatesmiths—"

"Hold up girl." Raul interrupted. "What do you mean, you were there?"

Ava grit her teeth. That memory had fangs. "I was in Parteno when the Remnant Magic storm arrived."

"Were you fierised?"

"What? No!"

Raul considered her for a moment. "You're lying."

Ava's hand drifted to the knives by her belt. "No, I'm not."

"No-one survives a Remnant Magic storm. Not unless they're fierised. "

"I did."

"How?"

Ava shrugged. "That's not your concern. Regardless, I saw it. I watched the city streets wiped from their foundation. It's real."

Katie's shoulders slumped. She heaved a sigh, shaking her head. "Okay. Well, the problem is this. A week ago, my friend..." She paused and collected herself. "They killed my friend Amber. Killed her with a knife that takes memories."

"Winterthorn," Ava said.

"Winterthorn?"

"That's our dagger. That dagger is from Vedmark."

"The ironhands used it to take Amber's memories, including the High Mage's plan to defeat them. Only they've killed the High Mage now, and they've melted every iron cast to nothing... And... And I have no idea what to do."

Ava sat down in the ash and tried to make sense of it. She couldn't. "Do you want to stop the blackcoats or not?"

"I want to..." Katie trailed off and glanced at her palm. Blood drained from her face. Whatever message had come across her palm, it wasn't good.

"What did they say?" Raul growled.

Katie didn't move. Forehead creased, she locked eyes with Raul. "The Directive are going to do it."

"Do what?" Ava asked.

Raul turned to Haberdeen. "We need to run. As far from here as possible."

Katie fell silent. Ava stamped her foot. "What are the Directive doing?"

"They're... They're going to use Sabriva Tower as a conduit to kill every person who has used fierisation. They're going to kill them all."

"When?" Ava asked.

Katie's pale skin paled further. "Three days."

"Then we're leaving," Raul said. "If Sabriva Tower is the conduit, we need to get out of its range."

"But the Fatesmiths know." Katie's voice trembled. "They're not going to make it easy for the Directive to kill them all."

Raul opened his mouth to respond. His face went grey. "They may not have to. Do you remember what Benjamin said? At Laroa?"

Katie shook her head.

"I didn't think much of it..." Raul's forehead creased in concern. "He said Remnant Magic was going to stop it, eventually. He said they ran out of time."

"What does that—" Realization cut Katie's question in half. "Sabriva's going to be hit by Remnant Magic?"

Ava's stomach dropped. *If the Head City falls, Euryma is done. I need to—*

"Ava, are you listening?" Katie asked. "The Directive are walking into a deathtrap. Sabriva is going to be destroyed by something they don't even believe in." Tears glistened in her eyes. "We need Declan."

"Kate... I'm sorry, I really am." Ava's hands dropped to her sides. "Nobody has seen Declan in months. I don't know where he is, or how to find him."

Tears rolled down Katie's cheeks, her shoulders shook beneath quiet sobs. Raul put a hand on her shoulder. "Get outta here. Find somewhere far away and leave it behind. There's no glory dying to save a doomed city." He walked to Haberdeen's side. "A deal is a deal. We'll be going now."

Katie continued to cry. Ava glanced at Raul. "Wait."

He turned back to her, eyebrows raised.

"Winterthorn," Ava said. "Where is it?"

"The impostor used it. Whoever she is. They've got it."

"An imposter? Who is it?"

"No idea," Raul said.

"Ward," Katie murmured. "He must have survived Anderma. He's pulled this trick before."

Raul's eyes flashed. "Whoever it is, I'd bet that knife is the source of her strength. No doubt she's using Haberdeen's memories to play the part."

Ava considered it. She pointed at Haberdeen. "Where did the knife come from in the first place?"

"I don't remember."

"I do," Raul said. "You told me it was a wanderer. He made you take it to see the truth of the coming storms."

"I'm sorry, Raul," Haberdeen said. "I remember nothing."

"No fault of yours, m'lady."

Wanderer. Ava repeated the words in her head. "A thief," she said at last.

"What do you mean?" Raul said.

"That dagger is a royal heirloom. It vanished after someone took it into a dangerous part of our kingdom."

Raul shrugged. "Means nothing to me. The knife is with whoever leads the Fatesmiths." He gestured to Katie. "Anything else before we leave?"

Katie wiped her tear-stained cheeks. "You won't come and help?"

"I told you. Get as far as you can. Either Sabriva falls or your murderous friends try to kill us all. We're not sticking around to see which comes first."

Ava produced a knife from her belt. "I'm not sure how I feel about just letting you go. You've hurt a lot of people."

"We were trying to save the world."

Ava raised an eyebrow. "And now?"

Raul shrugged. "We're trying to save our skins."

"Let them go," Katie said. "Raul was true to his word. I'm true to mine."

Ava didn't like it. Not at all. Still, she slipped the knife back into its sheath. Raul led Haberdeen out of the square. He glanced back one final time, then disappeared. Ava crouched down in the dirt. "You two formed a bit of a bond, hey?"

Katie shrugged. "He's not what I expected."

Ava pulled her to her feet. "You need to be careful. Mages are crafty. Whatever he said, take it with a grain of salt."

Katie didn't respond. She sat on the ground for a long

time, peering down the way they'd left. "I don't know what to do, Ava."

"Well, you only have two options." She raised one finger. "You can go to Sabriva and convince the Directive to leave before Remnant Magic turns them to dust." She lifted a second finger. "Or you can follow Raul's advice and get as far away as you want. It's fight or flee."

Katie wiped her eyes, leaving a patch of dirty ash across her cheek. "The Directive are a bunch of idiots." She shook her head. "But they want to do the right thing. I can't let them kill themselves."

"...You're facing a battle you can't win."

Katie nodded. "What do I do?"

Ava turned to the south. Distant green hills juxtaposed against Bruxelle's remains. *How long until those hills are destroyed too? How long until there's nothing left?* "How long have we got?"

"Three days."

"That'll have to do then. I'll get you on the train to Sabriva. You spread the word. Tell the people they need to evacuate."

"And you?"

"I'm going to find Declan."

Katie shook her head. "You said yourself. You don't know where he is."

"Then I better start looking."

"Why are you helping me, Ava?"

"You're not the only one who wants Euryma to survive unscathed." Ava started up the shattered road and motioned for Katie to follow. "There's a train station still standing, a few hours from here. Let's go save the Dominion."

CHAPTER 38
KATIE

THE TRAINS in Euryma were sleek and silver. Soft interiors with faux leather chairs in red or white. Every chair came with a table and a small screen for entertainment. The Northern Rail was a steel box on skates. Yellow foam flaked from holes in the seats; the carriage smelled of vinegar. At least, Katie hoped it was vinegar.

Distant hills bordered a horizon peppered with humble villages and bare forests. The train moved with a steady screech that made Katie's spine tingle. The constant sway of the locomotive—combined with the stress and exhaustion—soon lulled her into an uncomfortable sleep.

Sabriva gleamed in the distance. Its buildings reached high in a perfect sky. A crimson cloud swept over it and the city was gone. She was in Sabriva Square. At the base of a fallen tower, Mary-Lou stared from bloodshot eyes. "Why didn't you try harder? You could have saved us." Katie went to leave. Michael and Laurefen's corpses sprawled in the dirt. Laurefen's head turned to face her. His eyes were empty, his lips a cruel sneer. "You let us down. You let us die."

Katie woke with a start. Sweat drenched her forehead.

An old man seated nearby watched her with concern. Katie wiped her face, tried to regain some measure of composure. The man returned to his paper.

Mountain ranges replaced the forests. Katie shifted and a cardboard box fell from her lap. Complimentary lunch. A crushed sandwich and withered apple. She started unwrapping her meal when the man's newspaper caught her eye. The front page displayed a photo of Laurefen.

"Excuse me." She tapped the man's chair and touched the corner of the newspaper. "Can I borrow that page?"

The man smiled and handed it over. Katie opened the paper to a bold headline. *King's College Creates Chaos.*

"No good," the man said in a thick accent. "Sabriva no good."

Katie smiled politely and continued reading. *Laurefen Ember, the Dean of the prestigious King's College, has been accused of spreading anti-Dominion conspiracy theories in the Head City of Sabriva. Dean Ember has been observed speaking in front of large gatherings on multiple occasions, calling on them to rise against a threat to witch and wizard freedoms. Dean Ember is adamant that Sabriva Tower must be protected against an unknown threat. Citizens are cautioned against becoming involved in gatherings, which are frequently held in Sabriva Square. Acting High-Mage Phillip Fieldman has dismissed the gatherings as a blatant attempt to take power following Reginald Johannasberg's death.*

Katie's heart pounded as she read the report. It was everything she'd feared. War was headed to Sabriva.

CHAPTER 39
AVA

PAINT COVERED Misha and Grigory when Ava arrived. She looked from their sky-blue arms to the sky-blue wagon and laughed. "I take it someone spotted a yellow cart in Vedmark?"

Misha straightened up. "They did, and there were questions about a yellow cart carrying carpets through the Threshold."

"And so, you force your father to cover your own hide," Ava teased.

Grigory climbed to his feet. A streak of paint ran through his grey hair. "It needed some new color."

"Well, that's a convenient coincidence."

Misha ran a hand through his hair, leaving specks of color. "The witch is gone."

Ava nodded. "Traded for information. I'm afraid there's not much time."

"Not much time for..."

"I've got two days. Remnant Magic will hit Sabriva in two days and there's only one person I know who could stop it."

306

Misha's expression soured. "No."

"He's our only hope."

"He could've killed you."

"We've been over this," Ava said. "Declan lost control, but only because Rasporvin forced Haberdeen on him."

"I don't care."

Ava folded her arms. "Neither do I. I need to take Declan to Sabriva. If the Head City falls, Euryma is toast."

Misha dropped his paintbrush and turned back towards the cabin. "I want nothing to do with Declan Moore."

"As headstrong as his father." Grigory should have been angry. Instead, he pulled her into a hug.

Ava squeezed back. "I'm sorry. I'm glad you're okay. I thought the Knights would visit."

"Oh, they did." He let her go. "I'm old, though, and age is the best excuse to act a fool."

"Well, you're no fool to me," Ava said. "Ory, I need to find Declan. I don't even know where to start."

Grigory nodded. "He has been gone for months. I'm sorry. I wish I could be more—" Grigory froze. A steady clop of horse-hooves announced six black horses, each one carrying a Knight of Despair in full armor.

Grigory bowed as one dismounted. Urik. "How wonderful," he hissed. "The niece of the Steward returns at last." The man dipped into a mocking bow. "A pleasure, Madam Drakonov."

Ava bit her tongue behind a narrow smile. "The honor is mine, Knight Urik." The tension showed in the bands of Luck surrounding them. She had to tread carefully. They were all at risk, Grigory included. She dipped her head. "Grigory tells me you have been looking for me."

"We have," he said. "Ava Drakonov, the Grand Steward

desires your presence. Your whereabouts have been much of a mystery."

"Very well," Ava said. "You can let my uncle know I am on my way."

Urik turned to the Knights behind him. "We are curious where you have been."

Ava noticed a flash of panic in Grigory's eyes. She put a hand on his shoulder and smiled pleasantly. "Searching the forest for a traitor."

"A worthy cause." Urik sounded unconvinced. "No doubt your uncle will approve of such... *loyalty*."

Ava met his gaze. "We are *all* loyal to Vedmark here."

Luck let Ava picture all the ways things could turn bad fast. She willed the odds in a more peaceful trajectory. Urik nodded. "You will return with me to the City. The Grand Steward is a busy man. I am sure you have much to discuss."

Grigory stirred. Ava squeezed his hand. "I'm fine," she whispered. "Don't tell Misha what happened. He will make things worse." Grigory nodded against her shoulder and Ava let him go.

Urik climbed onto his horse and eyed the half-painted cart. "A beautiful shade of blue," he observed. "Your wagon has always been such a vivid shade."

"No," Ava slipped in. "Grigory prefers a green cart, a true shade of Vedmark. But I talked him into a change. I like blue. It matches my eyes."

"Delightful." Urik's lips curled into a thin smile. "Come, you will ride with me."

Ava eased onto the back of the saddle, then waved goodbye as they raced out of the clearing. The stallions moved like a storm, but Ava would not play the damsel. Instead, she used every ounce of Luck she could muster to keep herself from falling off the horse mid-stride. They approached Vedmark City at a gallop. Urik gestured the guards aside at the gate.

"You must be mistaken," she called, as they turned off the main road. "This is not the way to the Steward's Hall."

"The Hall is being rebuilt. The damage caused by the traitor is not yet repaired."

Liar, Ava thought. "My uncle seeks an alternative meeting place."

"He will meet you at the barracks."

Ava swallowed when they passed the blackened remains of the coppersmith. The odds of escape were stacked against her. She forced her racing pulse to calm.

They dismounted at the northern entry of the barracks. Urik threw the reigns to a pair of girls and stood over Ava, like a jailor supervising a prisoner. "The Grand Steward has struggled to find a suitable location to meet you. The holding cells will suffice for now."

Ava stiffened. "You must think I'm a fool."

Urik's confidence faltered. "I would never dream of—"

"If you're going to lead me to the dungeons, Urik, at least do yourself the justice of being honest."

"No tricks of Luck." It was not a question, but an order.

Ava glanced at the Knights watching from behind. "Luck can only take you so far."

"So cooperative." Urik's eyes narrowed. "You'll forgive my disbelief."

"I will cooperate on one condition. I wish to speak to Rasporvin."

Urik smiled darkly. "A deal. On my honour."

I'll need more than that, Ava thought as the Knights led her into the darkness below.

They locked her in Haberdeen's empty cell. Ava suspected it was on purpose. *Rasporvin wants you to know that he knows.* The iron bars were as thick as her arms, fixed in place by thick silwood beams. There was no Luck to manipulate. She sat on the floor and tried to rest. She needed her strength, but her mind would not stop moving. *You're running out of time! You need Declan. Katie is counting on you and instead you're locked in a cage.* Her attempts to squeeze through the gap between bars proved pointless.

A narrow strip of daylight crawled along the cell floor, marking time that moved too fast. *What does Rasporvin want? That's easy, he wants Winterthorn. Then he can kill the old king, lift the curse, and escape the Void. How can I use that?* Nothing came to mind. Ava buried her head in her hands, waiting for another option to present itself. The rectangle of sunlight continued across the stone. It had almost vanished when she heard someone approaching. *You'll have to make do.*

The footsteps grew louder. Ava grasped Luck and searched for the right move. Every choice had multiple outcomes. She sifted through the dominoes, searching for which one to knock down first. Ava stiffened, stunned, as the Emissary stepped into the light. "Ava?"

"Emissary!" Ava's plans dissolved. "Emissary, what are you doing here?"

The Emissary wore funeral black. She carried a leather duffel bag. She glanced behind her, then stepped closer to the barred cell. "Ava," she said in a stern voice. "We have little time."

"I know," Ava whispered back. "Sabriva is in danger. I need to find Declan."

"I agree." The Emissary nodded. "I can help, but I need you to listen and do as I say." From a pocket in her dress, the Emissary produced a long, brass key. She slid it into the keyhole and the lock clicked loose.

Ava scanned the hallway. "Where do we go?"

"It's not we, it's you." The Emissary handed her the bag. "You'll need this."

Ava opened it to see a pile of jingling shieldshards. "For Sabriva?"

The Emissary pulled a silver chain from beneath her robes. "And this too."

She dropped a sapphire pendant into her hands. It hung off a tarnished chain that looked ancient. "What is this?"

"That will lead you to Declan." She pointed to the bag of shieldshards. "Those should keep you alive. I am sorry it's come to this, Ava. I tried to convince the High Mage, but he's a fool. A dead fool. I wanted to keep you out of it for as long as I could."

"What do you mean?"

"There's no time. Go. Escape through the tunnels, head to the forest. Look through the sapphire. It will guide you to Declan.

Ava struggled to follow. "And what are you going to do?"

The Emissary motioned to the cell. "I'm going to wake up in here with a nasty bruise and complain to no end about how you tricked me."

"What?"

The Emissary's eyes burned with urgency. "Euryma is in your hands now, Ava. I can't imagine safer hands for the task. I'd wish you luck, but I don't think I need to."

Ava took a deep breath. "Thank you."

"It's time to go. Before you do, you must knock me out."

311

Ava released her and stepped back. "No... No, I can't!"

"It wouldn't be the first time. Or the last."

"But..."

"The harder you hit me, the more believable your escape." She lowered her arms and stepped backward into the cell. "No time to waste. Euryma needs you. Declan needs you."

CHAPTER 40
MICHAEL

EAGER LISTENERS STRETCHED across Sabriva Square, engulfing footpaths like noxious weeds, each one jostling to get the best view. The crowd surprised Michael. The headline article condemning them had doubled their numbers. *The people know something's not right. We've given them a standard to assemble beneath.*

Laurefen pointed to Sabriva Tower, which soared high above the city lawns. "Where are our leaders? Reginald Johannasberg was murdered, and the Magistri hide in their tower!" He boomed. "It is us—the people—who must fight this foe. It is up to us to save our cities, our friends and our families!" The square responded with scattered applause. Michael understood their hesitation. Laurefen continued. "It is up to us to protect our freedom. Euryma is a land of magic. We alone wield the unseen powers that founded this nation. Now, that power is threatened by those who would see you dead. Who are they to deny you your birthright? Who are they to withhold the legacy of this great Dominion?"

This garnered louder cheers. An overzealous follower to

313

their left fought through the assembly. As they got closer, Michael realized that whoever it was, they were not cheering. The people parted, and the perpetrator stepped into clear view. She was shouting. "Don't listen to him! You are all in danger! You need to get far away from here! You have to leave!"

It was Katie. Disheveled hair pointed in all directions. Her clothes were filthy. "You need to leave Sabriva!" she shouted. "You only have a few days! There's nothing you can do to stop it! If you stay here, you'll die!"

Mary-Lou streamed through the mass. Michael followed her.

"Lou!" Katie called. "Lou. You can't be here. The storm is coming. You don't have time."

Michael joined them. "What are you doing?"

Katie's eyes flashed. "I'm trying to save these people. What are *you* doing?"

"Now dear," Mary-Lou whispered. "We don't need to make a scene. Come, let's talk about it."

"I don't have time to talk," she said.

"If you don't explain yourself, we can't help you," Michael said.

Katie paused. Muttered something, then nodded. "Fine."

They left the square quickly, finding quiet in an information centre. Once inside, Michael shut the door behind them. Mary-Lou pulled Katie into a hug. "I was so worried about you!"

Katie smiled. "I'm sorry. I really am. I had to go. There's so much I have to tell you."

"Where is Raul?" Michael asked.

Katie's smile faltered. "Raul is gone. But I need to—"

"What do you mean, gone?"

"Michael, if you just listen—"

"No, you listen. We had one of the Fatesmith's ranking officers, and now we don't. So what do you mean, gone?"

"I made a deal. He delivered, so I let him go."

"You foolish girl."

Mary-Lou raised her hand. "Calm down, it's done now." She turned away from him. "Let's hear what she has to say."

"I've come from Bruxelle. It's gone, the same as Parteno, as Massalia. Remnant Magic has wiped it off the map."

"Not this again." Michael growled. The girl was insufferable.

Mary-Lou shook her head. "Katie, an earthquake destroyed it. It's been all over the news."

"Let me guess," Michael said. "Raul told you it was Remnant Magic. He told you what you wanted to believe, and you believed it. What did we tell you?"

Katie gritted her teeth. "I know what you told me. And I know what the aftermath of an earthquake looks like." She jabbed her finger at him. "You two need to stop being so thick-headed and listen. You expect to destroy the Fatesmiths, but you won't get the chance. Remnant Magic is on its way and you're standing in its path. The city needs to be evacuated. We can rebuild Sabriva. We can't rebuild dead people."

Michael slammed his hand on the table. The girl had gone mad. "Don't you care about Amber? Don't you care about *justice* for the witch that killed her?"

Katie glared at him. "Amber wouldn't have wanted us to commit mass murder. She was better than that. So was Dreyfus. And so am I."

Such arrogance. Michael shook his head. "We're not committing mass murder!"

315

"But you are. Call it what you will. If you use Johannas-berg's spell..."

"We're not," Mary-Lou said. "We can't. Johannasberg took his half of the spell to the grave."

Katie blinked. "But you said..."

"I sowed a seed and let it grow." She smiled sadly. "We've been spreading word everywhere. Without the High Mage, our best chance is to make the ironhands believe we're a threat. If we can draw them here, then we can meet them head on. We've had thousands show up to help. We're going to fight them. Finish this once and for all."

"But they're not coming," Katie said. "They don't have to. Remnant Magic will destroy you for them. Oh, you idiots, you've drawn all the Fatesmith's enemies into one spot to die."

Michael stood up. Just looking at the girl made him want to break something. "I'm not listening to this nonsense."

"You'd rather leave than have a hard conversation?"

Michael turned his back on her; a thread of air arced over his torso and spun him around. Katie let go of the aeronima, her expression fierce. "You can't walk away from this."

"Don't start something if you're not prepared to finish it," Michael said.

Mary-Lou stepped between them. "You both need to calm down. Kate, we understand you think you're doing the right thing, but Raul has bewitched you. You're too close to the situation to understand." She rounded on Michael. "And you need to consider things from Katie's point of view. All she's trying to do is help."

"Good intentions can be catastrophic," Michael replied. "Katie, do you have any evidence?"

"Massalia and Parteno aren't proof enough?"

Michael rolled his eyes. "I don't have time for this. We've got two days. We need to be ready."

"Aren't you listening?" Katie snapped. "You can't get ready for this. You must get people out. As many people as possible."

"Kate." Mary-Lou touched her shoulder. "Trust us. We know what we're doing."

Katie stamped her foot. "No!" she shouted. "No, Mary-Lou you don't! You're going to get all these people killed because you *think* you know better!" She stabbed a finger at Michael's chest. "And I'm sick of you! I will not let you lead these people to their doom. I can't!"

"What are you going to do?" Mary-Lou asked grimly.

"Whatever I have to."

Enough. Michael wove aeronima into a short lasso. Katie must have expected it, because she cut straight through it and launched a stack of thick tomes towards him. Mary-Lou blocked the books, and Michael redirected them back at her. The shelves emptied in seconds, and Mary-Lou sealed them—trapping Katie in a cocoon of literature. "I'm so sorry, dear."

"Let me go!" she screamed.

Michael gagged her with a knot of air. Katie fought and kicked in silence. "What do we do with her?" Mary-Lou asked.

"She just needs to see what we see. Tie off the nima, we'll keep her here for now."

"You think that's wise?"

Michael nodded. "When she sees that this Remnant Magic business is nothing but nonsense, she'll come around. If I hadn't seen the Well myself, I would be half inclined to believe her."

"We could tell her."

"The Well is not our secret to divulge," Michael said. "But maybe Laurefen will reconsider once he sees her like this." He looped his fingers through a strand of kinema and weaved them over Katie's shoulders. When he pulled tight, she hovered across the room. He fixed her to the seat with a thick coil of air.

Mary-Lou hesitated, then gave a weak smile. "We don't want to do this, but you'll see. Soon, you'll understand."

Katie glared daggers as they left the information centre. Michael locked the door behind them. "That didn't go well."

The lines in Mary-Lou's face seemed deeper than ever. "I agree. Poor girl. It's unpleasant, but it had to be done. She'll thank us for it one day."

Michael nodded. *Assuming we survive to see that day.*

CHAPTER 41

DECLAN

THE AXE no longer felt like an axe. It had become an extension of Declan's body. The handle was another limb, the axe head as dexterous as his fist.

He switched from Bull to Bear; the blade transforming from raging charge to swiping paw. Declan moved through the trees, stripping bark like butter, felling young pines like toothpicks. Arman clapped, his face split in a proud smile.

Declan slowed to prowling Lion. The weapon stretched ahead, testing and tasting the forest. Then, as fast as a viper, Declan spun around. The axe head severed a trunk as thick as his torso. The tree rumbled. Groaned. Creaks and snaps echoed amongst the pines.

"Now!" Arman directed.

Declan held the shaft loose and started the dance. The blade whistled over his ear, the neck of the handle rode his shoulder, then looped underneath his armpit. Declan caught it in his opposite hand and repeated the pattern on the other side. Catch. Swing. Catch, swing. Catch swing. Faster. Faster. Faster. The axe head transformed into a blur, a silver shell passing over his back again and again.

Branches peeled off the falling trunk. They hit the axe's force field and burst into sawdust. Declan marched toward the tumbling tree. *Catch, swing, faster. Always faster.* For one tiny moment, Declan doubted himself.

That was enough.

His grip slid an inch too high, and the rhythm evaporated. Declan dropped the axe and dove into the dirt. The tree exploded on the forest floor with a thunderous noise. Pine needles drifted in the air. Declan rolled onto his back. Sunlight pierced the canopy, only to be blocked by Arman's silhouette. "Almost," he said. He extended a hand and pulled Declan to his feet. "Very close, grandson. You were in the shell. A real Armadillo."

"Then I fell apart."

"Some take years to achieve what you have learned in months."

"When the big bits fall, that's when I lose my concentration. How do you keep it going?"

Arman picked up the axe. "Trust," he said. "You trust your weapon to do its job." He tossed it to him.

Declan caught the handle. "Trust the axe to do its job. Okay." The mangled forest looked like a war zone. "Let's go again."

Arman clapped his hands. In an emerald flash, the scene reversed. The thick fallen pine rumbled along the forest floor and leaped onto the stump as twigs and branches rushed to join it. In a flurry of wood chips, the surrounding trees repaired themselves. "Return to bull," Arman instructed. "Work your way into it. Trust your weapon will do its job."

Declan started again, finding his rhythm once more. Bull, Bear, Lion. Shattered timber strips littered the clearing. Declan cleaved the tall pine, then built his shell. The axe hummed like a nest of wasps until he again lost control. The falling trunk missed by inches as he threw himself into the dirt.

Arman chuckled. "Trust," he said, and set the forest right once more.

Declan squeezed the axe until his hands hurt. He took a long breath, relaxed his grip, and returned to the dance. The axe flowed from hand to hand. Bull. Bear. Lion. The Lion pounced, the tree split.

Trust. Declan closed his eyes and threw himself into the moment. *Axe to shoulder, hand to axe. Catch. Swing. Catch. Swing.* Declan risked a glance and regretted it. The tree collapsed. Its shadow enveloped him. His rhythm burst like a balloon. Declan lay in the dirt, seething. *Trust the axe! Why can't you just trust the axe?*

Arman's enormous boots stopped alongside him. "It is no simple task, grandson."

Declan rolled onto his back. "I don't know what to do! I keep telling myself to trust the axe, but I can't. My stupid brain just won't let me!"

"Blind trust can be a difficult feat," Arman said. "Sometimes it is born as a last resort."

"That doesn't help me now."

Arman laughed. "No, it does not. Perhaps we should call it a day. A good night's sleep may be all that is required."

"No." Declan climbed to his feet and retrieved his axe. "Please grandfather. One more attempt?"

Arman didn't reply. He peered into the trees westward, then stepped between Declan and the tree line.

"What is it?" Declan whispered.

"Someone's coming."

They retreated to the clearing's edge. As they did, a

voice caught up to them. "Please don't leave! I mean you no harm!"

The aches and pains of the day melted away. Declan stepped past his grandfather. "Ava?"

"Declan?" Ava dropped a bag and crunched through the forest carpet. Her hair was a nest of twigs and leaves. "I've been looking for... for you."

Declan leaped over the fallen trees and lifted her easily off her feet. "You're okay!"

Ava squeezed back. "I am. And you're here."

"I'm sorry." Declan lowered her to the ground. "I'm so sorry I hurt you."

"I should have told you about Haberdeen. I..." Ava paused. She stared at Arman.

Declan's grandfather cleared his throat with a broad smile. His eyes twinkled like starlight, his long beard twitched. "You must be Ava."

The color vanished from Ava's face. She pulled away from Declan and dropped to her knees. "Your Majesty!"

Arman winked at Declan. "I like her. She is as fantastic as you said. And beautiful too."

Declan blushed crimson. "Uh, it's okay Ava. This is Arman Moore. My grandfather."

Ava froze mid-bow. "What?"

"Well... Great, great, great... lots more greats... I don't know... grandfather."

Her bright blue eyes darted from Arman to Declan. She climbed slowly to her feet. "You're telling me... The King of Vedmark is your grandfather?"

Declan nodded.

Ava's jaw dropped.

"The King of Vedmark," Arman boomed. "Now that is a title I have not heard for a long time."

Ava bowed again. "Apologies, Majesty. I did not mean to offend."

Arman boomed a mighty laugh. "It is an honor to be seen as more than a *demon*..." Arman trailed off and stared into the forest. "My dear, were you followed?"

Ava shook her head. "No. I don't think so. I used this." Ava held up a gold chain with a blue jewel on the end. She turned back and a small cry escaped her lips. Three Knights entered the clearing, clad in scaled green with hands at the ready.

Declan recognized Urik. The others appeared just as dangerous.

Arman nodded. "Stay behind me."

"I... I didn't..." Ava trailed off. Three more Knights approached to their left, four more to the right.

Arman smiled at her. "Fear not, my dear. You are safe with me. Stay behind—all is well."

Declan stepped back. A hint of movement caught his eye. "Grandfather, they're behind us."

"It would appear we are surrounded," Arman whispered. "Perhaps thirty."

Movement surrounded them—the source of the movement stayed hidden in the trees. *This is bad.* He squeezed Ava's hand. She squeezed back.

Urik raised an open hand. The other Knights stopped on his command. "We have you surrounded, demon. You will return with us to Vedmark to be judged by the Grand Steward."

Arman Moore looked entirely at ease. He beckoned Declan behind him, then met Urik's eye. "You demand my return, Knight. Tell me, on whose authority?"

Urik's face darkened. "Do not question me. Surrender now or face our wrath."

Arman's laughter boomed through the forest. Declan noticed more than one of the Knight's exchange uneasy glances.

"Very well," Urik said. "Knights—"

A tsunami of emerald light surged from the ground. It swept the Knights up like rag dolls and swirled around the clearing. A titanic tidepool of Sila. Emerald attacks erupted from within. Arman waved them aside. The flood of Sila rose higher and higher, then rushed together. Fifty feet high, thirty Knights crashed into each other. The green haze vanished.

Some of the Knights managed to slow their descent. Others were not so lucky. Declan cringed as one landed with a crunch. Injured bodies covered the ground, some stumbled to their feet, others did not move.

Urik wobbled, unsteady on shaking legs. Blood ran from a gash above his eye. The remaining Knights gathered behind him. They eyed Arman like a wild dog.

"You live because I am merciful," he boomed. "Take your wounded. Take your pride. Return to your Steward and tell him of your failure."

Green flames swirled up Urik's arms and out of his palms. Arman caught the flames in one hand, where they swelled into an enormous orb. The Knights attacked in unison. None of it mattered. Arman collected every spell and added it to the ball. It grew to the size of a cart, the size of a cabin. By the time the Knights' assault stopped, the sphere filled the clearing. With the slightest push, Arman rolled it toward them. The Knights had no choice but to retreat. "Remember your fallen," Arman called.

The Knights rushed to drag their wounded from the orb's advance. Through the devastation, they fled into the pines. Arman waved a hand and the glowing ball vanished.

"Foolish puppets" He leaned forward, breathing deeply. "Come, let us return to our lodging."

Declan looked him up and down. "Are you okay, grandfather?"

"I am," Arman said. "Or at least, I will be by morning."

Declan nodded. Ava didn't move.

"You are well, Ava?" Arman asked.

"Yes... I... that..." Ava's mouth hung open. She released Declan's hand and waved around to the clearing. "That was incredible!"

Arman smiled. "You are a ray of sunshine. Come. Back to the cabin. There is much to discuss." He turned to Declan. "Be a gentleman, grandson, and gather the lady's bag."

Declan squeezed Ava's hand. "Gladly."

CHAPTER 42
AVA

AVA FOLLOWED IN STUNNED SILENCE. *The Deathless Demon is Declan's grandfather?* The King led them to a small cabin, a single room with two doors either side. He offered her a seat and she took it. Declan placed the bag of shield-shards down by her ankles and asked if she'd like a hot chocolate. When she nodded, he raised a questioning eyebrow.

"Uh, grandfather, can you conjure hot chocolate?"

"Chocolate?" The King smiled. "A speciality of Hispania. You have fine taste."

Ava's cheeks glowed. "Thank you, but it's okay. We need to talk about Euryma. We have little time."

The King settled into an armchair. "What do you need to tell us?"

"Sabriva is in danger." Ava held Declan's eye. "I met your friend Katie."

"Katie? From King's College?"

Ava told them everything—the phonecall, stealing Haberdeen and trading her for information, Parteno being destroyed, Amber's stolen memories, the High Mage's plan to defeat the Fatesmiths, the Remnant Magic headed to Sabriva. She spoke until her voice was hoarse.

When she finished, Declan stood at the window, his face unreadable. "Who killed Amber?"

"We don't know," Ava said. "Someone is pretending to be Haberdeen. Katie thinks it's Ward—"

"Ward?" Declan stiffened. "No. It couldn't be. He's... gone."

"Well, the real Haberdeen is powerless. I don't know who is leading the Fatesmiths."

The King had listened without speaking. When they fell silent, he cleared his throat. "Dangerous events, indeed. How long until these Directive wizards attempt to use the tower?"

"Tomorrow."

Declan's eyebrows vanished into his curls. "Tomorrow? And Katie wants us to protect them? How would we even get there in one day?" He shook his head. "It sounds like they're trying to commit mass murder."

"It's not the Directive she's worried about," Ava said. "It's Remnant Magic. If a storm hits Sabriva, it will burn everyone to dust."

"And Sabriva Tower will fall." Declan's eyes grew wide. He turned to his grandfather. "The curse."

"Curse?"

The King stroked his beard. "My unnatural longevity is bound to Sabriva Tower, Ava. If it falls, that curse will break. I will no longer be immortal, and once I die, the Knights of Despair will descend upon Euryma like vultures."

Ava's heart skipped a beat. Her shoulders slumped. "We have to stop them. If we don't, it's my damned uncle who will lead those vultures."

"You are not your uncle, Ava," The King said. "Quite the opposite, I believe. My Emissary tells me you have served Vedmark well."

"I... I'm sorry?"

A coy smile played at the King's lips. "Samantha is not the Steward's ambassador to Euryma. She is mine."

Ava's mind went blank. "You mean?"

"You have served *me* well. Thank you."

Ava's eyes darted from the King to Declan. A long unanswered question finally made sense. "That's why I was sent to get Declan, to bring him to Vedmark. It was you?" Declan's eyebrows vanished into his messy curls.

"It was," said the King.

"You never told me that," Declan said.

"You never asked."

Ava's whole world flipped upside down.

"We'll get to that later," Declan said. "Right now, we have to figure out how to save Sabriva Tower. Do these Fatesmiths know when the storm will arrive?"

"I don't know," Ava said. "But it will be soon. Raul said the Fatesmiths aren't bothered about Euryma, that Remnant Magic will do it for them."

"And who is helping the Directive? Have they brought back any of the fierised people?"

Ava's stomach plummeted. She had left that part out of her story. *He doesn't know.*

Declan must have seen it in her face. "What happened?" he asked.

"All the witches and wizards..." Ava trailed off. She took a deep breath. "I'm so sorry Declan. They're all gone."

"What?"

"After the fake Haberdeen took Amber's memories, she ordered every fierised witch and wizard to be melted."

Declan stared at Ava. She watched as the words made sense. He stumbled from the window and fell into a chair.

"How did this impostor take the girl's memories?" asked the King.

"Winterthorn," Ava said.

"Winterthorn?" Declan's head snapped upright. Tears stained his cheeks. "That's what the Grand Steward was after. He thought I took it from Haberdeen. What is a Winterthorn?"

"A curse." The King's expression hardened. "Forged by my brother, imbued to steal the blood and memory of any flesh it touches. It is the blade Morkurik used to kill my father and brother. The knife that stole the wisdom of Vedmark's ancient rulers." The King shook his head. "I should have destroyed that dagger."

"What do we do?" Declan asked.

The failing light cast a pink hue over the King's long beard. "We must fight," he said. "Sabriva cannot fall. We can save your friends and defeat this new enemy." He looked at Declan. "Do you agree, grandson?"

Declan wiped his bloodshot eyes. "First my parents, then Amber, now Ace. Everything I touch turns to ashes. Maybe it is best I stay here." He stared at the floor. "I can't use Sila. I'll probably just be in the way."

The King stood. "None of these things are of your doing, Declan." He knelt and squeezed Declan's shoulders. "You have a light within you, as I did within me when my brother came to destroy what I loved. It is your duty to let that light burn bright and banish the shadow."

Declan met his gaze and Ava could see the pain in his eyes. "How can I be a light when all I feel is darkness?"

The King lifted him to his feet with a tight embrace. "The light is always there, Declan. You just have to look."

Declan's arms hung limply beside him. He looked unconvinced. "I'll try, grandfather."

Ava looked from one to the other, uncertain they understood the urgency of the situation. "I'm not, uh, sure if I made myself clear. The attack arrives *tomorrow*. We have to leave now."

The King nodded. "Fear not, Ava. I will get us to Sabriva."

"But..." Ava stopped at the sight of Declan. He shook from head to toe. "What's wrong?"

"It's nothing."

"Grandson?"

Declan turned away. "I just need some sleep, that's all."

Ava caught his arm. "Declan," she whispered. "What is it?" She touched his shoulder to turn him around. Silent tears streamed down his cheeks. Ava threw her arms around him. "It wasn't your fault."

"It was," Declan sobbed. "I should have gone after Ace, but I stayed. I wanted to use Sila so bad, I wanted the power, so I stayed. I might've been able to save him, but I didn't. I was selfish and now he's dead." He looked to the King. "And then they said it was impossible. I had no family to sacrifice, and then I met you, grandfather. And for a moment I had the idea that..." he trailed off, his gaze dropped to his feet. "If... if I killed you, I would get the power."

"A natural thought to have," the King said.

"But I don't want that. I don't want you to die. I don't want a storm to destroy Sabriva and you to be at risk. You're the only family I have left."

Despite his serene smile, the King's eyes sparkled. "I understand. More than you know. I have lived life after life, and in every one, I have watched those I love grow old and pass away. I have no intention of letting Sabriva fall, nor the Knights break free, but I have lived my life. I do not fear death." He placed a hand on Declan's shoulder. "Death is not the end, Declan. It is a return. A return to those I have loved and lost."

Declan's face was stone. "I don't want you to go."

"Then we will burn bright together. Tomorrow. Rest now. Tomorrow we will save our land."

"I... I don't think I'll be able to sleep tonight."

The King's lips formed a gentle curve. "Nothing a little Sila won't fix." He clicked his fingers and a green haze wafted gently around him. "Rest well, Declan. For tomorrow we fight."

Declan nodded and stumbled towards his room. The door shut and Ava heard something heavy fall into a bed. The King returned to his chair. Ava remained standing. *Am I supposed to go to sleep too?*

"He is tired." The King's gaze settled on the door. "He has trained for many weeks. He is a hard worker, a fast learner. He has come far with the axe." He beckoned for Ava to sit down. "Declan speaks of you often—he admires you greatly."

Ava's stomach somersaulted, but she kept a straight face. "I'm glad to hear it. I was worried I'd done some damage when I came back." She examined the back of her hands, not daring to look up. "What did he say about me?"

The King's beard shook in silent laughter. "Perhaps one day he will have the courage to tell you."

"Your Majesty, I fear for him. Should he even come to Euryma if he can't use his powers?"

"He needs to be there. He does not realize it yet, but the Emerald Throne belongs to him. It is his birthright. A King must earn his place."

"But he cannot wield Sila."

"He can handle an axe. That will be enough." The King considered her for a moment—Ava tried not to squirm. She felt like a child beneath his ageless gaze. "You will be there too. Can I count on you to pull chance in his favor?"

"Of course."

The King smiled. "My Emissary has trained you well, but her knowledge limits her. The Lucks of old were different, though I fear much of what they could do is gone."

Ava leaned in. "How so?"

"It was beyond me. My first love was a Luck, but her description of her power was as poor as my explanation of mine. When Sabriva is saved, I will tell you what I remember."

"I look forward to it. Thank-you your Majesty."

The King waved his hands. The interior of the cabin shimmered, as if dipped underwater. When it settled, the far wall had three doors instead of two. "Your room is ready. I hope it is to your liking."

Ava shook her head in disbelief. "Amazing."

The King chuckled. It echoed off the walls. "Rest well," he said. "Tomorrow, we ink our quills and write history."

CHAPTER 43
KATIE

KATIE GLARED at Michael as he crossed the room. Her blood boiled. *You idiot! You're going to get us all killed because you're as blind and stubborn as a brick!* She had said as much when he last removed her gag. Now it was there to stay.

"Report?" Laurefen asked from a dark desk.

Michael handed him a folder of papers. "Two thousand, four hundred and twenty-five. We have Mary-Lou to thank. Those news stories travelled the Dominion. Many of those we saved from Haberdeen's holdhouses have come to our aid."

You're going to kill those people we saved! The people we sacrificed my mother to save!

Laurefen ignored her. "We may stand a chance after all. Are they aware of the plan?"

"They are. Groups of fifty. Half spread across the inner-city, the others watching the outskirts. We have planted rumors that we will perform the incantation at noon. Now, we wait for them to take the bait."

Laurefen flicked through the pages. "Very well. It appears everything is in order." He shut the folder and turned to Katie. She scowled at him. "I understand you do not agree with our methods, and I will not waste time trying to convince you otherwise. Regardless, the hour is upon us. Today we go to war against the enemy that has taken so many of our loved ones, your dear mother included."

Katie didn't blink. Her glare was as sharp as a knife.

"You are a capable witch—we could use your support. We will release you if you commit to working with us until Sabriva is safe." He nodded for Michael to release her gag, then turned back to her. "What do you say?"

Katie spat hot saliva at his feet. "You are a wretch of a fool. Two and half thousand will be dead before the day's out. My mother's legacy will be your idiocy, and *your* legacy will be failure."

Michael raised his hand, but Laurefen caught his wrist. "Katie."

"Their blood will be on *your* hands. *My* blood will be on your hands. But you won't be around to feel the guilt. You'll be dead too. They'll remember you as the idiot that handed the Fatesmiths what they wanted on a silver platter."

"That's enough," Michael growled.

"No," Katie hissed through clenched teeth. "No, it's not! I want you to know that when you see the storm coming, see your doom on the horizon, and you *finally* realize that you were wrong, I want you to remember that I was right, and you bound me up in nima." She spat again. "I hope your last thoughts are torture. You've wasted your legacy. You will have died for nothing because—" The gag returned.

"A shame, Katie," Laurefen said. "We need all the help we can muster. Raul has you under his spell. I will accept your apology when this is all over."

An urgent knock sounded at the door and Mary-Lou poked her head in, face flushed. "Movement to the north, Laurefen, Fatesmiths coming through Openings by their thousands. They've taken the bait."

"How long until they reach the city?"

"Not long enough. I expect they will be here by noon."

"Then we have no time to waste," Laurefen said. "Alert our forces. Wall the northern side and prepare the ambush sites."

Mary-Lou glanced at her palm. "Looptap from Fairborough, more approach from the south."

Laurefen turned to Michael. "An approach from both sides?"

Michael waved his hands, and a small triangle rotated to form a circular Opening. Through it, the level plains stretched for miles around the Sabriva.

"Where is that?" Mary-Lou asked.

"Top of Sabriva Tower." Michael disappeared through the Opening. "They're everywhere," he shouted from the other side. "Laurefen, you need to see this.."

Laurefen stepped through with Mary-Lou close behind. Frozen in the corner, Katie could only wait. When they returned, all three were pale. "Tell the wizards at Fairborough to prepare for battle," Laurefen directed. "Attack first, then retreat to the ambush sites."

Michael rubbed his jaw. "We can't hold every side of the city."

"We're outnumbered Laurefen." Mary-Lou squeezed her braid. "What do you propose we do?"

"We understand how their weaves work. We have ambush sites planned. This battle is our legacy. Our chance at victory." Laurefen stared out the window. "We stick to the plan. We fight."

Strips of light filtered through the closed blinds as Katie puzzled out her last encounter with the Directive. *Why would the Fatesmiths bring so many people if a Remnant Magic storm is on the way?* She had no idea how long had passed since they left her bound and gagged in the office. Occasionally, she heard faint shouts from outside. Mostly, it was silent.

Someone slipped inside the room, closing the door without a sound. Katie thought someone had found her—trapped, helpless—like a mouse in a trap. Then Mary-Lou knelt down. "Kate," she whispered. "This is bad."

The gag of compressed air vanished. "I could have told you that," Katie croaked.

"They have an army, over ten times the size of ours," Mary-Lou said. "They are coming from every side. Laurefen wants to fight. I fear we've backed ourselves into a corner."

"Good," Katie said. "Serves you right."

Mary-Lou's silhouette stiffened in the darkness. "I know you're angry at us. We're not perfect, but we're trying to do right by Euryma."

Katie closed her eyes and swallowed the choice words she had for the older woman. "What do you want from me?"

Her magical bonds vanished. Mary-Lou touched her shoulder. "We need you to fight. We need everyone."

"You're an idiot," Katie said. "A Remnant Magic storm is coming. The Fatesmiths—"

"Then why are they here?" Mary-Lou interrupted. Her voice wasn't harsh, it was the opposite. Earnest, pleading. "If Sabriva is about to be destroyed, why would an army show up and die with us?"

"I... I don't know. Maybe..." Katie trailed off. She didn't have an answer to that.

"Can you imagine a possibility?" Mary-Lou went on. "Even the smallest sliver of a chance that you might be wrong about all of this? That we might actually know what we're talking about?"

"Lou... I saw Bruxelle. This isn't Fatesmiths. This isn't Declan. This is something bigger."

"Perhaps it is." Mary-Lou squeezed Katie's arm. A gentle, motherly squeeze. The type her own mother would never give again. "But right now there's an army of Fatesmiths, and we need you."

Every inch of Katie's body wanted to knock the woman flat and run. Escape to safety, while she still could. *Amber would fight*, said a little voice. *Mom too. What if you're wrong?* Katie sighed. "I'll do what I can."

Outside, the sun hung at its peak. For the first time in Katie's life, the frantic inner-city traffic of Sabriva was gone. A unsettling emptiness replaced the city's rush.

"In here, dear," Mary-Lou called her to a maroon van.

"Cool wheels," she said, but the joke fell flat. Mary-Lou put the car into gear and accelerated down the vacant street. She rounded corners at speed. Katie took in the emptiness. "Where is everyone?"

"Hiding in their homes, I guess."

"They should have left."

Mary-Lou pursed her lips and continued driving. They went east until they reached the edge of the city. There, a line of Fatesmiths stood shoulder to shoulder at the end of the road. They didn't move; they didn't speak. A wall of blackcoats facing the city.

"What is going on?" Katie asked. Mary-Lou didn't reply. Instead, she pulled onto the curb outside a small restaurant. Katie followed her inside, up a set of old stairs and out onto the roof. Laurefen and Michael turned to face her.

Katie's cheeks burned. She drew herself up to Laurefen's eye despite every part of her screaming to look away. His lips twitched into the smallest smile. "Thank you for coming, Katie. I realize this is difficult for you."

A selection of choice curses rose to mind, but Katie bit her tongue. Her fingers brushed around the surrounding aeronima. She longed to rip the air out from underneath them. *Breathe,* she told herself. *Just get through the next day.* She gestured to the street below. The Fatesmiths still hadn't moved. "What are they doing?"

"We do not know," Laurefen said. "If we attack, they shield themselves. We cannot provoke them to follow. It is as if they are waiting for something."

Small groups of people waited on the surrounding rooftops, five or six at the most. Katie scanned the surrounding buildings. "This is all we've got?"

Michael shook his head. "This is the bait. The bulk of our numbers wait in the industrial district."

"So, how do we get them into the trap?"

"That's what we are trying to work out," Laurefen said.

Katie forced herself to hold his gaze. "Have you considered the possibility they are waiting for the storm?"

"It is impossible, Katie. What you consider Remnant Magic is welled up at Kingsbreak."

The words took a moment to make sense. "Welled up?" Katie blinked. "What... what does that mean?"

Laurefen did not meet her gaze. "It is Euryma's most well-guarded secret; the reason we know the Fatesmiths are lying. I should have told you sooner."

"I don't understand—"

"Movement. There." Michael pointed down to the line. "Discuss the Well later. What are they doing?"

A shimmering silver square coursed through the line. The Fatesmiths did not move. In moments, the line of men and women transformed into a line of iron casts.

"They're fierising themselves," Mary-Lou said.

Katie's confusion lasted moments. Then she remembered what Raul had told her on their way to Bruxelle. Her stomach plummeted into a hollow pit. "They're shielding themselves," she whispered. "I... I was right."

"What?" Laurefen shook his head. "Michael, take us down."

Michael attempted an Opening. A triangle appeared in the air, rippled and blinked away. He tried again with the same result. "They're blocking the spell somehow."

A faint glow rose over the horizon

"Blocking your spell. How?" Mary-Lou asked.

Katie swallowed. Her voice felt tiny. "You should have listened to me." None of them were listening. Michael tried again, but the Opening would not start.

"You stupid idiots," Katie growled. That caught their attention. She pointed to the sloping hills to Sabriva's east. Radiant orange light grew brighter. A sunset in reverse. Katie watched, transfixed, from the rooftop. *I knew it. I knew it was coming. What have I done? Nothing. All of it for nothing.* Frustration sparked a flame of fury. She turned on Laurefen. "You should have listened!" she screamed. He looked like a stunned deer. Michael and Mary-Lou were no better.

"What is that?" Mary-Lou asked.

"What do you think?" Katie had never been so angry. "I told you! I told you what was coming, and you tied me to a damned chair!"

"But... but... it can't..." Michael's voice failed. The orange light reflected off his bulging eyes. "The Well..."

The surge continued to grow. Katie couldn't believe how fast it moved. Tears of anger streamed down her face. "You idiots! You should have listened!"

"We need to move," Mary-Lou squeaked. "We need to go!"

"There is nowhere to go!" Katie shouted. "Look at it! We can't outrun that!"

"Go! Down to the van." Laurefen tried to wave to the people on the rooftops. None noticed. The strange light in the distance held their attention.

Michael grabbed his arm. "Laurefen! We need to go!"

The wave eclipsed the surrounding hills. It would be in the city in minutes. Katie followed down the stairs, two at a time, and jammed herself into the back seat of the van. Mary-Lou revved the engine and roared down the road.

"Sound your horn," Laurefen said. "Warn as many people as you can."

Mary-Lou leaned against the steering wheel. The car wailed down the street. Passing buildings became a blur. Sabriva Tower loomed ahead. "Where am I going?"

"Away!" Michael watched out the back window. "Faster!"

A vivid, fiery sunset replaced the sky. A wall of orange.

Mary-Lou took a corner, the side wheels lifted off the road, the van stank of burnt rubber. The engine whined as the van reached its limit and Mary-Lou banged a fist on the dash. "No, no, no, no!"

The surge flooded the city. Sections of buildings blew across it, smashing through the street like leaves in a breeze. Falling rubble chased them. Katie gripped her chair.

"Faster!" Laurefen shouted, looking in his rear mirror. "Watch out!"

A car-sized section of building rocketed past them, tearing the asphalt from the ground. Mary-Lou swerved, Katie's head hit the window. Architecture rained over them like missiles, destroying whatever they touched. Orange filled her view. *This is it.*

"Lou!" Michael cried as a stone arch collapsed in front of them. Mary-Lou spun the wheel, the tires screeched, they missed their deaths by a hair. The van mounted the curb. They tore across the grass of Sabriva Square as Remnant Magic swallowed the city.

"Get on the other side of Sabriva Tower!" Laurefen shouted. "It might block it!"

"Are you seeing this?" Michael shouted. "Nothing's going to stop that!"

"It's better than nothing!" Laurefen's white knuckles gripped the handle on the passenger door.

Mary-Lou sped towards the looming tower. Towering trees shattered like woodchips. *They should have listened!*

"Get ready to run!" Mary-Lou shouted. She slammed on the brakes, they skidded toward the tower wall. Michael had the door open before they stopped. He jumped out, Katie followed and came face to face with the oncoming storm. Deep orange, closer to red, engulfed the sky. It roared like a thousand wildfires. A devastating sense of fear cemented her feet to the ground. *There is no escaping this.* The sight of the surge was overwhelming.

Someone grabbed Katie's hand. It was Mary-Lou. Her face glowed in the red light. "I'm sorry," she whispered. Katie squeezed her hand and nodded.

They waited for the Remnant Magic to engulf them. *I'm sorry Amber. I failed. I'm sorry.*

Fierce heat built around them, but it was no ordinary heat. It came with a sting, a piercing sensation that brought her to her knees. Mary-Lou fell beside her. From the corner of her eye, she saw Michael and Laurefen already on the ground. She gasped—hot air burnt her lungs. She braced herself for death.

A flash of green exploded ahead of them. Three people stepped into the nightmare. Katie squinted into the glow. *Declan?*

CHAPTER 44

DECLAN

TERRIBLE HEAT ROLLED off the Remnant Magic. Declan fought to stay upright as his grandfather raised his hands. A glowing emerald web spread out from him in all directions, high into the sky and curving back over them. The surge hit it with the force of a volcano. Arman slid backward, his feet tearing tracks in the dirt. The storm shrieked like all the wind in the world. Trees, cars, buildings rent from foundations blew into the barrier of Sila, drawn up over the shield or burned to dust. Arman's jaw tensed, sweat beading about his temples.

"Are you okay?" Declan called.

"It is strong," he said. "I will hold it for as long as I can."

Ava dropped her bag. The shieldshards rattled inside. "I can help," she said. "I can use Luck to support you."

"Save your Luck," Arman said. "You know its role."

What does that mean? Declan turned and saw movement to his right. He drew his axe, then froze. Four familiar faces stumbled to their feet. Laurefen, Michael, Mary-Lou and Katie. They looked shattered. Declan lowered his weapon. "Laurefen?"

Katie rushed forward. "Declan! You came!" She threw herself onto him.

"Hi Kate." Declan stepped back from her. "What happened? Why are you still here?"

Katie's face darkened. She nodded to the other Directive members, who approached with guarded expressions. "The Fatesmiths knew Remnant Magic was headed to Sabriva. They surrounded the city and fierised themselves before it arrived." She gestured to Laurefen. "Meanwhile, our fearless leader caught himself in his own trap." Katie's eyes dropped. "Declan, they killed Amber."

"I know." Guilt turned Declan's stomach. "Ava told me."

Katie smiled at Ava. "You found him," she said. "Thank you. You saved our skins. "

"Looks like we got here just in time." Ava pointed to the tower. "As long as that building stands, we have a chance."

"What do you mean?" Laurefen studied them with caution; his eyes darted to Arman. "And who is that?"

Arman glanced back at them. Hands held high, a thin sheen of sweat coated his face. "I am Arman Moore," he said through gritted teeth. "King of Vedmark and grandfather to Declan Moore."

Declan blushed. Katie's eyes widened. Laurefen's jaw fell slack. "King of Vedmark..."

"And what we mean," Ava jumped in, "is if Sabriva Tower falls, you're going to have more than blackcoats to worry about. You said they fierised themselves?"

Katie nodded. "I think they did it to weather the storm."

Ava bit her lip. "You mean..."

Katie stared up at the orange sky. "When this is gone, whoever survives will have an army to deal with."

Michael cleared his throat. "You're telling me that once this is over, those ironhands will be waiting for us?"

"And it all could have been avoided if you listened to reason," Katie muttered.

The torrential wave of Remnant Magic stripped Sabriva of stone, brick and asphalt. Arman walled off the tower itself, but everything beyond it washed away like a city of sandcastles.

"That's... Forty thousand against seven." Mary-Lou tugged her braid.

Declan's shoulders slumped. "Those aren't promising odds."

"Can you use your power?" Mary-Lou asked.

Declan held up his axe. "I can use this."

Laurefen turned to Ava. "You said if the Tower falls, we'll have more than Fatesmiths to worry about. What does that mean?"

"Knights of Despair." Ava said. "As long as Sabriva Tower stands, the Knights cannot leave Vedmark."

"And if the Tower falls?"

"Vedmark's Knights shall return," Arman said. "Seeking to finish what they started a thousand years ago."

Michael and Laurefen appeared uncertain, but Mary-Lou's eyes contained a curious glint. "So, you're not a Knight of Despair?" she asked.

"No," Declan said. "No, I am a Warlock."

"There's a difference?"

"Knights can use Si—uh, green magic, whenever they want. Warlocks can only use it when terrible things happen, like when my parents were killed at Anderma. But they can't use it at will."

Mary-Lou hugged him. "I'm sorry Declan," she whispered. "We have made so many mistakes. How we treated you was one of them."

Ava considered the Directive. "Can you do anything?"

she asked. "Last time I was this close to this type of storm, it stopped your magic altogether."

Laurefen pulled a strip of grass from the ground with a twist of his wrist. "It appears the shield is blocking the disruption."

"Can't you use an Opening to get us out of here?" Mary-Lou asked.

Michael attempted as much. The doorway flickered and vanished. "Not yet."

"It wouldn't matter if you could," Declan said. "We cannot let them destroy the Tower." He turned to Arman, whose arms trembled in the green light. "Are you okay, grandfather?"

"It is a heavy burden," he replied. "But one that grows weaker by the moment. Even now, the ebbs and flows lessen from what they were. It should be over soon."

"How long have we got?" Ava asked.

"It is hard to tell. Minutes."

"It felt like hours in Parteno." Her gaze climbed the wall of Sila and she shook her head. "Incredible."

"So the storm passes, the Fatesmiths advance." Michael raised an eyebrow. "Forty thousand witches and wizards against *us*. What do we do?"

Declan looked up at Sabriva Tower. In the deep orange light, it glowed like a pillar of fire. "We don't have to beat them all. Just one." He turned to Laurefen. "Who leads the blackcoats?"

"Haber—"

"It is not Haberdeen," Ava interjected. "She is a shell of a witch, no memory of anything before Anderma."

"It's Ward," Katie said. "He must have tricked you, Declan. He's wearing Haberdeen's face the same way he pretended he was John."

346

Declan's expression darkened. *First my parents, then Amber and Ace.* Hate flared within him. "Then he is the one we need to kill. Cut the head off the snake."

Laurefen frowned. "If it is Ward, he would be foolish to fight on the front line."

"How do we get past their army?" Michael asked.

"Luck," Ava said. "There will be some chance Ward will come to us. I'll draw on that string of Luck. Once he's here, we can kill him and finish this."

Orange light above flickered as the tail-end of the storm passed by, flares of elongated clouds of magic that danced like flames. As suddenly as it arrived, it was gone. Sunlight broke over the skeleton of Sabriva Square. Arman lowered his hands. The emerald barrier faded away. Once it was gone, he sat on the grass and lay back. Declan rushed to his side.

"I am fine, Declan, just taking a moment to rest." Arman's chest heaved between breaths. "Your plan is good. Draw in the leader, then defeat them."

"I learned it from the best," Declan said with a tight smile.

Sabriva was rubble, the roads ragged dirt trails, the trees uprooted, the grass scorched blight. Everyone stood in stunned silence. Ava shook her head. "It's just like Parteno," she whispered, kneeling beside him. "Like Bruxelle. Complete destruction."

"Not exactly complete." Declan nodded to Sabriva Tower. It gleamed, victorious against the blue sky.

Ava squeezed his shoulder. "Then we had best protect what's left." She stood and held out her hand.

Declan let her pull him to his feet. "The Fatesmiths are on their way. We have one goal. Keep the tower safe. Whatever they try to do, we have to undo. Ava, find Ward. The sooner he's dead, the better."

Ava closed her eyes, her brow furrowed in concentration. When they opened, she was frowning.

"What is it?" Katie asked.

"They're on their way."

As if in reply, a faint clatter of footsteps echoed through the debris. A haze of pulverized stone blanketed the source of the sound, but the din of their march grew louder. Declan spun his axe and concentrated on his grip; he was holding it too tight, but it was the best he could manage. Butterflies fluttered in his stomach. Arman stood and put a hand on Declan's shoulder. "Do not fear, grandson. We will live, we will see."

A thunderous chorus of footsteps split the dusty haze as a mass of people stepped into the sun. They wore black coats with embroidery and glittering buttons, their faces were grim, eyes dark. A woman with auburn hair raised a fist and the advance stopped. A sea of blackcoats encircled them.

Declan gripped his axe a little tighter. These weren't the blackcoats he remembered. "Something isn't right," he whispered to Ava.

"See their hands?"

Declan focused on the front of the army. Their hands were rough and worn. *Those aren't the hands of wizards. Those are...* "They're LAMPs."

The auburn-haired woman stepped forward. Her hands were immaculate. "It's over," she shouted. "Your High Mage is dead. Sabriva has fallen. We are Euryma's future." She waved to the army behind her. "Surrender with a blood-spell oath, and we will let you live."

"What kind of oath?" Laurefen said. Katie shot him a look of disgust.

"An oath to give up the use of magic. To live as a LAMP and put an end to the destruction caused by Remnant Magic."

Laurefen exchanged a thoughtful glance with Michael. Mary-Lou touched his elbow and stepped forward. "We need time to consider it."

"No time. No tricks. Take our oath or we will overpower you. We are fifty-thousand strong. You cannot stop us all, even with your magic."

"What about the tower?" Ava asked. "Sabriva Tower is a beacon to Euryma. Allow it to stand."

"A beacon you planned to use against us." The woman spat on the ground. "Sabriva is no more. The old ways are no more. The Dominion will be ruled by people, not magic. As long as it stands, Sabriva Tower is a threat. It must fall."

Declan drew himself up. "No."

The woman's lips grew thin. "This is not a negotiation."

"Not with you." Declan searched the army of black-coats. "Who do you speak for? Where is your leader?"

"*That* is none of your concern," the woman growled.

"Ophelia. That's your name, right?" Katie asked. The woman nodded. Katie raised her open palms. "You have the city, Ophelia. Why waste the lives of your followers? We will take your oath if you move on. Leave the Tower untouched."

"This is *not* a negotiation!" Ophelia shouted. "We offer mercy, but our patience is running out. Sabriva Tower represents everything that is wrong with Euryma. This is your last chance. What is your choice?"

Katie turned to Declan, who looked to his grandfather.

Arman stepped forward, his arms burned green. He spoke with the voice of a winter storm. "Enough! If you seek to destroy this place, you will find only death. Yield or meet your end."

The woman's jaw softened at the sight of the Sila. She clenched her jaw. "We will not yield."

Arman's face hardened. "Nor shall we."

CHAPTER 45
DECLAN

OPHELIA RAISED an open palm and the mass of blackcoats drew swords; short with the dull glimmer of iron. Declan stared at them. They weren't swords. They were metal bars with wrapped leather handles. Others dug piles of what looked like ash from their coats. The Fatesmiths brandished the odd weapons and waited, eyes fixed on their auburn-haired leader.

She thrust her hand down at them. "Attack!"

A wall of emerald flame erupted from beneath them. Ophelia leaped back to safety. Blackcoats screamed and fell to the barren ash, rolling desperately to extinguish the flames. Others abandoned their burning coats and charged.

A swirling mist circled the tower. Shouts rang out in the chaos as Sila plucked Fatesmiths from the battlefield and dropped to the ground. Laurefen and Michael wrapped them in nima, then tossed them over the other side of the flames.

Declan turned to Ava. "Where is the leader?"

Ava pointed off in the distance, her finger tracing a path. "Out there." A blackcoat appeared behind her. Declan raised his axe, but before he could do anything, Ava caught him in the leg with a knife and in the face with her foot. More approached either side of them. The Fatesmiths had used rubble to create a bridge over the fire. They charged—iron rods held high.

A stream of knives flew from Ava's sleeve. Two men dropped, but more kept coming. Declan's anxiousness melted as he followed his axe into the Lion.

The blackcoat swung at his head—a novice error—and Declan parried the bar and jerked the pole to the ground. A quick counter found the man's cheek. Lights out. Three more ran towards him. Declan reset his grip and rushed to meet them.

Between the dancing axe and Ava's knives, a steady pile of bodies built between them. Declan did his best to only maim those he encountered—often turning his axe at the last moment to prevent a fatal blow. More than once, he let opponents retreat when he could have had their heads. The blackcoats showed no such mercy. They swung their iron rods like their lives depended on it, occasionally throwing out handfuls of black powder from their coat pockets to blind them.

Arman continued sweeping up the most of the Fatesmiths. Throwing them high into the air for others to deal with. Declan and Ava cleared the scraps. Some he beat, a few beat him, but magic always snatched them away before they could do him harm.

Declan edged closer to Ava. "This is useless," he said. A woman leaped forward. He ducked beneath her, side-stepped into Bear and spun the blunt end of his axe head into her stomach. Ribs cracked. The woman tried to stand. Ava extinguished her consciousness with a boot. "Where's Ward?"

352

"I don't know," Ava said. "I can't focus while we're under attack."

Declan scanned the battlefield. Katie and Mary-Lou stood back to back, fingers twitching like concert pianists, lashes of water whirled around them like tentacles, forcing blackcoats to the ground. He rushed towards them. "Katie! Ava needs a safe space to find Ward. Can you two cover her?"

Mary-Lou pointed ahead to Arman. "Only if you can protect your grandfather."

"I'll have to," Declan said. "We can't keep doing what we're doing. There's too many of them. We need to end this now."

Katie nodded. Mary-Lou looked more reluctant.

"Trust me." Declan told Ava. "Head to the Tower. Find Ward and bring him here." Declan saw a Fatesmith dash at his grandfather. He raised his iron rod, then exploded like glass.

"On second thought," Mary-Lou said. "Maybe your grandfather is just fine without us."

Declan leaped back into the battle. He moved from form to form, alternating between Bear and Lion, lost in the dance's rhythm. A hailstorm of boulders crashed over the clearing and a group of wizards burst through the flames. Their hands moved in a blur and the boulders rose into the air. Michael and Laurefen charged towards them. Declan sidestepped a new opponent, a grizzled old man with hair jutting in every direction. He swung his iron bar with the speed and precision of a swordsman. The man's eyes burned with delight as he pushed Declan into the ring of flame.

Declan could feel the flame's warmth on his back. He had nowhere to go. The man parried Lion easily and left little room for Bear. Declan retreated far as he dared, created some space and moved into the Bull. The change of pace caught the man off guard. Declan forced him back, but the victory was short-lived. He caught Declan's axe mid-swing and knocked the axe to the ground. The man smiled triumphantly, then disappeared beneath an enormous concrete boulder. Michael dusted off his hands and gave a stern nod.

Declan froze in shock. A half-dozen unfamiliar wizards lay scattered on the grass, glazed eyes wide open. There was nobody left to fight. Hundreds of bodies littered the grounds. At the foot of the stairs, the Directive stood together. Declan picked up his axe. "Where is everyone?"

"It appears your grandfather has turned the tide," Laurefen said. "He is immensely powerful, Declan. Your heritage explains many mysteries."

"But why retreat now?" Declan climbed the tower steps and searched the ruins of the city. Blackcoats waited in their thousands, but they no longer attacked. They were retreating, but at a snail's pace. "Something's not right."

Arman joined them. He looked as tired as Declan had ever seen him. He nodded to the wall of flames. "They carry their injured, and we have injured many." He sat against the tower.

"Watch out!" Ava's eyes were pools of panic. "Declan, he's coming!"

A column of purple light crackled high above them. Arman shot to his feet, but he was too slow. The beam split the tower with ground shaking force. Glass and concrete rained down on them. A panel of green wrapped itself around the building—Arman was holding the tower together. He dropped to one knee.

"Grandfather!" Declan slid through the dirt to his side. "Grandfather, no!"

Arman groaned as he stumbled forward. Declan caught him and lowered him to the grass. "The Tower," he muttered. "We must protect the Tower." He lay back and closed his eyes. The panel vanished.

"Grandfather!" Declan pressed his ear to Arman's chest. A faint heartbeat remained.

"Ire Tides," Mary-Lou hissed. "That purple light, those are Ire Tides! Ward has sacrificed humanity for power. We need to be careful."

"Up there!" Ava stared up at the sky.

A hooded figure soared through the air, flailing like a paper bag in the wind. The figure landed gracefully ahead of them. They straightened and tossed back their hood. It was Haberdeen.

"Now, now, who do we have here?" she sneered. "A couple of college elitists unwilling to take an oath? Do-gooders who care more about power than the lives of billions?"

"Who are you?" Katie said.

"I am Haberdeen, leader of the Fatesmiths."

"No, you're not!" Katie shouted. "Haberdeen is a shadow of a witch. You may have her memories, but you are not her!"

The red-haired woman considered Katie. Her lips twisted into a menacing grimace. "I know you. You're that coward from Anabar Bay. The one who abandoned her friend. The one who let her die."

Katie screamed and charged at her. The impostor laughed as her eyes flashed purple.

Declan waved to Ava. "Help her!"

A stray iron pole found Katie's foot and she stumbled to

the ground. A purple blast of magic missed her by a hair. She rolled to the side and her hands went to work. Haberdeen brandished a snow-white blade and sliced through the air. Katie gasped. Mary-Lou and Michael tried to help, but the knife somehow undid every spell they conjured. Declan watched in disbelief. "She's cutting through their nima," he whispered.

Laurefen lifted four boulders and heaved them at the woman. She blasted them to dust with thick beams of light. She waved a hand and threw Laurefen aside. He hit the ground hard, rolled through the grass and didn't get up.

A fresh beam of Ire Tides forced Michael and Mary-Lou backward. Katie was nowhere to be seen. The woman spun, her glowing eyes settled on Arman. *No!* Declan threw his axe at her. She raised a hand to stop it but the iron head cut through the magic. At the last minute, she ducked. The axe fell into the dirt.

Declan found an iron bar and began to swing. Over the shoulder, under the arm—*catch-swing, catch-swing, catch-swing, catch-swing.* Armadillo formed a protective shell around him. He moved towards the impostor as she staggered upright. He saw her eyes widen, saw them glow purple, saw light surge from her palm. *Catch-swing-catch-swing.* The Ire Tides bounced off. Declan continued to advance. *Catchswingcatchswing.* Another beam, another. The woman retreated. Then, with two hands, thrust a surge of violet energy towards him. It reflected off the barrier, straight back into her.

For a moment, the woman lifted from the ground, propelled skyward by her own spell. She slid backward through dirt and grass, then leaped to her feet. Only it was someone different now. Declan stopped and the iron bar fell from his hand. Haberdeen was gone. In her place stood a young man with a dark curtain of hair; not Ward, but someone else. Someone Declan never expected to see again.

"Ace?"

Horace's face contorted into a dark smile. Electric purple light blazed from his eyes, and he thrust out his hands. Declan flattened himself against the ground as a pillar of Ire Tides as thick as his torso hissed through the air. He rolled away and watched in horror as it blasted a gaping hole through the base of Sabriva Tower. *No!*

Declan scrambled to his feet, rushed back to his grandfather's side. High above, the tower groaned and shifted. With an awful roar, it began to shake. Declan wrapped his arms around his only family as stone rained over them. Through the chaos he saw Horace back away. The sky went dark.

Declan hugged his grandfather as Sabriva Tower collapsed around them.

CHAPTER 46
DECLAN

AMIDST A CHOKING plume of crushed masonry, Declan opened his eyes. He was alive. A shieldshard protruded from the ground. The dim glow of the amber hemisphere surrounded him and his grandfather. It crackled gently beneath the tower's weight.

Behind them, two more magical shields cast an eerie light in the darkness. Ava waved from inside one. She sat with Laurefen's unconscious body, while Katie, Michael and Mary-Lou huddled in another. As far as Declan could tell, they were buried deep below the debris. The cause of the collapse rushed back to him. *That was Ace, He's alive. He's leading the Fatesmiths. How did he get there? What's wrong with him? Why is he using Ire Tides?* Arman groaned; Declan's questions vanished. "Grandfather!"

"Declan..." Arman's eyes blinked open. "Where are we?"

"We..." *I failed you.* Declan gathered his voice. "We are under Sabriva Tower. I'm sorry, I couldn't stop it."

Arman struggled to sit up. Between labored breaths, he leaned over and spat on the ground. Blood. A crimson pool glistened in the shield's dim light. Arman's long beard was a mess. His skin seemed looser than before. "You did your best, grandson. Now there is one last thing you need to do."

"Yes, grandfather, anything."

Arman drew his axe from his belt and laid it in Declan's hands. "You must take this axe and end my life. Fell me like an old pine. Take your power, save our home."

Declan felt like someone had punched him in the stomach. He dropped the axe and shook his head. "No. Not that. Anything but that."

Arman Moore held his eye. "I am mortal now, Declan. The ravages of age find me at last. Spill my blood and gain access to your own Sila."

"Grandfather. I can't..." Declan trailed off. *All my life, I've wanted magical powers. Now it's here and I don't want it. I want my grandfather to live.* "You're all I have left..."

Arman smiled. "You're a good man, Declan. And sometimes, good men are required to make difficult choices."

"No. There's another way—there always is." He peered through the shields surrounding them. "Ava! Do you have any sanarmelon juice?"

"I do," she shouted back, the barrier muffled her voice. "But I can't get it to you. If I drop the shield, we'll be crushed."

Declan searched their crude sarcophagus. "Grandfather, can you shift the debris?"

"I can, but I will not." Arman's face was set. "You know what you must do."

Declan shook his head. "I already lost my parents. I can't lose you too."

"This is about more than you. I am old, I am weak and Winterthorn is here. My memories contain secrets too dangerous to share. They hold the key to the Ancellum, to

359

Euryma's magic." A shadow of pain crossed his face. "Those memories cannot fall into the wrong minds."

"We can't lose you," Declan said. "If I spill your blood, the Knights will be free. I'll get you the sanarmelon juice and Michael can create an Opening. We'll get you out of here. We'll fight another day." Declan squeezed his shoulder. "You can't give up."

"I am not giving up, Declan. I am accepting my fate. I am ready to see my family again. I am ready to go."

"You can't!"

Arman winced as he sat up by Declan's side. "Declan, my grandson. The role of a king is not an easy one. It requires courage to make the choices nobody else dares to make."

"Grandfa—"

An amethyst explosion bathed them in blinding light. White spots burned into Declan's retina. He blinked back his vision and his blood turned to ice. Horace stood over him, his thin face a mask of fury.

The Directive attacked first. Their shieldshards dissipated and they advanced as one, attacking from all sides, raining rubble from above and sabotaging Horace's footing from below. Horace withdrew behind a mound of broken stone. When he emerged, he had Winterthorn in hand. He moved with devastating speed, slicing through invisible threads, directing columns of purple light from the palm of his hand.

Michael ducked beneath the Ire Tides, leaving Mary-Lou exposed. The beam caught her side and knocked her to the ground. With a cry of pain, she curled into a ball. Katie skidded through the dirt to meet her. "Help!" she screamed.

Horace slid the white dagger into his coat and raised both hands, his eyes ignited. Michael tossed Katie a shieldshard, and she stabbed it into the ground. It erupted around them just in time to reflect the Ire Tides into an upturned section of stone stairs. The stairs exploded in Michael's direction. As far as Declan could see, he was buried underneath.

Horace advanced on the shieldshard, pressing a thick column of light onto its surface. At first, the purple beam reflected off the barrier—reducing the surrounding rubble to dust—but Horace refused to give up. The Ire Tides grew larger, thicker, until the shield flaked away. Declan watched in horror as the shield shattered like a fluorescent bulb. Katie tried to attack, but Horace grabbed her by the neck and tossed her to the ground.

"Let me go!" Katie screamed. Horace said nothing. He pinned her with his foot and raised a glowing purple fist. Then he turned and snarled as a knife lodged in his shoulder.

Ava sidestepped the remains of Sabriva Tower, a flurry of knives blooming from her belt. Horace retreated behind a twisted metal frame and Katie crawled to find cover. Mary-Lou hadn't moved. Declan's eyes darted from her stationary body to Ava. She was circling the rubble, knives in each hand. A flash of movement caught his eye. Horace appeared above her.

"I have to go, grandfather." Declan pressed the top of the shieldshard and dashed across the chaos. Horace crashed into Ava. She rolled out from his grasp and tried to escape. With a flick of Horace's hand, she was thrown skywards, soaring towards a jagged section of stonework. At the last moment, she stopped in mid-air. Declan spun to see Katie work furiously to lower her to safety. Horace noticed too. He shot a pulse in Katie's direction, forcing her to roll out of reach. Ava landed hard against the stone. Horace turned back to her, raising his hands.

With two arms, Declan launched Arman's axe across the clearing. It rotated in slow motion, the polished iron glinted like starlight as it cartwheeled through the air. Horace did not sense it until it was on him. He shrieked in agony. His left hand fell to the ground. He stumbled back, cradling a jagged stump. Blood poured out from under his elbow. He cauterized the stub with a purple flash.

Declan marched through the ruins of Sabriva Square. "What is wrong with you?" Declan shouted. "Look at what you've done!"

Horace's eyes burned like a violet caldera. "I'm doing what has to be done!"

"You're a murderer! How many have you killed? Thousands? Tens of thousands?"

Horace spat on Sabriva's ashes. "I'm saving billions! You don't know what I know! You can't see what I see! This is the *only* way!"

"This isn't you, Ace!" Declan stopped ten feet back from him. "That knife has taken your mind."

Horace's eyes gleamed purple. "I tried. I tried to do it the merciful way, to keep them in iron, to let people choose. How does the High Mage repay me? By planning to murder me where I stand!"

"It doesn't have to be like this!"

"Remnant Magic will destroy the world! Not Sabriva, not Euryma. The *entire* world! You think I like this? You think I enjoy the death?"

"Do you even remember me?" Declan asked.

Horace peered at him. The light in his eyes faded and his mouth formed a thin line. "I remember so much. Lifetimes on lifetimes, Declan. I remember everything."

"We're friends, Ace."

"Friends?" Horace raised his eyebrows. "Friends don't throw their friends in the fire."

"I... I never meant for that to happen. I was coming back for you. I was going to save you!"

"You?" Horace cackled. His eyes narrowed and began to glow. "The non-magical Declan Moore? The unremarkable LAMP? You are nothing. You can't do anything. You're part of the problem."

The barbs cut like razors. Declan tried to ignore them. *He's not himself. The Ire Tides are driving him mad.* "What problem?"

"As long as LAMPs are lesser people, the world will continue to suffer. Magic has caused this disaster. Someone has to end it."

"You're a hypocrite," Declan shouted. "You talk about stopping magic and here you are, blasting entire buildings to bits."

"I'm doing what has to be done!" Horace screamed. The violet in his eyes brightened; he thrust a glowing palm forward. Declan leaped to the side, Ire Tides roared past him. He sprinted towards a misshapen steel panel as the earth behind erupted in a cloud of dirt and rock.

"Come on, Dex, come out and face me," Horace called.

Declan could not get around him. The purple light followed wherever he went. If he tried to go left, it drove him right; if he veered right, it forced him left. *He's herding me into a corner.* No matter how fast he ran, there was nothing he could do.

Horace's voice echoed out over the rubble. "Do you know what day it is, Dex?"

Declan ducked beneath a row of stone columns. Ire

363

Tides blew them apart. He crawled through a narrow tunnel of fallen metal frames.

"November first!" Horace sang. "It's Offers Day!"

Declan didn't answer. He attempted to catch his breath. *He's on my left. He must want me to go right.*

"One year ago today my future was supposed to begin. A future *you* took from me."

Declan peeked out to his left. A familiar blade glinted in the dirt.

"I'm glad you're here, Declan," Horace said. "It's poetry. Today, I repay the favor."

In a wave of heat, the frames split in half. Declan dashed out and scooped up his axe. Ire Tides surged forward, Declan caught the beam, deflecting it off the axe head. Horace leaped through the dust and knocked the weapon aside. A pulse of magic threw Declan against a stone wall.

Horace's lips curved in a manic grin. "And here we are. What a difference a year can make."

"Ace..." Declan rasped. He felt like a tube of toothpaste being squeezed. "I didn't mean..."

"No doubt," Horace whispered. "I'm sure you had all the right *intentions.*" He slipped his remaining hand into his coat and withdrew a bone white dagger. "We will see."

Arman Moore launched himself into Horace's chest, knocking him to the ground. The spell dissipated, Declan fell to his feet. Horace staggered forward with his dagger and Arman sidestepped him. Declan tried to advance, but a wave of unseen energy tossed him backward. He hit the stone with a painful crunch. His vision doubled and blurred, but he refused to pass out. Ahead of him, Horace jabbed and stabbed at his grandfather. Flashes of green met sparks of purple. Arman was too slow, too weak. Declan pushed himself up.

"Declan." Ava huddled below a broken archway. She gestured to his feet.

Declan looked down. His axe lay in the rubble. *Just my luck.*

Declan glanced up and his hollow stomach vanished. Horace had Arman cornered, his wrists bound in violet light. He knelt down and picked up Winterthorn.

You can't let Horace gain those memories. It has to be done. Have the courage to make the hard choice. Declan stepped forward, tears building behind his eyes. *Grandfather asked for this, it's not your fault. It has to be done.* He raised the axe and launched it, aimed true at his grandfather's heart. It circled through the air in a perfect spin, its blade glinted like a noonday sun.

Horace flicked his knife and knocked it aside.

"No!"

Winterthorn plunged into his grandfather's chest. Arman roared in pain, a burst of green light, and he slumped over. His skin as white as his beard, his beard as white as the dagger in Horace's hand.

Declan collapsed to his knees. His grandfather's body collapsed to the ground. Horace stared up at the sky as if seeing it for the first time. "So much!" he shouted. "So many memories!"

Declan descended into a familiar blackness. Deep down at the bottom of the pit, a spark ignited. Declan considered it. It was no longer a glowing jade mitka, but now an emerald axe. Declan gripped the handle, squeezed tight, and let the unbridled power of Sila fill him. Horace turned around as Declan's vision burned green.

Horace stretched out his palm. He moved in slow motion. Violet lightning fizzled from the centre of his hand. A bright spark became a cylindrical pulse of purple light. It crept forward like a glacier, moving an inch at a time.

Declan waited until it reached his chest, then grabbed the beam. His fingers crackled with emerald electricity, the Ire Tides felt warm. Declan tensed and wrenched it in half. The pillar snapped. A chain reaction flowed in Horace's direction.

Horace stumbled, eyes wide. Flames ignited around Declan. "You've gone too far," he said.

"This... this isn't possible!" Horace tried to run. In one fluid motion, Declan summoned a glittering green spear and hurled it at Horace. It pierced his shoulder, skewering him like a chunk of meat. Horace screamed in pain as Declan drew the Sila back towards him, the spear dragged Horace with it. The surrounding fire burned higher. Horace grasped for his blade and sliced.

Winterthorn severed the spell. Declan staggered back. Horace stumbled, but stayed upright to retreat behind a pile of rubble. In a burst of emerald, the pile was gone, but so was Horace. "Come and fight!" Declan shouted. In one powerful bound, he leaped onto Sabriva Tower's fallen spire and searched the ruins below.

A spray of jagged purple spikes whistled in his direction. Declan pulled them together. Ground them to dust. Horace ran the other way. Declan knocked him down with a flash of Sila.

Horace crawled backward. "What- what are you?" he cried.

Declan stood over him. "You should know. It's in your stolen memories."

Horace closed his eyes. Declan resisted the urge to burn him from existence. A long moment passed before his eyes snapped open. "You're a coward, a coward who couldn't kill his own grandfather." He flashed forward and slashed at him with Winterthorn. Declan blocked the blow and followed with a glowing green fist. The punch threw Horace twenty feet back.

A violet pulse buffered his landing. Horace pushed himself off the ground. "This isn't over," he said. He opened his palm, a purple Opening appeared behind him.

No. Declan sent a tsunami of Sila surging towards it, but Horace was gone. Vanished, in the blink of an eye. Declan dropped to his knees and roared in anguish. It tore at his throat and filled the barren remains of the broken city.

CHAPTER 47
AVA

Ava SHIELDED her face from the blinding light. Flames cascaded from Declan's dark silhouette. The leader of the Fatesmiths had fled. Declan torched the area in pursuit. It was too late. He was gone.

Declan knelt in the dirt. Vibrant flashes rippled up and down his body. Ava struggled to her feet and limped beside him. "Declan, he's gone..." She stopped as he turned on her, his eyes burned like sunlit emeralds. He considered her for what felt like an eternity. The flames died down and Declan slumped to the ground. A boy consumed by loss.

Tears left tiny craters in the dust and blood. "It's over Ava," he said. "Horace has Arman's memories."

"Horace?" Ava stared at the spot where the Smith's leader had disappeared. "You said Horace was... *That* was Horace?"

"It was." Declan did not look up.

"But how? He's only young, your age. How is he so strong?"

"Ire Tides. Memories. He said he remembered lifetimes

on lifetimes." Declan's eyes were bloodshot and swollen. "How many memories are in that knife?"

"I don't know."

Declan climbed to his feet and started back through the ruins. Ava followed at a distance. He circled back to where the King's body lay, white, cold, like cut quartz. Declan cradled his head in his arms and cried. Ava didn't know what to say. *His parents. His friend. His grandfather. Oh Declan.* She opened her mouth and thought better of it. "Stay as long as you need. I'll be over here."

Ava wandered back between the piles of fallen stone. The army of blackcoats were gone. She followed a trail of Luck around the tower's foundations. "Katie! Are you there?"

"Over here!" Covered in dirt and bruises, Katie pulled rocks from a pile of rubble.

"What are you doing?"

A pained groan responded. The dark-skinned man, Michael, lay buried in the debris. Dry blood caked the left side of his face. Ava rushed to help.

"What happened?" he asked.

"The one leading the Fatesmiths escaped," Ava said. "He killed the King, then fled when Declan started using magic."

Katie stopped moving stones. "He killed Declan's grandfather?"

Ava nodded. "Declan's with his body now."

"The boy has had a rough run," said Michael.

"A rough run? Really?" Katie snapped. "They murdered his parents in front of him and now his grandfather too, and that's a rough run? You need to grow a heart." She shook her head and continued shifting rocks. Ava helped.

When they had moved enough, Katie and Ava dragged him out. Blood soaked Michael's lower body.

Ava tossed him a vial of sanarmelon juice. "That should fix you up."

Michael eyed the liquid, then threw it back. He suppressed a shiver as the concoction took effect. He crawled to his feet. He stared at his quivering legs in uncertain wonder.

"Where are the others?" Ava asked.

"Laurefen is out cold where you left him, still lying beside your bag of shields," Katie said.

"And the older woman?"

"Mary-Lou..." Katie shook her head. "She's not doing well."

"Where is she?" Michael asked.

Katie led them to Mary-Lou's body. She lay on her side by a small patch of grass. Mud crusted her messy braid. Michael knelt next to her. "Lou?" he said softly, squeezing her shoulders. She didn't respond. He turned her onto her back and gasped.

"I did as much as I could," Katie whispered.

A makeshift bandage—drenched in blood—wrapped tightly around her side. It came in too far, as if a section of her torso were missing. Michael held his ear to her lips. "She's breathing. It's weak."

Ava reached into her pocket and handed him her last vial of sanarmelon juice. "I'm not sure if it will be enough."

Michael pressed it to Mary-Lou's mouth and tipped her head. "How will we know if it's worked?"

"Give it a moment, then unwrap the bandage."

"You were right, Kate." Michael lowered her back to the ground. "We should have listened. Arrogance blinded us, and we've paid dearly. Remnant Magic is everything you told us." He nodded to Ava. "And if not for you, we would all be dead."

"I'm here because Katie asked," Ava said. "She risked a lot trying to find me. You owe her your life."

"We do." Michael touched Mary Lou's arm. "Is that enough time?"

"Only one way to know for sure."

Michael unwrapped the binding. It was saturated. His hands were soon red with her blood. When the last layer came off, Ava had to look away. *She'd need a bath in sanarmelon juice just to stand a chance.* Sections of bloody muscle hung from exposed bone.

"Wrap it back up," Katie said. "We have to stop the bleeding."

"There's too much." Michael shook his head. "This bandage isn't keeping it in, it's just absorbing it." He frowned at them. "There's nothing we can do."

"No," Katie said. "There has to be something!"

"Mary-Lou?" Declan staggered through the rubble and fell beside her. "What happened? Is she okay?"

"She's dying." Katie wiped her sleeves over her eyes. "That boy blasted her side out of her."

Declan leaned down over the wound. Blood dribbled from the exposed muscle. He held out his hand and—to Ava's surprise—it was green, like sunlight shining through a leaf. He pressed his palm to the Mary-Lou's side and closed his eyes. The glow turned blinding white, then it was gone. Skin replaced, fresh and smooth.

Michael's eyes were full moons. "You've... you've... is she?" He put his ear to her chest. A smile broke his lips. "Her heartbeat, it's strong."

Katie's hands trembled. "She'll be okay?"

"I think so," Declan said.

Ava touched his arm. "Declan, how? How are you still using magic?"

"I haven't let go," he replied. "As soon as I do, I'll lose it." His shoulders drooped. "At least until the next devastating thing happens."

"Can you hold it forever?"

Declan looked at his palms. "I don't think so. I'll have to sleep or rest, but for now... I'm in control. Where's Laurefen?"

Katie led them back to where Laurefen lay in the dirt. Declan pressed his hand to Laurefen's head. Green light flashed white, the old man stirred. He rolled onto his side. "What... what happened?"

Katie recounted what she had seen. When she got to the impostor, Declan stopped her. "His name is Horace. We were friends, we went to school together..." He stared at Mary-Lou's unconscious body..

"This isn't your fault Declan," Ava said.

Declan shook his head. "When the Fatesmiths first came to get me, after I lost you... I called him for help. I asked him to help me get away, even when you said to leave him alone. He had his whole life ahead of him. He'd been accepted into the best Mag-Ed schools in the Dominion and I dragged him into this... this mess. Ward got him. Fierised him. And now..."

"Horace made the choices that brought him to this point. Not you. Him." Ava squeezed his hand. "You made a choice with unplanned consequences. Who hasn't? We've all made mistakes, but this isn't on you."

"It is," Declan said. "Horace killed my grandfather, stabbed him with Winterthorn. All his knowledge, how to fight wars, how to win wars, it's all there in his head now."

"We'll work it out."

"And the Ancellum."

Laurefen straightened. "What about the Ancellum?"

Ava wanted to hug him, to take him away from the awful things that stalked him like a shadow. Declan's lip trembled. "My grandfather cast the Ancellum. It uses green magic." He took a long breath, his gaze wandered between each of them. "Now Horace has those memories. He may be able to undo it. Kingsbreak is no longer safe. Because of me."

"Stop it." Ava stamped her foot. "You did the best you could. We can't change what has happened, but we don't give up. We will live and see."

Declan opened his mouth. No words came out. Mary-Lou stirred behind them. Her eyes fluttered open. Her gaze drifted from Laurefen to Katie and to Declan. When she saw him, her face glowed. "Declan," she croaked. "You came."

Declan knelt beside her. She took his hands and he bowed his head. "I'm so sorry, Mary-Lou. I ruined everything!"

Mary-Lou shook her head. "We're alive, Declan. We're okay, we're here. We exist to see another day. Because of you."

Declan sobbed into her shoulder. Mary-Lou held him tight and smiled into the clear, blue sky.

CHAPTER 48
DECLAN

DECLAN CARRIED his grandfather through the Opening. A cocoon of Sila cradled his pale body. Clouds floated between Cedrus's branches, like hundreds of fluffy boats sailing east. The air smelled like Kingsbreak, its scent held a mix of wonderful and painful memories. The Opening shrank away, taking Sabriva's torn landscape with it. A fresh wave of despair washed over him. *This is not how it was supposed to end.*

Laurefen led them, but Declan was slow to follow. Ava remained by his side. They walked in silence; Declan replayed the day's events in his mind. When he reached the moment when Arman pressed his axe into Declan's hands and asked him to take his life, his legs turned to stone. *You should have listened.* Misery threatened to drown him, kept at bay only by the Sila coursing through his body. He clenched his jaw, continued walking.

"Declan..." Ava touched his forearm and they stopped. Katie glanced back at them, but did not stop. Ava's voice trembled as she spoke. "The last year has been, well, it's been terrible. I... I know you probably feel you have no-one left, but that's not true. You have me."

But for how long? Everything you touch turns to ashes. Declan forced the thought into the Sila, it burned away. He exhaled deeply. "Ava, I don't know what I'm doing. I thought it would all be okay. Arman was so strong. I didn't think it was possible for him to... go... but he did, and now... now there's no-one who can save us."

"There's you."

"Me? I'm barely more than a LAMP. I can only use Sila after I lose someone. Who else has to die before I can do anything useful?"

"You're more than the power within you. You are kind and smart and brave. We'll figure it out."

"How?" Declan asked. "There's so much against us. Horace and the Fatesmiths, Remnant Magic, and now the Knights of Despair are free. How can we beat that?"

"I don't know..." Ava trailed off as Katie rushed to meet them..

"Sorry to interrupt," Katie said. "There's a woman here to see you."

"To see me?" Declan blinked. "Did they give you a name?"

"Only a title. She introduced herself as the Emissary."

"She's here?" Ava asked, eyebrows climbing in surprise.

"In the hall," Katie said. "Do you know her?"

Ava still looked confused. "She was the one who sent me to find Declan and the King. She saved us."

Declan nodded to Katie. "Tell her I'll be there soon." Katie started to leave. "Oh and Kate," Declan called. She turned back.

"Yes?"

"I'm so sorry about Amber. I'm glad you're safe. I've missed you."

Katie smiled. "I've missed you too, Declan." She started back up the path. Ava watched her go, a small frown played on the edges of her lips.

"What is it?" Declan asked.

"The Emissary..." Ava's distant eyes focused on him. She shrugged. "I'm just surprised she's here, that's all."

"She worked for my grandfather. Is it too much to hope she'll have some answers?"

Ava frowned. "Maybe. Though my experience with her is that every answer creates three more questions."

Declan stared up at the grand buildings of King's College. "I guess we'll find out."

They made their way down the path, Ava beside him, his grandfather's body floating close behind.

———

The meeting hall at King's College was an artwork of carved wood. The timber floor was patterned with different stains that shone under layers of glossy lacquer. Sunlight poured through the open door and reflected into ornate rafters. In the centre of the building was a small square table where a familiar face waited.

"Mrs Winter?"

Declan's homeroom teacher stood as he drew closer. Her face glowed with a welcome warmth. "It is good to see you, Declan."

"Uh, I'm supposed to be meeting someone here."

"You are." Mrs Winter nodded. "The Emissary, I believe."

"Do you know when she'll be here?"

Mrs. Winter winked at him. "She already is."

Realization dawned and Declan's jaw dropped. "You're the Emissary?"

Mrs Winter's eyes sparkled. "I am." Her smile fell away. "Dean Ember has explained the circumstances of your arrival. Declan, I am so sorry for your loss. Your grandfather was a remarkable man. Kind, caring, with an unwavering compass for what was right. The world will miss the King of Vedmark."

Declan didn't know what to say. He settled for an awkward nod. "I have him with me.. or his body." He looked back towards the door. "I would like to return him to Vedmark to lay him to rest. Can you help me do that?"

"Of course I can. My family has served the Moore bloodline for generations. With Arman's passing, that service falls to you."

"But... You're a teacher..."

"The perfect role to monitor you. I took my post at Arman Moore's Preparatory School the year you started. I was overqualified for the position, but I took it on the condition they would assign me to your homeroom."

Declan didn't know what to say. All this time, his grandfather had watched over him from a distance. "You sent Ava?"

Mrs. Winter motioned to their surroundings. "Your application to King's College set the wheels in motion. I instructed poor Ava to collect you, a quick and easy task. What happened next was a complete surprise. We never expected things to turn out the way they did."

"What about my parents?" Declan asked. He still held the Sila, it sparked within him. "Arman was their ancestor too. Why didn't he protect them?"

"When events grew dangerous with the Fatesmiths,

your safety took priority." Mrs. Winter placed her hands in her lap. "You are a warlock, Declan. Only you could take his place."

The Sila burned brighter. "So, he didn't care?"

"He did. He cared, more than you know, but Arman knew the world would come to depend on you. You were the one person who was too important to lose."

Declan looked away. The despair of his grandfather's death returned. Tears built behind his eyes. He shook his head and fought to keep his voice steady. "He was wrong. I let him down. I failed to do what he asked, and he died. Even worse, Winterthorn killed him, took his memories. Now all hope is gone."

"Declan—"

"He asked me to kill him, to take my Sila and save everyone. I didn't want that. I didn't want him to die. I didn't want to be alone." Declan bit his lip, afraid to speak the truth that burned inside him. His gaze fell to his feet. "I didn't want the responsibility."

"You—"

"Now I've ruined everything. Horace is leading the Fatesmiths, and he has all grandfather's memories. He knows how to undo the Ancellum. He'll probably destroy Kingsbreak. The blackcoats will take over Euryma, Remnant Magic will burn whatever they don't and then..." He looked up through bitter, bloodshot eyes. "The Knights of Despair will take it all. Because of me." He released his Sila. The light left him, extinguished like a candle. Emptiness hit like a sledgehammer. Tears rolled down his cheeks.

Mrs Winter let him cry. Declan held his head and cried. For twenty minutes, all they did was sit while whimpers echoed off the walls. When the hall grew silent, she lifted a leather duffel onto her knees. "Shortly after you arrived in

Vedmark, Arman created these for you." She handed the bag to Declan. "He gave me orders to gift them to you when you were ready."

Declan opened the straps. Two short axes rested in purple silk. Their handles were made of a green-grey wood carved with a 'D' and an 'M'. The axe heads themselves were engraved with four pictures: a bull, a bear, a lion, and an armadillo. On the other side, one axe bore the crest of Euryma, the other the beaked dragon of Vedmark.

"Your greatest grandfather was the King of Vedmark, Declan. By birth, you are the heir to the Emerald Throne." Mrs Winter's kind voice turned stern. "There are challenges ahead, as you well know. The Fatesmiths. The Knights of Despair. The storms of Remnant Magic that ravage our world. We can no longer wait for you to be ready. It is time, Declan. Time to embrace your heritage and prove your worth."

Declan caught his reflection in the axe head. Bruised, battered, absolutely filthy. "How?" he asked. "How can I stand against so much power when I have none?"

Mrs. Winter's eyes sparkled like a glacier. "We burn bright in the darkness, Declan. What is it they say in Vedmark? We live and we see?"

Declan nodded. He lifted the axes from the bag. They felt like old friends. Carved into the base of each handle were two words. Declan read them. As he did, a fire ignited in his chest.

Burn. Bright.

CONTINUE THE ADVENTURE

facebook.com/ntaylorwrites

amazon.com/stores/Nathan-Taylor/author/B0CG649CZD

About Nathan

Nathan Taylor is an outstandingly distracted author with a penchant for imagining wizarding worlds and magical storms that could knock your socks off.

He gravitates towards ice baths (or rather the dopamine hit that follows), milk chocolate, and issuing stern warnings to his muggle children about the consequences of leaving dirty laundry on the bathroom floor.

Nathan lives in rural Queensland, Australia, which is the perfect place for snake bites, spider bites and picturesque sunsets.

Want More?

Join the Wintersmiths for a free short story collection at www.nathantaylorwrites.com

f facebook.com/ntaylorwrites

a amazon.com/stores/Nathan-Taylor/author/B0CG649CZD

www.ingramcontent.com/pod-product-compliance
Lightning Source LLC
Chambersburg PA
CBHW01025510726
47904CB00011B/2600

* 9 7 8 0 6 4 5 7 5 9 5 3 2 *